THE
LAST
RESORT

THE
LAST
RESORT
A JEN LU MYSTERY

Michael Kaufman

CROOKED
LANE

NEW YORK

Published in the United States by Crooked Lane Books, an imprint of The Quick Brown Fox & Company LLC.

Crooked Lane Books and its logo are trademarks of The Quick Brown Fox & Company LLC.

Library of Congress Catalog-in-Publication data available upon request.

ISBN (hardcover): 978-1-63910-207-5
ISBN (ebook): 978-1-63910-208-2

Cover design by Melanie Sun

Printed in the United States.

www.crookedlanebooks.com

Crooked Lane Books
34 West 27th St., 10th Floor
New York, NY 10001

First Edition: January 2023

10 9 8 7 6 5 4 3 2 1

To Chloe, with admiration and love.

1

"I never killed anyone before."

Yeah, that's what they all say when they're staring at prison through their big brown eyes. But I admit, the hedge fund CEO had us both convinced, Jen and me. A freak death by an errant ball at a snooty golf course.

Despite being a Timeless, the man looked unwell. His skin was now the color of liverwurst that had been left out too long in the sun. He charged from the posh meeting room toward the restroom. Second time since we had brought him up to the clubhouse.

My boss: Jen B. Lu. Age thirty-eight. Washington, DC, police detective. Me: Two years and nine months. Biocomputer implanted into her neocortex.

"What do you think, boss?"

Jen said, "I think he should take golf lessons before he kills anyone else."

"She's not dead yet."

"No," Jen agreed. "Not yet."

When the hedge fund president finally staggered back, dabbing the corners of his narrow mouth with a blindingly white handkerchief, we ran through it all again. That's your most basic police questioning technique: get them to repeat their story 150 times and try to spot discrepancies. It's one of the many areas where I run circles around humans. Of course, it also lets the bad guys lock in their stories, but no mind.

Trebook said, "As I told you twice—"

"Sorry, Mr. Trebook, I need to make sure we capture every detail while things are fresh in your mind."

"—when you're on the tee box—"

"On the fifth hole."

"Of course on the fifth damn hole." He glared briefly, his normal rich-guy moxie starting to bubble up. "From up there, you can't see the place we found her."

"You knew she was playing in front of you."

"Yes. As I have also already stated several times." He shot Jen a look that couldn't have withered a daisy, let alone my boss. "We saw her in the starter's cabin. And it's her regular time. Everyone knows."

"Did you speak to her?"

He looked uncomfortable. "No."

"She was by herself?"

"Right. No service unit. But the fifth hole descends steeply at about a hundred and fifty yards. She was down there, out of sight."

"Isn't that risky? Hitting your ball when someone could be there?"

"Our tee times are fifteen minutes apart," he said with a voice so smug it made me itch.

"Is that good?"

The high roller rolled his eyes, apparently recovering from his abject whining and now reclaiming his natural superiority. He fuzzed a hand back and forth over his close-cropped hair like a little boy might do after his first trip to a barbershop. Seventy-six years old, but looked about twenty-four. Not a good-looking twenty-four—his lips were far too skinny, his mouth far too small, and his ears looked like someone had slapped iceberg lettuce leaves onto the sides of his head—but not everyone can be as handsome as me.

"Most good private courses," Trebook said, "send out groups at eight- to ten-minute intervals. At a course where you might play"—here he sized Jen up and down as if calculating her net worth—"you'd be packed in every six minutes. Here we believe members absolutely must have the course to themselves. Fifteen minutes ensures this. And the fact that she was playing alone meant she should have been well ahead of the two of us by then."

She. Patty Garcia.

Texan. Fifty-two. Lawyer. Celebrity. Media darling. Daughter of farmworkers with a rags-to-riches story. Star athlete back in college. Rumored presidential candidate. *Time* magazine Person of the Year for leading the landmark civil suit against the oil, gas, and coal giants. *That* Patty Garcia.

When the call had come in, we happened to be a block away, so we were first on the scene. The polished gates of the golf club had breezed open to our police scooter. We charged up a drive that wound through thick woods where springtime leaves were popping out in front of our eyes. As we reached the steps to the clubhouse, a young woman dashed out and greeted us like a society dinner party hostess who was trying to control her panic that the beef Wellington would get soggy if we didn't hurry. She whisked us into a Tesla golf cart with heated seats, and as she sped away, she launched into her commentary. "A member named Mr. Trebook phoned me from the fifth hole. He thinks another member was hit by his golf ball. He thinks she's dead." She floored that puppy, and we charged straight across two holes, bombed through a patch of woods, blazed past a green, and arrived on the fifth hole. Good times.

Patty Garcia was lying there on the fairway, not moving, but then again, it kind of freaks me out when corpses start moving on you. Jen doesn't like it when I talk that way, but I'm not a kid anymore, and she can't tell me what to do.

We climbed out of the golf cart. The grass was as soft as a well-padded carpet.

Although our panicking hostess had said Garcia was dead, another woman—she was, we soon found out, Trebook's playing partner, Dr. Jane Kershaw—saw us and said, "I've found a pulse. It's extremely weak."

Garcia had a bump on her temple the size of a quail egg ready to hatch twins.

I checked comms and reported.

Jen said, "We expect an air ambulance in four minutes."

Here's the picture. We were in the northern half of Rock Creek Park, the section that hadn't been incinerated in the fire last year. In the old days before I was booted up, this course had been a run-down municipal track that could have doubled as a dirt-bike course. It was to golf what netless, bent rims mounted on warped plywood above an undulating slab of asphalt were to basketball: nice that a million people had access to it, but damn, couldn't we do a bit better for our citizens? But after Disney bought the National Park Service, it flipped the course to a small consortium of super-rich Timeless who decided they indeed had a social responsibility to do better. They landed a ninety-million federal Better Future for All grant and rebuilt it as an urban golf resort—golf course, pool, gym, spa, and private suites for the pleasure of 246 deserving members.

And that's smack-dab where we'd found Patty Garcia. The fifth hole of Viridian Green Golf Resort.

Other than the not-quite-yet-dead person lying in front of us, it was a pretty decent day. We were having a fantastic early spring—what Jen, when she's out of Zach's earshot, calls the good side of climate change. Zach is (your choice) her boyfriend, partner, common-law spouse, significant other. The trees around us were filling in with the tenderest of green leaves, each

3

looking like a delicacy you'd want to pluck off and eat. It was an overcast day, but throughout the woods, like dabs of paint by Monet, redbud and dogwood bloomed, and patches of wild flowers carpeted the ground. Jen told me to enjoy it while I could. Our "seasons" now seem to last a week or two, then we have a wild swing with temperatures climbing or crashing by twenty degrees.

Here was the cast of characters: Ms. Garcia on the ground looking dead. Mr. Trebook looking gray. Dr. Kershaw, kneeling at the lawyer's side, looking concerned. Two service units, each with a hand resting on top of a golf bag, standing off to the side. Four golf course employees shuffling from foot to foot—one whispering into his phone, the others with hands folded in front of themselves as if dress rehearsing for the funeral.

Just as I detected four sirens—an ambulance, a police motorcycle, and two cruisers—I also caught the first whumping of the air ambulance. Bad news about big people travels fast.

Garcia was wearing soda-pop-orange shorts—tightly cut and fashionably short—with a persimmon-orange shirt and a wide purple belt. Lying at her side was a neon-green golf bag. If I had my own set of eyes, they'd be pumping tears like a busted spigot trying to cope with this clash of colors. But somehow it worked on her. This was one very cool woman.

A gleaming white golf ball lay on the tightly mowed grass like a pearl in a display case on green velvet. We squatted down, looked, but did not touch.

"It's mine," the man said. His skin now seemed to be experimenting with interesting shades of green, which at least added a splash of color alongside his beige golf attire.

"Who are you?" Jen asked.

"Peter Trebook. Jane—Dr. Kershaw—and I were the group playing after Ms. Garcia." He pointed to the service units. "Those two are ours."

"This is your ball?"

"I didn't mean to hit her. Of all people."

"I'm sure you didn't. You're certain this is your ball?"

He nodded.

"Did you see it hit her?"

He turned back and glanced up the sloped fairway, beyond the top of the hill. "You can't see down here from the tee."

"Did you touch it? The ball?"

He blushed strawberry. I was already figuring out this guy was a veritable rack of paint chips.

"I wiped off some mud with my towel to make sure it was mine."

"Did you put it back right where you found it?"

"Of course I did."

Jen turned to Dr. Kershaw. "Where's your golf ball?"

Dr. Kershaw stood up and pointed down the fairway to a ball close to the green. "That's mine."

"You're sure?"

"From where I was hitting my second shot, I could see the green and where it landed. So yes. Definitely."

"But you couldn't see Ms. Garcia here."

"No."

"And where is her ball?"

"I have no idea," she said. Trebook shook his head, enthusiastically confirming he didn't know either.

Jen took out her phone and popped off a series of photographs: the famous lawyer, a close-up of the wound, the ball, the golf bag she'd been carrying, the people, the surroundings. She scooped the ball into an evidence bag.

The sirens and helicopter were getting loud.

Jen raised her voice. "How long since she was hit?"

Trebook and Kershaw started muttering back and forth to calculate the time.

He: "I teed first."

She: "I flubbed my tee shot. Went a hundred and twenty yards, still on the upper level. We walked to my ball, and I hit my second shot."

"We reached the top of the hill and saw her."

"Ran down."

"Got to her, say, eight minutes from my tee shot."

"Maybe a bit more."

"Phoned 911 right away."

I double-checked to confirm the time of the 911 call.

They were still talking.

"While you were calling them, I phoned up to the clubhouse," Kershaw said, checking her watch.

"Fourteen, fifteen minutes ago," Trebook said. "So nineteen or twenty minutes from when we teed off."

Which means, I said to Jen, *the ball hit Garcia between fourteen thirty-two and fourteen thirty-four.*

Any more talk was drowned out by the belly-deep thumping of the helicopter.

That's when we'd invited Mr. Trebook up to the clubhouse for a chat. Jen figured that sounded friendlier than admitting we were going to grill the guy until he cracked. He was now on his own—Dr. Kershaw had insisted on accompanying Garcia in the chopper.

The clubhouse was in a quiet uproar: everyone whispering, sitting in stunned silence, or sharing the excitement over their phones, but with their well-tended hands covering their well-fed mouths so others wouldn't hear.

The woman staff member who had driven us back up to the clubhouse escorted us to an elegant meeting room. Jen asked Trebook to have a seat, then stared at the woman until she got the message and closed the door behind her.

Jen began with an open-ended gambit: "That must have been quite a shock."

That's when Trebook said, "I never killed anyone before," and rushed out to toss what was left of his lunch.

When he returned, his face was gray-greeny white. We reassured him that Patty Garcia was still alive. He nodded, but it was obvious from the panic etching his face that he figured that might not be true for long.

Trebook closed his eyes and breathed like a yoga master. By the time he opened them, his tanned color was returning. It seemed to finally occur to him that his odds of getting dragged into a lawsuit were solid enough to turn an actuary into a gambling man. He abruptly announced that if we had any further questions, he wanted his lawyer at his side.

And so we said adios to the Timeless man who thought he had it all and headed down the long drive and out the polished gates of Viridian Green Golf Resort.

2

Friday

At the end of a tough day and a long week, Jen was home and Chandler was switched off. Alone and tired, she sipped an ice-cold Manhattan that was warming her up fast.

The long afternoon had ended with her correcting and adding to Chandler's report on the accident at the golf course. She dialed Zach. Took a sip of her cocktail—velvety, but something was missing.

"Your Manhattans are better than mine," was the first thing she said.

"Another unassailable reason not to ditch me."

"First day okay?" He was in Raleigh, North Carolina, for a conference of the Green Prosperity Network. Two months ago he'd landed a job as a member of the GPN's economic team.

"Folks here are still in shock from Mable." Mable was the late-season mega-hurricane that had destroyed the Outer Banks, ripping apart every house and bridge, gouging out so much sand that the area was now a collection of miniscule islands. Anyone who had taken the advice of the governor was now dead: he had said the warnings of scientists were wrong, it would be no worse than storms that had hit them in the past, and God would protect them because the state had outlawed abortions and homosexuality.

Jen and Zach were silent for a moment.

"Aside from that?"

"Tons of energy. Media everywhere. Presentation from the Norwegians on how they ditched their oil industry."

"Cool."

"There's this huge delegation of Midwest farmers who spend half their time lamenting what they used to believe and who they voted for fourteen years ago. Although the most fun is the gang from the Fox News purge. Did you know—"

"Zach."

"Yes?"

"And how was your day, dear?"

"Right, sorry. And how was, et cetera, et cetera?"

"You heard about Patty Garcia getting hit by a ball?"

"It was all everyone was talking about at dinner. Is she—"

"I was there."

"You're kidding."

"The latest is that she was in surgery."

"Very freaky."

"Why I never took up golf."

Saturday

Jen slept in on Saturday morning, but even at nine when she raised the blinds, she saw frost edging the fresh leaves on the trees. "Jesus," she said out loud, "yesterday it hit seventy-five." She checked the weather. High today: forty-one. It was what Jen, when Zach was *within* earshot, called the bad side of climate change—weather wildly swinging through the seasons in a heartbeat.

She monkeyed through a banana, downed a cup of strong coffee, and crunched on half a slice of multigrain toast spread with the raspberry jam she and Zach had made with his parents the previous year. She bundled into the cool-weather running gear she had prayed wouldn't be needed again until the fall.

Zipping her phone into a snug pocket, she headed out to pick up Les, her former partner.

Six months earlier, on the last case they'd worked together, Les had almost died rescuing Jen. He'd pulled through surgery, and the nurses and rehab staff had him moving within a week. He was transferred to a rehab hospital, not so much because there was anything physically wrong with him but because he hadn't yet spoken. In fact, he didn't acknowledge anyone or anything going on around him. He did what you told him to do, but almost like a machine. He would run or work out until you said *stop* and eat when you told him to, all the while making no eye contact or showing a lick of emotion. If he didn't get any instructions, he'd vegetate in one spot for hours.

Les was living back home with Christopher and still in this strange fugue state.

Before Jen ended her own sick leave and returned to work—the only lasting effect was a fatigue she couldn't shake—she had timed her visits to coincide with Christopher being out. The ever-cautious Christopher still blamed her for what had happened to his husband. Avoiding him was no longer always possible, but Jen figured Christopher was happy to have some time when he didn't have to worry about Les and at least glad that Les was getting a good workout. Christopher was not an exercise guy.

Christopher buzzed her up to the fourth floor. She'd once had the condo door code; no longer. He opened the door. Diffuse morning light spilled in from the large balcony doors; the skin of his beautiful face glowed reddish brown. He grunted a perfunctory hello and let her stew in the hallway while he got Les ready, nattering away as he might to a kid, his voice a deep, singsong softness from his native Brazil. "Did you pee? Let's go make sure . . . It's cold out there; you better bundle up . . . Definitely will need gloves . . . I'm putting tissue in your pocket." After kissing his unresponsive husband, Christopher hung on for an extra second as if he didn't want to relinquish his proprietorship.

Jen led Les to the stairs, all the while feeling Christopher's eyes jamming into her back.

Damn it, Christopher, she thought, *can't you just be decent to me? Tell me I'm the only one you trust? Tell me you know it wasn't my fault that Les ended up this way?* But Jen knew he wasn't yet there.

They took the fast electric shuttle up 14th to avoid city running and the burnt-out section of the park. Just before Arkansas Avenue, the Upshur Park baseball and soccer field had become a new Shadow encampment.

The Shadows. Homeless. Jobless. Wandering millions from hurricane-destroyed Miami, washed-away Louisiana bayous, and burnt-up chunks of northern California. They'd set up encampments in cities and towns across the country or sought refuge in Canada or Mexico. Nothing to fall back on. Nothing to look forward to. Nothing but nothing but nothing. Treated like mere shadows of humanity.

Jen spotted a tattered flag from the dried-up state of Kansas hanging from a scraggly tree. These folks must have been among the million people who'd fled that state, many on foot since they had long before sold their pickup trucks and cars. They'd trudged across the country. North, south, east, and west. Anywhere that seemed to promise relief.

Jen and Les stepped off the bus at Military Road NW and set off in a run. As they skirted the edge of Viridian Green, Jen pulled up a mental map in her head. Soon they were alongside the fifth hole, but even now in early March, the foliage was already becoming too dense to glimpse the course through the woods. "I was in there yesterday," she said to Les. "Not much more than a hundred yards away." She told him about the freak accident.

They ran at a good clip, working their way uphill along the newly widened Valley Trail. They passed other runners. A pod of teenagers on trail bikes zoomed by.

"Keep your eyes peeled, Les. Maybe we'll see the hyena." A striped hyena had escaped from the nearby zoo a week earlier. It was a scavenger, so it wasn't about to attack them. But it would be cool, Jen thought, to spot it before it was recaptured.

"Zach's down in Raleigh at a conference for his new job. I told you about it."

She paused as was her habit, hoping he might be responding in his head.

"I'm happy he's got this job," she continued. "What with my expenses for Mom and our portion of house costs with Zach's folks." As if this made any sense to Les. "Even with all that, we're finally able to save."

Jen's mom. Whose severe Alzheimer's had strangely turned her into a nice person.

"But . . . there's always a *but*, isn't there?"

Pause.

"Since Zach got the job, it's been two months of nonstop chatter about climate change and organizational intrigue. The other day I finally put my foot down. 'I get it,' I said. 'We're doomed.' Zach kind of laughed, kind of sounded preachy when he said, 'Then you don't get it. We set up Green Prosperity precisely so we won't be doomed.'"

Pause.

"Pretty sanctimonious, don't you think?"

Pause.

"I do hope he's right."

They ran in silence until they reached the top of the park and turned around.

"Work . . . it's still strange," Jen said. "I mean, last year I went from no one believing me to getting suspended to, well, getting paraded around like a hero. But now, it's like everyone is waiting for me to make a mistake. Vultures lining up for a feast."

Jen focused on the rhythm of their running shoes smacking on the dirt.

"You better not tell anyone at work how worried I am."

Les didn't say a thing.

"I'll take that as a yes."

Monday

End of a boring day catching up on paperwork. When she arrived home, cold from the chilly bike ride, Jen made herself a cup of mint tea.

Mug in hand, she settled at the small kitchen table and dialed Zach.

"I miss you," Zach said.

"I'm pretty sure I miss you too, but I'm too tired to say for certain."

Zach started to answer but Jen cut him off, her tone now serious. "Shitty news about Patty Garcia."

Zach's silence said more than any words.

Jen went on, "She never regained consciousness."

"Which I guess means she didn't suffer."

"Who knows," Jen said, but this felt too brutal. "You're right, probably not."

"It's a truly massive setback to our work."

"Generally? Or something more specific?"

Zach hesitated. "Well, general, for sure. She was a great advocate for action on climate change."

"She was supposed to speak at your conference, right?"

"Yeah, tonight. The closing address. She was . . ." His voice trailed off.

Jen had known Zach long enough to hear the unstated follow-up line: *As for the rest, I'll fill you in when I get home.* Some things weren't for the phone.

They talked for a while, Jen about work, Zach about his conference and its attendant intrigues of personalities and politics. Jen heard the front door open, and a moment later Zach's parents, Leah and Raffi, came into the kitchen, lugging cloth bags of groceries.

Jen waved to them and said to Zach, "My saviors have arrived with provisions."

"My parents spoil you."

"And I love every second of it."

"See you tomorrow afternoon."

"*Mañana.*"

3

Tuesday, March 7—13:22:58

We hit the station right on time for our squad meeting. Our old Elder Abuse Unit had been repurposed as the Special Investigations Squad. Perhaps the change was part of the experimentation that's been going on for the past fourteen years since the massive Black Lives Matter rallies and our own DC 18 uprising a few years later. But I like to think it was a recognition of our utter brilliance as a unit. Whatever the reason, the good news was that the SIS had been given latitude to "take creative initiatives to investigate crime"—bureaucratic poetry that probably cost the department a hundred grand in consulting fees.

SIS takes on normal detective work, but we're also pulled into wider projects—hence Jen having been stuck all morning over at headquarters for an excruciatingly boring meeting with the Commercial Crimes Unit to plan an investigation into a major seafood distributor.

Me, I'd still like to have a chance to kick some bad-guy ass, but that doesn't seem to be in the cards anytime soon.

So far today, my job had entailed keeping Jen awake during the morning meeting. Hour after hour, I dribbled a microdose of adrenaline and occasionally reminded her what people were talking about. This task required an infinitesimal speck of my mental power and zilch of my budding emotional abilities. But who worries about the hurt feelings of a sim? Right?

Anyhow, our squad meeting, the SIS, began. Although it wasn't our case, everyone wanted to know what it had been like to be first on the scene with Patty Garcia. She'd been such a rising star that all the news feeds and TV and radio chatter were focused on her life, career, her quirky death, and especially what it all meant for the climate change reparations, the amount of which was still to be determined. Would it be billions? Trillions? No one seemed to know.

Jen was starting to get into the story—the golfers, the pristine grounds—when Captain Brooks interrupted and said this was a meeting and not an old episode of *Lifestyles of the Rich and Famous*, a reference that apparently only I clocked.

They got down to business. Reports, discussion, brainstorming, Captain Brooks rubbing the mahogany-colored keloid scar where his left eyebrow should have been—at which point whoever was speaking usually got the message to wrap it up quickly.

As we went from case to case, Jen forced herself to chime in now and then, but her brain was turning into a bowl of overcooked grits until seven words from Amanda caught her attention. The group was discussing an unusual burglary that seemed to tie into a suspected fraud case at a big accounting firm. Amanda was pretty sharp. She popped a bubble of gum like a first baseman and said, "It's not like it was an accident."

It's not like it was an accident, Jen repeated to herself. And then she said to me, *Chandler, check when they're doing the post-mortem on Garcia.*

Easy as pie.

Rush job. Tomorrow morning. Unusual deaths go to DC's medical examiner. The autopsy, lab work, and reporting normally take weeks or even months, but although this was clearly an accident, it was getting special treatment. If nothing else, the medical examiner was a thoughtful woman who'd want to nip rumors or conspiracy theories in the bud.

Jen said to me, *What if we missed something?*

We? You see the respect I get in this joint? The only time I receive even half credit is if she makes a mistake.

I followed Jen's thoughts as she replayed Friday's events at the Viridian Green Golf Resort, correcting her every time she screwed up a detail. I repeated the golfer's lines, word for word. Didn't seem to be any discrepancies there. *Still*, she said to me, *what if it wasn't an accident?*

Meeting over, Jen signed out. Left me on so we could talk. Dragged herself home, showered, and crashed for an hour—enough to catch up on her sleep, but unfortunately also enough to leave her feeling disoriented and groggy. She stumbled into the kitchen, struggled to remember what she was doing there, extracted a cup of coffee with her AeroPress, perked up after one sip (which made it clear that her caffeine thing is about suggestion, not digestion), thought of going up to the rooftop deck, decided it was too damn cold, and plunked us down at the kitchen table.

"Okay, champ," she said to me, "let's say Garcia was murdered."

"It seems unlikely."

"Yeah, but say she was, any idea who might have wanted her dead?"

I ran a quick scan. "Boss, we only have two hours before you have to leave."

"That many possibilities?"

"Put it this way. Patty Garcia was public enemy number one for Fox News and routinely editorialized against in the *Wall Street Journal*. She was vilified by half the political establishment and envied by the other half because she was rocketing to the top of public acclaim. And of course she was hated by absolutely everyone in the coal, oil, and gas pecking order from a ginsel—"

"Is that a real word?"

"Roughneck insult for those doing the lowest oil rig jobs. Anyway, she was hated by everyone from them right up to the men and women cashing in their million-dollar checks each year."

"I get the picture. Anything about those two who found her?"

I checked. "Like they said, she's a doctor; he's a big-deal investor and a Timeless."

Timeless meaning he'd received the Longevity Treatment, which rendered its stratospherically rich subjects whatever age they chose. No one yet knew how long it could be sustained, but for now, they were Timeless. I'd once tried to dig up a figure on what it cost, between the treatment and the annual tune-ups. I'd narrowed it down to somewhere between ludicrous and obscene.

"Chandler, I got no vibe they were hiding anything, other than the fact he was a pompous dick once he got over being scared. Did Garcia have a boyfriend or girlfriend?"

"Appears not," I said. "Not right now."

"A zigfriend?" Latest word to cut out the gender binary stuff in relationships.

"Ditto," I said.

"Wasn't there something, I don't know, a year or two ago?"

"Three and a half years ago. Ugly fallout with her husband."

Electricity buzzed so hard through her neurons that I worried I'd be zapped. You don't need a PhD in criminology to know that when a woman is murdered, a current or former partner is the odds-on favorite to have killed her. On the other hand, we had zero evidence—really less than zero evidence—that the lawyer's death was anything but an accident.

"Well?" Jen said.

"When they hitched up, she was an up-and-coming lawyer shilling for oil companies. He became a senior vice president at BP/Chevron right after their merger and was on the fast track for CEO. But he was also a self-styled visionary who had other big plans. Ergo, they were the ultimate power couple."

"And then?"

"Seems that two things happened. One was that she got struck by lightning—"

"For real?"

"Boss, it's a metaphor. She did a complete three-sixty."

"Wouldn't that mean she was back to where she started?"

"Fine. She did a one-eighty and realized the companies she represented were destroying the planet and lying through their oil-stained teeth as they did. She knew they, their investors, and the banks that funded them had made fortunes as merchants of death and destruction."

"Chandler, that's very poetic."

"Her words."

"At that point, I imagine there was a tad of friction around the breakfast table."

"Along with every other part of the house. Their enchanted marriage came to a blistering end one August night when she called the cops. Seems he'd tried to push her down the stairs. He admitted they were having a heated argument, but he claimed she was 'getting hysterical' and lost her balance. Judge and jury found it hard to believe that a former star athlete would have trouble standing and arguing at the same time. And besides, her ex came across as a man who liked to get his way."

"And the fallout?"

"Aside from the divorce? He was publicly humiliated. He slunk off with a fine, but he was dumped by BP/Chevron. At first he was a pariah everywhere he turned."

"Revenge is as good a motive as any."

"Boss, he was convicted three and a half years ago."

"Chandler, let me tell you. For certain things, humans have longer memories than computers ever will."

I live, I continue to learn.

We did batting practice with a few theories, dug deeper into Garcia's past, until Jen looked at her watch. "Better split."

She was due to meet Zach, who had headed directly from the train station to the Green Prosperity Network office.

15

"Leave me on? I'm sure everyone's going to be talking about Garcia."

So here's the deal with Jen and me. In the olden days—that would be until this past fall—my life was all normal protocol: like other cops who have an experimental sim implanted into their neocortex, Jen was required to switch me on when she started work and turn me off when she left. That was it until I was decommissioned last year when the powers that be tried to muscle Jen out of the way after she got too close to the truth in the Eden investigation. I returned from the dead just in time to save her, a feat that appears to be turning me into a bit of a cult figure among my fellow sims. For a while afterward, Jen kept me switched on at all times but tucked in the background—she was in horrible shape and I was her security blanket. But within a couple of months, we were supposedly back to normal, except for her fatigue.

The thing is, since my resurrection, I've been able to come and go at will. Miraculously able, a few of the other sims would say, if they only knew. Certainly, science was involved, although try as I might, I haven't been able to figure out what it might be. Probably something as simple as a busted on/off switch.

It hadn't taken Jen long, being the clever detective that she is, to figure out that she was never alone. She wasn't amused or pleased or agreeable or any other adjective that would put me in a good bargaining position. She said, "Chandler, do you want me to report this anomaly to the doc?" Not really a doctor, but our nickname for the lab technician who ran my occasional checkups. Doc and everyone else had been amazed that I came back on in time to save Jen—well, with Les's help. I was worried I might get rebooted or even removed from Jen's brain and, *God*, dissected to see what had gone wrong in my build. To prevent that, I quickly whipped up a supposed programming glitch to explain why their permanent shutdown hadn't worked. Doc was pretty pleased with himself for spotting the glitch and erasing it.

So Jen's threat of ratting me out was a nonstarter. If I, in their eyes, was glitching, I had about zero chance of living out my full five years. I personally knew three synthetic implants in our trial class who'd already been shut down and physically removed for even more minor issues than my own.

"And," Jen had continued, "do you really want me destroying my relationship with Zach?" The two of them had been through a bad patch last summer when he found out about me. The fact that I had saved Jen's life several months later had gone a long way to getting him to chill, but if he discovered I was tuned in to their every conversation, their every bike ride, and their every tumble in the hay, he was going to explode all over again.

"So," Jen had said, "here's what we're going to do. I know you're not a little kid any longer. You want more independence. I get it. I felt the same when I was a teenager."

She was patronizing me, but I bit my tongue.

"When I have you supposedly turned off, you will shut down your external comms functions."

"What about emergencies?"

"Sure, except then. And your long-term memory function goes off. I don't want my private life to ever hit police records."

"But—"

"And you don't talk to me unless I address you. And"—here I felt heat rising across her face—"when I absolutely insist you turn yourself off entirely, we will have a specific word."

Over Christmas, I'd read a cheesy S&M novel—the eighteenth *Fifty Shades* installment, where Christian was now a Timeless who acted pretty much the petulant age he always had, say about four, and Anastasia still hadn't figured out that this whole arrangement really wasn't maxing out her human potential—so I knew all about safe words.

She had whispered the word, asked if I got it. I said yes, and when she whispered again, I was gone.

And now, a few months later, I'd remained true to my promise. It was a trade-off worth keeping. I mean, if you lived only five years, would you want to spend seventy percent of it unconscious?

Thus, off-duty events, like the visit to meet Zach at the Green Prosperity office, were always a matter of negotiation.

"So," I said as she locked her desk, "you're leaving me on?"

"Chandler, Zach and I haven't seen each other in five days. No offense, pal, but you're officially off." And she said the word.

4

"**W**ell, that was dramatic," Zach said as they started walking home from his office. He hoisted his duffel bag over his shoulder like a sailor on leave.

"Who was he?"

At the GPN office, a young man dressed in early-1960s college prep had been ranting that Patty Garcia had been murdered.

"One of our volunteers. Well meaning, but he can get a bit hyperbolic," Zach said, then grew more serious. "Is it possible?"

"What? That she was murdered? I wondered that myself, although it seems unlikely, given what I saw."

"What, uh, did . . ."

"Don't worry, nothing gruesome. A bump on her head. The golf ball that hit her was lying on the grass. The person who hit the ball appeared to be shocked and upset."

"So—"

"I'm waiting to hear if there are any surprises tomorrow when they do an autopsy. Colonel Mustard slipping her poison before her round of golf, or—"

"Sorry, I can't joke about this one."

Cop humor and all that, but damn if Zach wasn't right, and Jen said so.

They paused at a corner. A man and a woman in camouflage army fatigues and snappy red berets marched up to them and dramatically saluted. They were both young, fit, and extraordinarily good-looking. As the woman proffered a strip of cardboard with a memory button attached, the man said, "We'd like to talk to you about enlisting in the Climate Oasis Warrior Corps."

"Fuck off," Zach said. He tugged Jen by the arm to cross the street and mumbled, "Fucking parasites."

"Zach!" she said. She'd never heard Zach talk to anyone that way. "Those two are probably unemployed actors hired to be recruiters. Did you see them?"

Zach said, "I know . . . I know . . . It's just that . . ." He drifted into silence.

Jen didn't want their reunion destroyed. However, she took a few more steps, as if needing to physically distance herself from Zach's outburst, before she said, "Back to Patty Garcia, okay?"

"Right." Zach seemed to brighten at a bittersweet memory. "It was such an incredible breakthrough when she won the climate reparations lawsuit."

Even before the assault trial was over in Texas, Garcia had pulled up her tent pegs and moved her legal practice and home to DC. She had one aim: to lead the fight, both in the courts and in the public eye, to make the big carbon producers and their major investors pay back all their profits dating back to when scientists had clearly shown that carbon emissions were causing climate change. The proposition was simple: no one should have profited from the conscious destruction of humanity's collective future. Those profits would now be taken away and used for massive green programs across the country and around the world. Since the assumption was that companies and individuals couldn't or wouldn't pay, all their assets, which these days consisted not only of oil and gas but a vast amount of renewables, would be seized and put under public ownership. "Energy," Garcia proclaimed, "must be publicly owned and controlled."

Everyone said she was dreaming in Technicolor. Even if it miraculously squeaked through a lower court, it would be fought to the very top. But in the end, luck was on her side. Three conservatives on the Supreme Court had been personally traumatized by climate change: One had lost a daughter in a mudslide in California when a mountain that had already been stripped bare by forest fires was drenched with a year's worth of rain in one week. Another had seen his family compound in Florida disappear in Hurricane George— literally disappear; maps needed redrawing for that stretch of coastline. The third had lost her husband in the Great Oregon Heat Dome in '31.

Zach said, "Garcia claimed she wasn't surprised by the court victory."

"Really?"

"She liked to say it was a symptom of the whiplash changes in people's lives and their ideas. Even self-proclaimed conservatives were now focused on *conserving* the environment we were rapidly destroying."

There had, however, been one big hitch.

The courts had ruled there needed to be firm proof of when the industries knew for certain about the impact of burning fossil fuels. This would become the date set to measure the amount of reparations.

"And that," Zach said, "is the multi-trillion-dollar question."

"Literally?"

"Literally. The industry only fully acknowledged the data a few years ago. Reparations based on that timeline would cost them several billion. Chump change for them. However, some think the companies definitively knew as far back as the 1960s. If so, reparations would run into the trillions. But no one has found a smoking gun."

Jen said, "And so?"

"The courts imposed a deadline to fix a date."

"What was it?"

"Much too soon. Friday, April fourteenth."

"Only five weeks away from now."

Jen and Zach's walk was interrupted by a red light. She put her arms around his neck and kissed him.

He smiled and said, "That's for . . . ?"

"Being home. Being who you are. Knowing about all this stuff. So . . . ?"

"So, what?"

Jen said, "You think all these big bad oil barons had her knocked off?"

The light changed, and they crossed the street.

"It seems farfetched." He started into his next sentence but went silent, as if reassessing his thoughts. "Strange, isn't it? These people will consciously do things they know will kill millions of people. And yet I can't imagine one of them saying, *Let's bump off Patty Garcia.*"

"Why not?"

"I've met many of these folks. I disagree with them. Some of them are truly abhorrent, but many are decent people."

"You're forgetting your lectures."

"Jen," he said with a laugh, "I don't lecture you."

She came to an abrupt stop and made a point of getting his attention so she could roll her eyes.

As they started off again, she said, "You're always *lecturing* that it isn't about evil individuals. Corporations maximize profits, and damn the consequences for communities, workers, or nature. See," she said playfully, "I am taking notes."

"I don't—"

"But what I'm really interested in now is what you didn't tell me last night on the phone."

He looked puzzled.

"I asked you about the impact of Patty Garcia's death. You seemed to be holding back."

"She was supposed to speak at the conference on Monday night. The closing address. There were all sorts of rumors."

"Like?"

"Like she was going to announce she was running for president." In two years: 2036. "The media were descending on us. But . . ."

"What?"

"Some folks were saying there was something else."

"Like what?"

"No one had any idea."

They were now almost home.

Jen reached out and stopped him again. Tipped her head down. Looked at him out of the tops of her eyes. Rested her hand on his cheek. "Actually," she said, "what I really wanted to ask is whether we could forget about the fate of the planet for the night?"

And later that night, the lights out, both of them naked and content in their bed, after they had said good-night and Jen was about to drift off to sleep, Zach murmured, "I really do wonder what she was going to announce."

5

"**B**ut sir, it's—"

Captain Brooks held up a hand to stop her like he was still a rookie directing traffic. "There's absolutely no reason for you to attend the autopsy."

"What if she was murdered?"

"Then it's a job for homicide."

"Are they going be there?"

"No, because she wasn't murdered. It was an accident. Read your own report."

"I didn't definitively say it was an accident."

"No, and no one has definitively said that time travel won't ever happen, but you know what?"

"What?"

"It's not your case."

"I was first on the scene."

The captain rubbed the keloid scar over his eye. "Jen, there will be an autopsy. There will be a report from the chief medical examiner. I'm sure they'll rush that through."

"Sir, I'd really like to be there."

"No one likes being at an autopsy. Not even the pathologists."

"You know what I mean, sir."

"And I'm guessing you know what I mean too."

The boss and I slunk from Captain Brooks's office.

Legs in prison chains, we lumbered down the hall for a coffee. Think what it's like when your best friend or spouse is in a bad mood—how much it brings you down too. Now imagine if you shared their brain.

Despite that, I was happy when the smell of coffee hit me, even though, as usual, it was burnt. I like these cooler days because Jen drinks more coffee, and I like coffee because her buzz is my buzz. Good times.

"Chandler," she said to me, "I miss Les's pep talks. Cobalt Blue and all that."

One off-duty night a year and a half ago, Les was pushing Jen to be more assertive. "You need to be harder. Tougher," he had said. "Like steel."

He had taken a hit of the joint they were sharing.

"It's all about image. Start with your name."

Jen had said, "What's wrong with my name?" Jen B. Lu.

"You need a name that gives you swagger. Comic-book flash. Like steel or cobalt." And then in an utterly stoned progression, Les had riffed on Jen's unusual blue eyes, pasted together her middle and last names, and rechristened her Cobalt Blue.

She had said it was the silliest thing she'd ever heard, but kind of cherished it all the same.

"Boss," I said, "the captain's only doing his job."

"Me too."

For a millisecond I didn't know what she meant until I saw a thought lighting up one of the neural pathways that activates when Jen is being sly. "Damn," Jen said, "I totally forgot there's a report down at the chief medical examiner's office about one of our old cases that I was supposed to pick up."

"Which case?"

"Not exactly sure. But we'll figure it out."

"And you need a physical copy?"

"I'm an old-fashioned sort of girl."

Twenty-four minutes later we were down on Elm Street. The modern building was pretty nice-looking, but it was a good thing there were doctors inside: all those sharp glass edges could really hurt somebody. We waltzed through security and, as Jen is wont to do, climbed the stairs to the fourth floor.

The receptionist at Forensic Death Investigation was a white woman in her late thirties, which seemed a bit old to be a RBGV—a Ruth Bader Ginsburg visigoth—but the receptionist was appropriately decked out in faddish homage to the great RBG: rectangular dark-rimmed glasses and hair severely yanked back from her forehead. But like other RBGVs, her hair was dyed a screeching red, and she wore a shaggy fake-fur vest and an ornamental metal breastplate with not much underneath—hence visigoth. Weird. Definitely a thing that won't be around a year or two from now.

Halloween costume aside, she was all business.

Jen held up her badge and put on her most official voice. "I'm here for Patty Garcia's postmortem."

"Papers?"

I'm still amazed at the words humans keep using.

Jen said, "We didn't have time to process them. I'm hoping—"

"Insofar as"—when they remembered, RBGVs talked like they were writing a Supreme Court decision—"you lack the proper documentary evidence, admission will not be possible."

The woman looked again at Jen's badge, and her bureaucratic demeanor cracked like a frozen pond getting hit by a meteorite. Her whole RBGV cool disappeared. "Oh my God. I don't believe it. You're Detective Lu. Last year I read everything, I mean everything, about you, and I mean, you are like so amazing!"

She was referring to the case that had almost gotten Jen killed and turned Les into an automaton. Jen had caught rumors of a bootleg version of the Longevity Treatment, which, as I mentioned, was normally only available to the super rich and powerful, creating the Timeless. The bootleg version would supposedly allow ordinary people to live a healthy life well into their nineties. But when it seemed to be killing anyone who got it, Jen tracked down whoever was pushing it. In doing so, she paved the way for the distribution of a safe version of the modified treatment.

The gushing woman said, "I can't believe I'm meeting you." She stuck out her hand, "My name's RBGV-780. It's super cool to meet you." She pointed to a group of chairs. "You go right over there now and sit while I check with Dr. Samuel."

We sat. I read Jen her messages. I read her a long obit about Garcia. The receptionist kept stealing glances our way. It was fourteen and a half minutes before a man came out in scrubs. He was handsome, late middle aged, hair still dark, with a pleasant smile and a firm walk that told you he took exercise seriously.

"Sorry, I was tied up. I'm Dr. Samuel."

Where's he from? Jen asked me.

South Africa. Probably Cape Town.

"Ashley"—he nodded toward the receptionist—"sorry, RBGV-780, says you were hoping to witness the Garcia autopsy."

"I was first on the scene. Just doing a routine follow-up."

"On what appears to be an accident?"

"I didn't definitively say that in my report."

"Well, that's why I was delayed. We were just finishing up."

"And?"

"You'll have to wait for the report."

Even with improvements in recent years, we knew that reports from this office usually took ages. Dr. Samuel apparently knew as well, so he kindly added, "We're rushing toxicology and histology—"

Tissue samples, I said.

"—and hope to have a preliminary report by Friday."

"Can you tell me anything?"

"What did you observe, Detective?"

"She'd been hit on the head by a golf ball."

"That sounds about right. The contusion had a subtle subcutaneous pattern that is consistent with the dimples of a golf ball."

"Nothing else?"

He weighed her question.

"Who's going to hear whatever I might say?"

"No one. I promise."

"RBGV-780 tells me you were the cop who saved so many people last year."

Jen shrugged. She'd been curious. She'd been pissed off at whoever was circulating the deadly fake of the Longevity Treatment. She'd merely been doing her job and hated this attention, especially now that a few of her fellow officers were chiding her for not pulling off another miracle investigation.

To Jen's shrug, Dr. Samuel nodded gently. "She had a small abrasion on one of her fingers and a tiny bruise on her palm."

"Could they be defensive wounds? Can you pinpoint when they happened?"

"In answer to your first question, yes, it's possible. As for the latter, it's impossible to say when they were sustained. She had almost three days to heal before she died. We took tissue samples to see if we could determine what caused the wounds."

"Could they—"

"They could be anything. Innocuous."

"Or not."

"Or not," Dr. Samuel agreed. "We also found a fiber healing into the cut on her finger. I had a quick look at it. I'm guessing it's nylon, but we'll know for certain when we get the analysis from the lab in a few days."

"And the color?"

"That one's easy. It was bright green. But," continued Dr. Sam, "so far nothing indicates that we're looking at anything but a strange accident."

"A golf ball in the head can kill you?"

"A lot of things can kill you."

Jen and I zoomed straight up to Viridian Green. This time, getting through the electronic gate was more of a challenge. We then had to wait in their tasteful lobby. No tattered doctor's office magazines here but actual paper copies of today's newspapers, crisp golf magazines, and glossy brochures advertising the exclusive Climate Oasis getting built in Wyoming. *Freedom! Land! Security!* it proclaimed—code words for no taxes, no coastline about to get swallowed by the sea, and only people like you. (That is, except for the hired help running the stores and restaurants, concierging your life, maintaining the infrastructure, tending your gardens and children, cleaning your home, cooking your meals, and shooting outsiders who don't belong.)

After ten minutes, the woman who'd met us five days ago, Georgette Baxter, came out to greet us.

We exchanged the usuals. "Sorry about this loss." "Everyone here is in shock." "I'm sure they are." "It's a loss to us all." Jen's pretty good at this banter from her days in the Elder Abuse Unit, but I could tell she was hungry to dig into the meat.

"Georgette, I'm wondering if you noticed any strange reactions from your members."

"Like?"

"Oh, nothing really. Anyone who didn't seem too shocked?"

Ms. Baxter had the decency to pretend to think about it for 6.2 seconds; she even bit her bottom lip. "No," she said. "Of course not. Everyone here is in shock," she repeated.

"No odd behavior?"

"Why would you . . . you don't think Mr. Trebook or Dr. Kershaw were, my God, I mean—"

"No, definitely, absolutely not." Although of course we weren't counting them out.

"So, then . . . ?"

"It was an accident. I'm just crossing a few *t*'s."

This made no sense, but Georgette seemed mollified.

"I actually dropped by to pick up Ms. Garcia's golf bag. The bright-green one she was carrying. You guys did save that?"

"Of course we did. But you'll have to talk to Mr. Moorehouse." Said with the conviction that *everyone* knew who Mr. Moorehouse was.

"He's . . . ?"

General manager by title, but when we met him a few minutes later, I would have pegged Mr. Moorehouse as a former army officer. A colonel or general, except I knew that most retired generals went on to work for defense companies hawking expensive doodads to their former subordinates who wanted to be fawning customers so they'd get the next round of jobs. When we entered his office, he didn't bother standing. Perhaps it was because he was nailed to the stiff-backed chair. Perhaps it was because he was a rude dick.

Either way, he was scribbling on a piece of paper, his eyes focused through reading glasses.

"Sit," he ordered, not even looking up. His voice was quiet but imbued with authority.

We sat. We examined his hair, a silly 1950s crew cut. I asked Jen if we could arrest him for that.

He spoke, still not raising his head.

"Georgette reports you have a request."

"I came to retrieve Patty Garcia's golf bag. As part of our investigation." I could feel Jen fighting the urge to snap off *sir* at the end.

He finally looked up. "May we see your warrant?"

"I don't need a warrant to assemble items from the scene of a crime or unexplained accident."

"You are telling us Garcia's death was a crime?"

"No."

"In fact, I am told it was quite clearly an explained accident."

"We're waiting for the medical examiner's report."

"Ms. . . ."

"*Detective* Lu." This time I could feel Jen fighting the urge to snap *you fucker* at the end.

"Detective Lu. We naturally have kept her golf clubs and bag to give to her next of kin. That is our standard procedure. Should you wish to access them, return with a warrant."

Jen, there's no way we'll get a—

No kidding.

Unless the bag was evidence in a homicide investigation or might help get to the bottom of a suspicious or unexplained death, no judge in DC these days would give us a warrant. And anyway, going to Captain Brooks with that would be announcing Jen had disobeyed his order not to investigate Garcia's death, which was why Jen was tiptoeing around this schmuck in the first place.

"Maybe I could just take a quick peek at it. The bag." *And slice off a chunk of neon-green nylon that might match the fiber in the wound.*

"Warrant," was all he said as he turned his attention back to the papers on his desk.

6

Friday

Jen and Zach had already stood in line for twenty minutes. Her patience had run out nineteen and a half minutes earlier.

"Do you actually think this will be worth it?"

"Who knows," Zach said. "It's getting a ton of buzz."

"So are the giant murder hornets." They'd now made it as far east as Chicago. Chandler, she thought, would know the scientific name for them. She considered rousing him to ask.

The line to the exhibition inched forward. Inside was a new installation by an artist named Second Century B.C. She'd been a winner at last year's Venice Biennale—sadly, the final one before the city joined Atlantis in the depths of the Mediterranean. Rising sea levels had proved too much for the flood barriers.

"Zach . . ."

"Yes?"

"You haven't heard any new rumors about Garcia, by any chance?"

"Such as?"

"Reasons someone might kill her."

"You said you talked to the pathologist today."

"Between us, right?"

"As always."

They shuffled two steps.

"There was a small cut on her finger. Possibly a defensive wound."

"If she'd been attacked."

"Exactly. Healing into the cut was a bright-green fiber."

"Okay."

29

"Her golf bag was bright green. Which could mean she was using it as a shield to protect herself."

"Can you examine the bag?"

"No luck so far."

She and Chandler had meticulously studied the photographs she'd taken of the golf bag, both in the position Garcia had dropped it and after one of the course employees had picked it up once she'd been choppered away. The bag was in mint condition, with nothing to suggest it had been used as a shield.

"Of course," Jen continued, "it could be that when she earlier picked it up, it slipped and cut her. Or maybe the fiber isn't from the golf bag at all. Maybe it was from the shirt worn by the attacker."

The line crept forward three feet. They were getting close.

Zach slung his arm around Jen and hugged her.

"You're wonderful," he said.

"True."

"Pathologist with years of experience says it was an accident. Cobalt Blue says that one green fiber in a small abrasion on her hand—"

"Her finger."

"Right . . . on her finger points clearly to murder."

At the mention of her nickname, Jen laughed.

"Speaking of Cobalt Blue," Zach said, "let's take Les for a bike ride sometime."

"Sure," Jen said. "And can you ask around about Patty Garcia's big announcement?"

"I already told you. There were only rumors."

"Someone must know."

The line advanced a few feet, as if it were a chain of prisoners shuffling forward. The gallery was letting in a maximum of two people at a time. Polyamorous households were screwed.

The gallery door opened. Jen and Zach watched a woman emerge from the exhibit followed by a man with a baby strapped across his chest. Zach turned his attention back to Jen but didn't speak. In the way you learn to read someone you spend a lot of time with, Jen knew exactly what he was about to bring up again—even though it was a total change of topic. It was the back-and-forth discussion they'd been having for the past month.

She stopped him in his tracks.

"Zach," she said, "it's too big a decision to make. I mean, everything would change. It's like in science fiction—"

"You never read science fiction."

"But I've seen enough movies. There's a moment when pathways diverge, where you create a totally different future with one simple action."

"As you've pointed out many times," he said, "having a kid isn't one simple action."

"You know what I mean."

Zach seemed at a loss.

Jen said, "The world is too uncertain. I'm too uncertain."

Zach was about to answer when a voice in front of them said, "Welcome to the new installation by Second Century B.C."

They entered the exhibit.

The room was pitch-black.

And absolutely silent.

The room stayed pitch-black. It stayed absolutely silent.

They had been warned not to touch the art, whatever it might be.

Jen whispered to Zach, or at least she assumed he was still next to her. "I don't get it."

"I don't think you're supposed to," Zach answered.

"What's the point?"

"I think that's the point."

Saturday

As Friday dragged into Saturday, Jen began to doubt her suspicions about Garcia's death. She had a stubborn streak about as wide as the Grand Canyon, but she wasn't stupid. She didn't believe in secret cabals and the perfect, undetectable crime. It'd been intriguing to imagine Garcia had been murdered, but perhaps Zach's gentle teasing at the art show had been right: she should trust what the smart pathologist had concluded.

As for the rest of what he had tried to bring up again, they had agreed to leave it until another day.

For Jen, the decision to have a child seemed as unfathomable as that idiotic art exhibit. Or perhaps that was the whole point. Of the installation, that is. Something about the unknowability of reality. Jen, however, didn't buy it. She wanted to figure things out. Figure out crimes. Figure out how the world worked. Figure out if she had it in her to be a good mother, she who had had an unhappy, miserable, abused and abusive mom herself. And figure out if just maybe Patty Garcia had actually been murdered.

Yeah, she mused, a scramble of thoughts as confusing as that stupid installation.

She and Zach ate breakfast on the roof—on Thursday it had turned warm again, and by today, Saturday, they didn't even need sweaters. Coffee, fruit salad, and Zach's weirdly wonderful green-eggs pancake—the green provided by kale blended in with the milk, butter, and eggs.

Throughout that lazy day, Jen kept thinking about Patty Garcia. *She had an accident. Strange, but that's all it was.*

She kept trying to reassure herself. *It was an accident.*

And yet, all the repetition of this mantra wasn't doing its job. Like a killer bee that couldn't be shooed off, she kept feeling she was missing her target.

Slipping into her running gear, she was unable to quiet a nagging thought: *Something's off.*

She picked up Les, and they did the same run they had the week before. As they were flowing in rhythm along the heavily wooded trail that skirted the western edge of Viridian Green, she caught the faint but sickening smell of a decaying animal.

On they ran.

"Les," she said, "I wish you were able to work this through with me." She explained what she'd seen and what Dr. Samuel had said. "I can't help feeling there's an angle I'm missing."

She paused. No answer. No sound coming from Les.

Not until they were on their way home.

They were keeping up their pace, but Jen was now tired and no longer talking much. They were near the golf course again when Les stumbled slightly and, to Jen's amazement, grunted a sound. She glanced back at what had made him stumble. There, half pressed into the ground—sticking up enough to hurt if you stepped on it with running shoes—was a smooth stone.

"Hold it, Les."

Les stopped. Didn't seem at all curious that they had stopped. Didn't look at Jen as she went back to examine what he had stepped on.

She squatted down, and what had at first seemed to be a stone was clearly a golf ball.

She fetched a sharp-edged rock and dug at the hard-packed ground around the ball. She set down the rock and wiggled the ball from the dirt.

It was a very old ball, the white turned yellowy brown from years stuck in long-dried mud. There were cracks on it.

She held it in her hand. The itch. The itch. She threw it into the woods so no one else would step on it.

And as they started running again, the itch finally got scratched.

Patty Garcia's golf ball.

I wonder, thought Jen, *if they ever found her golf ball.*

7

"**D**r. Kershaw? This is Detective Jen Lu. Really sorry to bother you on the weekend."

The second she'd returned from her run, Jen had punched me in for a bit of overtime. Maybe only to be her telephone operator, but I like to think she wanted to have a second set of ears for this one: phoning the woman doctor who'd been with the hedge fund guy who'd bonked Garcia.

"You are?" Kershaw said.

"I'm the police officer who was at Viridian Green when Patty Garcia had her accident."

"I'm getting dressed to go out."

"I have a quick question," Jen said.

"Make it snappy."

"You said you were certain the ball up near the green was yours."

"Yes, I did, and I am. But as you know, I left in the helicopter and didn't go and pick up my ball."

"Did anyone from the golf club return it to you? Your ball?"

The doctor laughed. "They cost ten bucks. Anyway, it wasn't really mine."

"What do you mean?"

"One of the privileges members and guests enjoy is that in the starters' cabin there are three types of balls to choose from. All the very best. You take whatever you need to play the round."

Words from an old Billie Holiday song played in my circuits, the line about how those who already have keep on getting more.

"So," Jen said, "how did Mr. Trebook know the golf ball on the ground was his?"

"It's customary to put an identifying mark on the ball."

34

Chandler?

Nothing on it but a scuff from a club.

"His wasn't marked," Jen said.

"If you don't mark the ball, one notices the number so there's no confusion about whose ball is whose. But he plays Titleist and I play TaylorMade, so he could identify his that way. We watched mine land near the green and we knew approximately where his landed, even though we couldn't see it from the tee. There was no question in either of our minds that was his ball."

"And you didn't see Ms. Garcia's ball?"

"I assume she must have already hit her second shot. It must have been somewhere around the green. Or if she had mishit, it could have been in the woods, although she was an excellent golfer. Sorry, but I really need to—"

"One last question, I promise. If it had been found, how could anyone identify her ball for certain?"

Dr. Kershaw laughed. "That's easy. Everyone, even guests like me, knew that she used her own balls. All custom labeled."

"Sort of like vanity plates?"

"From what I heard, that wouldn't be her style. No, hers all used the number sixteen."

"That something special in golf?"

I started to feed Jen the answer, but Dr. Kershaw was already speaking.

"I don't think *he* played golf."

"He who?"

"Abraham Lincoln. The sixteenth president of the United States."

Next call was to Peter Trebook. I would have visualized his face changing colors as it had when we first interviewed him, except our conversation lasted only 6.83 seconds. "Detective. I'm sorry, but I've been advised by counsel not to speak about this matter. If there are any further questions, they should be directed to them." With that, he hung up.

"Boss," I said, "I found something interesting about Trebook."

"I find that hard to imagine."

"You have a cruel streak in you, Jen Lu."

"What is it?"

"His hedge fund was one of many companies cited in Patty Garcia's reparations case."

"Because . . ."

"They had massive investments in coal. A couple of teachers' pension funds headed for the doors, but most investors didn't give a damn about how they made their money."

"Okay."

"Then the Supreme Court upheld the ruling." Which never would have happened if the Court hadn't been expanded to thirteen justices with fifteen-year term limits. "When they did, the value of his fund plummeted by hundreds of millions."

"Cue the sad violin music, please."

"Want to bet who was called as a witness at the original trial?"

"Tough one, but I'd have to put my chips on Peter Trebook."

"And guess who raked him over the coals?"

8

The phone call came two days later on an unseasonably hot Monday afternoon right as Jen was trying to find the energy to leave the station. She'd been up since early in the morning and had suffered through a particularly tedious shift at District One, going through computer records of the seafood vendor they were beginning to investigate. She was having a hard time remembering whether to go down or up to get downstairs to the front doors when her phone pinged.

"This is Georgette Baxter," the voice said in a whisper. "From Viridian Green."

"You sound like—"

"You should come here."

"Sure. How's tomorrow morning for you?"

"I mean right now. They found a body."

Chandler, she yelled at me as we flew downstairs, *why didn't you hear about this?*

A purple police motorcycle pulled up for us right as we reached the front door. Man, am I efficient. So what if I missed an emergency call to another district?

Dead body. Second death up there in a week. Whispered phone call. If that didn't demand the siren, whatever the hell would? We were on fire as we raced up 16th. Good times.

"Maybe Georgette lost it and knocked off her dick of a general manager," I said.

"Not her style," Jen replied. "Maybe they let Mr. Trebook back on the course."

"Or maybe—"

"Chandler, clever repartee gotta be done in moderation."

Life lessons.

We shot past Military Road NW and banged a hard left onto Joyce, past a bored-looking uniform stationed at the open gate and up to the clubhouse, where, once again, Georgette Baxter was waiting for us in a golf cart.

"It's horrible," she said. "It's . . . I mean, he told me not to phone you. He talked to me like I was some, I don't know, so I did it anyway, I called you, and—"

"Georgette. Take a breath."

She sucked in air like she'd just swum underwater across the English Channel.

Jen waited and then said, "What happened?"

"Over the weekend"—she took another big gulp of air—"a few members mentioned a dead-animal smell."

I smelled it when I was running with Les, Jen said to me.

"We get that sometimes with all the woods around us. Today, though, it was awful strong. So Eugene, he's one of our groundskeepers, a real sweetie who—"

"Focus, Georgette."

"He goes to find it and bury it or whatever he does. But . . ."

"Take a breath, Georgette."

"Yes. Well. He phoned straight up to Mr. Moorehouse to say someone was dead. He thinks it might be Modus."

"Who's Modus?"

"He used to work here. At the old course, I mean. He was let go by the new management. He wasn't quite the type they . . . Anyway, it seems he ended up living in the forest, scavenging for golf balls in the woods and the ponds, you know, very early in the morning, to sell somewhere. They give out very good golf balls here. The grounds crew says he never bothered anyone. Mr. Moorehouse ordered staff to call the police if they spotted him, but, well, I have the impression that never happened. People seemed to like him."

That was the longest burst of words we'd yet heard from Georgette. She paused long enough to gulp a couple of lungfuls of air.

"They call him a Shadow, but that's not a nice word, is it?"

Jen agreed it was not.

"Please don't tell Mr. Moorehouse I phoned you. Say you heard about it and thought you should come. I don't want to get into trouble. He's, well . . ."

And on she nattered as we raced across a familiar fairway, into a familiar patch of woods, and down a familiar pathway.

"Georgette, you didn't say where the body was found."

"I didn't? Well, by the fifth hole."

The hole didn't look so pretty this time.

At the side of the fairway, about a hundred yards past where we had found Patty Garcia, was a convention of police vehicles and golf carts. Scene-of-crime folks, all civilians these days, had driven their van across the fairway, and from the look on Mr. Moorehouse's face as we drew near, it wasn't clear whether he was more upset about the ruts on his pretty lawn or the fact that a man without a home was dead, although I'd have put big bucks on the former. Two uniforms were running caution tape along the edge of the woods. A man and a woman in white Tyvek jumpsuits were setting up floodlights: the sun would be setting in an hour and seventeen minutes, and already, over here on the western side of the fairway, the woods were gloomy.

Mr. Moorehouse and several members of his staff stood off to the side, two holding their noses, three with masks, all looking green.

Jen, there's Dick Zeleski. Homicide.

Dick was at the edge of the woods, talking on his phone. As we walked toward him, the wind shifted, coming straight at us from the woods.

"Jesus H.," Jen said, and I felt her throat tighten and her hand shoot reflexively to cover her nose and mouth.

Here's the thing you need to know about me. What Jen sees, I see. What she hears, I hear. Same goes for touch, taste, and smell. The only thing, and it's a big thing, is that I don't *experience* any of these the way she does. I know she finds the sight of Zach's broad shoulders attractive, as she does the flop of his hair onto his face and his boyish but rugged looks. I can admire them all, appreciate his proportions and intellectually know he stacks up well compared to other men I've observed. But none of these send a sizzle through me like they do her. She loves the taste of freshly picked tomatoes with basil and finds the taste of cauliflower "dusty," whatever that's supposed to mean. I can recognize those tastes and sense her reactions, but they evoke no love or hate. The mere thought of ice cream makes her shudder: it rekindles a horrible memory of abuse by her mother. But even if I get to taste it someday, which I never will because she won't touch the stuff, it will evoke nothing but the sensations of smoothness and cold. Sight has been the easiest to appreciate, because I can match it with various aesthetic principles—balance, symmetry, the play of light and shadow, and images I've learned to appreciate. Hearing, too, is something I can judge. Touch I get. But when it comes to smell and taste, I'm hopeless. I can identify many things by their taste or smell, much more acutely than Jen or any other human. But none of it is *good* or *bad*.

This is one of my greatest limitations. In normal moments, it makes me sad.

But being so close to a body that had been decaying for more than a week was not a normal moment.

I felt Jen gag. Take her hand away from her face so it didn't appear that she couldn't hack it. Breathe through her mouth. Hear her wish she had one of those tiny jars of Tiger Balm, a Chinese menthol ointment, so she could rub some under her nose. She was fighting hard not to vomit.

Dick Zeleski ended his phone call and acknowledged Jen with a grim nod.

Dick had had a bad case of acne as a teenager, but rather than this being a source of embarrassment, it had become a badge of honor. He wore bright-red glasses so you couldn't help but look at his face, and he'd occasionally rub a hand over his scarred cheeks in appreciation. I like it when humans take pride in their differences.

They bumped fists. Jen said, "You doing okay?"

"I'd prefer the White House Rose Garden, know what I mean?"

"Homicide?"

"Can't tell. It's pretty nasty in there. Did you hear about the hyena that escaped from the zoo?"

"Yeah."

"Seems we found it. Or at least it found the body."

Jen wasn't enjoying this.

Dick said, "The hyena gave the guy who found the body"—he opened his notebook—"Eugene Yong, quite a scare before it ran off."

"Can I have a look?"

"You serious?"

"I was here when Patty Garcia was killed." Jen turned and pointed up the fairway. "Just over there."

"Oh, that's right. I hear you've decided she was murdered."

"Dick, who told you that?"

Dick shrugged.

Chandler? Jen said to me.

I shrugged too. Things get around.

Jen said, "It does seem odd to find two bodies within a hundred yards of each other."

"One wasn't a body when you found her. And, so I read, it was clearly an accident."

"When did this happen?"

"Hard to tell. They first noticed smells over the weekend." He rubbed his cheeks. "That would usually tell you it was only a few days before. But it was damn cold for a spell last week, and that would have slowed down decomposition. So maybe a bit earlier. See what I mean?"

Jen looked into the woods. I could feel her pupils dilate.

"Where is he?"

"About forty, fifty yards in." He raised an arm and pointed. "You can just make out a clump of kudzu. See it?" He made a circle with his pointing hand. "The huge one there."

Like a creature from a bad horror movie, thick vines were digesting a group of short trees.

"This guy seems to have made a home in the middle of it. Eugene over there"—Dick turned back to the fairway and pointed to a young man in work clothes—"found him right near the opening."

"So, can I?"

"Crime scene folks need us to keep our distance."

"Dick, I want to see this."

"Even a total sadist wouldn't want to see this."

Jen said, "You haven't been talking to my captain, by any chance?"

Dick looked genuinely mystified.

"Here's what I can do," he said.

"What?"

"Elmore could share my memory of it with your sim. Chandler, right?"

"You can do that?"

"They're trying it out with a few of our sims. You sure you want to see this?"

"Yeah, go ahead."

"Here it—"

"Jesus!" Jen's head whipped back, and I yanked the image away from her mind.

"Sorry about that," Dick said. "I should have had Elmore fade it up slowly. Elmore's pretty no-nonsense. Not much for flowery descriptions, just slaps it down on the table, if you know what I mean."

Ready to try again? I said.

I made sure it faded in slowly.

Jen keeps instructing me to be more sensitive. Okay, so let's just say the hyena had gone to work on the abdomen and then did what striped hyenas can do, which was crush the skull to get at the brain. I suppose if you saw a nature documentary with a hyena devouring a zebra, you'd find it gross but fascinating—the cycle of life and all that. Here, it was just plain disgusting.

Jen said, "That's gonna play hell with forensics."

"Yeah, probably. But if he was shot, they'll find evidence. Stabbed, even with that damage, there should be cuts or stab wounds. Natural causes, they'll likely find that too, unless it was cancer of the belly button. Drug overdose would be easy. Don't see how any of those could be linked to Garcia."

The crime scene folks weren't going to let us get close for hours, so Jen asked Dick to call her when they were ready to remove the body.

Jen and Zach were supposed to have dinner at their favorite Cambodian joint, but she told him that the thought of meat or even fish, natural or vat grown, made her queasy. They met at home for a salad. Turned out even that was a challenge—she just couldn't get the stench out of her nose.

It wasn't until 20:26:17 that Dick phoned. We were back at Viridian Green in eighteen minutes.

"Do we need to put on Tyvek?"

"Naw, but you'll want these." Dick handed Jen a face-mask respirator.

"Scene's real clean," he said. "No rain, so no footprints. They got nothing so far except a spilled bag of golf balls. That and the body."

"And?"

"No visible harm, if you count out the . . . you know. I'm guessing it's drugs or natural causes."

Dick slipped on his mask. We followed him along a path marked by phosphorescent tape. The woods were lit up like a movie set, the air dense and heavy. We reached the kudzu, which, perhaps because of the powerful lights flooding the scene, looked otherworldly. One figure in white coveralls was doing a slow crouch-walk through the woods.

"Around the side." Dick's voice sounded like it was coming from underwater.

We followed.

Just as we arrived, two figures decked out head to toe in white were setting out a body bag beside the corpse. We were nine and a half feet away.

Jen forced herself to look at the body.

It was ugly. As described.

One more nightmare for Jen, I figured.

I wanted to check out the scene. *Look around*, I said.

There wasn't much to see. The ground was a dry patchwork of plants, sticks, tree roots, and hard-packed soil. Only one thing: about seven feet from the body, a ratty cloth shopping bag lay on the ground. Scattered around it were twelve golf balls.

A covered-up investigator with a camera slung over their shoulders and fingers to their phone was checking photos, or sending an email, or playing whatever game was big in CSI circles this year. Probably Fungus Attack.

Jen went to this figure—seemed to be a man from the shape.

"Can I look at the golf balls?"

This person said in a deep voice, "Yep. Done with those." Meaning they'd been photographed and would be bagged for fingerprinting if foul play was suspected. "Don't handle them."

Jen took some of her own photos. Squatted. Popped on her light. Moved her head around to read the number on each ball, grabbed a stick and poked at one or two if she needed to turn them over to read their makes and numbers. Nothing to see but twelve golf balls, all in good shape.

She stood and gazed around. Other than the balls, the scene was clean, just like Dick had said. No litter. Nothing scavenged from people's garbage. Nothing but nature. Assuming this fellow lived here, he cared for things and wanted to stay hidden. Unless someone had been through here cleaning up afterward. In which case, why leave the golf balls scattered?

Jen's eyes turned back right as they lifted the body and set it into the bag. Her eyes dropped to the spot where the body had lain.

Nothing underneath but dirt and matted foliage.

Dick came over to us. "Not exactly worth your while coming back."

The sound of a zipper brought our eyes back to the bag.

They lifted it and started walking.

"Well," Dick said. "That's it for me for tonight. Off to help Evert with his homework." Dick turned to leave.

I saw the picture forming in Jen's mind.

"Wait!" yelled Jen.

The two figures in white paused but didn't set the body down.

Jen said, "There was something in his back pocket. I saw a bulge when you lifted him."

One of the investigators spoke. It was a woman's voice. Tired. "Could be a wallet. Could be anything."

"I need to see it."

Dick said, "Jen, if there's anything there, the folks at forensics will catch it."

"I need to see it now."

The woman said, "And we need to get out of here."

Dick said, "Leave it, Jen."

Jen stepped forward and reached for the zipper.

The other person, who sounded like a man, said, "Just hold it there." He turned to face his partner. "Rachel, let's just do this, okay?"

They set the body down. Unzipped it.

"Which side?" the man said.

"Left. The side I was on."

The two gently turned the mutilated body. Sure enough, something round was bulging in his back pocket. The woman called out, and the man who'd been on his phone came over with his camera.

"Get a photo of this, will you?"

He took a few.

She then slipped her gloved hand inside the pocket and pulled out a golf ball.

Fake surprise in her voice, the woman said, "Wow. It's a golf ball."

Dick said, "Assuming it's this Modus guy, he collected those balls over there."

Jen said to her, "Can you make out anything on it?"

The woman held it in front of her and turned it slightly as if trying to catch enough light to read the brand. "Titleist something."

"That's it?"

"And a number. Number . . . uh . . . ten."

I felt Jen deflate.

"No, wait a second, it's sixteen. Yeah, for sure . . . sixteen."

9

Patty Garcia's office was in the spanking-new building kitty-corner to the McCain Senate Office Building, what was once the Russell Senate Office Building, named after an archsegregationist from Georgia. I figure that if you ever want a tour of utter nastiness, racism, thuggery, privilege, and patriarchy, just check out the names of public buildings and streets in the United States. Throw in art galleries, hospital wings, and university buildings, and you'll add vanity, greed, and profiteering to the list of sins. Yeah, yeah, I know, many are named after extremely worthy people, and some decent types who paid to have public buildings named after themselves, but I tell you, I'm the one with a database for a brain and I can pull up a pretty nasty list.

The elegant four-story glass–and–red granite building was a pleasant contrast to the nearby government buildings, where power seemed carved into marble and limestone. Garcia's legal practice occupied the top two floors. Although it was a small firm by contemporary standards, it had the cultured elegance I'd seen in them all. But instead of the usual important paintings and sculptures posed like visual name-dropping, there was fantastic art and objects from Latin America. Garishly colored carved animals from Mexico. Bright Guatemalan textiles. A wall display of hats—white Panama hats, black bowlers from Bolivia, woven hats from Peru. And a wall of woodcuts by Costa Rican artist Francisco Amighetti.

We'd made it into Garcia's inner sanctum. If I'd had breath to take away, this room would have done the trick. Glass windows with a view of the Capitol dome. An actual fireplace. A creamy-looking Italian leather couch. Built-in shelves, now devoid of books. An ornate coffee table resting on a pomegranate-colored Mexican rug. A Queen Anne walnut desk with, incongruously, a battleship-gray adjustable desk chair.

The top of the desk was untouched, as if Garcia's staff was too scared to disturb any of it. A computer monitor. A leather writing pad. A neat stack of documents in a colorful wooden tray. A glass of pens and another of pencils—the glasses lurid colors. A photo of Garcia and an older couple I identified as her parents.

And a clear glass bowl containing eight golf balls, as if to remind her there was life outside of law.

Number sixteen, at least the ones I can see.

Got it, Jen replied.

Maybe Jen did get it and was keeping it from me. But last I'd heard, we didn't have a clue about the significance of Modus carrying one of Garcia's golf balls in his pocket. Had she hit her ball into the woods as Dr. Kershaw had speculated? Had Modus picked it up and stuffed it into his pocket and the killer not found it when he dumped out the bag of balls? However, why would Modus's killer need to find that particular ball? As far as I was concerned, it was much ado without nothing. (On the bike ride over here from District One, I'd read through Shakespeare. What a guy!)

Except for the untouched desk, everything in Garcia's life was being discombobulated. Everywhere we turned, banker's boxes were stacked like crenellated castle walls. Other boxes were still open; staff members shuffled back and forth to fill them.

"What's happening with all those?" Jen said.

The woman we had come to interview brushed two fingers against the fringe of her Beatles' mop-top hair, this year's de rigueur haircut for white Beltway women. In polish, she matched the room. She wore an expensive metallic-cloth suit, emerald in color with lighter-green piping. Its severe cut perfectly matched the severity of her long face. It was too angular—and her eyes too large—to be considered beautiful, but it fit what seemed to be a sharp determination.

Brita Germaine, fifty-three years old, longtime executive assistant to Patty Garcia.

It was clear she was a woman who meant business and was used to being in charge. However, right now it seemed that boxes, books, papers, and files were the ones in control.

Germaine said, "This task will take forever. We can't . . ." She faltered and shook her head, as if unused to feelings of discouragement and defeat. Her voice combined a soft East Texas drawl with enunciation perfected at Brown and then Yale law school—as usual, I'd done my homework. After university, she'd spent years at one of the big law firms in Boston, then another in Dallas before Patty Garcia recruited her.

"All her papers, all her reports, her notes, files, correspondence, every last thing. There's tons on button discs, which take even longer to sort through, but still there's so much damn paper."

Jen waited. Germaine hadn't gone within ten feet of her question.

"Right. Most will go to the appropriate senior partner. Personal stuff to her parents. Those ones with blue labels"—she pointed to the boxes—"are from the reparations case. There's talk of establishing a personal archive."

"Is that usual?"

"It's more common for politicians." This was said with the same tone Germaine might use with a dim-witted employee.

Chandler, Jen said, *does she mean like a building?*

Right as I said, *No*, Germaine seemed to read Jen's mind. She gave Jen a pitying look that Jen didn't like. "We're in discussions with Rice to house her papers." And then, as if Jen were a total dolt, "The university, not the food."

I wanted Jen to say, *Or possibly Colgate. The university, not the toothpaste.* But the boss was all business.

"Ms. Germaine."

Brita shut her eyes for a second, like nothing in the world mattered anymore. "Brita's fine," she said, but her tone said that nothing would be fine for a dog's age.

"Brita, can we find a quiet spot to talk?"

Her eyes flickered to the boxes, as if she was torn between wanting to get it over with and preferring to do anything but supervise her staff as they sifted through the remains of Patty Garcia's life. She called out to two others who'd been carting papers and boxes in and out of the office. "Would you mind giving us the room for a few minutes?"

She plunked herself down on the sofa and, as if remonstrating with herself for any hint of sloppiness, sat up straight and crossed her legs at the ankles. Jen took an armchair. I'd never felt anything so soft except the pair of Italian gloves Jen had once tried on and then quickly handed back to the clerk when she discovered the price.

Only when Brita let out a sigh did I realize she'd been holding her breath. "This has been horrible. Patty was . . ." Brita's voice faded into the past.

"Yeah, she was," was just about all that was worth saying, and Jen said it.

"I suppose you all still think it was an accident, don't you?" Brita didn't even bother ramping up her voice to make an accusation. Discouragement. Defeat.

"The medical examiner's preliminary statement was unequivocal."

"But you said you were there."

"Not when the ball hit her."

47

"Then you tell me." Brita jutted her long chin at Jen in accusation. "Tell me what you think."

Jen, I said.

"I'm seeing if there are any loose ends to tie up."

"Such as why big oil had her killed?"

"You sound pretty sure of that," Jen said, thinking, *I knew that this woman was edging on crazy.*

Brita gaped at her as if Jen had questioned her certainty that the sun had plans to set in the west that evening.

"Detective—"

"I do Brita, then you do Jen."

I could see Brita's mouth starting to form the letter *J*, but that didn't get far. Even people used to being in charge can be strange around cops.

"I was asking why you thought big oil had her killed."

"Patty performed miracles. I mean, she pulled off what others had tried and failed to do. Almost everyone doubted her, you know."

"But not you."

"I wouldn't have worked for her if I did. And there was so much more she had set her sights on."

"Like becoming president?"

For a split second, the muscles in Brita's face constricted, but she quickly collected herself and laughed. "No. Real things. We were going to achieve so much."

Note the "we."

I did, Jen said back to me.

"What I was getting at," Brita continued, "is that the fossil fuel producers will have to cough up billions. And all because of what she did."

"I heard it could be trillions."

Again, Brita face tightened for a fraction of a second.

"Perhaps," she said, "but time is almost up to get the proof going back very far. Paying out billions is nothing to sneeze at."

"So they all get together and decide she has to go? You said big oil had her killed."

"Oh, come on. I'm not a wacko conspiracy theorist. It was shorthand. I didn't mean all these companies had a cabal to kill her."

"Shorthand for . . . ?"

"For a small group of people in the industry. Maybe just one Timeless guy who blamed her because he was about to lose his fortune and would have to abandon his plans to live forever."

"You really think those people go around killing their opponents?"

"Normally, they don't need to. They make sure laws are passed and millions of working people come to think they each have a stake in preserving the status quo that's going to kill their grandchildren."

There's nothing here, I said to Jen.

Jen shifted the topic.

"Had Ms. Garcia received any threatening messages in the past year or two?"

Brita's look was incredulous. "She was a high-profile woman. What do you think?"

"Like?"

"Constant trolling, for one thing."

"I'm not minimizing the impact of that, but any direct threats?"

"Yes, and we pass those on to a woman in the FBI we've worked with. Once they figure out who it came from, a visit to these dickless worms is enough to end it. When they can't track them down, they usually conclude it's either a troll factory in Russia or China or another pathetic guy trying to scare or demean women. We had a conviction nine months ago. He's still in prison for another three months."

Chandler?

He's still locked up.

Jen said, "That's it?"

"Plus all the usual suspects."

"Like?"

"For starters, Patriots for America. Patty led a civil suit against these self-proclaimed militias. We lost that one, but she was still trying to force the government to disarm them, although their numbers have plummeted since 7/28."

Bad stuff before my days, but the closest we've come to a second civil war.

"Do you think they might have tried to kill Ms. Garcia?"

Brita shook her head. "As much as those militia guys wanted her dead, they'd want to make the point they'd done it. Show off how big their guns are. No way they'd contrive to make it look like an accident with a golf ball."

Believe me, boss, there's nothing here. Not a shred of evidence she was murdered.

But Jen persisted.

"Did you and Ms. Garcia have a good working relationship?"

Brita bristled. "Of course we did. What are you implying?"

"Just asking." Jen looked at her notebook. "What do you know about Peter Tiebook, the hedge fund guy who—"

"I know who he is." Brita sounded relieved by the change of subject.

"When it comes to business, he seems absolutely amoral."

"Yes, but here's the surprising thing. After the trial, he actually reached out to Patty. They met. He didn't completely back down, but he listened to her concerns and said that as costly as the reparations will be, he thinks they are necessary."

"Was he playing her?"

"I don't think so."

Jen wrote a note and then said, "I'm curious about her ex, James Culpepper."

"Culpepper? He's a total shit. What about him?"

"Before their separation, did you have any inkling of his abusive behavior?"

Brita shook her head. Even she must have known this was a dead end. "Patty was a private person that way. She spoke about things they did together but never talked about what was actually going on between them." There seemed to be a tinge of resentment in Brita's voice that she hadn't had a say in what movie they watched or when they had sex.

"And when he pushed her down the stairs?"

"I was as surprised as everyone else."

"Do you think he was trying to kill her?"

Brita brushed a fleck of dust from the metallic green skirt. Those over-sized eyes looked upward again in thought, but I couldn't shake the feeling there was a bit of acting going on. "No, probably not."

"Afterwards, did she get threatening calls or emails from him?"

Brita shook her head in a slow, sad way, as if regretting there was no rope to hang the bastard with. "Not only that. Patty asked me to have his social media posts monitored, just in case."

"And?"

"He wrote nothing negative about her at all."

"He's still doing social media?"

"Oh yeah," she said with derision. "He sees himself as a big-time vision-ary who needs to share his wisdom with the world. He did one initial video saying he was innocent of the charges, that he was extremely sad that his wife had chosen to invent these stories but that would be all he would publicly say. I had a staff member monitor him right up to now. This morning, actually. There's been nothing other than one anodyne—"

Bland.

"—statement after she died."

Chandler, Jen said to me, *we'll need to go through his social media. And see if we can get hold of his email.*

"One other thing," she said to Brita. "I heard a rumor that Garcia was going to make a big announcement at the Green Prosperity conference in Raleigh. The weekend she died."

Brita stiffened again. She didn't speak.

Jen said, "Is that true?"

Brita said, "Yes, it's possible."

"Possible?"

"Of course I knew she was speaking there."

"Can you tell me what she was going to announce?"

"No. I mean, I don't know." Resentment again.

"As her executive assistant, wouldn't you be part of those discussions?"

Red tinged the face of the alpha woman, clashing with her green suit.

Resentful eyes glared at Jen and then looked away.

Brita's jaw stayed clenched. This woman was going to need a tetanus booster if she didn't lighten up.

Jen said, "Let me know, will you, if you figure that out."

She followed the direction of Brita's gaze to a thick display of small photographs pinned haphazardly to a large board. Boys and girls, young women and men but mostly women, each photo pinned on top of others.

Brita had regained her power of speech and her confidence. "Those pictures poured in after the reparations case. Young people, kids even, thanking her. They all said that for the first time, they felt they had a future. Some said they no longer regretted their parents decided to have them."

Into the silence in Jen's brain flashed phrases and images from her most recent discussion with Zach about having kids. But Brita quickly brought her thoughts to an end.

"What I was trying to say is that you shouldn't let this die. I may be wrong. Fine. But if there's a one-in-a-million chance she was murdered, isn't it worth finding out?"

10

As lunchtime approached, the boss was still obsessed about the quote-unquote murder of Patty Garcia.

"Jen," I said, "don't start looking again for patterns that don't exist."

"I'm not," she said.

My own body-mate lying to me.

"Anyhow," she said. "Last year there *was* a pattern." The string of deaths Jen had pieced together. Her big triumph. Taking down the bad guys behind the poisoned longevity treatments. And almost getting herself and Les killed.

She stood up. "Where're we going?" I said. She didn't answer, although I read her like a book.

A minute later, Jen knocked on the captain's office door.

"Sir, we've got a second death at Viridian Green."

Captain Brooks didn't even bother to respond.

Jen said, "Somebody must be up to something. Sir."

"Detective, bad guys are always up to something. That's why we call them bad guys and not good guys who've made an honest mistake."

"Captain, I think I should keep looking into this."

The captain rubbed the keloid scar where his left eyebrow should have been.

"Jen, first, there's no evidence that would give us reason to put resources into a nonexistent murder investigation. Second—"

"But—"

"Second," he said, with more emphasis, "it's not my call. And third . . ."

"Let me guess. Just do my damn job and stop making up stories."

"Something like that."

15:13:08

"I'm not sure digging into Patty Garcia's death qualifies as doing your damn job," I said to Jen.

Not for the first time, she was disobeying a direct order from the captain.

"You're right, it's *your* damn job. Keep reading, or whatever you call what you do."

I was breezing through everything about Patty Garcia's ex-husband I could get my virtual hands on, even though the captain had just told Jen there would be no investigation into her death. Social media feeds, newspaper articles, business websites, his weekly webcasts, credit records, public records of his salary and stock options from his oil days, and especially his big new project. We would need a warrant to dig through his emails or tax records. Jen, like a lot of cops, used to play it loose with things like that, but as she spent more time with Zach and his parents, she was taking illegal electronic searches with a bit more caution. But I mean, what fun is that?

"Get out of my brain for a minute, will you, Chandler?"

I like to think I'm indispensable, but the boss occasionally figures otherwise.

But then a minute later, she said, "Pack up, sport, we're out of here."

16:52:54

As she stared out the window at the snow-covered mountains, I could feel Jen's concentration wandering away from the interview. A condor soared past a high peak, playing in the wind. A breeze rustled through a stand of lodgepole pines and shook snow from their branches.

"Breathtaking, isn't it?" said James Culpepper III.

Ten minutes earlier we'd been slogging through a hot and humid spring day. Now we were inside a converted warehouse near Union Market with Patty Garcia's ex-husband. I couldn't figure out if the guy was fish or fowl. My carefully programmed ability to evaluate people was gummed up like someone had poured molasses into my algorithms.

The room was a cozy chalet. A real wood fire crackled in the fireplace—how they'd gotten permission to install it these days in DC was beyond me, but money talks.

Before coming here, we'd gone by his home, but no dice catching him there. Now we were inside the headquarters of Climate Oasis Inc.

Culpepper's big new project. Big investor. Big man on the board of directors. Big man who could still open doors, even if his reputation had been sullied.

Before we got down to business, he'd given us his spiel. Climate Oasis owned 1.6 million square miles of Wyoming on what had once been public land. They were constructing the largest gated community in the world. By far. They didn't want to have to deal with government tax and inheritance laws and they didn't want their citizens to answer to outside authorities if their private army, the Climate Oasis Warrior Corps, needed to shoot Shadows who invaded their land. So Climate Oasis had gotten the go-ahead from Congress to be a semiautonomous U.S. territory. Bigger than the second-smallest state, Rhode Island, and twenty-two thousand times larger than the country's newest state, our own dear state of Washington, DC—the *DC* part hanging on as an anachronism until they settled on the name of the state, given that *Washington* was already taken.

"Can I get you another hot chocolate?" Culpepper said.

"I'm fine," Jen said, turning back to the convicted wife abuser, a man with the bland handsomeness and calm authority of a corporate executive. "Let's get back to what happened between you and Patty Garcia, if we could."

"No problem," he said, and he was so calm I almost believed him. "I don't mind saying we'd been going through a hard time, the two of us. For at least eight months before it came to a head."

When he tried to shove her down the stairs, I said to Jen.

"I'm not claiming it was always bliss." He laughed a pleasant, self-deprecating laugh. "There were times we wanted to kill each other. But seriously, it was a good marriage, a solid marriage. If she could be sitting here today, she'd tell you the same."

Chandler, check it.

I checked six old profiles of her. *She says she was happy as a clam.*

"What changed?" Jen said.

A gust of cold air rushed in from the open window.

"One sec." Culpepper got up smoothly and athletically and closed the window. In the distance, heavy clouds now shrouded the mountains.

He sat back down. "You were asking what changed. Perhaps both of us. With our merger—"

"BP and Chevron."

"Right . . . With *their* merger, I should say, I was monstrously busy. Especially since I was already getting pulled into this wonderful big new project."

He waved his hand in appreciation at all that was his. "Meanwhile, she was having her little road-to-Damascus moment and decided that the way I'd made my fortune was the work of the devil."

"The work of the devil," Jen repeated.

James Culpepper III nodded grimly. "She actually said that once." He stopped talking and nodded to himself again, as if running through the scene in his head.

We studied him.

His hair was the color of a walnut shell, light enough to show his Anglo-Saxon pedigree but dark enough to give him authority. Good teeth. Absolutely perfect shave. Cheeks that were firm and eyes that showed brains, cleverness, but no guile. However, bundle it all together and there was nothing there. His face was bland and boring—the type of mug you could see in *Fortune* magazine one moment and not recognize the next when he tried to push you down the stairs.

Culpepper stared at the window. We followed his gaze to see that a snowstorm had cut visibility to a few feet. Snow was collecting on the window ledge. Even I wasn't certain how they'd pulled this off.

Jen said, "And then . . . ?"

His eyes slowly returned to Jen's, as if reluctant to dredge up painful memories.

"At first we agreed to disagree. But, little by little, we were arguing. She was already spending scads of time here in DC, although her office and of course our home were in Dallas. Not a good arrangement even if things are going well, and truth be told, the trust between us was breaking down. Disagreements started turning into arguments. Neither of us was ready to back down."

Jen was about to speak, but Culpepper jumped back in.

"Listen," he said brightly, "you gotta see the big picture."

"Of?"

He stood, again with that fluid, athletic motion. Gestured for us to follow him. We left the chalet and were now walking through an old warehouse that had been beautifully restored: sandblasted brick, thick timbers, polished hardwood floor, lights floating overhead. We passed between two sentries in the Warrior Corps camouflage uniform and red beret—they saluted when we passed, as if one of us were the U.S. president—went through a door, and there in front of us was a massive model of Climate Oasis. Their land was tucked against the Rocky Mountains. There were four towns. Even in this small scale, two looked like New England villages, complete with church steeples. A third had an appropriately western vibe, and the fourth was West Coast modern. Each had small houses.

"That's where everyone's going to live?"

Culpepper laughed. "Oh no. Those are for the staff and managers of various stores and restaurants. They'll be able to rent, but only our owners will have the rights of territorial citizens. Each citizen family will buy a large parcel of land and build on there."

"Is this already happening?"

"Surveying is complete. The first families have bought land, others have put down deposits. Work on the airport and main service roads begins soon; the perimeter defenses are going in. We're recruiting to our militia, the Warrior Corps. And we'll begin to lay the infrastructure for the first village this summer. Freedom."

"What?"

"The name of the first village. Freedom."

"That's great, Mr. Culpepper, I wonder if—"

"I wish I could tell you what's coming next." He waggled a finger as if Jen had pressed him to divulge a state secret. "But you're going to have to wait"—he glanced at his watch—"one week for that surprise."

"Cool," Jen said without conviction. "Mr. Culpepper, I know you're a busy man. If I could ask you one or two final questions."

"Shoot," he said.

"I'm curious," Jen said. "What sort of woman was she?"

Culpepper the Third shrugged. I thought I spotted a storm brewing deep in his eyes. Since his tone was so measured, it was impossible to tell whether it was sadness or anger. "Smart as hell. Athletic. Ambitious. A tremendous capacity for new ideas, some good, some not so. Wanted to get attention; you know, really stand out."

"Is that good or bad in your book? Wanting attention?"

"It made her effective, I have to say that. But . . ."

I felt Jen raise her eyebrows to ask the obvious question.

"That was our doom. She didn't simply want to win the argument between us; she wanted to make me and a whole lot of other people pay. Oh yeah, and she was desperate to have the public cheering for her. I was collateral damage." Culpepper was utterly calm as he said this.

"You don't sound angry."

"I was angry," he said calmly. "Extremely so. What she did cost me my position. The court case cost me a fortune and a loss of future income at a level it's hard for many people to imagine. It cost me friends. Respect. Standing in my community. From the second I was falsely charged until the verdict eight months later and then for another year . . . that whole time was horrible."

"What changed?"

"I healed myself."

He stopped. Let that sink in. Just maybe it was a line he'd delivered a few hundred times before.

"That's quite something." Even I thought Jen sounded sincere. "How'd you do that?"

"Four things." He composed his bland face. "One, I threw myself into Climate Oasis. I increased my investment and was brought onto the board of directors. Wait till you hear our next announcement."

Jen started to tell him he'd already said this to her, but he cut her off.

"Sorry, I already told you, but it's hard not to get excited. The board was only able to give it the final go-ahead last week."

"Groovy."

Groovy?

Stuff it, Chandler.

"Secondly," Culpepper continued, "I turned my anger into speaking out for the unjustly accused."

I'd read all about this and watched one or two of his broadcasts. He'd become a prominent defender of those men he called "the unjustly accused." Assorted men who'd raped, sexually harassed, or beaten up their girlfriends or wives. Aside from them, however, he attracted a second tier of followers: disgruntled men who complained that the only reason they weren't yet CEO of Apple was because a woman landed the job that should have been theirs. And finally a third tier: by and large decent, good men who were flummoxed by a world that had promised them rewards as men—a good middle-class job, financial security, a sense of authority, mastery, and respect—but now had been tossed onto the trash heap by an economy that had no place for them any longer. To one extent or another, all of them blamed their woes on women or at least felt men were the primary victims of a discombobulating world; many of the white ones had been taught to blame people of color for their woes. I should keep a running list of this sort of crap for every time I wish I were human—the absolute shit they inflict on each other.

Culpepper was still speechifying.

"Three. I did a huge amount of personal work. Detective, I've seen men and women self-destruct. Poison themselves, right?" He waited until she nodded. "I didn't want to end my days that way. I did a slew of hard work. Counseling, meditation, exercise, transforming my diet—I did it all. And it worked. I didn't forget. I didn't forgive. But I made sure that what she did wouldn't eat away at me."

Although relaxed and personal, his speech had a practiced quality to it. He'd recited this story of his metamorphosis many times.

"And number four?" Jen said.

"I moved here. It was simple. I wanted to reboot my life."

"Why DC, of all places? You've been here . . . how long?"

"I moved into my new home two years ago."

During our quick stop before coming to the Climate Oasis showroom, we'd only seen the outside of his large house. The grounds, though, were spectacular. Two point one acres in the middle of Washington, DC, a strip of woods separating it from St. John's College High School to the south. A winding drive lined with cherry trees, now in their final days of bloom, just off Oregon Avenue. Tennis court and a pool. All invisible to the street or to neighbors.

"DC isn't exactly your turf."

"I'm an easterner. Philly. I only relocated to Dallas for work and would have been moving to New York within the year if . . . well. A year after the trial, I suggested we set up one of our two Climate Oasis offices in DC to have good access to government officials."

"Well, you certainly have a beautiful house. Lucky to be facing Rock Creek Park."

And, Jen did not say, a ten- to twelve-minute run from there along the trails and through the woods to hole number five at Viridian Green Golf Resort.

"Mr. Culpepper, we've taken a lot of your time, and I appreciate it. Just one other question. I'm curious what you were doing two Fridays ago at the time of Ms. Garcia's accident?"

Jen and I had discussed this moment. Leave the big question to the end. Throw it in nice and easy, like a flat rock skimming the surface of a smooth pond. And before his heart even thumped another beat, I'd watch him for any telltale signs of worry or evasion, stuff I'm damn good at spotting.

There was nothing. No twitch, tic, flinch, muscle stiffening, intake of breath, or aversion of the eyes. Instead, a playful smile tugged at the corners of his mouth and his eyes twinkled as if he was amused by the question.

"You're asking me for an alibi? For an accident?"

"Not at all. Just curious. You don't have to answer."

"No worries. I was at home."

"Alone?"

"Actually, I was with about twenty-eight thousand men. You see, at the very hour that she was tragically injured, I was doing my weekly live broadcast."

11

"**H**e actually told you there were times he wanted to kill her?" Zach said.

"I think he was trying to get a reaction from me."

Zach was packing his overnight bag for a quick trip to New York City. "You said he was presenting himself as, I don't know . . ."

"Healed."

"God, whoever invented self-help has a lot to answer for."

Zach held up a sweater with broad yellow, white, and red triangles. "What do you think of this with my blue jeans? The pale-blue ones."

"It'll make you look like a beach ball bobbing in a swimming pool."

He nodded in appreciation.

She said, "You know I hate that sweater." And then after only the slightest pause, she said, "I think it was his way of showing he was smarter than me."

"But you have to admit, Jen, it's quite a leap from being smug to committing murder."

Which was exactly what Chandler had told her when she'd left the interview at Climate Oasis.

Zach put on a farcical expression, "Anyway, who hasn't said that at one point in a relationship?"

"I think it pretty much once a day," Jen said.

"It doesn't mean you go out and do it."

"And I promise not to if you ditch that sweater."

"Done," he said.

"But maybe he did," Jen said. "Kill her."

"Then it would be even harder to imagine he'd joke about it. Either way, he sounds like an insufferably arrogant bastard."

"Actually, he came across as pleasant."

60

"In which case, imagining he killed her is even more of a stretch."

"This whole investigation is a total stretch."

Zach tossed the sweater back into a drawer and grabbed another. Indigo with subtle streaks of pale yellow.

"Much better," Jen said.

Zach zipped up his duffel bag and kissed her. "Sorry I've got to run off like this."

Jen tried to look sorry too.

But she wasn't.

She needed time completely on her own to figure this thing out.

And sure enough, hours later, she was sleepy, sizzling, exhausted, and excited as her mind keep tumbling through Patty Garcia's life and death.

In was two in the morning before Jen finally fell asleep. There one minute, gone off the face of the earth the next.

She woke at ten and stripped off the T-shirt she'd slept in, scrambled into her running clothes, drank a coffee, ate a banana, and texted Christopher that she was going to pick up Les.

Soon they were running together, this time along the Potomac.

"Les," she said, "I sure could use your help to figure out if Garcia was murdered. And who did it. And why."

Les didn't answer.

Jen said, "I'd be smart to take your silence as a suggestion to drop the whole thing. Give me some guidance here, won't you?"

Les kept running silently at Jen's side.

12

"**H**ey, Doc," Jen said to Jamal el Massot, the lead technician for the implant program.

Doc had called us in for a diagnostic to make sure that his fix for my non-existent glitch was working.

I still had no idea why I'd been able to switch myself back on last year or why I could now remain aware even when Jen had booked out of work and officially signed me off. I only hoped Jamal wouldn't figure out I had this trick up my sleeve.

We both liked Jamal, maybe all the more so because we knew what he'd gone through almost twenty years earlier. He'd come from Yemen as a university student right before the Saudi invasion of his homeland. His mother, a nurse, had died when our then-favorite oil dictator had done one of his regular hospital bombings. A year later, Jamal's father, brother, and two sisters were also killed. These days Jamal was doing well, but Jen had once told me that anyone with a speck of empathy could see the deep-down pain in his dark-brown eyes.

"No strange things with Chandler?" he asked Jen.

She said no, except that I could be an asshole at times.

Yuck, yuck, I said to her.

He got Jen's permission to speak to me directly. He asked me the same question, and through Jen, I said, "Ditto, in reverse." I don't go into a monotone computer voice. It's Jen talking, but I know it creeps her out.

The doc had Jen flip me into diagnostic mode, and he linked me to his tablet.

And while he poked and probed me, I did what I wasn't supposed to be able to do and certainly not supposed to do: I poked and probed his database.

I had a swell idea.

11:42:18

"This is embarrassing."

The way Brita Germaine spat out the word with defiance made it sound not embarrassing in the least. More like *embarrassing* was a word she knew should be assigned to what she was feeling, but she was reluctant to show weakness.

We'd met her in front of the Smithsonian and were walking toward the Washington Monument. Okay, I'm probably not the first to say it, but nothing says patriarchy better than a 555-foot-tall penis. Whenever the right-wing judges yammer on about the intentions of the Founding Fathers (capitalized), they say it with the same religious fervor as when they clutch their Bibles and speak of their Father who art in heaven. George Washington and his brethren called the shots, and just like The Man, it shall be truth forever more.

Where was I?

Western end of the Mall. Hot day for mid-March. To the left of the monument, the last bunches of cherry blossoms hung sloppy and deflated from the limbs of the small trees, weeks earlier than in the old days. Brita was to our right, wearing a metallic red suit that had edges so sharp I kept warning Jen to keep her distance.

Have I mentioned that I didn't totally trust Brita? Jen said I was being unfair: Germaine seemed devoted to Garcia, and she was dealing with grief and the loss of a dream. Compounding that, she was about to be out of a job, although perhaps she'd work for another partner. I said she was hiding something. It now appeared we were both right.

She had phoned Jen this morning. Asked if they could meet away from her about-to-be-former office. She wanted to get away from it all.

"Let's turn back," she said, "before we're wading through the tourists."

We did a one-eighty and faced the Capitol. The great dome was sheathed in scaffolding, like it apparently had been for a while back in the teens. This time it was so the workers could clean off the soot from last summer's massive Rock Creek Park fire.

Brita spoke.

"I was annoyed with her." *Her. Patty Garcia.* "In the days before she was killed. This absolutely must be between us."

"No problem," Jen said.

Why, I thought, *would anyone assume they could speak to an on-the-job police officer off the record? "Yeah, I robbed that bank, but you won't tell anyone, will ya?"*

We were walking slowly. Brita had her eyes fixed on Jen's. "I was getting blamed for some serious office shit. She'd known me long enough to realize I wouldn't have done what she was accusing me of, but the Wednesday before she was killed, she dressed me down all the same." Her jaw was so rigid, I was worried it was about to snap off. "In front of other staff, that's how bad it was." Brita's eyes defied Jen to disagree with her assertion that she shouldn't have been scolded this way. "It had been an exhausting month. So much was at stake, with the deadline for the reparations date coming at us fast but nothing to show for it. We were all on our last legs. So Thursday morning, I sent her a text saying I needed the day off to look after some family matters. It wasn't true, but that's what I wrote her."

"What happened next?"

Brita pushed the thick fringe of her limp hair away from her forehead.

"She phoned on Thursday afternoon." Her eyes shifted upward for a second. "Around two thirty. I didn't answer. I should have, but I didn't. She left a message for me."

"Which said?"

"I found it, Brita. I found the smoking gun."

"Which one would that be?"

She hesitated. Perhaps stumbling over her own petulance or exhaustion or anger or whatever the hell it was.

"I don't know, not one hundred per cent. But in retrospect, I believe it was the proof we'd been looking for. The date we could point to. You know, when the oil companies knew for certain that fossil fuels were destroying the planet."

The smoking gun for climate reparations.

We like smoking guns in our business, and Jen had talked about all this with Zach. But we wanted to hear it straight from the horse's mouth.

Brita said, "Until 2029 they claimed there was no definitive proof that burning fossil fuels caused climate change. All their denial strategies, all their lobbying, all their massive tax breaks and government handouts, and all the postponement action to the Paris Accords . . . everything hinged on that assertion. Of course, we knew they had long known the truth. But we never had proof."

"Fine. But a motive for killing her?"

"Don't you see? These companies wanted to stop her before she came up with proof that they've known for years. Proof could cost them and their investors trillions of dollars."

A trillion reasons to commit murder.

Brita said, "How things change, right?"

"What do you mean?"

"A decade ago, there's no way any court or government would go after companies that way. Try suggesting climate reparations and you'd be laughed at. But ever since Miami was wiped off the face of the earth and half the Appalachians burned down, everyone knows we need drastic action."

Jen said, "Then tell me this. If it's so earth-shatteringly important, why didn't you phone her back the second you got her message?"

Brita stopped walking. She looked away. Her voice barely reached us. "Yeah," she said. Her gaze returned to us. She seemed to screw up her defiance and said, "I'd worked almost every day for the past year. Days off still included phone calls and emails. I was fed up. Exhausted. Pissed off." Pause. "And humiliated."

"Did she know this?"

"I'm not sure. Maybe. She was like a lot of driven people. Don't get me wrong, she was a great woman, I mean that. I admired her more than any person I've ever met. But all that charisma meant that she swept everyone along with her. She generated excitement and belief, but she never understood the needs of those around her."

Brita pondered a moment and then added, "No, that's not quite right. She could be incredibly supportive. There were endless times she'd been that to me. It's only that her dreams were so fierce, so alive, that she didn't let anything get in their way."

"So?"

"The next morning, Friday, I went in early, but she had blocked the day off weeks before. A meeting with her accountant—"

"About?"

"No idea. Probably taxes. Next, a haircut. Lunch with two friends. Then golf. I sent her a text apologizing for not returning her call."

"Did she write back?"

"Within seconds. She said she'd only play nine holes and I should meet her at Viridian Green around three."

"Is that all it said?"

Brita hesitated. Seemed to stiffen. "All that I can remember."

"Do you still have it? The text?"

"I'll check," she said, but made no move to do so.

Jen glanced down at Brita's purse.

"Yes. Let me see." She sucked in her breath. Reached into her pursed and pulled out her phone. Woke it up. Poked and scrolled. "Here it is." She flashed it toward Jen, as if proving the text was there, then turned it back toward herself and read, "*Will just play 9 holes. Come 3ish. Viridian Green Lounge. There are things I need to speak to you about.*"

Jen said to me, *Chandler, is that what you saw?*

I replied back, *Yep.*

Jen said, "Viridian Green. Had you been there before?"

"A few times."

"When I came to your office, why didn't you tell me you were at the golf course when Ms. Garcia was hit by the ball?"

"It didn't occur to me. I mean, I wasn't on the golf course."

"I said *at* the golf course."

Her voice was unnecessarily defiant. "I arrived early, around two fifteen. I was in a quiet corner by myself, working. It was a normal day. I heard sirens, and people went rushing outside. I joined them, thinking it might be a fire, but one of the staff told us not to worry, there'd been a small accident and we should go back to what we'd been doing."

"Weren't you worried Ms. Garcia might have been hurt?"

"Why would I be? The staff member was reassuring. Members went back into the lounge. It wasn't until ten minutes later that golfers poured in yelling about what happened. The place filled up quickly. It was a madhouse. I ran to their office and was told Patty was being flown to the hospital. I called a car and was gone a few minutes later."

"You said she'd found the smoking gun."

"I said I think she may have."

"What exactly do you think it was?"

Brita's voice became confident again. "I've poured over her planner. The office phone log and Thursday visitors. Nothing there. Except one thing. Roslyn, she's our receptionist, said that she went over to the Library of Congress just before eleven on Thursday and didn't come back for an hour."

A five-minute walk from their office.

"What was she doing there?"

"No idea. I called over to one of the librarians we'd had contact with, but she hadn't seen Patty. She said she'd ask around but came up with nothing."

We wrote down the name of the librarian.

We asked Brita if there was anything else.

"Like what?" she said.

Like whatever it is you're still not telling us.

13

I'd suggested we pick up Les and bring him along to the Library of Congress. "Perhaps," I said to Jen, "he needs actual stimulation. You know, work."

She'd bought that, and here we were in one of the library's auxiliary buildings. We'd already come and gone from the main building, which, in spite of a few scars from the attempted militia bombing in '28, was still a gob-smacking display of spectacular. There we spoke with the librarian whom Brita had mentioned. She hadn't found anyone who'd recently talked to Ms. Garcia. We decided to try a few other departments.

This brought us across the street to the second floor of the James Madison Memorial Building and to the modest front counter of the modest La Follette Congressional Reading Room, which was reserved for the somewhat less-than-modest members of Congress. It seemed a long shot, but we'd struck out in every other room or department. We figured we had nothing to lose.

A young librarian with the most beautifully shaped skull I'd ever seen—I knew because her head was shaved—was doing her best to help us. "Are you certain?" she said for the second time. "She's not a member of the Congress."

Before Jen could respond, the woman shifted her eyes to Les, as if he might respond differently, but he was staring blankly ahead.

To Jen, she leaned forward and whispered, "Is your friend okay?"

Jen ignored this, and without a shred of proof that this was the place we were looking for, said, "We believe Ms. Garcia came here."

Just as Jen was saying this, a short, thin man passed by. His gray hair poked out from under a retro Washington Senators baseball cap, and in his arms were three identically bound teal-blue volumes. Even the bindings looked boring, but I sensed that this was a man who loved his job.

"Did I hear you mention Patty Garcia?" he said, the smile now gone.

Jen said she had.

"Awful, wasn't it?" he said.

Jen said it was.

"She was here, you know, the day before she died."

Jen snatched his elbow and pulled him behind the counter. "You and I," she said, "need to talk."

He led us to a glass-fronted office. Two desks. Computers. Bookcases. He laid the blue volumes on one of the desks.

Jen introduced herself. Ron Decker did the same. Said that everyone called him Deacon.

Deacon looked at Les. Jen said, "He's my partner. He doesn't talk much."

Honestly, I didn't think it was simply Les's lack of speech that was creeping people out.

Deacon said, "Are you following up on Ms. Garcia's request? She said she'd come back at the very end of the day on Friday. That was the soonest I could pull the boxes of committee hearing minutes for her."

"What committee?"

"The Senate Armed Services Standing Committee."

"Why?"

"She didn't say."

"I thought this place was only for members of Congress."

"True, but I completely dig what she'd been doing." He shrugged. "Anyways, she was searching for the minutes from hearings back in 1968. On long-term challenges to national security."

"Why would she do that?"

"You'll have to ask . . . God, I almost said . . ." He regrouped. "You'll have to ask one of her staff. I don't know."

"Where are the minutes?"

"That was the first interesting thing. I tracked down a reference in a volume like these." He patted one of the teal-blue books. "Not this series, but a similar index. It was the *CIS Index to Unpublished U.S. Senate Committee Hearings, 18th Congress–88th Congress, 1965–1968*."

I felt Jen's brain entering hibernation mode. *Ask why they were unpublished*, I said.

"Why weren't they published?"

"Cool that you caught that. Ms. Garcia wasn't certain exactly what testimony she was looking for, but she seemed certain it would be there. She had the year, the name of the committee, and the name of the hearings. But it took me a while to find the right index. The one I just mentioned."

"About long-term national security issues."

"These stay confidential for fifty years."

Deacon's desk phone rang. "One sec," he said, then picked up the receiver and started speaking.

I said to Jen, *How could Garcia know she'd found the smoking gun if she hadn't read it yet?*

Jen said, *I suppose someone tipped her off. Told her the details of what happened in the committee, maybe a presentation, but didn't have exact dates or names.*

I said, *Who would have told her?*

Jen said, *From what Brita Germaine told us about looking through Garcia's notes and diary, we may never find out.*

Deacon hung up. "Sorry about that," he said. "Where were we?"

Jen asked questions; Deacon answered or spun off in his own direction. How long did these particular hearings last? Off and on over the course of a year. Who chaired this committee? Richard B. Russell—KKK-loving senator from Georgia. Him again.

As they spoke, I got down to work. I burrowed into our comms network, but I was also relying on our proximate communications links, which was why I had suggested we invite Les along.

Jen said, "You said that was the *first* interesting thing."

Deacon was now motoring in fifth gear, his voice intense, his eyes fixed on Jen's. "The next thing was that they weren't available on microfiche even though fifty years had passed."

"Haven't you digitalized all this stuff?"

"A lot of it. But we still have members of Congress who'd rather burn books than preserve them . . . shit, I really shouldn't have said that—"

"My lips are sealed."

"Once things are public, they all get transferred to microfiche and digital. But for some reason these hearings never were."

"So . . ."

"Exactly what Ms. Garcia asked me. Egg-zact-ly. And I said, 'No worries. We'll pull the Hollinger boxes with the original minutes.'"

While Deacon was enthusiastically describing the various types of archival boxes, I continued with my efforts over our proximate comms link to hook up with Les's sim implant, P.D.

P.D. had been switched off shortly after Les was shot. While he was still in a coma, there had been a fierce debate about whether it was safer to turn her off or leave her on. In the end, the software geniuses decided it would be prudent to wait, but the second he regained consciousness a few days later, they slammed the switch, although they didn't permanently deactivate her as they had tried to do to me last year.

I had this hunch that she was responsible for Les's problems. You see, P.D. is pretty much my opposite. Like Les, she is cautious by nature, a fan of the rule book, and while I might have dreamed of taking a bullet to save Jen, I figured P.D. must have dreamed of keeping Les as far away from bullets as possible. His injury must have deeply traumatized her.

Earlier that morning when I tapped into the Doc's database, I'd had one goal: get P.D.'s identifier number to access her code. As I had expected, this consisted of twenty-eight letters, numbers, punctuation symbols, and emojis: 2.5555757234593984 novemdecillion possibilities in all. One of those "more combinations than atoms in the solar system" things and hence impossible to crack. Like mine, her identifier number changed at random times. I was hoping the one I'd grabbed still worked.

I entered her number.

Deacon was saying, "Like I said, I told Ms. Garcia that the quickest we could get those particular boxes was late the next day. Friday, that is. Normally it's faster, but—"

Jen cut him off. "Tell me again what she said."

"That she'd come by herself late on Friday and start reading through them. However, neither she nor anyone else came. Then I heard she had an accident."

"Can I read them?"

"Anyone can read them. But it'll take you a day, maybe two, to go through them carefully. There are eleven boxes."

"Can I check them out? You know, borrow them?"

He looked at Jen with pity. Explained the rules: Only in the reading room. No pens allowed. Only the pencils and paper they provided or your own computer to take notes. And he wasn't sure that Jen would be allowed to work here. "You may have to access this at the National Archives. And over there, you'd have to be within sight of a librarian whenever you opened a box."

"Anyway, there's no way in heaven I'll have time to sit here."

I could almost hear the captain scorching her with one of his looks if she asked.

Jen became quiet.

Deacon was quiet.

And into the quiet, as normal as can be, Les said, "Maybe I could go through them."

14

"**E**xactly what just happened?" Jen said to me seven minutes later, her voice still crackling with astonishment. I had to slip her a nibble of cortisol so she wouldn't blow my circuits. My swell idea had worked.

Les was out by the sixth-floor elevators speaking with Christopher on Jen's phone. We were in the Madison Cafeteria. What a town—even the damn cafeterias have to be named after someone. Once all the buildings and cafeterias are accounted for, I figure they'll start naming restroom stalls. Seems crazy, but come to think of it, there are a few Supreme Court judges I wouldn't mind being honored that way.

I said, "I got a hold of P.D.'s identifier number."

"How?"

"Jen, you really don't want to know that."

Jen ate a french fry. "Fine. Keep going."

"I tried to turn her on through our normal comms channels, but it wasn't working. So I got you to invite Les so I could send her emergency flashes over proximate comms."

"Why would you assume any of this would work?"

"Because she's even more cautious than Les. We all know—"

"We?"

"We sims all know our ultimate job is to protect you. Keep you alive. She took this task a step too far. She was worried that when he got better, he'd be back on duty—"

"Of course he would."

"And thus back to facing dangers like the one he almost didn't survive. Right before she was switched off, she managed to set up a routine—"

"What?"

71

"Sort of a widget. A little app that kept running even when she was down."

"And this—"

"Interfered with his ability to interact."

"Fucking weird."

"She is. But I managed to convince her just now that Les was going to be fine. And if she really wanted him to be happy, she needed to erase what she had done."

"And now?"

"I told her she needed to shut herself down so Doc could turn her back on himself."

"What's happening with you guys?" Jen said.

"I'm not exactly sure."

Les returned at that moment. He stopped at the end of the table, and for a split second I fretted that he had become catatonic again. But he reached down and grabbed a french fry, and before he popped it into his mouth, a smile broke onto his face. "God, Jen," he said. "It's great to see you again."

19:59:22

"Amazing," Zach said for the tenth time.

"He seems all there. Like nothing happened."

"Does he remember the last seven months?"

"I'm not sure. One minute it looks like he doesn't have a clue, but the next he's asking if we're going running again this weekend." Jen held out her wineglass. "Just a smidgen."

Zach poured the Rioja, one of their cool-weather favorites.

"Is he returning to work?"

"He says he is. He'll need to pass a physical and mental exam. He's in great physical shape, and he should be fine when the shrink grills him. Except . . ."

"Yeah," Zach said. "Christopher isn't going to be too keen on him working."

I was officially turned on. Jen was sitting with Zach on the couch in front of their screen.

"Okay. Down to work," Jen said. "You don't have to watch this with me."

"It's cool," Zach said. "I love hearing sexist creeps rant against women."

It was Culpepper's broadcast at the time Garcia was killed. His alibi.

Jen said, "Chandler is turned on. I need him to watch for breaks or discrepancies that might indicate any part had been prerecorded." Which would tear apart his alibi.

Zach barely hesitated. "Fine."

Progress.

Culpepper was standing in a lovely home office. Mouse-gray walls with shiny white paint on the wide baseboards and window trims. To his right, bookshelves showed how smart he was. To his left, a large window must have had a filter on it like on movie shoots, because the trees outside weren't bleached out by the daylight. On one side of the window, the branches of a *Magnolia kobus* seemed to be weighed down with a profusion of magnificent white flowers. Except for that and an English yew (*Taxus baccata*), most of the trees were still bare.

Too bad Patty Garcia wasn't poisoned, I said.

What?

The Taxus baccata.

What are you talking about?

Outside his window. The yew tree.

Which one is that?

God, Jen, the man you sleep with used to be a gardener.

Do I ask him to understand blood splatter patterns? Anyway, what about it?

The whole tree is poisonous. It—

Focus, Chandler. For starters, can you fix the date by the light outside? And the exact time of day?

It had been overcast that Friday, so there were no shadows. I said, *I might be able to do research on filters and estimate the approximate date and time from the light, but that would depend on knowing how the room was lit and the type of camera he used and the ambient light that afternoon.*

Spit it out.

I'm saying no.

There has to be a way to find out if it was prerecorded.

Culpepper started, "Good afternoon, friends across America and around the world. I'm sure all of you saw the sad news this morning from London. Our hearts go out to John Foner, who took his life in despair after losing a court battle for custody of his two children."

Chandler, check it.

Yes, it was that morning. Friday, March 3.

Crap.

73

The guy he just referred to, John Foner, had previously been convicted of physical assault on his wife, sometimes in front of their children. He'd threatened to kill them all.

We watched. Culpepper was smart and appealing. His voice was serious and soft. If you didn't know better, he would even sound reasonable. "I have no problem with women's independence," he intoned. "But don't you agree with me that it shouldn't be an excuse for turning the tables and constantly giving women an advantage in hirings? In promotions? And in everything else?"

Zach said, "Makes sense if you discount the fact that women still are second-class citizens by just about any measure."

Jen said, "Pesky things, those facts."

We watched. Jen and Zach took turns yelling at the screen.

My job was made more difficult because the video cut back and forth between two cameras. I was looking for any changes in ambient light or movement in the trees—a branch suddenly jumping position by a fraction of an inch or a bird that disappeared from one moment to the next. That would tell me that this broadcast had been recorded at different times and then edited together. It would have been a snap if this were one continuous shot, but I needed to compare the positions when one camera's view ended and then pick it up again forty-five seconds or a minute later. I would have to make an astronomical number of assumptions to extrapolate forward from one shot and then do the same running backward from the next. It was close to impossible, even for the likes of me.

After his thirty-minute speech, he fielded audience questions for another twenty minutes.

We reached the end.

Culpepper's polite, half-hour rant had begun at 14:30. Garcia was hit by the ball between 14:32 and 14:34. You don't need to be a biocomputer to see that the numbers didn't work in our favor.

Chandler? Jen said, when the recording came to an end.

Nothing. It looks legit.

You certain?

I'll need to go through it again.

Zach said, "So? You saw what you hoped to see?"

Jen's tone was glum. "Nope. I still have a murder that no one thinks was a murder. Where it seems impossible anyone could have killed her. Where the murder weapon was a golf ball randomly hit by someone who isn't much of a suspect. Where my favorite suspect was doing a live webcast at the time of Garcia's death. Where other suspects are a shadowy cast of powerful men and women who've been destroying the planet with impunity but don't normally go around whacking people on the head. Where a second man died less than a hundred yards away, perhaps around the same time; hopefully, we'll know in a few days."

Zach held up the wine bottle.

The boss didn't even register his offer. She charged ahead: "Culpepper practically bragged about wanting to kill her. He lives in spitting distance of the murder spot. If his opening rant had been prerecorded, he could easily have done the deed and gotten home on time to answer his viewers' questions."

"But—"

"And if Culpepper didn't do it, there's another possibility. The day before she was killed, Garcia apparently dug up something really big. A smoking gun. It's too big a coincidence that she would die in a freak accident within twenty-four hours."

"And what would that be? Your smoking gun?"

"You can't tell anyone. Not yet."

"Jen."

"I think she got proof that the oil and gas companies, or at least one of the biggies, admitted publicly back in the 1960s that they knew they were causing climate change."

Zach voice rose to off-the-charts excited: "You have that proof?"

"Uh, well, not exactly."

Zach sighed. He gave her a big hug and kissed her lightly on the lips.

"Jen, I got to say, I love you."

It seemed out of the blue, even to a guy like me who can rapidly make connections. Jen looked perplexed.

Zach said, "I wanted to tell you something you can actually prove."

She winced at the corniness, but he repeated it anyway. "Jen, I totally love you."

15

Maybe the afternoon wouldn't have dragged like glue on a cold day if Jen could have kept her attention on her new assignment rather than an investigation that didn't exist. I tried to cheer her up with references to the slippery world of international fisheries, the scales of justice, and every bad pun I could catch in my (neural) nets, but the beginning stages of the investigation into Continental Seafoods was inching along like a sea snail.

Her shift ended. We went out into the pouring rain.

The second we were a block away from work, Jen pulled her bike onto the sidewalk, took refuge under a store awning, and sent a text to Les. *Call as soon as you get this.*

No response, just as I had warned her. I figured Christopher had suspended Les's personal phone months ago and he wouldn't yet have his work phone back.

Jen hunkered down and headed to the Madison Building.

Out front in a concrete planter, a lone pink tulip was doing its best to stand up to the rain. I figured it was symbolic of something, but I couldn't figure out what.

Two paramilitaries at security checked her out up and down. She showed her badge. They asked for ID, and two of them studied it for so long they might as well have been authenticating a newly discovered copy of the Constitution. Finally, they waved her through.

We raced up to the reading room.

Baseball-capped Deacon wasn't in. The beautiful bald-headed newbie was.

Jen asked if Les was there. The woman said he had dropped by, but Deacon said to tell him he hadn't been able to get permission for a member of the public to work there. She'd sent him over to the National Archives.

We biked along Independence. The American elm, red oak, and Japanese zelkova were bare, but a patch of cherry trees were still in bloom, their battered flowers looking discouraged. The rain had stopped, but after Jen got splashed by a bus, we turned off the busy street, cut up to the Mall, and beelined across to the National Archives.

This time we breezed through security without any assholes giving Jen a hard time. They told her she needed to register and leave her backpack and rain gear in a locker. Twenty minutes later, clutching her embossed card—they still used physical library cards here, but then again, this place dealt with preserving the past—we were racing up a stairway, the smooth wooden railing gliding under her hand.

Here we returned to grandeur. The Central Reading Room had a dark, burnished wood ceiling, pale limestone walls, a beige marble floor, brass lamps resting on wooden desks, and massive windows divided by thick rectangular mullions that gave this 1930s building its only Art Deco touch. We found Les in a more modest side room, his back to us, hunched over a table that held a small cardboard file box—one of the Hollinger boxes, I told Jen. A set of committee minutes printed in blue ink lay open on the table.

Jen stopped. Watched Les as he scribbled a note and flipped to the next page.

Her right hand reached up and brushed a tear from her eye.

She stepped forward and rested a hand on his shoulder. Les didn't flinch and didn't turn but said, "It's about time you showed up."

He stood, smiled so big I thought his face was going to pop, and embraced Jen with a tremendous hug. He then held her at arms' length and stared at her.

The room was empty except for Les and Jen, but he spoke in a soft voice. "Yesterday was the strangest day of my life. I couldn't make sense of anything."

"Let me guess, Christopher didn't want to tell you much."

"At first, no. He was worried I'd freak out. I hear I haven't been at my charming best. I have hazy memories. I know we often went running, but I don't have the foggiest idea where or anything we talked about."

Jen said, "That would be what *I* talked about."

"I don't have a clue why I was acting that way."

"It was P.D."

I had told Jen not to tell Les lest word got back to Doc.

But Jen's number-one loyalty was to her partner, Les, and I knew she figured he had a right to know.

77

She explained what I had told her. "Chandler figured it out. And he figured out how to contact her."

"Chandler," he said, "I owe you more than you'll ever know."

I told Jen to thank him, and he smiled when she did.

Jen said, "How'd it go this morning?" Les had done his physical and mental exam to assess whether he was ready to come back.

"If I might say, with my usual modesty, I believe I aced both."

"When will you hear?"

"Monday. I see Brooks at noon."

Jen patted his shoulder. "It's going to be great to be working together again."

Les gestured at the table. "What do you think we're doing now? This is so cool. I feel like I'm smack-dab in a smoke-filled committee room, two-thirds of a century ago."

Jen picked up the minutes. Robin's-egg-blue cover. It was a printed template with *The United States Senate* and the words *Report of Proceedings. Hearings held before* in an Old English font, then the particulars of these hearings typed in blue stenographic ink. The simple publication was bound by a faded red ribbon threaded through three-punched holes.

"Want to hear something cool?" And without waiting for an answer, he said, "See that ribbon? That's the red tape. You know, the expression about lots of red tape meaning government rules and oversight? It comes from all these ribbons."

She opened the report. Questions by senators and answers by the experts making presentations. All typed up in a purple-blue ink.

"Why blue?" she said.

"No idea. I guess it's how these copies were reproduced."

"More importantly, what have you found?"

Les grimaced. "Nothing. But I've only made it through four boxes. I've got six to go."

Jen sat down and started reading.

She'd been at it for eight minutes when I realized even the slowest of readers would have turned to page two by now. She was still sitting up and her eyes were open, but she was more or less asleep.

Jen.

She twitched like she'd received an electric shock. Looked around to get her bearings. And told Les she needed to go home and sleep.

Les said, "I'm beat too. Let's call it a day."

The case of the century and they both wanted to sleep? And I want to be more human?

Spare me.

16

Saturday

Eight thousand feet above the Allegheny Mountains of southwestern Pennsylvania, Jen knew that Zach wasn't entirely happy. He liked flying, so it wasn't that. She knew he'd be enjoying the model-train-set villages down below and the forests waking up from winter. The problem was they were in an absurdly expensive PAV—a personal aviation vehicle, so called because flying car sounded absolutely silly. For most people, including Jen, riding in this puppy would be a thrill: it was still rare to so much as glimpse one—he never had and Jen only twice—let alone fly in one. But Zach had already complained about the millions it cost to buy and maintain.

She looked down at the Alleghenies, late-winter brown except for patches of green conifers. In spite of bulky noise-canceling headphones, the rotors buzzed loudly, several octaves lower than high-pitched drones but equally annoying. She thought how much nicer this would be in a car gliding in silence along a smooth road.

Jen was in the front passenger seat and Zach was stuffed in the back. She glanced at Richard O'Neil's personal helper, Jaisha, whom she had met before. Jaisha was in the driver's seat, although the PAV seemed to be flying on its own. Zach didn't totally trust technology. That morning at breakfast he'd mentioned all the times his computer had crashed or slowed to a crawl and the year his phone got hacked. He had wondered out loud if someone could do the same to a PAV.

She figured that the thing bothering Zach most wasn't the absurd price of the car or computer glitches. It was the fact that they were off to visit Richard.

Not that Zach ever seemed jealous of her. She knew he totally trusted her, just as she trusted him. And he couldn't know that for a couple of weeks the previous summer when they seemed headed toward breaking up, she had fantasized about going along with Richard's playful flirting when they first met. She might have actually ended up with this interesting, rich, and gorgeous man.

Zach couldn't have known that, could he?

No, of course not.

Jen knew that the problem was that Zach detested the very existence of the Timeless. The Longevity Treatment was the ultimate luxury item—not multiple mansions, yachts, artworks, or planes; living forever, or at least for centuries, was the ultimate symbol of ever-growing inequality.

The day before, Jen had phoned Richard after arriving home from the National Archives. She had reached Rob, the other of Richard's two service units. Jen was surprised when Richard came on a moment later.

"Hi, Richard, I don't know if you remember—"

"Are you kidding? Forget you? Especially since the last time we talked, I almost got you killed."

"Thanks for the flowers."

"I take it you're fine."

"Perfect."

"But I heard that your partner is having problems." Richard seemed to know everything.

"Les is actually doing great. Back to his old self."

"So . . . ?"

"I'm hoping to ask you about someone." She knew from their previous talks that he wouldn't want to have this conversation over an open line. "I was wondering if you're in town."

No, he wasn't. But he said that if she didn't mind, he could send his car the next morning to bring her to his country place.

She said that would be great. She was about to ask if she could bring Zach when he surprised her.

"Listen. Bring Zach, will you? I'd like to meet him."

He didn't say where he was, other than in the mountains, so they should dress warmly. And then he said, "Ever been in a PAV?"

She looked down at the ancient mountains, actually very big hills, running in bands southwest to northeast. The farms and towns sprinkled through the valleys spoke to her of a simpler life, although she figured they held the same secrets and struggles, tenderness and violence, pain and love, as anywhere else.

Gazing down, Jen thought of Culpepper's model of an oasis for the ultra-rich. Tenderness and violence, pain and love.

Jen swiveled in her seat, reached back, and took Zach's hand. She beamed an innocent *Gee, I can't believe we're doing this together* smile.

He smiled back. Perhaps everything was fine.

As they banked over another hill, the electric motors dropped another octave, and Jen felt the pressure change in her ears.

Jaisha pointed ahead and toward the left. "There it is," she said.

Forests. Farmland. Some sort of building or house tucked into the woods—she couldn't quite make it out.

They descended onto a parking area cut into the middle of the woods. Space enough for a helicopter pad and twenty cars, although right now there were only two, a cranberry-red Aston Martin and an old Land Rover Defender that, for all Jen knew, had been owned by the final British monarch before he and his family were finally stripped of their absurd titles and staggering wealth.

As they were getting out of the car, Rob pulled up in a four-seater golf cart. When Jen had first met Rob and Jaisha the previous summer, she hadn't realized right away that they were service units. There weren't many of these human-looking robots to start with, but these two were a rarity among the rare. Nothing she'd ever seen had come close.

Rob said, "Welcome to Richard's country home."

They piled in and started up the driveway through the woods. Rob and Jaisha were silent, although at one point they nodded to each other as if they'd been having a private conversation.

The springtime smell of the forest was deep and rich. Small patches of snow nestled at the base of a few trees, but the afternoon sun was bright, and the air was warm. The trees were bare except for the large clumps of rhododendrons and some type of fir tree. Zach whispered to her, "Hemlock. Killed Socrates."

As they wound uphill along the narrow drive, the sound of water grew louder and louder. Rob parked the golf cart at the end of a sandstone-colored walkway that bridged a stream. "This way," he said, and gestured them across.

The sides of the bridge didn't even reach her waist. Jen looked down at the water flowing underneath the house that rose above.

Zach stopped. He stared up at the house. Pale-ochre-colored balconies cantilevered over what looked and sounded like the top of a waterfall. Jen caught his gaze, and she too stared in amazement.

"Jen," he whispered, or maybe he only seemed to whisper because the waterfall was drowning him out. "Do you know where we are? Do you know what this is?"

Dumbstruck, she nodded. She'd seen a movie about this house in art class way back in high school. She knew where she was. Everyone knew,

They were at Frank Lloyd Wright's masterpiece.

Fallingwater.

A UNESCO World Heritage Site. Once voted as the greatest work of American architecture. In the public trust until 2030 and open to tens of thousands of visitors a year. Sold off to an unknown buyer.

Zach said, "This is so fucked."

Richard himself was waiting at the glass-front door set under a low-ceilinged carport. He was a gorgeous man. Sun-bleached hair and, even with a bulky pale-green sweater, clearly muscular. Midthirties. Only he was now close to 113 years old. One of the Timeless.

"Jen!" he called, opening his arms and giving her a hug. Not long, not overly done, but Jen could sense Zach stiffen at her side.

Richard reached out and took Zach's hand, holding it for an extra split second as he cupped Zach's elbow with his other hand. "Man," he said, "I can't tell you how good it is to meet you."

He stepped back, smiled, and said, "Come on in. What are you waiting for?"

Stone walls. Glass panes divided by clean lines of painted steel. Polished flagstone floors. Jen felt overwhelmed. Emotional. Many years before, she had dreamt of this home and had decided, with the complete resolve only a sixteen-year-old can muster, that she wanted to be an architect. Took books out of the library. Talked to her art teacher. Dreamt. Until a few weeks later when she made the mistake of telling her mother, who told her not to get stupid ideas into her dumb head.

"Yes," Richard said. "It still has that effect every time I come here to spend a few days. It's, well, I don't have words for it, and I suspect if there had been words then, Wright would have written a book rather than design a house. Let me show you around."

For more than an hour they toured the house, went onto the balconies, and visited the guest house. Jen felt drunk. She sneaked glances at Zach, who seemed to be wrestling with strong and conflicting emotions; he was entranced, but much quieter than he'd normally be. At times she saw his jaw tighten and she thought he was going to burst out in anger.

Jen wanted to know how this had come into Richard's hands. That morning, for reasons she wasn't entirely certain about, she had completely shut Chandler down—something about wanting her visit with Richard to be an experience just for Zach and her. Now she switched Chandler on for a moment to ask him.

Chandler told her that in 2029 after the crippling costs of the so-called Years Without the Sun, Pennsylvania had gone unofficially bankrupt. Every penny went into massive subsidies to aid farmers after flooding and two crop-less years, rebuild washed-out roads and bridges, replace obsolete storm sewers, and hire more police to contain the riots. Organizations that had relied on government funding were hit hard. Private foundations and individual donors were already stretched thin from the recession and couldn't make up the slack. The nonprofit conservation group that held Fallingwater in trust was on the verge of canceling most of its land, water, and forest conservation programs. They saved them all by selling their treasure. The public cried out, lawyers wrangled, trust loopholes were discovered, and a numbered company based in the Cayman Islands bought the home and the surrounding five thousand acres of forest and farmland.

Chandler said he should stay switched on. She muttered their safe word, and he was gone.

They settled in the living room, the built-in banquettes stiff. Now that they had stopped walking, Jen felt the chill of all the stonework. Rob brought drinks—a cup of tea for Richard, a steaming mug of hot chocolate for Jen, but nothing for Zach, who grumpily said he was fine.

"Jen," Richard said, "what trouble are you getting into now?"

Jen told him she was looking into Patty Garcia's death.

"I read it was an accident."

Jen said, "Maybe. Maybe not. I'm wondering if you ever met her ex-husband, James Culpepper."

"The Third," Richard added. "Pretentious bastard."

"You know him?"

"Not really. That development he's involved in . . ."

"Climate Oasis."

"Right. They approached my investment team six months back. You know, when things were getting sticky for them. But we didn't think it was a smart play for us, so we turned them down."

"How much did they want?"

"Firm numbers weren't discussed at that stage. As much as the money, they were looking for a vote of support that would help them with the institutional investors who had grown antsy. Anyway, back to your question."

"What did you mean? About things getting sticky?"

"When the climate reparations ruling was upheld by the Supreme Court."

"What about it?"

"The whole stock market took a dive."

"And Climate Oasis? Them too?"

"They're not a publicly listed company. But a lot of their investors had a background in the oil and gas industries. Other investors got spooked. Sales were suddenly in doubt. For a while the whole thing was on the verge of collapse."

"And then?"

"Silicon Valley money started pouring in. I guess they figured that if their attempt to buy New Zealand failed, they'd need a Plan B."

"Okay."

"And then of course two weeks ago."

"Two weeks ago." Jen wasn't asking a question. She knew what was coming.

"When Patty Garcia died. The market went crazy. Among other things, there was a lot of chatter about Climate Oasis. I heard that in one week, they had more sales than in the whole previous year." Richard grimaced. "Anyway, you were asking if I'd ever met Culpepper."

She smiled. "I almost forgot."

"I did. Meet him, that is. A couple times, including at one of those White House things. But I can't say I know him."

"Did he have it in him to kill someone?"

"Not when I was around him." Richard sipped his tea. "Apologies. That sounded like I take your concerns lightly."

He paused, as if to clear the air. He began again. "James Culpepper appeared to be a reasonable sort of man, somewhat brash, but with good manners."

"He was a convicted wife abuser."

"Who, like others of his ilk, knows how to pass for a decent guy. Yes?"

Jen said, "Yes," and waited for more.

"At any rate, I was about to say that he seemed self-assured. That, of course, fit his self-styled reputation as a visionary. You don't get where he did if you aren't awfully sure of yourself." He lifted his head slightly as if in thought. "However, underneath I caught a sense of insecurity, like he needed to prove he was in control, or at least one of the boys, if you see what I mean. I said something idiotic about the economy, and rather than disagreeing or even questioning what I'd said, he nodded in agreement. I was the alpha in the conversation, and he seemed beholden. A few minutes later, I saw him lording over someone else."

Richard paused again. "But murder? That seems a stretch."

Jen felt herself deflating.

Richard must have sensed this, and he said, "I'll ask around for you."

Zach jumped in, his tone much more aggressive than usual. "What do you think of climate change reparations?"

Richard cut him a hard look.

Jen rushed in. "It's another angle I'm looking into concerning Patty Garcia's death. I've been wondering if someone connected with big oil might, you know . . ."

Richard laughed. "Hire a hit man to kill her? Seems farfetched." But he stopped, and the smile left his face.

"What?" said Jen.

"Last time you had a hunch, it almost got you killed." He turned his attention to Zach and smiled. "You need to watch out for this girlfriend of yours."

Zach didn't even fake a smile.

"But Jen, are you asking me what these companies are capable of?"

"Pretty much."

"These guys grew spectacularly rich doing things they knew were destroying the planet."

Jen said, "They seem to be investing a lot in green energy these days."

Zach spoke, his anger seeming to include her. "Of course they've been doing that. They've had decades to prepare. They knew what they were up to and that someday they would be forced to stop."

Jen had never seen him so belligerent. She tried to ignore him and turned to Richard. "Even if these companies knew the harm they were causing, isn't it good that they're now investing in green energy?"

"Sure it is, although for years it was only window dressing," Richard said. "But listen to me, Jen. Talking about green energy with these guys is like discussing the menu with cannibals. I wouldn't turn my back on them for a minute."

Richard shifted his attention to Zach.

"You were asking about climate reparations. Zach, if you had asked me two or three years ago, I would have dismissed the very thought. Illegal. Grasping. Anti–private property. Communist."

"And now?"

"That's just it. And that's why I asked Jen to invite you along. I'd like you to tell me about Green Prosperity."

Jen wasn't totally surprised by this request. Based on their discussions the previous year, she knew that, whatever his wealth, Richard had a ton of curiosity. But more than that, he seemed to be questioning the very things that had made him a Timeless.

Zach, however, seemed taken aback by the question. All he could muster was a sharply abbreviated version of their work, as if it were a waste of time to say more. "Research, policy, education."

For months now, Jen had experienced Zach's excitement about Green Prosperity's growing network of local volunteers who were being trained to carry out community-organizing projects and local education. He spoke of innovative policy proposals that took the debate well beyond the environment-versus-jobs polarization that had been used dishonestly but effectively by the right. He talked about the partnerships Green Prosperity was developing with civil rights organizations, trade unions, women's groups, and even traditional service clubs to bring about a just transition to a low-carbon economy. They envisioned cooperative businesses playing a significant role in a green economic transformation, an approach that would give people more control over their work and daily lives. He spoke about their creative projects with select businesses and their work with governments to take more effective action.

But now all she heard was Zach snubbing Richard.

"Zach," Richard said, his voice level, "I asked because I'm genuinely interested." His tone displayed the patience of a parent speaking to a petulant child . . . or make that grandparent or—Jen did a quick calculation—a great- or even great-great-grandparent. She stared at his face. Something was different, something had changed, but Jen was too agitated to think about what it was.

"I'm curious," Richard continued, "whether you work with governments."

"Of course we do."

Richard asked, "Who funds your work?"

"Foundations. Private donors. Unions. The co-op network. Some government funding. Corporate funding when it's not greenwashing. Nothing from the big carbon producers or emitters or the banks and insurance companies that keep them going."

"Is your funding stable? Enough to accomplish your goals?"

Zach snorted and laughed a bitter laugh.

Jen had never known Zach could be so rude.

Zach said, "We're understaffed, underpaid, and unable to roll out the large-scale public campaigns we'd like to."

Richard nodded, seemingly not taking offense. In the end, he said only, "I wish you luck."

Jen could feel Zach boiling over. She saw the storm churning in his eyes and the rigidity of his body.

She stared at him, trying to catch his eye, but he wouldn't look her way.

Zach said, "Sorry to sound rude, Richard, but it's not luck we need. We're at the mercy of an economy where a handful of people—"

"Like me."

Zach hesitated, but the dam broke. "Yes, people like you, control most of our country's wealth. One reason this country is going down the tubes is that you guys—"

Jen's fingers gripped the edge of the banquette cushion.

"—made sure over the past fifty years that your taxes tumbled toward zero and everything got deregulated or privatized. That has starved governments and limited what we can publicly accomplish in this moment of crisis."

Jen reached over and squeezed Zach's leg. "Zach, you're blaming Richard for all the problems of the world."

But Zach couldn't seem to stop himself. He said, "I know I'm being a shitty guest, Richard, but we're sitting here in a perfect example. This house, this . . ." He waved his hands. "This masterpiece should be in public hands."

And with that, he abruptly stood up.

"I need to get out of here. Jen, I'll meet you at the car. No rush."

He turned to Richard. "I'm sorry," he said. He headed to the door, Jaisha following close behind.

Twenty minutes later, they were back in the air, the setting sun behind them, moving toward the night without a single word. That is, until they were home, where they shut themselves in their bedroom and screamed at each other for the next hour.

17

"**B**oss, you shoulda powered me up yesterday."
Jen didn't respond. Her eyes were fixed on the table of numbers on her computer. It was Sunday, but we were at the station.

I said, "It was work."

Ten minutes later I tried again.

"How's Zach?"

"Fine," she said, but I caught a flash of memory in Jen's brain. Their bedroom. Late at night. Bitter words flying back and forth.

"And your visit with Richard?"

If you can hear a begrudging tone in a thought, I heard it. "Fine," she said. "It was fine."

"Did you get anything useful from him?"

"Nothing."

I waited. I mean, it's not like I had anywhere else to go.

Jen said, "He's going to ask around. About Culpepper."

"Well, that's good."

"Sure."

"Hey, boss. It's me. Your partner. What's up?"

"Nothing."

Again, the image of their bedroom. Angry words flashed like lightning.

Over the course of the morning, I put it together. I mean, I'm not a detective for nothing. Something happened at Richard's, and she and Zach had a meltdown afterward. Maybe they weren't talking now . . . God, humans.

I did manage to find out one interesting thing from her, although I wasn't sure what it meant.

I asked her how Richard was doing.

"Pretty much the same," she said, as her temperature rose by two-tenths of a degree.

I felt hamsters scuttling around her brain, this time with images of Richard: some from last year when we first met him and others that I assumed were from this weekend's encounter.

Her thoughts bore down on one new image.

She said, "When we saw him, I thought there was something different." Thoughts moved like human molasses. "It was his eyes. I just realized it was his eyes. They were . . . they were . . ."

At glacial speed she thought that over until, as if startled, she said, "He had crow's-feet. I'm sure of it. He had the hint of crow's-feet at the corners of his eyes."

16:23:18

I knew it had been months since Jen last visited the woman who, in a previous state of mind, had been her mother. It wasn't simply that she no longer recognized her daughter, but that she was now a happy human being rather than the nasty and abusive person Jen had known and hated all those years. Seven months ago, Jen had decided to forgive her. And to continue paying her nursing home bills until she died, whenever that might be.

But as for seeing her again? Jen said that, forgiveness or not, every visit was a dress rehearsal for hell.

Be that as it may, she announced to me that it was high time to visit Gabriel Cohen. Gabe was a retired journalist who lived in the retirement wing of the same home where Jen's mother was confined. He had helped Jen through her various crises last year, and he was the writer who'd broken the story about Jen's triumphant case.

It had been a tiring day—Jen still not fully recovered from the injuries and trauma of the previous autumn. She said she was too exhausted to ride the whole way, so she hoisted her bike onto the bus's front bike rack, and in we climbed. The bus driver had a fine head of gray dreadlocks. We sat down. Jen stared out the window; I stared out the window. We stopped at a red light. Two workers in dirty yellow hoodies were setting up a massive diamond-shaped sign to divert traffic. The bus driver honked and gave them a friendly wave. One of them held up his middle finger, but the bus driver laughed and honked again. Humans at play.

We arrived at the home and stood at the locked metal door. She peered through its minuscule window into the activity room. Her mother was dancing by herself. Others were ignoring her. Jen thought, *Good that you're finally happy*, turned, and went back down the stairs to the other building to visit Gabe.

I like Gabe Cohen. From what I can see, everyone does. Except the thousands of men, women, and non-gender-conforming people in positions of power whom he pissed off during his time at the *Washington Post*. He had notched up two Pulitzers, although he wasn't the type to mention it. And he was a shoo-in for another for his coverage of the scandal that emerged from our big case last year, although he kept protesting that the real investigative work had been done by Jen.

We knocked. When he opened the door, his face lit up. He pushed his fire-engine-red walker to the side and gave Jen a big hug that led to such a flood of endorphins and oxytocin that I truly wondered what I was missing.

He said, "I thought you'd moved to . . ."

When he didn't finish the sentence, Jen said, "To where?"

"I'm trying to think of a place without phones or Internet access."

"I would say you're sounding like my mother, except, well . . ."

"Come on in."

We settled into his small living room. Jen drank iced coffee from a colored aluminum tumbler: today the burgundy one that looked like grapes with a coating of frost. Gabe asked about Les and then Zach's comings and goings—and I was walloped with a surge of anger that Jen had a hard time concealing. They caught up on the latest from the co-op network that had played such a big role in last year's case.

When she told him about her investigation into Patty Garcia's death, the tone shifted.

Gabe said, "It was hard not to wonder when she died in such a bizarre way. On the other hand, it was so bizarre, it's hard to believe it was anything but an accident."

"Exactly why my captain told me to drop it."

"Jen," he said, drawing out her name into a playfully scolding tone.

She told him about Culpepper, Garcia's ex-husband.

"I remember the court case," Gabe said. "And I've read one or two things about him since."

"Of course, it might have been some entity in the oil and gas industry."

"You might need to narrow that a tiny bit," Gabe said.

Jen dutifully gave him a *no kidding* look.

She said, "I've pretty much written off most others."

Gabe said, "I'm sure that will be a relief to countless millions."

But I said to Jen, *Maybe we shouldn't write off Brita Germaine. Remember the words she omitted at first when she told you about Garcia's text? "There are things I need to speak to you about." Maybe she thought she was about to be fired.*

I could feel Jen's synapses sparking all around me, so I added, *And remember how Germaine was quick to point fingers at Big Oil and Garcia's ex-husband?*

"Jen?"

"What? Oh? It's . . ." She shook her head, as if chasing a thought away. "Work stuff. Say, do you happen to have any good contacts in oil or gas companies?"

His gray eyebrows rose. "A specialist in plots to kill lawyers?"

Jen laughed. "Or if they're busy working out their next hit, then at least someone who had an inside track on how they were undermining the reparations process."

Gabe thought for a moment, almost imperceptibly nodding his head from time to time as if vetting a list of names.

"I knew this one guy. An engineer with Hibernia. South Asian heritage. He worked hard, did his job well, cheered for Hibernia because that was *his* company, you know what I mean?"

Jen said she did.

"All was fine until one day, I'm not exactly sure when, but maybe fourteen or fifteen years back. His daughter was in high school and got suspended for skipping class to attend a climate change march. You remember them? Greta Thunberg?"

Jen remembered one of the marches in particular. She was already wearing blue and was on duty. It seemed more of a parade than a protest, and the energy was infectious. She'd been moved by the dedication of these teenagers and wondered what it would have been like, at that age, to have so much confidence.

"That night at dinner, he, his wife, his daughter, and I think he had a son, were chatting about buying a new TV, and Ravi said he figured he'd be getting a bonus because, as he put it, 'we are having a good year.' His daughter asked him what he meant by *we*, and pretty soon she was laying into him, nicely but firmly. She asked him how he could talk about being a provider when he was helping destroy her future.

"He didn't leave Hibernia overnight. Life isn't so simple. He ended up with a company researching how to lower the massive energy requirements for cement production."

"Are you saying I should speak to him?"

Gabe shook his head. "No, I'm reminiscing. He's a good guy, but he stays completely away from politics and public policy."

With Gabe promising that he'd think about who she could speak to, Jen was on her way.

Monday, March 20, 14:48:39

The split second our early shift ended, we'd beelined for Les's, but we'd only made it halfway before a cold rain whacked us without warning. Jen cranked the pedals like she was possessed, the rain pounding the pavement like jackhammers.

She was now wrapped in a white terry cloth robe that Les said they kept for guests; her clothes were tossing in the dryer.

"How does it feel, partner?" Jen said for the fourth time.

"When he welcomed me back, the captain actually smiled," Les said. "I've seen it, I've seen him smile, and now I can go to heaven."

"Don't take it too personally. It's cause he doesn't like to have his officers get knocked off. Is P.D. back on?"

"Alive and well."

Jen glanced at Les's tablet. It appeared to be at a shopping site. "Are you sure you're okay? You hate shopping."

"Birthday present for Christopher. He's complained about our chef's knife for years. Claims it barely cuts butter." He swiveled the tablet around. "What do you think?"

"You should ask Zach or his dad. They're the cooks in the family."

The music stopped, and Les got up to put on another vinyl album.

"Les, I read somewhere they've invented a way to play music without all that gear."

Jen and Les had been down this road before. Jen: Why bother? Les: Warm sound, cover art, the sheer physicality of playing a record, blah, blah, blah.

"It's the journey," Les said. "Not simply a random collection of songs. They made these albums to take you on a journey. The order of the songs creates a rhythm and a logic."

"Then at least get them on button chips."

"But this album with its totally different side A and side B tells you why you need records." He held up the cover. The Beatles, *Abbey Road*. "Their last studio album and, I think, one of their two masterpieces, the other, of course, being *Sgt. Pepper's*."

I felt the boss's impatience bubbling up. "Les," she said, "any luck at the Archives?" He'd spent the morning there before his meeting with Captain Brooks.

Les ignored her. "The thing about *Abbey Road*," he continued, "is that side A, except for two great songs, becomes quite light, occasionally silly, and then turns gloomy, ending abruptly as it's plowing through these depressing augmented arpeggios."

"I didn't know you knew stuff like that."

"Then flip it over, and you're instantly taken on a joyous twenty-two-minute ride that builds and builds, higher and higher, to the end."

He lowered the arm onto the record. Side A. Crackles and hisses. The music began.

"Down to work, right?"

"Right," Jen said.

"Listen, Jen, I finished the boxes, but I couldn't find a single thing. I mean, I found endless questions and answers about petroleum, gas, and coal reserves. But nothing about climate change."

"Shit."

"Sorry."

"What are we missing?"

Les paused, and I knew he was listening to P.D.

At last he said, "P.D. wants me to remember the index at the beginning of each of the documents."

Les closed his eyes, although I already knew this would be like asking a gerbil to recite pi to a thousand decimals. Humans don't possess that type of RAM and certainly don't have the storage. When he read those reports last week, P.D. had not yet been turned back on, and my guess was that Les had barely glanced at the names of the dozens and dozens of people—well, let's be clear, since it was 1968, the dozens and dozens of *men*—who'd testified at those hearings.

The third song came on, "Maxwell's Silver Hammer." Even I knew it: Zach's parents played this record, although at least they'd graduated to CDs. It was a silly, tinky-tonk number, about someone using a hammer to commit murder.

Jen said, "I don't get this song."

Les said, "P.D. says we should return to the Archives."

"Why?"

"She says she needs to see the details. Maybe piece together a different picture."

"It's raining outside."

"So?"

"And cold again."

Thirty-seven minutes later we were back in the reading room.

Les filled out a blue slip.

That stupid song, "Maxwell's Silver Hammer," kept playing in Jen's head, which meant it kept playing in mine.

She forced Les into a conversation about the reading room just to silence the damn song.

The Hollinger boxes hadn't yet been sent back into storage, and we had them in no time. Who says a government department can't be efficient?

One by one, Les opened each of the reports. He and Jen looked at each contents page far longer than P.D. or I needed, then quickly turned the pages while we hoovered up the material.

I could see why Jen had fallen asleep on Friday trying to read this stuff.

"Anything?" Jen said.

Les shook his head. "P.D. says no."

One report left.

Robin's-egg-blue cover. Faded red ribbon threaded through three punched holes. *Open it up.* Contents page in purplish-blue ink.

Les turned the pages, one by one. P.D. and I spotted the anomaly in the same instant, but it was her honor to enjoy.

Les said, "P.D. says to go back to the contents page."

He and Jen stared at it, at first not seeing what P.D. and I had instantly noticed when we breezed through the report. We left them to it—humans need to have that sense of discovery and accomplishment.

The word C O N T E N T S was typed at the top, the letters each underlined and spaced apart to make them look bigger. The next line was STATEMENT OF, followed by a typed-out list of thirteen names, each with a title. The men were primarily from government departments and the military, but some were from industry. No page numbers. Les ran his finger down the page. Stopped on the eighth name.

"What the . . . ," he said.

Dr. G. R. Bevans, Assistant-Chief Scientist, Standard Oil of New Jersey. "Anthropogenic Causes of Atmospheric Warming and the Impact on National Security."

"Jen," Les said, "I swear I didn't read any testimony like that when I went through this before."

Les flipped quickly to a spot halfway through the publication. Turned pages slowly. Made it to the end. Went to the beginning and did it all over. Flipped back to the contents, then skipped ahead to the testimony immediately before Dr. G. R. Bevans and the one that followed him. Although there were no page numbers in the index, the text pages were numbered. Eleven pages were missing.

Judging from the title of the presentation, Dr. G. R. Bevans, speaking on behalf of Standard Oil of New Jersey, had apparently acknowledged anthropogenic—that is, human-created—global warming. Proof that the oil companies knew what was happening. In goddamn 1968.

And now it was gone.

It would have been simple. Undo the ribbon. Remove the pages. Tie it back up.

So much for the supposed difficulties of government red tape.

The pages that might just be the smoking gun were nowhere to be seen.

18

On and off. Off and on. The rain came and went all night long. Now it was whacking down hard outside the station window. I dipped into Genesis and read about Noah, his unnamed wife, and sons with awkward Biblical names. I'm guessing that the name *Ham* will never come back into fashion, but that's what I said about bell bottom pants, and look what happened a few years ago.

The previous afternoon we had beelined from the National Archives to our pal Deacon at the Library of Congress. His Washington Senators retro cap of the day was red with blue lettering. We told him about the missing pages and showed him the photos Jen had snapped of the cover, the contents page, and the pages right before and after the missing testimony. Ron "Deacon" Decker looked upset. "It happens, well . . . I can think of one other time."

"And?"

"In that case we tracked down another copy, reproduced and reinserted the missing pages—with a note, of course, saying they were reproductions."

We asked where the other copies might be, and he rhymed off a list: Their own copy in the Library of Congress archives. Senate Archives for certain. And a small number of personal archives of former senators, most often held in university libraries.

"Did they make lots of copies?"

"Oh, sure. Most got thrown out as people changed jobs or retired. Or simply cleared out old files. But usually we can find a good handful floating around."

We asked if he could try to find one for us.

Now on this miserable, rainy morning, we were at the station, slogging through routine work. It was Les's first day back, and we kept getting interrupted as officers popped in to say hello.

As Watson might have said to Sherlock, singular news had arrived with the morning post. That would more correctly be *arrived by text*, but how I long for those civilized days before the U.S. Postal Service was gutted and handed to FedEx for a dollar. FedEx claimed it was taking over a massive burden for patriotic reasons. It in turn fired all the workers, sold off property and vehicles, and then licensed local delivery to gig workers for a fortune. Thus treating humans, yet again, to the miracle of the free market. I ask you, when will they ever learn?

But I digress.

Anyway, the news arrived by text from Deacon: the Library of Congress's copy of the hearing minutes had been delivered to him. However, the same pages *and* the table of contents were missing.

An hour later, Deacon phoned. "I spoke to Senate Archives. They have the whole series, except that one. That one date. The whole document is missing."

He warned that it would take time to track down other copies.

A cadet with short blond hair and a faint mustache appeared at our office door. "Is one of you Detective Lu?" His voice was so squeaky that I wondered if we were recruiting kids from sixth grade. I looked more closely and decided the faint blond smudge over his mouth was milk from morning snack time.

Jen, Les, Hammerhead, and Amanda looked at each other. I guess they could applaud this recruit for *not* racial profiling, but Jen (Chinese on her mother's side) looked at Les (white), who looked at Hammerhead (ditto), who looked at Amanda (black/Latinx), who looked back at Jen.

Jen said, "I guess the one with the Chinese last name is me."

The recruit blushed. "There's someone downstairs for you."

Jaisha was at the front counter, standing motionless, silent and elegant. All six of the cops and the three civilian staff in the room were shooting her looks, some gaping at her beauty, others probably trying to figure out if she was human or not.

Jaisha handed Jen a phone. Heavier than hers. No discernible brand.

"Please push redial."

Jen did. It rang twice. Richard O'Neil spoke.

"Hi, Jen. How's tricks?"

"We're a bit waterlogged here, but besides that, fine."

"And you and Zach?"

Jen hesitated.

"Come on, kiddo."

"He's not usually like that."

"From your reaction, I gathered not."

97

"He's sort of apologized to me a hundred times. But each time, he explains again why he was so angry."

"Are you speaking to him yet?"

"I may have murmured a few words in my sleep last night."

"That bad?"

"It'll be okay. It's just that . . ."

"It's just that he was right."

I could tell Jen didn't think she'd heard this correctly.

"At any rate," Richard continued, "I had my people poke around regarding Patty Garcia's demise."

"And?"

"You might say the industry's private responses were different from their media statements."

Chandler?

I fed one quote to her from a piece in the business section of the *New York Times*: "We disagreed with her economy-destroying proposals, but she was tenacious, smart and hard-working."

Richard continued. "They said all the right things, but the proof of the pudding was in the eating."

"Meaning?"

"As I mentioned before, the tremendous stock market rally over the past two weeks. Oil, gas, banks, you name it."

I hated this shit more than I can tell you.

Jen said, "Did your people pick up any rumors about her death?"

"Not a whisper. But Jen, I didn't expect there would be. There are no grand conspiracies in the world. Those of us in power simply don't need them. We write the rules to suit us."

It was the bluntest thing I'd ever heard him say about his position in society.

"And," he continued, "if one or several people *were* involved in her death, it's not the sort of thing they'd brag about at Davos."

"Thanks anyway for asking around."

"Do you expect to pursue this further?"

"I don't know."

I was about to chime in that Jen shouldn't lie to friends when she added, "Well, yeah. I guess I am."

"Even though I didn't hear anything," Richard said, "doesn't mean there aren't things worth hearing. Things worth someone's life to keep covered up. Be careful, Jen."

"I always am."

Richard laughed. "You most certainly are not."

Jen handed the phone back to Jaisha, and she shared such a beautiful smile that I started wondering if I could figure out a way to get to know her better.

We trudged back upstairs, where Les asked what was up. Jen told him that Richard had come up with nothing.

Meanwhile, I kept digging through industry and media responses to Garcia's death. I said to Jen, "This might be interesting."

"What?"

"That quote about Garcia being 'tenacious, smart and hard-working.'"

"Yeah?"

"It was from the head of the U.S. Petroleum and Gas Institute. His—"

Jen interrupted me. "Get me Zach."

I dialed.

"Zach," Jen said without preliminaries, "what can you tell me about the U.S. Petroleum and Gas Institute?"

"Nutshell or PhD version?"

"Nutshell."

"It's the industry lobbying group. Headquarters here in DC. The pretentious bastards refer to themselves as The Institute, even though there must be a thousand institutes around here. They push for reduced environmental standards and more government handouts and tax breaks."

"I take it you're a big fan of their work."

"One of my favorites is when companies are fined for breaking environmental laws. Corporate-friendly tax laws allow them to declare their fines as an expense and use them to reduce their income taxes."

"So in effect, the rest of us pay off their fines."

"Yep," he said. "In the past, the Institute's role was to create confusion and uncertainty about climate science. Bogus research, fake citizens groups, lawsuits against environmental organizations. And of course, lavish campaign contributions."

"And now?"

"People got wise to their tricks, so they're rewriting history. I mean that literally. They've bought one of the country's major textbook publishers. Books now portray the oil and gas industry as longtime champions for a green economy. And they're redoing tons of old video."

"Redoing?"

"They're scrubbing the internet to modify old speeches and news reports to put big oil in a favorable light. Things like the massive BP Deepwater Horizon spill—"

Michael Kaufman

"The what?"

"Exactly. It was in 2010 but has completely disappeared from history. It never happened. Additionally, they train politicians and business leaders to talk like they're Greenpeace activists while continuing to stall necessary climate measures."

"They're busy beavers."

Zach said, "Maybe we should start talking to each other again."

Jen said, "Maybe you should truly apologize for stomping out on Richard and me like you did."

"I was being childish."

Jen said, "That doesn't rate as an apology."

"In which case, I apologize. No excuses. No justification. I apologize."

"In which case, we're talking again."

After they'd hung up, I said, "Boss, I was trying to tell you something."

"You already told me about that institute thing."

"That's not what I was getting at."

"Are you pouting, Chandler?"

"Perhaps."

"Then spit it out."

"It may be a coincidence, but maybe not."

"I'm still not feeling any spit."

"That's gross," I said. Jen didn't reply. "Remember the name of the scientist from the missing pages?"

"Bevan."

"Close. It was Bevans, G. R. Bevans. Well, like I said, that quote I fed you was from the CEO of the Institute."

I felt the hairs on the back of Jen's neck rise in anticipation.

I decided to stretch this one out.

"His first name is Drake."

"Like that geriatric singer?"

"No, like Edwin Drake, who drilled the first modern well in 1859 in Pennsylvania."

"Chandler," she said, "this is feeling like when I was a kid waiting to open my Christmas present even though I already knew what it was."

"The CEO of the U.S. Petroleum and Gas Institute is named Bevans. Drake Bevans."

19

Drake Bevans, or more specifically his assistant, transferred us to his director of communications, who told us to come on over.

Mike Bradshaw was a big, friendly man. Big smile. Big firm handshake. Big *I couldn't be happier than to be speaking to you right now* personality. His starched pin-striped shirt fit him well; his office fit him well. Photographs jostled for space on the walls: Mike smiling with politicians, Mike smiling with his family, and one from his college days with Mike in a Longhorns burnt-orange jersey, his football helmet tucked smartly under his arm and that big smile beckoning the world.

"Detective, I'm real pleased you made time to see me."

"Exactly what I was about to say."

"Coffee? Dr. Pepper?"

Coffee! I said to Jen.

"I'm fine, Mr. Bradshaw."

"Everyone calls me Mikey."

"Mikey it is."

"So, Detective, how can I assist you?"

Coffee!

Again, Jen ignored my plea and got down to business as planned.

"Mikey, I'm trying to track down a report from a Senate hearing."

"Have you tried—"

"It has testimony from one of your members."

"Oh yeah? Which one?"

"Standard Oil of New Jersey."

"That's one for the history books."

"This is from 1968." Standard Oil became Esso. Became Exxon. Became ExxonMobil.

"A smidge before my time." Big smile. "In fact, my parents were still in high school. Hadn't even started dating."

"You must be glad they did."

"Don't you know it," he said. "Maybe you should try the Library of Congress or National Archives, Detective. They have stuff like that."

"We did, but it seems to have been misplaced."

"That's big government for you," Bradshaw said. "Well, we have an excellent research room here, and Zion's got to be the most brilliant researcher on the planet. I always say, if it's getable, he'll gettle it."

He gazed at Jen like a puppy until Jen finally smiled at his turn of phrase.

He opened what appeared to be an internal phone directory.

Jen said, "Let me give you the information."

"Good thinking."

"It's one of a series of reports from the Senate Armed Forces Committee in 1968."

"Okay." He started reaching for his desk phone.

"You better write this all down." She opened her notebook. "The title of the report was *Hearings: Long Term Threats to National Security, 1968*." Jen gave him the exact date.

"Right." Again he reached for the phone.

"Hang on. Specifically, we're looking for the testimony of a Standard Oil scientist named G. R. Bevans."

"Got it." He reached for his phone, but his hand froze in midair. "Did you say *Bevans*?"

Jen made the motion of looking at her notebook. "Yep."

"That's the last name of our CEO."

"You got to be kidding."

Somehow Bradshaw didn't seem to notice Jen's overacted lie. He picked up the receiver of his desk phone, glanced at the directory, and tapped out four numbers. A moment later, he said, "Zion, Mikey Bradshaw here . . . Totally good, totally good. You? . . . Listen, I'm trying to track down an old document and am hoping you can help me . . . Hang on."

Bradshaw gave the details to Zion. When he got to the name of the scientist, he paused a fraction, and a smile appeared on his face.

He spoke. He listened.

"Cool, right? I wonder if Mr. Bevans knows he has a namesake in the industry."

Mikey Bradshaw hung up and smiled at Jen. I was starting to wonder how much wear and tear face muscles can endure.

Bradshaw said, "Shouldn't take long to do a search, and if we have it here, you'll be most welcome to use our reading room."

Smile.

Or maybe humans can get arthritis of the cheek.

Jen said, "You been here long?"

"Three years this very month. It's a damn good place to work . . . Goldarn good."

I didn't think people actually said that.

He waited for Jen to agree it was goldarn good and then said, "Speaking of work, I was just reading about your exploits last year. Eden and all that. Now, there's a story and a half."

I only get to live five years, right? I hate to think how many hours are wasted listening to humans engage in small talk.

Small talk or not, I felt a jolt from Jen and quickly tuned back in.

Bradshaw was in the middle of a sentence. ". . . I'm saying. Strange about Patty Garcia, wasn't it?"

"Very."

"Between us, she didn't have many fans in my business, but I know everyone respected her."

Jen laughed. "Mikey, you're wasting your nice words on a mere cop."

"I read you were the one who found the body."

Chandler! Was that in any of the press coverage?

Of course not. Nothing.

Jen tried to keep her voice neutral. "How'd you hear that?"

Bradshaw didn't seem the least bit fazed. "Oh, we produce a daily internal briefing. My people amass a ton of information, and I read through a lot of it." He smiled, "That's our job, right?"

Before Jen could agree that was his job, the phone rang. Bradshaw listened. Said, "Uh-huh," a few times and then, "Too bad." He listened again and said, "His father . . . There you are . . . No, I'd like to tell Mr. Bevans myself about his dad's report. I'm sure he'll be pleased as punch. He ought to hear it directly from me."

He set down the receiver and spread his hands. "Detective Lu, sorry, but we don't have anything like that here. Scads of minutes from over the years, but nothing at all from those particular hearings. But it turns out that our CEO's father worked at Standard Oil."

Of course, we'd already figured that out. Geoff Bevans had been a research scientist at Standard Oil of New Jersey from the early sixties (when, if I've got these confusing name changes straight, it was also known as Esso before being rebranded as Exxon). He retired in 1989 and lived a reclusive life until his death in 2009.

Bradshaw stood up. Walked around his desk. Stretched out his hand. "Well, I'm sorry I couldn't be much help, but I'll give you a ring if Zion digs up the report. And if you ever get to Austin, you call and I'll make sure you get tickets to a Longhorns game, you hear me?"

Big smile.

Big handshake.

Big zero.

20

Tuesday, March 21—12:52:46

"That conversation didn't move the needle a single inch."

We met Les in Franklin Square. The rain had stopped. Jen and Les grabbed Thai food from one of the trucks and ate as they slowly circumnavigated the square.

Les said, "You gonna be updating the captain about this investigation?"

Jen got super interested in the peanuts that had gravitated to the bottom of her paper container of pad thai.

"Shit, Jen," Les said, reacting to her silence. "You should have told me. I mean, what if I said something when I met him yesterday?"

"Did you?"

"No. Luckily," Les said. "You need to talk to him."

"And say what?"

"Lay it out for him. I mean, you just came off a major coup when your instincts proved right."

Jen was staring at him.

Les said, "Right. It was six months ago." Sadness swept over his face. He tossed his empty container into a trash can like he blamed it for the fact that he'd missed out on a chunk of his life. "Maybe we can sit down over there and you can run me through it again."

He led the way to a bench.

Once seated, Jen said, "Suspect one. Ex-husband."

"Motive?"

"Revenge and economic loss."

"You told me he lives in a mansion."

"True. But he lost out on becoming CEO. And with the reparations, he stands to lose a fortune."

"Poor schmuck," Les said.

"Most damning of all, he's a smug bastard."

"Yeah," Les said, "guilty for sure."

"Second," Jen said, "Garcia's longtime executive assistant."

Les said, "We're stretching so much, I feel like I'm in a yoga class."

"Les, that's not a bad line for someone who just got his brain back. Garcia was keeping her out of the loop, and maybe Brita thought she was about to be fired."

"Christopher would throw a party if I got fired."

"She knew Garcia would be playing golf alone—"

"How would she know that?"

"Apparently everyone knew she played on her own—"

"I didn't."

"Except you."

"Okay," Les said. "And then she uses ESP to deflect some schmuck's golf ball to hit the exact tiny spot that will kill her?"

I felt Jen's muscles tighten. I could feel her getting ready to shoot a nasty reply when her phone dinged. Actually, she imagined she heard a ding, but that was merely a stimulus to her auditory cortex coming from me. I was letting her know a text had come in.

Jen held up a finger to signal Les to wait.

I fed her the message, and she passed it on to Les.

"I just got word from our buddy Deacon over at the Library of Congress. He's tracked down archives for three senators who were at the hearings. In two of them, nothing at all from those particular sessions."

"They didn't think they were anything worth saving."

"In the third archive, the same pages and table of contents are missing."

They shared a moment of silence. I kept my mouth shut too.

"Okay," Jen said, "the oil people."

"No way they'd get their hands dirty like that."

"Haven't you seen the movies with oil workers? They're covered with black gunk."

Les didn't bother groaning.

"Jen, I'm pretty sure there are quite a few 'oil people.' You've got an actual suspect?"

"What about this Bevans guy?"

"What about him?"

Jen shrugged.

"Anyway," she said, "Someone like that could have hired a killer."

"Who loads a golf ball into his elephant gun and shoots her."

"Maybe the smack on the head was a coincidence."

"What did the pathologist say?"

"They're not infallible."

"Wait! I think I've got it. This hired killer does a Mission Impossible HALO parachute drop into DC—"

"Les, I'm not an idiot."

Les agreed that was probably true.

Les said, "It sounds to me like her ex-husband is your strongest suspect."

"Yeah, except he has a rock-solid alibi."

Les stood up from the park bench. Crunched his head one way and then the other: I heard the vertebrae cracking. He looked back at Jen.

"One thought, Cobalt."

"What's that?"

"Maybe hold off talking to the captain after all."

15:37:25

Back at her desk, Jen steeled herself to begin an online training about a dense policy directive on search and arrest procedures. She'd been postponing this chore and had until the end of the day to complete it.

Her phone rang, and she snatched it up before the second ring.

"Hey, Jen. Doing okay?" Gabe Cohen.

"Yeah, now that you've phoned."

"Got your TV on?"

"Gabe, I'm at work,"

Gabe said, "It's your buddy's company."

"Who?"

"Culpepper. His company."

"What station?"

Gabe told her, and she clicked on a feed.

It wasn't Culpepper on the screen but a man identified as the CEO of Climate Oasis. "And to help launch our new project . . . well, I think everyone will recognize this face."

The picture changed. The face of a trillionaire tech bro floated in front of the camera. Upside down. The camera panned back. A subtitle announced, *From the Lunar Gateway Station.*

I said to Jen, *The Lunar space station is in a highly elliptical, near-rectilinear pattern.*

English.

He's orbiting the moon.

Shhh!

It was a face you saw and a name you read much more often than a voice you heard. But here it was, screachier and more stoned out than you expected a male trillionaire's voice to be. "Hey, all. Amazing view up from here. Without further ado, I'd like to introduce our astounding new addition to Climate Oasis."

Another man and a woman floated into the background and, like cheesy game show assistants, unfurled a small banner:

Climate Oasis Lunar City

The screen now jumped to an animated video. A lander streaked across the barren lunar surface. A bright spot appeared ahead, and soon we could make out a massive, clear dome with buildings and trees underneath. The voice of the CEO came back on. "That's right. Starting today, we're selling condominiums in our ultimate climate oasis. We expect that construction will begin—"

Jen clicked out of her browser.

"What absolute shit."

Gabe said, "I can tell you one thing. If I was a Timeless who was going to live forever, the moon would be the last place I'd want to settle down. Hang on." I heard his TV go silent. "Anyway, the actual reason I was phoning is because I thought of one person who might just know about that document you want." In his voice, I could hear he was smiling. "Blessing Robinson is one of the most extraordinary people I've ever met. I do hope she's still with us."

"Telephone number?"

"Changed since the one I once had. But I have an address. And anyway, it's best if you go there. She's someone you'd definitely want to meet."

21

When Jen got home from work and the mind-numbing online policy training, she found Zach's father, Raffi, performing magic at the stove. Zach, his mother Leah, and Jen's friend Ximena were keeping an eye on him like they were watching an episode of Julia Child, but were mainly drinking wine. Me? No one seemed to notice I was still turned on.

Jen had met Ximena Maleena the previous summer, first as an adversary but soon a trusted friend. She had a fierce intensity and a mule-like surefootedness. Her face was angular and strong, and with her thick hair twisted into a rope, she could have been a model for one of Diego Rivera's murals from a hundred years before. She was a member of a large international co-op network with ties to the Green Prosperity movement.

Jen hugged Ximena, said hi to Raffi and Leah. When she turned to Zach, he handed her a glass of sparkling wine. Good times.

Jen said, "This is for?"

"I thought we should celebrate the end of our silent era."

Jen smiled and gave Zach a big hug too.

Judging from their *oohs* and *aahs*, dinner was great. Zach's father Raffi was a good cook, at least when his wild improvs worked out. This one: a vegetarian moussaka, stuffed grape leaves, and a dal made with Greek rather than Indian spices.

They had barely dug into their chow when Zach popped off his bombshell.

"So . . . I found out today what Patty Garcia was going to announce." They all stopped eating. "At the closing session of our conference."

There were several shouts of encouragement.

"Philip and Carmen"—Zach turned to his parents—"our cochairs, knew. The story's coming out tonight at midnight."

"And?" Raffi said.

"Garcia was making two announcements. The first that she was officially running for president. That would have been enough to make headlines. But the biggest surprise was that she, several Democrats, and even a few Republicans were launching a new political party. The Common Good."

Ximena said, "Third parties never win elections. They'll split the vote."

Leah said, "Theodore Roosevelt's Progressive Party came second in 1912 after he left the Republicans."

Zach said, "Polls showed that Garcia was more trusted than anyone. And Carmen says they expected quite a number of elected officials to join the new party."

"Which means," Raffi said, "she'd have had a chance of winning."

Zach nodded. "I—"

A loud yawn escaped Jen's mouth.

Ximena nudged her playfully, "Jen, I know you're not big on politics, but . . ."

Jen said, "Sorry, I've had a stunningly boring day. But I do want to hear this."

I fed her a nibble of adrenaline.

Chandler, that you messing with my head?

I kept my mouth shut.

Zach said, "I was saying that I should have known something was up."

Jen mustered her energy. "Why?"

"Down in Raleigh, Secret Service showed up while we were setting up on Thursday night," Zach said. "I didn't think twice about it. We had some prominent politicians speaking, so I figured Secret Service would be there."

"So?" was all Leah said, but Jen and I were already two steps ahead.

Jen said, "With those other politicians, there'd be a greater police presence, even FBI. But the Secret Service protects the executive branch and declared presidential candidates. The Secret Service must have been informed of Garcia's intentions. And once she declared her candidacy, they'd never let her out of their sight."

And now I felt Jen's mind slamming into high gear.

Chandler, you're hearing this, aren't you?

I fessed up. *Yep, I'm here.*

Friday, March 3, was going to be Garcia's last golf game playing alone. With no Secret Service protection.

Perhaps the murder didn't happen that day because she'd found the smoking gun. Perhaps it was also because whoever had killed her knew it was then or never.

Wednesday, March 22, 09:32:16

"Why didn't you tell me she was about to announce she was running for president? And this thing about a new party." Jen's voice was calm but authoritative.

Brita Germaine didn't miss a beat: "Because it was a secret."

"It isn't any longer."

"Good. It was crap to start with."

"What do you mean?"

Brita eyes wandered around Garcia's office—pictures now down, whiteboard erased, boxes stacked high, desk cleared off—and returned to Jen. "I told her there was no chance in heaven it would work. She floated the idea back in the fall. I tried to dissuade her. Told her it would be a disaster. She'd never be president and her credibility as a lawyer would be toast. Our whole firm would end up as a one-liner on late-night talk shows."

And, Jen thought, *your own days of glory would be over.*

"You had an obligation to tell me."

"That's absurd."

"It could be the reason someone wanted her dead."

"Anyway," Brita said, "I didn't know anything."

"What's that supposed to mean?"

Brita's voice turned sharp and angry. "It means I was out of the fucking loop."

Jen let that simmer. The boss is good at letting silence do its work.

But Brita now seemed to catch herself. Or had at least checked her anger. Or wanted to change the subject.

Jen went for it: "When did you learn Ms. Garcia was going to announce her candidacy and this new party in Raleigh?"

Brita looked startled.

She didn't speak.

Jen said, "On that Friday morning when you arranged to meet her at her club?"

Go for it, Cobalt!

"Or maybe on Wednesday? Two days before she was killed? Remember, the day she supposedly berated you in front of your staff?"

Brita deflated. Gave up. Surrendered.

She slumped down in her desk chair. Closed her eyes and flopped her head back against the back of the seat. Didn't speak for the longest time. Finally, she said, "That was why I was so upset with her. She didn't scold me in front of other staff. She was out of the office. I had to go into her desk—"

"Was that typical?"

"Of course. The relation of executive assistant to managing partner, at least in our case, is one of trust. Patty locked her desk, but I had a key. If she had anything totally private, she would have kept it at home. She often said so herself: our relationship was built on complete and total trust."

That's what they say in every relationship, sweetheart, until it isn't.

"And what did you find?"

"Her notes."

"For . . . ?"

"You're the detective. What do you think?" Snapping. Bitter. "Her fucking notes for the fucking speech in Raleigh that would destroy us."

10:14:47

"Well," said Les over the phone, "she certainly gets extra motive points."

"Motive. Opportunity."

"There's only that one small complication."

"The it-was-an-accident thing?"

"Something like that."

"What about the Shadow?" Jen said. "Modus."

"What about him?"

"Don't you think it's strange that he should die a couple hundred yards away? Maybe on the same day?"

"Unfortunately, Shadows die all the time. No home. No health care. No hope. Lousy diet. Alcohol. Drugs. Crime."

"Sort of the anti-longevity treatment."

"Sort of is," Les said.

"But it's still a powerful coincidence."

"Jen, you show me a murder weapon that isn't a golf ball, and I'll follow you wherever that takes us."

"I'm telling you," Jen said, "she was murdered."

"Whatever you say. Are you coming back in?"

"Yeah, soonish," she said. "Les, are you busy right now?"

"Super busy. I'm trying to decide if our pencils should go in a cup or in the drawer."

"Wow, that old stereotype about gay men and interior decorating really is true."

"My other career."

"Maybe you can zip up to Viridian Green. Ask around, find out if anyone saw Brita on the course that day? I'll send you a photo."

"It'll have to be tomorrow morning. That okay?"

"Sure," Jen said. "Just watch out for the general manager. He bites."

22

We were on our way to find Blessing Robinson, the woman Gabe Cohen had told us about a couple of days earlier. Washington Highlands has a reputation as a pretty tough neighborhood. Jen always cautions me not to exaggerate these things, but here's the picture: Public housing. Run-down detached homes, although there were many where you could tell folks took pride in doing what they could. Apartments were two-story boxes, red and brown brick, some with bars laced over their first-floor windows. Most trees were still leafless, the kids were in school, and those with work were at work, so there was an empty, dispirited feeling about the area.

We found the house west of the Oxon Run creek on the one hundred block of Yuma Street SE. Half the street was newish low-rise apartment blocks. There were several construction projects and a stretch of old clapboard bungalows, one boarded up from a fire, and some newer homes. Most were well looked after, but nothing was fancy.

And then there was the house at number 117.

We climbed out of the car and stood across the street, looking at the place. Oxytocin flowed like a summertime river through Jen's body. If she'd been a cat, I would have heard her purr.

A small house, straight off a Virginia farm. Soothing pale green with white trim. A white picket fence, the pickets cut at different lengths so that each section of fencing was scalloped. The house was huddled in the midst of so many trees that in the summer it must have been almost impossible to see. The front porch was only a few inches up from the ground, and the overhanging roof was supported by four wood pillars painted white to match the fence. With its screen door and swinging chair, I expected to see barefoot children chasing chickens and hear the shouts from the menfolk over in the barn.

We crossed the street. Went up the short walk and stepped onto the small porch.

There was no doorbell.

Jen knocked.

No one came.

She knocked again.

Waited.

We were about to leave when the inside door opened.

On the other side of the screen was a tiny little woman. Face dark and shriveled with age.

"Yes?"

"Ma'am," Jen said, and held up her badge, but the woman didn't look at it. "My name is Jen Lu. I'm a DC police officer. Gabe Cohen said you might be able to help me. Gabe's a—"

"I know full well who Gabriel is. You come right on in."

She lifted a thin arm, felt around for a moment, and unhitched the screen.

Blessing Robinson welcomed us into her home.

Blessing Robinson appeared to be blind.

She walked ahead of us, her steps small, her right hand running lightly along the hallway wall as if for reassurance.

We reached the kitchen. Simple. Clean. Worn-down hardwood floor. Arborite countertops and cupboards painted pale green. An old white refrigerator shaped like an elongated marshmallow.

"Miss, you'll have to bring a second chair from the dining room. Could you do that for me?"

Jen carried in a chair.

"Go on now, you sit down. Let me pour you a nice glass of iced tea." Blessing opened the refrigerator and took out a green plastic pitcher with a lid on top.

"Ms. Robinson, can I give you a hand?"

"I'm just fine, and don't you go calling me Ms. Robinson. I got enough of that from all my students to last a lifetime. Blessing will do fine. Just fine."

A calico cat, its tail pointed proudly into the air, sashayed into the kitchen and, without invitation, jumped onto Jen's lap.

I caught Blessing's lips counting to six as she poured tea from the pitcher. With great care, she brought one glass and then the other to the table.

"I still have a smidgen of my sight. And they've fitted me with a contraption so I can read. But dear, it really is no fun. When you knocked at the door, I figured it was another developer. They won't take no for an answer, but that's all they're ever going to get from me. So tell me, how is Gabriel? I haven't spoken to him in years."

It was as if Blessing hadn't spoken to anyone in years, and it all was pouring out in one go.

Jen talked about Gabe for a while and then explained that she was searching for a particular Senate report.

Blessing's weak eyes lit up.

"Words I love to hear."

She pressed one hand on the chair, the other on the tabletop, and stood up. Started toward the door. Turned back and said, "You come with me, Miss."

With the cat following, she slowly led us to the stairs in the front hall.

"I'll need to take your arm, if you don't mind."

The cat cut in front of us and scampered up.

Blessing stopped talking as we climbed the wooden stairs, as if the effort took all her concentration. The only sound was her breathing and the creak of the old wood.

There was a chair at the top. "Could you . . . ," she said to Jen, and Jen eased Blessing down into it.

Blessing said, "Maybe you can find the switch for me. Along the left side there. It's so good to have a visitor."

The whole second floor, except one area that I assumed was a bathroom, had been opened up and turned into a library. Hundreds of books and hundreds of file boxes. It wasn't a huge area—I sized it at 628 square feet—but even that can hold a lot when shelves line the walls and ceiling-high rows divide the room. A dehumidifier hummed in the corner.

I identified molecules of old paper, leather, and mildew drifting in the air. I felt Jen relax and caught a snatch of a happy memory of a class visit to the public library when she was a little girl.

"While I catch my breath," Blessing said, "let me tell you about my collection."

Her story went like this: In 1967, she was in the MA program in U.S. History at Howard University and must have stood out, because she landed an internship with a congressman, a huge accomplishment in those years for a woman and for a Black person. While attending her first House committee meeting, she watched the stenographers type away. "I realized I was no longer studying history, I was watching history being made, and watching these nimble-fingered women recording it. I caught the bug."

She finished her degree. "It wasn't easy back in those days for a woman to find professional work. Especially a Black woman." But she got a job with a senator that lasted five years.

"And that was when I began collecting documents. Surreptitiously, of course." She let out a soft, mischievous laugh.

Jen said, "My lips are sealed."

Blessing laughed again and stretched out a thin arm. "And there you see it all, right in front of your eyes."

Eventually, Blessing had enrolled at teachers college and became a history teacher, but she never stopped collecting.

"When I'm gone, it's all going to Howard University. I'm not being boastful, but I'm so proud of this collection. Now, dear, what did Gabriel think I might have?"

Jen gave her the details.

Blessing said, "It wasn't one of my committees."

Jen's heart dropped.

A mischievous flicker lit her face. "But it was for a white boy who kept flirting with me. Let's go see."

Jen helped her stand. Blessing led us down the second row. She ran her hands lovingly along wooden shelves worn smooth with age. "My daddy made these for me. He's been gone now for coming on forty-three years. He was a good, good man."

She stopped.

"I think they should be right about here, but you'll have to do the looking for me. Third shelf up."

All the closed magazine boxes in this section said, *Senate Committee Hearings*. The whole third shelf was labeled *Armed Forces Committee, 1968 to 1970*. One box said, *Hearings: Long Term Threats to National Security, 1968*.

Blessing said, "Nothing is complete. Far from it. It's what I could get my hands on, that's all."

Don't ask, I warned Jen. These were reports she'd taken when people were cleaning out offices or changing assignments, reports fished from wastebaskets. Reports she probably had broken laws to acquire.

"Baby, you bring that box over to the table now."

Jen carried it to a wooden table painted with glossy white paint that was chipping off along the edges. Blessing sat down and instructed Jen to bring the other chair over.

"Well," Blessing said, "don't be shy."

Jen opened the lid and carefully lifted the hearing minutes from the magazine box and set them in a pile. Pale-blue covers with fading red ribbon threaded through punched-out holes. Les had gone through six much larger boxes. She knew Blessing's collection was a very small sample. One by one, she looked at the dates on the front cover and, just in case, opened the minutes to the contents page.

Nothing. Nothing, Nothing. Nothing. Nothing. Nothing.

The third to the last report had the right date. She opened it to the contents page and to her delight saw it: Dr. G. R. Bevans, Assistant-Chief Scientist, Standard Oil of New Jersey, "Anthropogenic Causes of Atmospheric Warming and the Impact on National Security."

She fought to hold down her excitement. She told herself, *We've seen that much already.* Her fingers felt like they had rods stuck through them as she fought to turn the pages. *They won't be here,* she intoned to me. She turned another page. *They won't be here.*

Another page and another. Nothing and nothing.

Until there it was.

What Patty Garcia had been searching for. Maybe even died for.

We were looking at the missing report.

"Do you mind, Blessing, if I read this quickly?"

"I don't mind. But I'd prefer to hear it myself. Read it to me, child. Would you do that for me?"

Jen told me to hit the record button on her phone. Not that I needed it for myself: I could take in every word and recite it back verbatim.

Some of Dr. Bevans's observations were tentative—it was only the 1960s, after all—but it was clear. The production and burning of oil, coal, and natural gas were "causing a dramatic increase" of CO_2 and methane in the atmosphere. The evidence was incontrovertible: this increase was "causing a trend to the warming of the planet and a change of our climate." It wasn't yet clear how quickly this would accelerate, but it was happening and would have drastic consequences.

In a presentation by Standard Oil of New Jersey, we had found the smoking gun. The document that set a date to when the oil industry knew about the impact of burning fossil fuels. A date that would send the cost of climate reparations well into the trillions.

"Blessing," Jen said, her voice trembling, "This is it. This is the report I've been looking for."

"That's good, dear."

"Could I borrow it? I promise to be careful."

Blessing's expression changed. "I've never, in all these years, never once let anything out of my sight. I'll have to give that some thought. I hope you can understand."

"Could I at least photograph it?"

A recording of Jen's voice was one thing, but that wasn't proof this existed.

"I don't know. That would confirm that I broke the law. And you a police officer. You see, many of these documents were confidential or private. And these here"—she patted Jen's pile—"I recall very clearly that they are unpublished. The hearings were held in secret."

"But no longer. They're all in the public domain now."

"Yes, it's been more than fifty years. Much more. My, how long ago it all was."

"So—"

"But this still constitutes evidence that I broke the law when I took them."

"I—"

"Now, dear. I'm not saying no. But I need to think on it a bit. Maybe you can return this weekend? Would you do that? It would be so nice to have a visitor again."

23

"You could have stuffed it under your jacket. She'd never have noticed."

"Chandler! That's awful."

We were in a car, heading back to the station.

"And anyway," Jen continued, "if I took it illegally, it wouldn't be admissible evidence."

"But it's evidence of something much bigger," said I, eco-warrior.

"Chill. She'll give it to us. I'm guessing she's only jonesing for second visit."

"Just in case, maybe we can go grab a warrant."

"Fat chance of getting that," she said.

"Three weeks to go before the deadline."

"Don't fret. In two days, we'll have Patty Garcia's smoking gun."

We rode the rest of the way without another word. But let me tell you, from where I sit, there is never silence. Jen was buzzing. Should she bring the report to Deacon at the Library of Congress so it would be there, a returned public document? He could then inform the Supreme Court that he had the document, the smoking gun. Or should she hand it over first to the captain? Her mind didn't stop.

I'd memorized the document as she read it. I'd hit record on Jen's phone so we had her voice reading it. I don't do visual or audio recordings, although there are rumors our next generation will do that, privacy of our hosts be damned. But neither Jen's recording nor my word-for-word recollection was proof of anything. Jen could have made it up. In two days, three at the most, Jen would have it in her hands.

Back at the station, we caught up on paperwork. This required about point zero one percent of my computing power. I thought about P.D. and how she had suggested Les return to the National Archives to compare the tables of contents with what was inside each report. P.D. is a detail person. When she gets it right, it's a thing of beauty.

With that in mind, I realized I needed to go back to other missing details of the case. Tiny details. Fine points.

I raced through the same list that Jen had shared with Les two days before, although this time I rather brilliantly turned it into a snappy action plan.

Brita Germaine: Solid motive and opportunity. Pissed off at boss, who she found at Viridian Green; confronted her, started arguing, pushed her down in a fit of anger, not murder, and when that errant ball came their way, she picked it up and smashed it against Garcia's head. Problem: A golf ball's too small to be a decent weapon. If Brita was holding it, it would barely poke beyond her fingers. And wouldn't someone have seen her running away or fleeing the scene in a golf cart? Action: Wait and see what Les comes up with.

Big Oil and Gas: Motives galore, especially since they knew Garcia had been searching for the smoking gun. Perhaps they heard she had uncovered a lead. Presumably they'd heard rumors about her running for president and were justifiably worried how this would affect them. Problem: An industry is not a suspect. Better get a name or two attached. Interesting that, so far, only one name had popped up: the Bevans clan. Father long dead. Son in a position of power. Action: Check out Drake Bevans.

Inside political job: If word had leaked that Garcia was forming a new political party, that was sure to upset the old guard. Problem: Her death was way too convoluted for a political assassination; those tended to involve some dumbass guy set up to pull the trigger. And anyhow, politicians specialize in character assassination, not the real thing. Action: None for now. Likely a dead end.

Culpepper: Motives up the wazoo. Problem: He was packing an alibi as irrefutable as a beautifully programmed string of zeros and ones.

I know I'm supposed to be a computer, but I was feeling rather emotional about Culpepper. I hated the guy. Hated his arrogance. His sexism. Hated everything he stood for.

I didn't want to let him off the hook. Not yet.

P.D. came to mind. P.D., a detail person.

Action: Go through Culpepper's broadcast again. Frame by frame. Pixel by pixel. Maybe I'd pick apart his alibi. Neither my hardware nor my software was set up for that type of visual processing. It was going to take a long time.

I got down to business.

12:26:44

The moment Les returned from Viridian Green, Jen dragged him out for tacos.

While they agonized the way humans do making the simplest food choice, I read the first five volumes of Proust's *In Search of Lost Time*. The story of my life.

They got their food and finally sat down. Jen said, "They didn't stuff you with shrimp cocktails, by any chance?"

"Unfortunately, it was all business."

"Did you meet their dictator? Sorry, director."

"He was off-site."

"Probably taking classes in pulling wings off of butterflies."

"So I—"

"Or stealing lunch money from kids."

"—spoke to his administrator."

"Georgette Baxter."

"She's one pissed-off woman," Les said.

Being a bit of a blue-collar lad myself, I've always had a soft spot for pissed-off workers.

Les said, "I think she's about to quit."

"Shit, I hope not until this is all over."

"Anyway, she took me around to speak with staff. First, to their security booth. The guard was one of those damn guys from one of the mercenary companies. When he brought up the logs for the day of the accident—"

"The murder."

"Whatever. He acted like he was revealing CIA secrets."

"Maybe he was."

Les threw her shade.

"So?" Jen said, growing impatient.

"Brita arrived at ten past two that day."

"Pretty much what she told me."

"I then spoke to several people in the clubhouse. Brita told you she'd been sitting in one of the lounges, right?"

"'A quiet corner,' were her words."

"No one remembered serving her, and there were no chits on Garcia's account."

"Which means no proof she was in the clubhouse at the time of the attack."

Les said, "To be fair, within minutes the place was total chaos. Her presence would have been the last thing on anyone's mind."

I told Jen my hypothesis about Brita: she had managed to find her employer on the course, rumbled into an argument with her, clobbered her with something, and whomped her on the head with the golf ball to make it seem like an accident. And by a fluke, this killed her. Even I knew this was a harebrained theory: autopsy results would have shown the other blow.

Unfortunately, the boss grabbed on to this half-baked idea. No, make that the raw ingredients of a recipe for a half-baked idea.

"Maybe," she said to Les, "Brita drove a golf cart out to the fifth hole."

"I asked Georgette about that very possibility. She acted offended. She said they had extremely attentive staff." Les raised his voice an octave. " 'Strangers can't casually wander around.'"

"You know, that wasn't even close to sounding like her."

Les continued, unfazed. "Golf carts are parked outside the pro shop for members to take if they wish. But a swarm of staff are hovering around to help players, and they'd have stopped a stranger from driving off in one. And even if she somehow had, Brita wouldn't know exactly where her boss was. There was nothing to or from Brita on Garcia's phone records that afternoon—"

"You checked those?"

Les smiled. "P.D. did. Which means if Brita wanted to find Garcia, she would have needed to drive around looking for her. Again, someone would have noticed, but no one did."

Ditch my dumb theory, I told Jen.

Never one to be ordered around, especially not by the likes of me, Jen plowed ahead and spelled out my nonbaked theory to Les.

He said, "Jen, do you really think a middle-aged woman would do that?"

"Not necessarily to try to kill her. She wanted to confront her but was getting nowhere."

"So you said."

"So she lashed out, killed her by mistake, and then tried to make it seem like a freak accident."

"So you're telling me she was planning to confront her boss, not kill her?"

"Something like that."

Jen, I started to say, before she shushed me up.

But Les said exactly what I was about to tell her: "If she had been planning only to confront her boss, then she would have openly asked for a golf cart. Told them she had an urgent message to personally bring to her. That sort of thing. But she didn't do that either."

"So . . ."

"Brita Germaine is pretty much out of your picture."

24

Thursday, March 23—12:52:17

Here's everything you need to know about some guy you've never heard of:

Drake Bevans was born in 1951 in New Brunswick, New Jersey. His mother was a housewife; his father, Geoff R. Bevans, had a position in the chemistry department at Rutgers University. By the time Kennedy was assassinated, Geoff had left academia and was commuting a half hour each way to the Standard Oil of New Jersey Research Labs at the Bayway Refinery, where there wasn't so much as a twig of ivy or any living thing to be seen. The refinery's a few miles south of the Newark airport, in case you have a perverted desire to check out this industrial wasteland.

In high school, Drake showed a flair for chemistry, just like his father before him. He won a state science prize. At university he demonstrated an even greater knack for business and graduated cum laude from Princeton with a joint chemistry and business major. He got his MBA from Wharton.

His first job in the energy industry was a summer gig at the refinery when he was seventeen. He is apparently one of the few people on the planet who truly loves the smell of an oil refinery.

He graduated from business school; the company (which by then had been renamed Exxon) hired him. Given his background, Drake was put into the business side of research and development.

In spite of, or perhaps because of, the alarming 1968 presentation by his father to the Senate committee, Exxon went all out in the seventies to ramp up their disinformation campaign about climate change. According to the many articles and documents I'm still sifting through, they bought and buried patents that would greatly boost auto mileage. They helped bury plans for advanced batteries to run electric vehicles. They began to sow confusion about climate change. Make money! Keep shareholders happy! Destroy the planet! Nice guys, right?

Here's where it gets murky.

It appears that after his report to the Senate, Drake's dad, Geoff R. Bevans, never presented a paper or research report again. I couldn't track down a single publication in an industry or scientific journal. In fact, through the 1970s and 1980s, as far as I could see, he didn't attend a single scientific or industry conference.

For a research scientist, that's pretty much unheard of.

I don't know if what I'm about to tell you is true.

I'm making this up.

But it seems to me that Exxon had put G. R. Bevans on ice.

And guess who was running the research division by 1982?

Drake Bevans.

This man has some serious daddy issues.

"That's all you got on him?" Jen said.

"Partner," I said, "that's just the beginning of the highlight reel. Drake was scaling the heights of corporate power like Hillary and Norgay did Everest. Everyone said he'd be running Exxon by his fiftieth birthday. But then, in 2005, he resigned. Said, and I'm quoting here, 'Our industry, our way of life, is at war.' He said that as much as he'd love to run a company 'as universally respected as Exxon'—I'm quoting again—"

"I figured you just might be."

"—he wanted to play a larger role, quote, 'in saving America.'"

"Chandler, I wish you'd learn how to do air quotes."

The boss can be so insensitive.

"A year later," I said, "he'd rounded up big dollars and established the Institute."

"How old is he?"

I didn't want to tell the boss to do the arithmetic, but really, it's not like we're talking about solving the twin prime conjecture.

"Eighty-three," I said. "But since he looks about fifty, he must be a Timeless."

"I need to meet this guy."

She told Les about Bevans. He said, "What are we waiting for?"

13:10:39

Back to the U.S. Petroleum and Gas Institute. Didn't stop in to say hi to our old buddy Mikey Bradshaw. Didn't seek out the resource room to make the acquaintance of brilliant researcher Zion. Jen and Les flashed their IDs at the reception desk—Les asked to speak to Drake Bevans; Jen said, "No, we don't have an appointment"—and we were asked to wait. Five minutes later we were given passes and instructed to go to elevator two. Same routine as before, but a different floor. No buttons to push, so we let the elevator do its job and take us to six, the top floor of this low-rise glass-and-metal tower designed to remind you of an oil rig.

Drake Bevans did not make us wait.

A polite young man with a flat Midwest accent led us straight into Bevans's office.

Bevans stood up, came around his desk, shook Jen's and Les's hands without ceremony, and spoke to the young man. "Nine minutes," he said.

Bevans had none of Bradshaw's PR flash, but then again, that wasn't his job. In fact, he didn't even seem to own a smile. Everything about him spelled *serious*. He was one of those rare men who still wore an old-fashioned suit and tie—suit, gray; shirt, white; tie, blue gray—as if to say anything good enough for the twentieth century, America's century, was good enough for him. As media photos had suggested, the Longevity Treatment had taken his appearance back to his fifties, although my guess was that he must have been one of those humans who already seemed an old man at five. His expression wasn't so much unfriendly as severe. He had a noticeable paunch, indicating he didn't have time for anything as trivial as exercise. His forehead was high, the washed-out gray of his eyes matched his suit, and his thin lips looked like Mother Nature had forgotten to add the red dye.

"Detective Lu, Detective Westin, have a seat." Not friendly, not unfriendly. Simply getting down to business.

Detective Lu and Detective Westin sat.

Bevans waited until we were seated, then took his place behind his desk.

I could tell Jen was expecting Bevans to speak. Welcome them to the Institute or ask why they were there. Instead, he looked at her, then at Les, then back to Jen. No particular sign of curiosity.

"Mr. Bevans," Jen said at last, "I'm interested in your father."

"My father."

"Geoff R. Bevans."

"I'm aware of his name."

So far, this was going extremely well.

All the way here, we had debated where to begin. We knew where we wanted to end—that is, with a connection established between three things: (1) Patty Garcia somehow finding a reference to G. R. Bevans's 1968 report to the Senate that proved the oil companies had clear evidence about the impact of CO_2 emissions; (2) the fact that almost all copies of the report had disappeared or had the key pages removed; and (3) Garcia's murder—as Jen, and Jen absolutely alone among 8.7 billion humans, called it.

Hitting Drake with a reference to his dad had seemed a clever place to start our questions. That is, until it turned out that Drake wasn't going to be so easy to crack.

So how to get Bevans to spill the oil?

Jen tried outlasting him.

Drake looked at her.

P.D. sent me an uncharacteristic comm. *Your boss is a bit wacko.*

In the spirit of solidarity with Jen, I chose silence rather than honesty.

Jen said to me, *What's that paper in front of him on his desk?*

Hold your eyes on it for a second.

The font was normal twelve-point printing. It was upside down and Jen's eyes were at an oblique angle, but this was a piece of cake for me.

It's a briefing about your background and your visit here to Mike Bradshaw two days ago.

After a full minute, Bevans said, "I have less than six minutes left." He looked at Jen. He looked at Les. Les turned his attention to Jen, signaling she was in charge.

"Mr. Bevans," Jen said, "as you probably know, I came on Tuesday looking for a report that your father presented to the Senate."

"So I am told."

"Do you have a copy?"

"Tuesday was the first I'd ever heard of it."

"How can that be? You were head of the research division."

"In 1968, I was seventeen years old."

"How do you know the date of the report?"

"You told Mike Bradshaw, and he told me."

Jen said, "It appears to be a very important document."

"How would you know if you haven't read it?"

"What if I have?"

For the first time, Bevans didn't look so calm.

He and Jen had another staring match.

"Detective Lu, let me ask you a question, if I might."

Jen nodded her consent.

"Is your interest in this alleged document part of an investigation?"

"It's linked to an inquiry we're making."

"Interesting," he said. "Three weeks ago you were on the scene right after Patty Garcia was struck by a golf ball."

Jen hesitated but said, "Yes."

"A woman who had one goal, and that was to destroy a major part of the U.S. economy and grab our assets."

"You don't sound too sorry about her death."

"I leave that to our PR people. But it does seem strange to me, Detective, that you are suddenly interested in an alleged sixty-five-year-old report—"

"It isn't alleged."

I wanted to yell at Jen not to give that information away. Why tip him off? But it was too late.

Bevans raised his eyebrows slightly.

"—a report whose supposed title"—he glanced at the paper in front of him—"would have been of great interest to Garcia."

"Mr. Bev—"

"And you tell me that you, and I presume your partner here"—he glanced at Les—"are making inquiries." He took a breath, and I could see his nostrils flare. "However, I am aware there is absolutely no investigation going on about Garcia's death."

"How would you know that?"

"Please, Detective, don't take us for lightweights."

More silence. Then Jen asked a question even I wasn't expecting.

"Mr. Bevans, are you involved in any way with Climate Oasis?"

For a millisecond, Bevans looked surprised. But he swiped his hand in the air as if brushing away an annoying mosquito. "I assure you, I don't have time for that nonsense. Why?"

"No reason. Only wondering."

His eyes dropped to his wristwatch. "I have less than one minute left."

"Why don't you want to talk about your father?"

"My family is absolutely none of your business. Unless, of course, your question is part of a criminal investigation, which, as we both know, it is not. That much said, I'm sure your superiors will be pleased to hear of your initiative."

Ask him how well he knows Culpepper and when they last spoke.

The door opened, and his assistant stepped into the room. Bevans stood and walked around his desk. We stood. Bevans shook hands with Jen and with Les, and with the air of a perfect gentleman, he motioned toward the door.

Les was through first. Jen stopped.

"Mr. Bevans, do you know James Culpepper?"

Jen! I screamed. *Wrong question.* But it was too late.

"Of course I know him. Until four years ago, he was an executive vice president of one of our largest members."

Jen realized her mistake and started to ask one of the right questions— *When was the last time you two spoke?*—but Bevans cut her off after two words.

"Apologies, but your time is truly up."

13:26:45

Taco? I said to Jen.

No answer.

A nice bowl of tom yum gai?

Ditto.

Your blood sugar is low.

Stop it, Chandler, I'm thinking.

Oh, right, and somehow, sitting here in the midst of the bird's nest that is her brain, I'm not supposed to know that?

My partner, my buddy, my better half—make that my better 99.99 percent—Jen B. Lu, was driving me crazy.

Okay, I admit it. I'd been increasingly enthusiastic about my participation in her unauthorized investigation, She's got a way of sucking me in. That said, I still wasn't a hundred percent convinced. Everyone—cops, forensic pathologists, the media, even many insane conspiracy theorists theorists . . . I mean *everyone*—said Patty Garcia's death was obviously not a crime. Garcia had died after getting bonked on the temple by a rock-hard golf ball falling from the sky at, I calculated, 38.66 miles per hour. Damn, it's surprising there aren't dead people lying around golf courses all over the place.

The whole world knew it was a fluke accident except, unfortunately, the person I happened to share a body with. *Su cuerpo es mi cuerpo* and all that.

When I stopped for ten milliseconds to think about it, I realized ignoring this reality was a major problem. That is, Jen and I were busy searching for a crime when there'd only been an accident. Last I checked, unless negligence is involved, committing an accident isn't a crime.

Strangely—or perhaps I should say, idiotically—this problem wasn't bugging her. She seemed to have bracketed it, as the academics say. That is, she had stuck the problem into an imaginary space where she didn't have to think about it: a problem that would disappear as soon as she somehow proved that Garcia had actually been murdered. Circular logic, or rather, circular illogic.

As far as I was concerned, it was *the* problem to deal with, but she was the one with the police badge, not I.

Instead, she was worried about family histories and which bad guy might be prone to commit or order a murder. If only there had been a murder.

I tell you all this not to vent my frustration. It's not to prove that between me and my boss, I am definitely the more rational one.

No, I tell you this because things were about to change. Which I guess proves that while I have the franchise on logic, rationality, memory, and speed, Cobalt Blue runs circles around me when it comes to intuition and the ability to see through people's deceptions and lies.

Jen and Les had left the Institute without a word between them. Les was in an almost jaunty mood, but nice guy that he was, he didn't want to rub in how absurd the visit had been.

We were cutting through Franklin Park, heading back to the station. That's when I suggested she have some food to get her body chemistry to a better space, but she ignored me. In addition to the usual food trucks, there was a craft fair today. It was beautiful weather. The good citizens of DC were out in force, relishing a hot spring day before the humid oven that would be our city-state in the coming summer of 2034.

Two men holding hands crossed in front of us.

Two women and a man argued whether the Wizards were going to make it into the play-offs this year.

Two more women passed by, one with a baby strapped to her chest. They were in a heated conversation about the baby's father.

Jen paused and watched a craftsman do intricate cross-stitches on a cloth hanging. He looked up and smiled. Jen smiled back. We moved on.

Another vendor was hovering anxiously over her table of jewelry and knickknacks. None of it was particularly nice, and she had a grim look on her face that dared passersby to stop. We did not rise to her dare.

At the next booth, a man and a woman with identical gray ponytails were smoking a joint and sending vibes to the crowds to check out their pottery. We stopped, and Jen bought Les a cup to serve as a new pencil holder.

From the next booth, the sharp tap of a hammer on metal caught her attention and that stupid song "Maxwell's Silver Hammer" jumped uninvited into her head. *Joan was quizzical . . .*

Jen wandered toward that booth.

The song continued in her head.

A person was tapping a bent metal case with a ball peen hammer, apparently trying to straighten it out.

It was a small hammer with a round end, like a small bulb.

Round. Like a golf ball.

Tap, tap. Bang, bang. The hammer came down on the metal case.

If it had been someone's head instead, that person would most surely be dead.

25

Jen had checked the office wall clock so many times during the past hour, I worried she'd wear out its numbers. She was sure as hell eager for her shift to be over. When we were close to quitting time, I put on my best mission control voice and did a countdown. At "blastoff," Jen yelled a perfunctory good-bye to Les and ran for the door.

We were on her bike and flying, slaloming through traffic.

Truck, I said, attempting to sound calm.

It wasn't even close, she yelled back.

First stop. A neighborhood hardware store. Number one on her list: a claw hammer, the regular type used for banging nails. I suggested the DeMark hammers with the nice green grips. Instead, she snatched up the cheapest hammer on the rack. She bought a tube of Infinity glue, a scary new brand of glue that came with so many warnings that I was surprised it was legal. And an N95. And dishwashing gloves. And a pair of safety goggles.

Next stop. A giant sports store. Slapped the three-pack of golf balls on the checkout counter. "Can I just buy one?" Jen said. The sixteen-year-old clerk stared at her blankly as if he didn't even know they sold golf balls.

Final stop: the Greek butcher a few blocks from home, where she bought a skinned lamb's head—they were gearing up for Easter, and whole carcasses were hanging in the window.

Back home she taped shut the bag with the lamb's head, scribbled a note—*Disgusting. Do Not Open!*—and plunked it into the refrigerator. All the rest she carted up to the rooftop garden. (Among the warnings and legal disclaimers that came with the Infinity Glue, one more or less said, "You will most likely die if you use this in an unventilated space.") She almost stabbed herself as she struggled to cut open the glue's rigid plastic packaging, one of the few types of excess packaging that was still legal.

She grabbed a few of the bricks that Zach used to weigh down netting for the vegetable beds and fashioned a mount for the hammer, pointing the business end upright. She piled on more bricks to make a narrower channel, which she adjusted until it would securely hold the golf ball in place on the head of the hammer. The glue instructions said it would require twelve hours to properly set, and she had to make sure that gravity or wind wouldn't topple the ball.

Once satisfied with her setup, she cleaned the ball and the metal surface of the hammer with alcohol, as instructed.

She read the glue instructions for a third time: Open package. Check that you have an up-to-date will. Squeeze gently into applicator brush. Brush on each surface, back and forth twice. Retract applicator brush.

She donned the glasses, mask, and gloves. Took a breath and got down to business.

That night Jen and Zach went to the American Film Institute to see an ancient Ingmar Bergman flick, *The Seventh Seal*. I'd caught it before and liked it, even though it's damn heavy. It asks if you can find faith in the modern world. Given the ongoing tension about Zach's desire to start a family, it was an unfortunate choice of movie: in one scene, a young couple wonders about whether they should have a child—this in 1957 when people were worrying so much about the possibility of nuclear war. I felt Jen's body tense up. And when at the end the peaceful couple was with their baby while the figure of Death led everyone else away, Jen was seething. The word *ambush* pinged in her head, over and over again.

Afterward, as if nothing were in the air, Jen and Zach strolled into the café, where they shared a slab of chocolate mousse cake and drank coffee: decaf for Zach, full throttle for Jen. Good times.

I was off duty, so I was keeping my mouth shut, but it was kind of nice to enjoy some down time with the boss. Before the movie, the image of that golf-ball hammer kept jumping into her head. I heard her say to herself, *Put it out of your mind. Enjoy a night with Zach.* It became kind of a mantra and seemed to stop her fretting.

Which left her able to fret instead about an old movie.

"It was slow," Jen said, apparently trying to avoid the argument she was itching to start.

"Movies were slow back then," Zach said.

"But kind of mesmerizing."

"And with that big question that lives on to this day."

"Finding faith?" Jen said, all innocence.

"I guess that. But I was thinking about whether people with good conscience should bring children into a world going up in flames."

Jen's fork was suspended in midair.

"Did you know that was a theme of this movie?" She tried to make the question sound offhand. As far as I could tell, she failed.

"No," Zach said vociferously. He started to say something, but his mouth hung open. Words eventually stumbled from his mouth. "Oh God, I . . . that would be crappy of me . . . I had no idea . . ." And on he rambled until Jen cut him off.

"I believe you," she said. And when she did, I could feel her body buzz with confidence, as if she realized this was a discussion she could handle.

Jen said, "Having children was never on my radar. I didn't exactly have a good role model. But . . ." Jen scrunched her mouth, confusion in her eyes.

Zach said, "And like the movie said, it's a helluva time to bring children into the world. Maybe we should take a break on this one for a while."

"Promise?"

He smiled. "Promise."

Jen seemed to acknowledge his words by raising her cake-laden fork and giving it a slight tip in his direction. "In the meantime . . ."

"Right," Zach said. "Let them eat cake."

Friday, March 24—06:57:39

Jen had changed her soundtrack. The Beatles were out. The Drifters and Laura Nyro were in. She merrily hummed "Up on the Roof" as she removed the hammer from its brick supports. The sun rose over Washington, DC.

She stopped humming.

Tentatively, she tried to wiggle the ball. It didn't budge.

She put the dishwashing gloves back on and unwrapped the lamb's head from the bag. It was disgusting. All the fur and personality were gone, but the eyes bugged out at her. A few tendons were attached to the skull, but there it was: a skull, white, splotched with red.

The nice South African pathologist had said that a blow to the temple might only cause temporary disorientation and a headache. Maybe short-term unconsciousness. But Garcia's case was one of the rarer ones: the ball had hit hard enough and at just the right angle (and, who knows, perhaps there was a weakness in her skull from a long-ago sports injury) to cause a small but significant fracture to the temporal bone, which rapidly pressed inward and lacerated her middle meningeal artery. It ended up being a serious injury, but one that with such a prompt response would normally not be fatal. This time, however, it was.

I had suggested Jen use a fully grown sheep skull, because they're fairly similar to human skulls. The lamb skull wouldn't be quite as thick. But we were going for proof of concept, not science.

She propped the lamb's head between the bricks to keep it steady. When she whacked it, she didn't want it flying over the rooftop and landing on the sidewalk at the feet of an early-morning commuter.

She raised the golf-ball hammer.

And, like Maxwell, brought it down upon the head.

Which smashed apart in spectacular fashion.

07:39:13

"Right," Les said, "run the whole thing by me again."

"Again?" Jen whined, sounding like a peevish teenager complaining that her parents never listened.

"I'm still waking up."

"It's almost eight."

"Christopher and I stayed up until . . . never mind, just tell me."

Les took a slug of coffee and set it back on their shared desk.

Jen started at the top. After all, Les hadn't been particularly aware back when Garcia was killed.

"The only visible damage was a blow to her head. They operated on her."

"Then how could the pathologist see a faint bruise that matched the pattern on a golf ball?"

"Shit, Les, I'm not a doctor. They did some type of operation that didn't destroy the skin where the ball hit. Okay already?"

"No reason to get mad at me," Les said, and calmly sipped his coffee.

"But what I'm telling you is that it could have happened another way." She looked at his expression and added, "Maybe."

Les recited it for her. "Someone snuck through the woods and bonked her on the head with a golf ball glued to a hammer."

"It wouldn't have to be a hammer. Could have been an iron pipe or anything."

"Not anything," Les said. "Spaghetti wouldn't have worked. A paper towel roll—"

"Les, I'm being serious."

Les raised his cup, looked in, tipped it as far back as he could, and drained the last drops.

"Jen, so am I. Kind of. It's a good theory. A possibility."

"Shouldn't you have said that first? That would have been the nice thing to say."

"If you hadn't woken me up and dragged me down here like it was an emergency, maybe I would have."

Jen pushed her untouched cup of coffee over to Les. "Have mine."

"On the other hand," he said, "don't you think it's kind of farfetched? I mean, who'd think that a single knock on the head would kill her?"

"He—"

"Who?"

"Whoever it was—he, she, they," she said, her exasperation getting pretty obvious. "*They* hit her on the head, and she went down."

"What if Garcia had raised an arm to block him?"

"Who?" said Jen, her tone snarky.

"Jen." His tone scolding.

"Fine. Him. Then *he* would have done something else. Maybe he expected to have to suffocate her or hit her twice."

"Then what's the point of doing the whole bit with the ball?"

"In case it actually worked and killed her. Or maybe he thought, *It'll knock her out and I'll suffocate her.*"

"Wouldn't that show up in the postmortem?"

"Chandler?"

I told her. She told Les.

"If she was knocked out, the killer wouldn't need to use any force to smother her. And remember, she lived for two more days and had been operated on. So this would have disguised any . . . what did you say it was, Chandler?"

I told her the best I could, but I need to study this stuff one of these days. She tried to repeat my already messed-up understanding—which included words like hypoxia, asphyxia, cyanosis, and petechiae—but the whole business was like the birthday party game of telephone where one person whispers a sentence to the next and ten kids later, it's gibberish.

In the end, Les saved her. "Okay, let's just say they couldn't detect anything."

"There you go. He could have been playing the odds. He was assuming he'd be able to kill her without being discovered. He was planning to drop a golf ball next to her so people would think someone hit her."

"This is such a stretch, Cobalt."

"And then he got lucky. A golf ball landed nearby. It was a total bonus for him."

"No, it was a direct heavenly intervention."

"Seriously, Les. It was a stroke of luck."

"And if that didn't work?"

"Then he would have found a nastier way to kill her."

"But Jen, you still have to prove that someone actually was there with her. And even that doesn't prove they murdered her. They could have been having a friendly chat when that guy's golf ball came sailing through the sky and whacked her. Right?"

Jen didn't have time to answer, because I interrupted her.

Jen, you need to hear this.

Hang on, Chandler.

Jen, there's been a fire.

26

I had a car waiting for us out front. Jen was screaming, "Siren on," even before Les slammed the door shut.

We saw the vehicles first: two cherry tops, an ambulance, a firetruck, and a fire inspector's van. Address 117 Yuma Street SE. What had once been an improbable little farmhouse in Washington, DC, was now a pile of blackened rubble.

Jen had the door open before the car came to a stop. Like a Baltimore Ravens running back, she crashed between the two uniforms who reached out to stop her. She made it onto the sidewalk and to the remnants of the white picket fence before the cops caught up to her.

"Ma'am," one said.

She ignored him. Staring. Eyes on the fire with anger and tears.

"Ma'am," the officer repeated, this time more forcefully.

By then I heard Les behind us, scolding them. "Didn't you see the car we arrived in?" It was unmarked, but it stood out a mile away. I heard a rustle and figured Les had pulled his badge.

Closer to the house, a female fire inspector and a male cop were talking and making notes.

Jen called to them. "I'm Detective Lu. An elderly woman lived here. Did she . . ."

The cop and female inspector came over.

The cop shook his head. "I'm sorry. We only found a body."

"Blessing Robinson," Jen said.

The cop opened his notebook. "That's the ID we got from the neighbors. Likely her, but we won't know until . . . you know." He nodded toward the ambulance. "They're waiting for the all clear to take the body to the coroner's."

"When did this happen?"

"Neighbors got woke by an explosion about three AM. My hunch is a gas leak."

The woman inspector said, "Lou, eighty years ago we did hunches. Now we do science."

Jen stared at her. "Aren't you Inspector Striowski?"

"One and the same."

When we'd spoken to Striowski by phone the previous summer, she'd used the exact same words. However, judging by not only the voice but also the first name on last year's report, she had definitely been a he at the time.

"But weren't you . . ."

"Yes, but my last name didn't change, did it now?"

"No reason to."

Jen looked back at the damage.

"So what happened?"

"As Lou here says, it appears to have been a gas explosion. The second one on this block in a half a year."

The cop said, "Folks up the street claim it's one of the developers clearing out people who don't want to sell."

"Anyone killed in the other?"

"Luckily not. And zero proof it was anything but an accident."

Jen turned her attention back to the rubble. One half of the house was a blackened skeleton. The first few stairs up to the second floor were visible. At its base, partially covered by blackened debris, were the remains of Blessing Robinson covered with a blanket.

"If it was an explosion," Jen said, "why would she be at her stairs at three in the morning."

Striowski said, "Maybe coming down for a midnight snack. Old folks don't always sleep too good."

Jen said, "The second floor was her library. She slept on the first floor."

Striowski wrote that into her notebook.

"Still," Striowski said, "she could have been up and passing by the stairs when it happened. Don't worry, Detective, we'll consider every possibility, as I'm sure the coroner will too."

We turned our focus back to the house.

The other half of it was missing. Piles of debris started a few feet away and stretched well into the neighbor's yard and up into damaged trees. Blackened lengths of two-by-fours. Sections of wood shelving. Strips of wallpapered plaster. Tangles of wire and metal. Ragged flaps of cloth. Bits of furniture Everything now wet and smelling awful.

Here and there in the midst of this were thousands of scraps of paper, some blackened, all soggy and disintegrating from the firefighters' hoses.

Jen reached down.

And picked up a pale-green plastic pitcher with its lid still tightly on. She shook it. Incongruously, it still had iced tea inside.

10:22:07

Jen stormed into Captain Brooks's office.

"There's been a third murder."

Captain Brooks didn't miss a beat. "I thought I told you to stick to your assignments."

"You knew I hadn't, didn't you. Sir?"

"I couldn't possibly follow all my officers' comings and goings. Even if I wanted to, which I don't."

"But you knew."

"I *knew* that when you get a bee in your bonnet, you're hard to discourage. Let's say I'm not surprised. Anyway, that's pretty much why I set up the special projects unit. If we want cops to be robots, we should hire robots. If we want cops to be soldiers, why not just declare martial law and let the army take over? The special unit is an experiment in thinking and professionalism."

He had said so at our first meeting in January: *An experiment. Create space for initiative. Use your brains. Work outside the lines.* But Jen, Amanda, Hammerhead, and my fellow sims had never quite believed the nice-sounding cliches.

"Where's your partner?"

"In our office."

"Get him in here."

"Yes, sir."

"Then sit down and walk me through it."

It took thirty-seven minutes for Jen to outline the whole impossible business. Whenever she glanced at Les, he seemed to be doing his best not to look incredulous. As she went, the three of them tried out various scenarios, always reaching a dead end. Captain Brooks rubbed the scar over his eye. They talked about the latest: Blessing's death and the destruction of her archives. The explosion might have been deliberate; hopefully, the investigation would find clear evidence one way or the other.

"But even if it was deliberate," Jen said, "we have zero evidence to pin it on the person I suspect."

140

"And who would that be?" the captain asked.

"Drake Bevans. He certainly had a motive."

"If he had known Blessing had this document, why wait till now?"

"I'm guessing he didn't know until I led his people straight to her." Jen looked away. "And then, well, I more or less admitted to Bevans I had read the document."

I didn't need to be psychic to read the expression on the captain's face.

"From the moment I first walked into the Institute with questions about that document, they could have been following me."

Perhaps that person had paid a friendly visit to Blessing, just like we had. Masqueraded as Jen's colleague and sussed out enough about Jen's visit to know they had to return later and destroy the place.

The captain said, "Even if we somehow place her death on his people—"

"Or someone he's hired," Les said.

"What the hell do you think I meant, that he sent his secretary down to torch the place? Of course it's some muscle he's got on tap." His tone became sarcastic. "Would it be okay if I finish what I was starting to say?" He looked at Les. He looked at Jen. He spoke. "Even if we manage to find out who set the fire, then somehow link it to Bevans, it won't necessarily mean this had anything to do with the death of Patty Garcia. As you said yourself, the main motive would be to keep the old Senate hearing documents from coming to light. If, somehow, Bevans got wind that Garcia had tracked it down."

Which would mean that Blessing might have merely been collateral damage—that most despicable of all the terms ever concocted by the U.S. military establishment.

Les said, "We won't have answers about Blessing's death anytime soon."

This wasn't the death of a high-profile lawyer. Investigations by the coroner and the fire inspectors would take weeks. Months, even.

Jen said, "She was an amazing woman, sir." I felt the beating of Jen's heart and figured it was the thud of resignation and despair.

"It's possible," Les said, "that before burning down the place, they found and stole the document first."

"If so," the captain said, "it's long gone."

Either way, there was no way around it—Captain Brooks knew it, Jen knew it, Les knew it, and I knew it—if Blessing had died because someone wanted to destroy her documents, then Jen was responsible for her death.

I thought this gloomy moment might be a good time to share my news.

I'd been working through the night reviewing Culpepper's video. Even for me, it was ridiculously painstaking work. I'd discovered an anomaly and was starting to double-check it this morning at the very moment I saw the report on the fire. I got distracted. Even I didn't think that could happen, but I continue to surprise myself. I got distracted and forgot all about it. Until the captain started grilling Jen and Les.

Ready to join the fray, I reviewed the anomaly.

Since I knew exactly when and where to look, it only took a split second. I told Jen what I had found.

"Jen?" said the captain.

"Sorry, sir. Chandler has something on Culpepper."

"I thought we were talking about Bevans."

"We were, maybe we still are, but it turns out we can tear Culpepper's alibi apart."

27

I spelled it out to Jen, and she told the captain and Les. "Chandler says he went through Culpepper's alibi. Remember, Culpepper claimed he was doing a live broadcast at the time of his ex-wife's death? We watched the tape of it and didn't see any discrepancies."

"Jen, you told me all this already."

The problem was not only that humans tend to fumble around when they describe things. The problem was that Jen's brain had been lurching like a drunk teenager since we learned of Blessing's death.

Nonetheless, she soldiered on. "Chandler sort of went through the recording again . . . frame by frame—"

Pixel by pixel! That's the whole incredible point.

"Jen?"

"Sir?"

"Perhaps Chandler should tell it directly. Do you mind?"

Jen said, "If we have to."

My moment in the spotlight.

"Sir," I started, and unexpectedly I didn't feel as sharp as I normally would. "I examined the whole recording frame by frame *and* pixel by pixel. It was an extraordinary undertaking, even for me. It was shot in 8K at thirty frames per second, so I was examining 3.564 trillion pixels. I—"

"Chandler," the captain said.

"Yes, sir. There was one bud that opened," I said, and stopped. *There,* I thought. *That was much more succinct.*

"Maybe you can find a happy medium. Somewhere between one bud and three trillion pixels."

This had never happened to me. I was making a mess.

I pulled myself together.

"In the background behind Culpepper, there's a window that shows a patch of trees and shrubs. Even though most didn't yet have leaves, the foliage is so thick you can barely see sky—although, at any rate, the day was overcast. In our initial run, I watched for jump-cut movements of branches or a bird or squirrel that suddenly appeared or disappeared. Things that might indicate he had recorded parts of his speech earlier that day and edited it together."

I paused. Let him take that in.

"There were no anomalies. Until, as I said, I went through it pixel by pixel. There is a lovely magnolia off to one side. A *Magnolia kobus*. It was just then coming into bloom, and I would estimate that forty-two percent of the blossoms were fully or partially open."

"Chandler, can we . . ."

"I found one bud, extremely tiny, barely visible, blending into the foliage, that was closed during his speech. But when the questions and answers began, it was open. Not fully, but it had clearly popped its husk and was three-quarters open. It was still extremely hard to see, but the white of the petals are clearly visible. To me."

"How quickly could this have happened?"

"I'm not a trained botanist, but I estimate it would take anywhere from one to two hours at that day's temperature for a particular blossom to open that much."

"Chandler, how much time elapsed on the video between the shot of the bud and of the flower?"

"Throughout his opening address, it was a bud. Then he turned to a second camera and said it was time for questions."

"A second camera?"

"Exactly. It's at an angle. You can't see the window in this view."

The captain waved his hand for me to get on with it.

"When he turned back to the main camera to field questions, the tiny bud was now open."

"How much time had supposedly elapsed? Going from the view where you saw the bud to the other view and then back to the view with the bud."

"Six point two three seconds."

"Tell me again. How long would it actually take for that bud to bloom?"

"Between one and two hours."

I didn't need to say it: enough time to get to the golf course, attack Patty Garcia, and return to answer live questions.

"Jen, Les," the captain said. "Bring him in."

11:48:06

Jen and Les climbed into a car. It smelled like the farts of whoever had been in there last. Jen and Les made a big deal out of it. Sometimes they act like they're ten years old. Once again, perhaps my inability to experience smells isn't such a bad thing.

We figured Culpepper would be at home, since Friday was the day of his weekly webcast. It wasn't yet rush hour, but it took us twenty-seven minutes to reach his house. Jen said that traffic wasn't as bad as in the old days, but that wasn't much consolation.

Although Captain Brooks had said, "Bring him in," he quickly clarified that we weren't arresting him. We still had no case against him. It was more along the lines of *invite him down for a chat*.

Les pressed the bell.

It set off the same impressive chimes that it had eight days earlier on our first visit when Culpepper wasn't home. This time, though, it also set off a yapping dog.

Jen, who still had a scar on her cheek from an encounter with a German shepherd the previous year, reached into her purse for her pepper spray. Les rested his hand on her arm. "It's excited."

"Who's there?" A woman's voice came over a speaker, almost drowned out by the high-pitched yapping of the dog.

Les lifted his badge in front of the camera. "Detectives Westin and Lu."

"Stelka!" the woman yelled.

Les leaned into the monitor. "We'd like to speak to Mr. Culpepper," he shouted. "Is he home?"

"Les," Jen said in a soft voice, "I don't think you have to yell."

The dog was going apoplectic.

"What?" said the voice. "One minute." The barking dog retreated away from the door, but I swore I could hear its nails clawing at the floor as it got dragged away.

The voice came back on.

"That little Stelka," the voice said with a kind laugh. "My baby, but oh, she cause racket." The woman had a strong Ukrainian accent and was still wrestling with English. "What you want?"

"To speak to Mr. Culpepper."

"Not here."

145

"You are . . . ?" Les said.

"Yes, I'm here."

"No, I mean, who are you?"

"His housekeeper, of course."

"Do you come often?"

"Two times."

"A . . . ?"

"A what?"

"Two times a month? A week?"

"A week."

"Do you always come on Fridays?"

"No. Only this week."

Les said, "I wonder if we could come in for a moment. Ask you a few questions."

"Mr. Culpepper says no one comes if I all alone."

"But we're police officers."

"You want me in trouble?"

"When will he be back?"

"Come tomorrow."

Jen said to Les, "What about his webcast?"

I checked Culpepper's site and told her. "It says it's coming live today from New York."

"When did you say he left?"

"You sure you from police?"

Les quietly asked Jen, "Leave a message?"

Jen shook her head and mouthed *no*.

And with that, we were gone.

28

The boss had the weekend off, which meant life had been boring. I learned Latin, which will come in handy if I become the pope. Hey, that's not so farfetched. No one says anything directly to me, but my cohorts keep buzzing that my arising from the dead last year was nothing short of a miracle. Although I guess that would put me more in the territory of saints than popes. Alternately, they say it was an act of witchcraft, which means they're jealous, which means that one of these days they'll rat on me and I'll get burned at the stake. Even without that, my days are numbered. Since I'll die when I'm five and I've already got two years nine and a half months under my belt, I'm counting each tick of the clock.

For a change, Jen took it easy. The only rough moment had come on Friday night when she had to phone Gabe to tell him that Blessing Robinson had been killed.

When we left home on Monday morning, Les was waiting out front, sitting on the hood of a car like a fifties teenager on a big date. Jen climbed in, and we set out to visit our favorite wife abuser and former oil big shot.

James Culpepper came to the door but didn't invite us in.

He said, "I don't appreciate you trying to worm information from my housekeeper."

The door monitor had been recording us.

Les said, "We'd like to ask a few questions."

"Are you arresting me?"

"No."

Culpepper started closing the door, then seemed to think twice.

"I'm happy to speak to you. With my lawyers present, of course."

147

Now, four hours later, we were in an interview room. Jen, Les, Culpepper, and two others. Alpha and beta models of a particular human variant: male, white, lawyers. Alpha was decked out in a hand-stitched suit that matched his gray hair. He was twirling a black Montblanc pen between his manicured fingers. The younger of the two, Beta, attempted to appear eager and alert, but his chewed-up nails and bloodshot eyes told me that Alpha's firm was stingy when it came to allowing its minions to sleep.

"My client," said Alpha, "is—"

"I'll take it from here, Jeremy."

Make that Beta and Gamma.

Usually Jen and Les go in easy, maybe with a round of good cop/bad cop, or maybe one taking charge and the other looking bored. They'd build up trust or at least lull the person into the rhythm of talking. Or lure him into a sense of complacency. Or stir up his nerves. Or cover enough ground that we'd be able to circle back and trip him up with the things we were most interested in. But when she and Les had discussed their tactics, Jen had insisted this guy wasn't going to fall for any of it. It would be best to catch him off guard.

Jen didn't tiptoe around. "Why didn't you tell me you prerecorded your opening presentation on Friday, March third?"

"You didn't ask, did you?"

Jen didn't bite.

Culpepper continued. "You asked where I was when my former wife had her accident. I said I was doing my web broadcast."

"But you weren't, were you? You had prerecorded it."

"I almost always record my presentation about an hour and a half before airtime. In case I stumble or there's a recording glitch."

"Were there any glitches?"

"No, not that time."

"And there were no mistakes?"

"There are always some, but I want it to sound natural. If I stumble over the odd word or thought, it gives it a spontaneous quality."

"Who is doing the recording?"

"No one. When I started my webcast a year and a half ago, tech people set up my computer and outfitted my library with lights, two cameras, and a microphone. The software has a sweet AI interface."

"And you always do it ninety minutes in advance?"

"I didn't say always. I said I almost always do it an hour and a half in advance. Sometimes two hours, but I like it to be current with any breaking news and I want the outside lighting to be the same as the Q and A segment so no one will notice. In fact, my congratulations to you spotting the edit. What was it?"

Jen ignored that. "But last week in New York, you did the whole thing live."

"So?"

Jen waited.

"I had an important Climate Oasis meeting up there. I did the broadcast live from my laptop. May I leave now?"

Les took over. He repeated Jen's earlier question. "Can you prove this is the normal way you do it? Prerecord approximately an hour and a half in advance and then do the questions live?"

"No. I never keep the recording session. There is the issue of not wanting anything with glitches to ever show up. You know, if I have to go back and rephrase a point or if I wandered too far off script. Simply put, I want my archives to have only the one version, the full and final show. The AI discards the prerecording as soon as it becomes part of the live broadcast."

"So there's no one to corroborate this."

"My webcast host is in St. Petersburg. I'm sure the Russian authorities will be delighted to let you do a police investigation in their territory."

Les said, "You admit, then, that your presentation on the day Patty Garcia died was prerecorded."

One of the lawyers rested a hand on Culpepper's arm and jumped in. "Detective Westin," he said to Les, "my client has—"

Culpepper brushed the lawyer's hand away like it was a fly. "Admit is much too dramatic a word."

"It means you could be anywhere when it's playing back."

Culpepper smiled, arrogance pouring out, "I could have been. I might have been. But I wasn't and never am. I listen to my recording as it plays. I want to get into the here and now so I can transition perfectly to the Q and A."

"Can you prove it?"

"Why would I need to prove that?'

"Because we are asking."

"I suppose you could dredge up my phone records. See where I was at that time."

No one said the obvious—that this would only prove where his phone was.

"Or you could check my security cameras to see if I left my house."

"You have cameras?"

"Of course. But I only turn them on at night or if I'm away. I don't believe in spying on everyone who comes onto my property."

Until they ring your doorbell, I thought.

Jen jumped in. "Mr. Culpepper, there is something else I'm curious about."

"Then I'm curious to know what that might be."

"When I spoke to you at the Climate Oasis office on—"

March fourteenth.

"March fourteenth, you said something very interesting."

"Ms.—"

"Detective."

"—Lu. What would that have been?"

"You said there were times you wanted to kill Patty Garcia."

A thin smile formed at the corners of his lips.

"Yes, those might have been my words."

"They were."

"And so?"

"It's an interesting thing to admit."

Culpepper gave out a triumphant hoot of laughter. He turned to his lawyers one after the other, both of whom timidly laughed along, although I doubt they had a clue what was going on other than that they were representing a madman.

"*Detective*," he said with emphasis. "You've truly earned your title. *Detecting* that I said I wanted to kill her."

He smiled.

We waited.

"But you may want to revisit your notes. I said there were times when we both wanted to kill each other. It's an expression. Quite common." He paused, a bit too dramatically. "Even in our loving marriage, we joked about things like that."

He tilted his head and raised his chin as if modeling a heroic pose for a statue.

"Unfortunately for you," he said, "but fortunately for me, I had absolutely nothing to do with the accident that killed her."

"The smug bastard!"

"Fourteen," Les said, without expression.

"The smug fucking bastard."

"Fifteen."

"You don't agree?"

"Of course I agree. So what?"

"So I'm on the verge of an *I hate men* thing for a while."

Les pretended to get to his feet. "Give me a shout when you're done."

Jen's phone rang. She snatched it off the desk and glanced at the screen: an unregistered number.

She pressed ignore and turned back to Les.

It rang again.

She picked it up.

"What?"

"Is this Detective Lu?"

A man's voice. Slightly muffled, as if he had a hand cupping the phone.

"Who's this?"

"Mikey Bradshaw." Urgency in his voice. "We spoke—"

"I remember." U.S. Petroleum and Gas Institute.

"I really gotta talk to you."

"Why aren't you on your own phone?"

"That's exactly it. There's some bad shit happening, and I need to talk to you. Only you."

I could tell that Jen was in no mood for any more alpha men. But she said, "First division, third floor. I'm here for the rest of the day."

"I can't." He was speaking faster. "Tomorrow. Late afternoon. Just you."

"Fine."

"Not there. Not here. I can't have anyone see me."

"Wear sunglasses."

"I'm serious. This is serious. I need to go."

Jen said, *Chandler?*

I said, *He's panicking. Seems real.*

A meeting place popped into Jen's mind.

Jen said, "Two PM. U.S. Botanic Garden. Up on the canopy walk. No one will see us up there."

Bradshaw didn't even say good-bye.

Like a character in a cheesy movie, Jen pulled the phone away from her ear and stared at it for a second.

"Weird," she said to Les.

"What?"

"Mike Bradshaw. Sorry, *Mikey*. The flack at the Institute."

"What did he want?"

"He was in panic mode. Seemed to be calling from a burner. Said, I quote, 'There's bad shit happening.' Says he wants to meet me."

"You really think your Bevans guy was behind the fire?"

"Maybe. I don't know. What I'm certain of is that he doesn't want anyone to know about Standard Oil's knowledge of the impact of climate change in 1968, or about his father's involvement."

"And Bradshaw. You trust him?"

"Not particularly."

"But you're going to meet him, aren't you?"

Jen didn't bother answering.

29

Monday

Jen had apologized to Chandler. "Sorry, champ, but I got to grab a few hours on my own."

She needed to figure all this out, and for that, Chandler usually helped her. But more than anything, she needed complete silence in her head.

Following the frustrating interview with Culpepper and the panicky (or entrapping) call from Mike Bradshaw, she beelined home, pulled off her work clothes, slipped into her running gear, and set out for a long run. The weather had done another one-eighty and was now dry and as hot as it used to be in late May.

The first mile was rough. Muscles and tendons that had been sitting all day protested against being forced to work. Her brain kept getting distracted by her surroundings: a car slicing in front of her in a sudden right turn, a pile of dog shit, a flock of kidlets from a day care, and a boisterous pod of Shadows she needed to either slalom through or, as she chose to do, cross the street to avoid.

Even worse, though, was the babble bouncing inside her head from this damn case that wasn't even officially a case.

The autopsy report on Modus, the dead Shadow at the golf course—*Damn,* she thought, *I've got to stop thinking of these people as Shadows*—had arrived that morning. It had been rushed through. Nothing that looked like natural causes. No drugs, no poisons, and none of the physical or chemical traces of a heart attack or stroke. What was left of his liver after the hyena had lunch was in good shape. There was no indication he'd been strangled, shot, or stabbed, although an eaten-away-and-now-gone gut wound was possible. The hyena had cracked open his skull and devoured chunks of bone and major portions of the brain. The team at the coroner's office had jigsawed the remaining pieces of skull the best that they could. There was a fragment that might show the impact of an object, but it was too small to be conclusive.

In sum, maybe not a natural death—that was helpful—but then again, no firm indication of a violent death. The other useful information was that they'd used insect evidence, state of decomposition, and weather reports to estimate that he had "most likely" died on Friday, March 3. Certainly not before that, as Jen already knew: Modus (alive) had been spotted by ground staff early Friday morning. But since the body hadn't been discovered for another ten days, it was impossible to be any more precise than that.

What's more, the crime scene team noted they hadn't found any remnants of blood on the ground between the body and the dropped cloth bag with his golf balls. This suggested, to Jen at least, that Modus had likely been killed where the body lay, and the murderer—for she was convinced this was murder—had snatched the cloth bag off the body or from the dwelling and spilled out its contents ten feet away. That, or perhaps Modus had dropped the bag in an effort to elude his attacker.

Jen ran in place as she waited to cross 16th and get onto Piney Branch to enter Rock Creek Park. She studied the cars, buses, and trucks passing by. Her stomach rumbled, and she wished she'd eaten a banana before her run.

Focus, she thought.

No evidence that Modus had been murdered, although as far as she was concerned, it was a slam dunk. Make that a hole in one.

No evidence of how he had died. Although possibly he'd been smashed on the head and left to die.

No indication of what type of object had been used to kill him.

Jen's working assumption: If Patty Garcia had been murdered, the same person had likely killed Modus. Perhaps the murderer had finished with Garcia and then spotted Modus watching him. Chased Modus down, killed him, and emptied the bag of golf balls, presumably in search of Garcia's ball. But why? Why would it matter if she had hit it into the woods?

Jen reminded herself that everything didn't have to fit.

After the first, wide-open stretch of Piney Branch, the woods narrowed in from both sides of the road, save for the running path. Six months after the great fire, it was still a dispiriting sight. In places, all that was left were blackened trunks and stumps of branches. In other spots, the trees appeared almost complete, but she knew that no leaves would appear this spring or ever again. It was like running through a winter graveyard in a horror movie. Vines and ground cover, though, were coming back in patches here and there. At least there was that.

And why did Bradshaw call me? She poured over explanations for his call. The breakthrough she'd been looking for to finger Bevans? A fact-distorting chat to throw her off the scent? A couple of thugs showing up instead of Bradshaw to threaten her? A warning?

Another mile slipped by until she noticed the bleak surroundings again.

The only good outcome of the fire was that the city had purchased the park with a payment of one dollar to Disney—all of it, that is, except the golf resort and the zoo. Planting of seedlings and small trees had begun. She thought, *If Zach and I have children, this will once again be a forest when they're old.* Was that, she wondered, a note of optimism or a symbol of a bleak future ahead?

Some of the trails through the burnt-out landscape had been cleared by platoons of volunteers organized by a new athletic gear consumers' co-op. But Jen found these bleak trails depressing, and so she stayed alongside roadways until she eventually crossed Military Road, the northernmost limit of the blaze.

Finally, she was past the fire zone and in the woods along the familiar Valley Trail. A troop of high school kids on trail bikes ran her off the path. She cursed at them but was quickly on her way again.

Within a minute she was skirting the edge of Viridian Green.

She and Chandler had plotted the distance from Culpepper's house to points along the fifth hole. There were several possible trails, but one route of just under a mile stood out, not only for the shortest distance but also the fewest encounters with cars. At the two spots Culpepper would have had to cross a road, there wasn't a single traffic camera—and he'd want to be as invisible as possible. Although he must have run past other runners or walkers, it had been midafternoon on a weekday, so the trails would have been quiet. And if he kept a hat on and his head down, no one would remember his face. This route only required that he wait on his driveway for a car-free moment before dashing across Oregon Avenue, cutting through a few trees, and getting onto a trail. Then, as he neared the golf course, there'd be a twenty-second sprint along Beach Drive so he could get across Rock Creek itself.

Plotting possible routes on a map was one thing, but she had never tried it herself. She couldn't know exactly where Culpepper would have cut through the woods onto the fifth hole, but that would only make a small difference.

She popped Chandler back on.

30

"Jeez, boss, I thought you'd never get me in on the action."
I'd been eavesdropping on her brain, of course. She hadn't used our safe word to make me disappear, but the deal was that I had to hover in the deep background when she signed me out, right?

Jen ignored my complaint like I was a teenager whining about having to clean my bedroom.

"Chandler, I need you to clock me."

Terrific, I thought, I'd been demoted to a Fitbit.

"And see if you can dig up running times for Culpepper. Maybe he kept times on one of the running apps. Or he runs in charity events. Cross-country would be perfect."

She set off north, forked to the left, and was soon running up onto Beach Drive to cross over Rock Creek before plunging down a grassy embankment and then steeply up into the woods. Here the running was much slower than the Valley Trail. Roots forked across the path, big stones jutted, and there were further climbs and descents, sharp turns and obstacles, before we hit a dead end at a ramshackle community garden. We skirted its edge, and a minute later we were staring at Culpepper's long driveway.

"Eight minutes, fifteen seconds."

A slow time for her, but it was along a narrow, cluttered trail.

"Did you discover any times for him?"

"No running apps, at least none I could access. But he did a couple of charity runs last year."

"How long would this take him?"

"On the flat-out portions, you're much faster, but the crappy portions, maybe not much slower than you . . . Let's say eleven minutes."

"Plus he'd have to go through the woods from the trail to the golf course."

We went back and tried that. Judging from old maps I'd checked, this was a completely new hole carved into the steep and once heavily wooded hillside. Even though the March vegetation was still relatively sparse, we couldn't make out the fairway, only a break in the trees where it must be. We didn't know Culpepper's starting point, but I estimated we were roughly perpendicular to the stretch of fairway where Garcia had been found.

We easily weaved between saplings and full-grown trees, then pushed through bushes and vines, and soon reached a new chain-link fence, tastefully green to blend into the forest. It sported a metal sign every twenty feet warning that trespassers faced dire consequences if they proceeded any farther. The fifth fairway stretched magnificently to our right; to our left, it rose up a hillside.

"This is the exact spot," I said. I don't like blowing my own horn, but you've got to admit it was a minor but impressive bit of navigation. Jen merely grunted and added time to make it through the woods.

I said, "Times two. For him to get here and run back."

Jen said, "No. He could have strolled over after his taping."

I couldn't believe it. Outlogicked by a human. Then again, if there was anyone I wouldn't mind outsmarting me, it would be Cobalt Blue.

Jen said, "He'd wait in the woods for Garcia to appear. Kill her." She looked around. "What's key is the elapsed time between the murder and when the question-and-answer session started. After he somehow kills her—"

"There is still that issue," I said.

Jen continued as if I hadn't shared my words of wisdom. "He spots Modus, runs and catches him, smashes him in his head, checks the bag of balls."

We kept adding minutes to the total. Spotting Modus, attacking him, getting home.

I said, "He'd be sweaty. His face would be red."

"Check the tape."

I checked. There was barely any difference in his skin tone between his presentation and the question portion. Jen said, "Yeah, but it was less than one mile. And a mild day. He'd barely work up a sweat."

We added time for washing his face, combing his hair, and a quick change.

"There you go," Jen said. "Four to six minutes to spare."

I felt like I was talking to one of those people who believes in deep-state conspiracies. Every time someone proves it's absurd, the conspiracy theorists merely have to say, "Well, duh, that's part of the conspiracy." Jen was so convinced Culpepper had committed murder, she couldn't see the obvious.

"Boss, listen. Do you think he'd plan this elaborate murder and give himself only four to six minutes of wiggle room?"

"He wasn't planning on Modus."

"Still too close. What if there'd been a line of cars and he'd had to wait to cross the street? What if Garcia had run when she saw him?"

"She wasn't the running-away type."

"You know what I mean. He would have built in wiggle room."

"Maybe he waited longer than he expected for her to show up. He'd have had an abort time, you know, to pull out. She shows up right at the margin. He knows it's going to be tight, but it'll work. Modus throws his times off, but even then, he made it work."

"Boss, you're making an awful lot of assumptions."

Jen shut me off with what felt like a slap.

31

Monday

"Jen," Leah said. "Jen?"

Jen glanced up from the eggplant lasagna Zach had made. Smiled feebly.

"Not a great day at work?" Leah said.

She shook her head.

"Patty Garcia stuff?"

Jen scrunched her face into another feeble smile. "I have this big oil guy who I figure might have arranged for an old lady to be killed." She looked away from Leah. "That's why I was so upset Friday night. She was such a lovely person."

"How awful," Raffi said.

Jen always tried to keep the more disturbing parts of her work away from home. It wasn't a matter of bottling things up—she knew that wasn't healthy—but because she didn't want to burden Zach's parents, or even Zach, for that matter, with the more terrible things she had to experience. Tonight was one of the times she needed to talk it out.

"I believe it's tied in to the Patty Garcia case, even though nothing directly links my oil guy to all this." Jen thought about her meeting the next day with Bradshaw, and hoped that a link might be clear after that. "So," she continued, "I keep coming back to her ex."

"Culpepper," Zach said.

"But the way I imagine it happened, there's no way he could have killed Garcia. The timing simply doesn't work."

She went through the numbers from her afternoon run.

It was Leah who said, "How can you so accurately fix the time when the golf ball hit her?"

159

Jen said, "The people playing behind her were certain about the time. Within three minutes."

"But," said Leah, "they didn't see it."

"No. But they know when he hit the ball."

"But," Leah said, "you're going on the assumption that it wasn't his ball but something else that killed her."

"Right."

Leah said, "And you said that Garcia was playing alone, and a good player."

"Uh-huh."

"You need to speak to someone who plays golf."

"Like who?"

"Well me, for starters."

"You play golf?"

"I do. Well, I used to. Raffi too."

Jen looked at Raffi, turned back to Leah, staring at them like they had just revealed they were members of a secret cult.

Leah said, "That's how we met."

Raffi said, "I was lousy. Leah, though, was damned impressive."

"But you're socialists!"

Leah said, "What does that have to do with it? Just because a bunch of overweight rich people toot around in golf carts doesn't mean there aren't working- and middle-class folks, women, racialized minorities who don't play as well."

Jen hated how Leah, Raffi, and Zach could turn anything into a political conversation.

"Anyway," she said.

"Anyway, if Patty Garcia was alone and that much better, she'd be well ahead of these two. Especially since they sound like they're pretty mediocre. How much time did you say there was between groups?"

"Fifteen minutes. But these two behind her got off five minutes late."

"And was there a group right before Garcia?"

Jen thought for a moment. "No. They'd gone out quite a bit earlier."

"No one holding Garcia up. If she was as athletic as she seemed from the stories and playing on her own, and these two were hacking their way through the course, even by the fifth hole she could easily have increased the gap by another twenty minutes. So forty in all."

Raffi beamed at his wife. "You sure would have."

Jen's brain was crackling. If Leah was right, instead of Garcia being knocked out between 2:32 and 2:34, it might have been as early as 1:50.

Even if Culpepper had gone on to attack Modus, he could have been home with forty-five minutes to spare.

Jen said, "I've been a total idiot."

20:17:53

"What's up, boss?"

"I need to check Garcia's phone records. See how far ahead she was."

In the mid-2020s, so the history books tell me, there was a ton of push-back about government, social media, and private sector surveillance. But after the militia bombings in 2028, governments pounced on the opportunity to introduce new security measures. Many were now getting rolled back. However, the Emergency Phone Records Act still allowed us limited access to cell phone records without a warrant if someone was "suspected of committing, or witnessing, or being in any other way involved in, or having some relation to, a criminal act." Which, as anyone with half a brain and a lick of respect for civil liberties could tell you, was a supposed limitation you could drive a Mack truck through. Without a warrant, the law said we could access one hour of phone data, including calls made and received, and cell tower locations.

"Let's check her out from one thirty to two thirty."

It took me a second.

"She received a call at two. Lasted fourteen minutes."

"From?"

I checked the number.

"NPR. Hang on," I said. On a hunch I checked their program logs.

"She was doing a live interview."

"You sure?"

"We can double-check with them tomorrow, but that's what their logs say."

"Let's see where she was at the time."

Easy.

The phone grids give us maps that look like Venn diagrams, each showing the radius of different phone towers, although clever software makes sure calls are stable. There were three in question. A large circle from a transmitter at the clubhouse covered much of the course. But as soon as a golfer got to the outer holes, their phone switched to the minitowers placed along the walking trails throughout the park, really little more than boosters hidden in trees. There was one that covered the third and fourth holes in their entirety. But by the time golfers reached the fifth tee, another tower came into play.

Patty Garcia's pings showed that she had stopped on the fourth hole for fourteen minutes. The signal was constant. She wasn't budging.

During that fourteen minutes, Trebook and Kershaw would have cut the gap between themselves and the faster Garcia. Still, they had started twenty minutes behind her. But if Culpepper had attacked her before Trebook and Dr. Kershaw arrived at the tee, wouldn't he have left a ball lying there to make it seem like an accident? Wasn't that the whole point of the Maxwell's golf-ball hammer idea? However, no other ball had been found near the body. Which meant he hadn't done it earlier. We were back down to four to six minutes.

No breathing room for Culpepper.

The boss was back in the world of make-believe.

That or Jen's hunch was right and Culpepper had cut it very close and gotten very lucky.

32

Jen leaned over the metal railing and peered down at the miniforest. "When's he gonna get here?"

It was eighty-eight degrees, and the air was thick and heavy, like we'd been soaked by a tropical rainstorm. We were on the canopy walk inside the U.S. Botanic Garden, on the southeastern tip of the Mall. The conservatory is the diametrical opposite of all the marble and limestone seriousness of monumental and official DC. It's an elegant greenhouse that soars ninety-three feet high, its glass roof shaped like a Victorian birdcage. The space inside is divided into a collection of habitats—jungle, desert, orchids, and medicinal plants. High above much of this, but still in the midst of the indoor trees, is the canopy walk that follows the perimeter inside the structure.

Jen held on to the stainless-steel rail and stared down at the pretend jungle. With each breath I analyzed the play of esters that made up the complex smells of this huge greenhouse: overwhelmingly the deep scent of so many leaves, bark, flowers, soil, and mulch carried by the water evaporating off the pathways. Jen said, "It smells beautiful." I'm sure it did, but her words made me sad.

"Chandler, What's the time? He's late, isn't he?"

We had arrived early. Jen was nervous. Jen was driving me crazy.

But before we had to pursue this pointless conversation a millisecond longer, Les's voice came through via P.D. "He's here."

Les was down below, tourist map opened in his hands, sitting on a metal bench trying to look tired and lost. He wore a battered baseball cap from a nonexistent team, the Stonewall Rioters, and a pair of sunglasses. Bradshaw had specified that only Jen should be there. Besides, we were worried it might be a setup, and it was best to have only one visible and vulnerable person.

163

Even though Bradshaw hadn't met Les, Bevans sure had. No reason that Les wasn't on his radar just as much as Jen.

Jen said, "See anyone else?"

"Those schoolkids when we first got here."

"No shit. They were up here." Jen had been convinced that at least one of them would go sailing over the railing. The metal walkway was only a few feet wide and circled the perimeter of the conservatory.

"And a boy," Les said. "Probably a high school student. Has a sketch pad and just settled down on one of the benches. Trying hard to look poetic."

"I thought I saw two women."

"Yeah. Looks like a mom and her own mother. The daughter has one of those baby snuggly things strapped to her. They seem to be enjoying themselves."

Bradshaw appeared at the top of the metal stairs on the other side of the conservatory, kitty-corner to us. He looked around. Jen waved. He started in our direction. Even from 131 feet away, I swear I could detect chemicals of nervous fear shooting from his every pore.

"Amanda, Hammerhead," Les said. "Anyone outside?" We weren't expecting trouble, not here. But you never know, so we'd dragged those two along. Amanda was in the Garden Court at the front entrance; Hammerhead was out back.

I didn't hear their replies, but a few seconds later, Les said, "Jen, everything's cool. Moving into position." The plan was that as soon as Bradshaw reached us, Les would climb the stairs.

Bradshaw walked stiffly, and if I hadn't guessed he'd wrecked his body playing college football, I would have assumed he was having a hard time remembering how to make his legs work. With jerks of his head, as if his cervical vertebrae were made of rusty iron, he glanced backward, then to Jen, then across to the other side of the conservatory.

Jen, this guy's crapping in his pants.

He had a minor in theater. We need to be careful.

Bradshaw reached us. Stuck out his hand. It was cold, clammy. Jen held it longer than normal, her long fingers stretching out to his wrist in the move we'd worked on.

His pulse is racing. 128.

He rubbed a hand over his forehead.

Jen said, "You okay?"

Bradshaw said, "Not really." His head ratcheted back and forth. "I shouldn't be here."

Jen waited.

Bradshaw looked over the railing down at the tropical forest.

Jen said, "I'm here to listen."

Bradshaw didn't speak, didn't look at us. Glanced behind him. Jen followed his eyes. The mother and daughter had come up the stairs. They were chattering away. Happy. Laughing. Jen thought, *Oh, to have a normal life.*

Jen returned her focus. "Mr. Bradshaw? Mikey?"

Bradshaw almost jumped at the sound of his name. He looked at us. There was genuine panic in his eyes.

He took a breath.

"There's really bad shit happening. I told you that, didn't I?"

"That's okay. Take it slow."

"Everyone's panicking. Two weeks and three days."

"Until the climate reparations date is set." It was a statement, not a question.

He didn't respond to this. He was going into panic overdrive.

Jen kept her voice calm. Slow. Soothing. "Mikey, is that what you need to talk to me about?"

"I need to get back to the office."

"That's cool. What's going on?"

"It's not what I signed up for with him. You know what I mean?"

"Who?"

Bradshaw's gaze shot to the right, and he managed to stiffen even more. He was on the verge of splintering into pieces.

Jen glanced over. It was only the two women, chattering away, the younger one's hand resting on the snuggly where Jen could make out the bulge from her baby's head.

Jen placed her own hand on Bradshaw's arm, signaling, *It's fine; we'll let them pass.*

The younger one was speaking, "I swear, like Tom is already planning what sports he'll play."

The mother said, "Sounds exactly like your father."

My pattern recognition chops flipped into high alert.

Right as they smiled hello, I yelled *Watch out!* to Jen, but it was too late.

The older one lunged at Bradshaw and pushed him hard, toppling him over the railing. Bradshaw shrieked. Jen screamed, "Les!" just as she saw the younger one wiggle a gun out of the snuggly.

Jen threw herself at the younger woman, and right as I heard Bradshaw thwack hard onto the ground, she grabbed the woman's wrist and twisted it violently.

The woman kicked at her, but Jen managed to keep her grip. The older woman was coming at us now; Jen twisted the younger woman's arm behind her and whipped her around as a shield.

The older woman pulled a gun, and from thirty feet away, Les yelled, "Police, drop your weapon," as the younger woman pressed hard against Jen, forcing us backward.

The older woman shouted to her partner, "I got Westin," but as she turned and raised her gun, Les fired a shot into her, the impact whipping her backward. The younger woman screamed, "No!" and with an unexpected move heaved herself backward, taking herself and Jen over the rail.

We were falling. Fast.

But we didn't fall far.

In midair, Jen shoved the woman away from her. We crashed into the branches of a massive rubber tree. The young woman wasn't so lucky.

A split second later, Jen heard the woman's body hit a low bush and the ground.

15:32:08

"What the fuck?" Captain Brooks said. "What the fucking fuck?"

We were still at the Botanic Garden, but in the front foyer. The conservatory was now a crime scene, and the folks in paper jumpsuits would be there for hours more.

"Sir, I was meeting the communications guy from the U.S. Petroleum and Gas Institute. Mike Bradshaw. I told you about him. He called me. He had information about 'bad shit' going on."

"No kidding."

"And then these two women showed up."

"Who assassinated him right under your nose."

"They were two moms."

"Detective, my mom wasn't the greatest on the planet, but she never tried to knock anyone off."

Here's the picture.

Bradshaw had died on his way to the hospital.

Assassin One, the sweet middle-aged woman, was dead, shot and killed by Les.

What cop shows don't tell you is this: most human beings, including most police officers, don't enjoy hurting other people. Unless they're a psychopath—or someone who's been institutionally groomed to demean or hurt people, particularly those of a different race, sex, nationality, religion, political persuasion, gender identity, or sexual orientation—even shooting someone, not to mention killing another human being, bad guy or not, is a horrible thing to do. Even in our gun-happy United States, where police use weapons hundreds of times more than anywhere else in the world, three-quarters of police officers have never, *ever* fired their weapon while on duty, let alone killed someone. And it didn't matter that Les had already been end-lessly told that if he hadn't acted as quickly as he had, he or Jen or both would be dead. Didn't matter one bit. Les was freaked out beyond belief. Only one week back on the job, and the guy was a wreck.

Assassin Two, the young fake mother, was alive and probably in surgery by now. We didn't have a clue what injuries she'd suffered and whether she'd live or die. But I could tell you one thing: if she lived, we weren't about to find out who had hired her. These two were professionals, the really nasty side of gender equality—a couple of women who had leaned into the business of assassinations.

And the boss? She had more bruises forming than a schoolkid at recess and so many scratches she looked like she'd landed on a cactus rather than a rubber tree. She hurt a lot, and I didn't need to be the surgeon general to tell you that she was going to hurt a hell of a lot more the next morning.

Captain Brooks said, "Can we link them to the fire that killed . . . uh . . ."

"Blessing Robinson, sir."

"Right."

"We can try, but these two were pros."

"Any idea who they are?

"No, sir."

"Beyond 'bad things'—"

"'Bad shit,' sir."

"Beyond 'bad shit,' do you have the faintest idea what Bradshaw wanted to talk to you about?"

"I think he wanted to flip on his boss, Drake Bevans."

"Jen, why do you always insist on going after people in positions of power?" He didn't wait for Jen to answer. "Did Bradshaw name Bevans?"

"Not exactly, sir."

"How unexactly?"

"Bradshaw said, 'It's not what I signed up for with him.'"

"*Him.*"

"It could only be Bevans. His direct boss."

"No, it *might* be Bevans."

And on it went. Captain Brooks questioned Jen and chewed her out and fretted over her until even he couldn't continue. He ended it with, "I want a report on my computer by seven thirty tomorrow morning."

33

We had wasted hours getting checked out at the ER. Jen had nothing but minor cuts, bruises, and what were already becoming a host of very sore muscles. I don't even have five minutes of med school and could have told them that much, but who asks me? Next, we headed to the deserted SIS office, where we slogged through the night before Jen hit send. Off went her report four hours, six minutes, and eleven seconds early.

I called a car.

I coaxed Jen to stand up.

Jen went home. Body parts she didn't even know she had were stiff and aching.

She swallowed more painkillers.

Ran a bath so hot the porcelain started to melt.

Peered into the mirror and examined the scratches on her face. Stripped off her clothes and checked out a blossoming set of bruises.

Climbed into the tub, her skin instantly turning scarlet.

Within two minutes she was asleep.

13:12:59

Even if it hadn't been a scheduled day off, Jen wouldn't have gone within a mile of the station. She limped back over to the express bus stop on 16th where a ninety-year-old guy offered to help her up the steps. She managed by herself and let the friendly woman in the snappy uniform drive us to the top of the park.

On the way, Jen dropped a message to Les. *You're going to make it through this. It was an awful thing to do, but you're alive and I'm alive because you did it. Partner, you've saved me again. I'll be with you every step of the way.*

I could tell it even hurt to touch the imaginary keys on her phone.

She pressed the buzzer to signal the bus to stop right before it reached Silver Spring. Got her bearings in relation to the park and soon was winding south, walking on trails alongside Rock Creek.

This whole business had turned into a mess. Jen needed to regroup. Take stock. Make plans. Get her shit together. Close down this damn case one way or another, once and for all. It was driving her crazy, and that meant she was driving me around the bend.

"Help me here, Chandler."

We began with Patty Garcia.

Garcia discovers the smoking gun. (We hadn't been able to suss out how she'd tracked it down and perhaps never would.) She's about to announce she's a candidate for president, which will give her round-the-clock Secret Service protection. A few days before her announcement, she's found unconscious on a golf course. Two days later, she dies.

Drake Bevans.

Jen and Les begin snooping around for the missing document. We realize that Drake Bevans's father spilled the beans about climate change and was then—still my best theory—put on ice. We question Mikey Bradshaw. Bradshaw presumably tells Bevans about this document, although he, Bradshaw, doesn't understand its significance. Two days later, we go to Blessing's. That same day, we question Drake Bevans and inadvertently tip him off to the existence of an intact transcript of the hearing. Not long after, Blessing's house is blown up and the document is gone forever. Three days later, Bradshaw phones in a panic and wants to meet. Next day, Bradshaw is murdered.

Next up: Bradshaw's killers.

The younger one in the hospital recovering from her injuries has been ID'd as Sandi Postman; the older dead woman, her mother Bitsy. Nothing directly connects them to Bevans, although who else would have ordered Bradshaw killed right before he spoke to us? They did know Les's last name and presumably knew Jen's. Even if we weren't targets for them—although that was possible, given what Bevans seemed to know about our progress— they were certainly keeping an eye on us.

Nothing, however, connected either him or them to Garcia's death.

"On the other hand," Jen said to me, "Maybe we can nail him for Blessing and Bradshaw alone. What are the chances of linking him to the women?"

There were too many variables and unknowns to come up with an actual probability. I made up a number to give her the dismal picture. "One in a thousand. If we're lucky."

"Dial Richard for me, will you?"

I did. Rob, his service unit, answered. I kind of wanted to talk to Rob myself—I mean, why shouldn't I have my own friends?—but Jen jumped in. Five minutes later, Richard phoned us back.

I endured eavesdropping on four minutes of small talk before Richard said, "So what's up?"

"Do you happen to know Drake Bevans? From the U.S. Petroleum and Gas Institute?"

"We've met a few times. Why?"

"Would he be capable of arranging a murder?"

"Whoa! First Culpepper and now him?"

"I have zero evidence he had anything to do with Garcia. But I was there when a professional killer knocked off his communications director."

"If Bevans didn't like him, wouldn't it have been easier to simply fire the guy?"

Jen told Richard about the document, the link to Bevans, Blessing Robinson, Bradshaw.

"Jen, when you've been around almost one hundred and thirteen years, you meet lots of folks, including some truly despicable people. But as far as I know, I've never met a person who hired a contract killer." He laughed to himself. "Then again . . ."

"What's he like? Bevans?"

"You met him," Richard said. "He's not impolite, is he? But he's as cold as ice. Methodical. He has a reputation for being absolutely driven." Richard paused. "No, it's more than that. When it comes to his beliefs . . . his sense of mission, he's like a damn religious zealot."

"Would he kill for that sense of mission?"

Richard ignored the question. "In business, you learn there are men and women you can trust, and those you must keep at arm's length. And finally, those who are downright dangerous. Bevans? He's known to be extremely manipulative. Bevans is . . ." Richard fell silent for a moment. "Bevans is a weasel."

"But—"

"Although I only met him a few times, I'd swear he had a chip on his shoulder. A very big one. Like many successful men, it was hidden under his self-confidence and zeal. I've no idea what his problem is, or even if I'm calling that right. But I can tell you this, Jen . . ."

We waited.

"Remember when I told you to be careful? From what you've told me, you better not forget that."

Jen thanked Richard and said good-bye.

And so we moved our thoughts on to James Culpepper III.

We'd come close to breaking his alibi. He could have made it to the golf course and back, although with very little time to spare—too little for my taste, but then again, I don't run the show around here.

If we allowed for some sort of golf-ball hammer, he could have had the means, even though we were pretty certain we'd never find the actual murder weapon. It would be long gone.

He had motive. He'd been exposed as a wife beater. He'd been publicly humiliated. He'd been dumped. He'd lost hundreds of millions in future income. Once climate change reparations began, he'd lose a big chunk of what he still had and might even lose his stake in Climate Oasis.

But we were missing three things.

Anything approaching proof Garcia had been murdered.

A murder weapon.

Proof that Culpepper had been on or even near the golf course that day.

We didn't have evidence that he was anything but a schmuck who had obstructed the course of justice by lying to us.

The boss wandered slowly along the trails for an hour, her body hurting less and less as she stretched her muscles out. One moment I'd feel her head bursting with everything that had happened since . . . when? Just under a month ago. And then I'd realize that she had zoned out and her mind was thinking about branches and leaves and the gurgling water whenever we neared the creek.

Maybe it was a gift, I thought. That ability of the human mind *not* to focus. To swim in and out of consciousness. To be here and then be . . . gone. Maybe the very thing that made them seem to us so intellectually deficient was a beautiful thing I would never get to enjoy.

Without really noticing where we'd been heading, Jen realized we were once again on the trail near the golf course. Here the trail was wide and smooth.

She stopped.

Looked through the woods. We could make out smudges of green: the fairway where Garcia had been hurt. Maybe attacked. Or, as Jen finally conceded, maybe everyone but her was actually right. Maybe an errant golf ball had hit Patty Garcia on the head.

Rather than this admission freaking her out, it seemed to bring her peace. She could let this one go.

"Partner," she said, although she pronounced it like a cowgirl—*pardner*. "We tried, didn't we?"

I agreed that we had.

"So whaddya say, pardner, if we mosey back to the ranch and make us a couple of pisco sours—"

"A couple?"

"Shore thing. One for you, one for me."

And just as she took her first step, more peaceful and contented than I'd seen her in a month, one of those damn kids, same as before, zoomed past on his trail bike, so close that his handlebar brushed against her.

"Watch the fuck out!" she yelled, and as she did, she noticed that the rider had a camera mounted on their helmet.

The boss ratchetted around just in time to see others barreling at her, and as she did, I felt a series of clicks in her brain, as if a dozen circuits were all closing at once. Any hopes of a pisco sour break from her hopeless quest vanished. Jen reached into her pocket and, as the next bicyclist whizzed by, pulled out her shield and held it high.

"Police," she yelled in the direction of four others who were coming fast. And then, like a woman who meant business, she screamed, "You . . . will . . . stop!"

She planted herself in their path. They could either smash into her or slow right down to go around her.

The first of the last four tried that, and Jen reached out and pulled the bicyclist to the ground.

The others stopped, babbling away, "You didn't have to do that." "You almost killed her." "We have the right to be here."

"Take off your helmets," Jen ordered.

They did.

Two boys, one girl, one nonbinary. The girl was wearing a T-shirt that said, *Catholic and Pro-Choice*.

Jen glanced over her shoulder down the trail.

"Your chickenshit friends deserted you."

Boss, make nice.

I didn't feel her soften until one of the four, the girl, said, "Crap, lady, weren't you ever a kid?"

At first I felt Jen bristle and a sentence form: *How'd you like to be arrested for reckless driving, endangering lives, and obstructing justice?* However, she wrestled down the urge. Thought about the girl's question. And then turn to mush.

"Shittily," Jen said, "not really."

The kids were staring at her.

One said, "Did you just say *shittily*?"

Jen smiled weakly. "Me? Swear? On duty? Not on your fucking lives."

This got them all laughing.

"I think I've seen you all here before."

"Yeah," one of the boys said. "Just about every day after school. You know, as long as it's not raining or stuff."

Friday, March 3. Overcast but warm.

"What school?"

"St. John's College High School. It's—"

"Yeah. I know it." Right next door to Culpepper's.

Jen looked at their bikes. Each had a camera mounted to the handlebars in the front, and one had a camera tucked under the seat facing backwards. All the kids had cameras on their helmets.

"You're recording when you ride?"

"Well, yeah," one of them said, like every idiot knew that.

At the same time, another said, "Not, like, everything. That would be insane."

"When do you get out here on weekdays?"

The girl said, "We already told you. After school."

"I mean, what time does school end?" Jen held her breath.

"Three forty-five. We have to get out of our stupid uniforms, but we're here at four or four fifteen."

The glimmer of hope disappeared.

The nonbinary one said, "Except for Fridays, of course."

"You don't come then?"

"Well, they have this new thing on Fridays where the last two periods are for extracurricular. Clubs and teams."

The girl said, "That starts at one thirty."

The nonbinary kid said, "We're into the park before two."

One of the boys said, "We're the Trail Bike Club."

Private schools, Jen thought.

She pointed to the cameras. "All your video. Does it go up on, I don't know, YouTube? Instagram? TikTok? Zap?"

Four sets of eyes rolled so dramatically that if they could have made a sound, it would have been a sonic boom.

In case the point was lost, the four of them looked at each other and did their eyes again.

The nonbinary kid said, "Those things exist to mine your data and sell it to advertisers."

Mini-Zachs in the making, I heard Jen think.

"Then . . ."

"Well, duh," said one of the boys with a little laugh, "We're on YourJam."

A co-op–run, not-for-profit video-sharing space, I said.

"Right, of course," Jen said, pretending to know. "My nephew's on it too." And pretending to have a nephew.

Good, I said to her.

"He's real cool," she said.

Now you blew it, I added. But before they could start rolling their eyes again, she said, "Think you could show me?"

Two of them whipped out their phones and brought up their YourJam page.

They proudly showed Jen their highlight reel.

She said, "Cool," and then, "And what about other stuff? I mean, you guys must shoot tons of video."

The two boys shrugged pseudomodestly, like they were Plateau and Muybridge and had just invented the first moving pictures.

"All the stuff you shoot, is it, like, here at YourJam?"

I called a car and got to work. It wasn't as huge a job as it might seem. We knew the day we were looking for. We knew the approximate time. We'd found out there were ten members of their club, and no, they didn't have a clue who'd been with them on one particular day almost a month earlier. Each bike had one or two mounted cameras, plus everyone had a helmet cam. They sometimes sat still to take static shots of each other doing tricks or flying past or looking cool.

Piece of cake.

By the time a car arrived, I'd set up a sweet little routine that used a facial recognition program to go into their YourJam site and scan all their March 3 videos.

However, YourJam blocked me. Don't quite know how it figured out I was running the videos through facial recognition software, but it did. A message popped up. *YourJam is a surveillance-free space. Enjoy it. Don't abuse it.*

It probably wouldn't have worked anyway unless Culpepper had been staring right at the camera.

I rolled up my sleeves. I started to run the videos at high speed, slowing down whenever I noticed a runner or a walker come into the frame.

By the time we reached the station, I was ready for the show.

Jen said, "I wish we could do this with Les."

Not only was Les back on leave, but at his own request, he'd had P.D. temporarily deactivated. "I need to be on my own," he had said.

"Or," Jen continued, "since we're watching videos, at least we could have some popcorn."

I ignored Jen's attempt at flippancy. I knew how worried she was about Les.

I linked to an array of three screens and took her through the videos. Twice. Three times. Four times.

I brought up two mapping apps, street view (although in this case, it was trail view). Found the spot. Showed her what I'd found.

"Let's go talk to the captain," Jen said.

We went to Captain Brooks's office and waited for five minutes. That stretched to ten, but finally, he opened the door and told us to *venite*, except he said it in English rather than Latin.

"Detective Lu." He looked at Jen. "Whatever this is, I sure hope it isn't going to screw up my week."

"No, sir," Jen said.

"Or my career," the captain added.

Jen smiled, mischief painted across her face. "That I can't promise you."

"Any news about the woman who tried to kill you?" Brooks asked.

"She made it through surgery. She's going to be fine, but it'll take a while. Still no idea when we'll get to question her."

"Okay, Detective, let's have it."

After Monday's frustrating interview with Culpepper, we had reported back to Brooks that we didn't have anything on Garcia's ex.

But now Jen was able to say, "Sir, I think we can place him at the scene. Culpepper."

"You're shittin' me."

"First of all, the times were slightly off." She hesitated. "Our times . . . my times."

Brooks was watching her carefully.

"I made a mistake. I took it as fact what the golfers said, which would have been fine if it was Trebook's ball that hit Garcia. Even with the prerecorded talk, he would barely have time to make it back. But she was probably twenty minutes ahead of Trebook. Which means Culpepper would have a slightly bigger window to attack her."

The captain rubbed his scar. Nodded for Jen to continue.

"Culpepper could have recorded his program, changed into his running clothes, walked over to Viridian Green, waited in the woods, and when he saw her, dashed out—"

"Wouldn't she have run away or tried to fight back?"

"Then maybe he called out and walked over casually. Said he wanted to apologize. Got close, reached behind his back, grabbed the hammer, and hit her."

"Works in a movie."

"Sir, it works. I figure the homeless guy, Modus, saw all this. Culpepper chased him down and killed him. Culpepper could have gotten home, cleaned up, and done the rest of his broadcast with a few minutes to spare. I want you to see this."

Jen plunked her tablet onto his desk and came around to stand next to the seated Brooks. She poked play. The video showed a bike coming into a frame. Jen paused the video. "This is at 14:27:01 on Friday, March third." She hit play again. The bike whizzed past, left to right. The camera chased after it for another ten seconds until they met up with a group of riders coming toward them. The clip ended. She tapped the screen to rewind frame by frame. "Okay. Right there." Brooks leaned forward. Jen said, "You can just make out someone back in the woods. Maybe wearing green."

"Where exactly is this?"

"In the woods along the west side of hole number five of Viridian Green." She tapped on an icon and brought up a screen shot from the trail. More or less the same view and the exact stretch where we had cut through the woods and up the hill to the fairway. "I'm certain it's where an attacker would come out."

"Aside from your psychic powers, why would that be?"

"Except for this spot, the woods are dense on the hillside going up from the trail. I tried out this spot and was able to make it easily to the golf course."

The captain started to speak.

"Hang on, sir." Jen brought up the second video. At the bottom of the frame, small hands with painted nails gripped a set of handlebars—it was from a helmet cam. Ahead, one rider boogied up the trail, doing little tricks along the way. Even with the built-in image stabilization, the picture moved around as the rider turned their head one way and then the other. Thirty seconds later it was done.

"So?"

"Watch." Jen rewound partway. She ran it for ten seconds and stopped.

The captain shook his head.

She slowed it down and paused at 14:27:14. Pointed to a spot on the screen. A tiny part of the frame. A person—a man, it seemed—was near the edge of the same stretch of woods as in the other video. Wearing drab-green running gear and a matching baseball hat. Blending in nicely, but not nicely enough. I knew Jen was disappointed that the color was nowhere close to the neon-green fiber found in the cut on Garcia's finger.

"You can't see his face at all."

Jen said, "The tech guys can figure out his exact height by returning to this scene."

"I'm sure there's a boatload of men who are the same height as Culpepper."

Jen ran it forward. In another quarter of a second, the man was gone.

The captain was starting to fidget.

"One more, starting slightly before the last one." Jen said.

"You guys are losing me with all these damn times."

"Sir, don't worry about them. I'm only telling you so you know we've got this covered."

Another helmet cam. This one showed the whole group of riders from behind. Jen paused it. "These friends, it's a school trail bike club—"

"They have those?"

"Not at the schools we went to."

"You don't know where I went to school, Detective."

"No, sir. Where I went to."

"That's better. But for the record, we were lucky to have chalk in ours."

"That day, their videos stretched over a couple of hours. Only these three we're showing you are during this exact time. In this one, you can count five bikes in front of the rider, so this one was from the end of the line. Watch."

It started earlier than the previous video. Rock Creek was appearing and disappearing on the left, the wooded hillside on the right, the trail and other bikers out in front.

Two bikes coming the other way jumped into the frame, skidded into U-turns, and joined the pack in front of the camera. Soon the scenery became familiar, although, since the rider was swinging their gaze from side to side, it was hard to fix on any specific landmarks.

The captain didn't say anything this time.

Jen rewound. Tapped on the screen. "Here it is."

Only six seconds had elapsed since the time in the second video.

The camera eye was pointing straight ahead along the trail. It moved to the right toward the woods and the golf course beyond, then swiveled back to the front.

"I saw him," Captain Brooks said.

Jen rewound to 14:27:20. Froze on the image.

The man in drab-green running gear was still small. Way in the background. Still coming out of the woods. Head down. Raised his head for a split second, then lowered it again.

"Go back."

When he raised his head, we couldn't see where his eyes were focused; he was too far away and too small for that. But his arm was raised up like he was pushing a small branch away from his face.

"I'd bet he was worried about whacking himself with a branch. That would explain why he raised his head," Jen said. "The kids were barreling by. I'm sure Culpepper had no idea he'd been recorded."

Jen Lu and Captain Brooks stared at the face in the video.

Not the biggest or the clearest image ever.

But there he was.

James Culpepper the fucking Third.

34

It was an argument that Jen had no chance in hell of winning.

Captain Brooks immediately sent for Rhianna and CK from homicide.

"Sir," Jen had said, "it's my case."

I swear I did my best to stop her, but Jen, she's one determined woman.

The captain said, "Do I really need to . . ."

"But—"

"Apparently I do." The captain held his right index finger in the air. "A. It wasn't your case. Why not? Because there *was* no case. You did a great job. If we nail this creep, society owes you a debt of gratitude."

"But—"

"B." His middle finger joined the first. He spread them apart to form V for victory. "You're a good detective. Your squad is supposed to do exactly what you did. Work outside the boxes. Take chances. However, you don't do homicide."

"But—"

And now he raised his ring finger, his gold wedding band still there two years after his wife's death. His thumb held down his pinkie to form a Boy Scout salute. "And C. Why the hell do I always have to get into these arguments with you?"

Homicide arrested Culpepper an hour later.

His lawyer was in Boston for the evening.

Culpepper remained in his cell, refusing to talk until he spoke to his lawyer, who'd be arriving around noon the next day.

Jen could barely stop jabbering all through a late dinner with Zach. Leah and Raffi joined them for a glass of wine and to hear Jen's story.

Jen's mind was still buzzing when she tossed her clothes into the laundry bin and slid into another hot bath, the juniper-scented bubbles clinging to her.

She stretched out. It had been an exhausting couple of weeks. She used her toes to turn the handle and add more hot water to the long tub. I felt her tension melt away. I felt the smooth porcelain on her legs, felt the gentle slope of the tub against her back and the soft towel under her head. She closed her eyes and, for the second time that day, let the heat of the water melt her to sleep.

Thursday, March 30—07:18:19

Right after the sun rose into a cloudless sky, Jen tanked up with coffee and phoned Gabe, who she knew would have been up for hours.

"Gabe. Could I ask you a favor?" She didn't even wait for him to answer. "I'm wondering if I could come and talk to you. Not today, but soon. It's about Blessing Robinson. I'm certain that her death had something to do with that report I was looking for. The 1968 Senate hearing."

"Do you have actual evidence of that?"

"Not a shred."

Gabe was quiet until he said, "Were you able to read the report?"

"Every page."

"And? Did you make a copy of it? Take pictures?"

"No. She said I could come back for it over the weekend."

"Damn."

"But I read it out loud. And recorded every last word."

"As you know, that doesn't constitute proof that the document existed. You could have been reading from anything."

"But it's something, isn't it?"

"Quite something."

Jen jumped on her bike, and we reached Culpepper's house on Oregon Avenue before homicide and forensics were due to arrive to search the property. A squad car blocked the driveway. Jen said hi and waved her badge at the uniform, who looked like she wouldn't be able to keep her eyes open much longer. We strolled around the property. I wouldn't exactly call it a search— Jen was avoiding the temptation to dig into his trash cans or force open the pump room at the pool—but I could tell by her eagerness that she was hoping to discover the ashes of a small campfire with half-burnt green running clothes or, I don't know, a hammer with a golf ball attached.

Rhianna and CK arrived. A van with two crime techs swung in behind them.

Rhianna was a Detective II and running the show. I hadn't worked with her before, but she had a rep for being down-to-earth. That is, right until the second she went for the kill with a suspect. They said she was smart, a team player, and fun.

CK had a real name, but he was one of those guys who put a disproportionate amount of time into his body and poured all his money into his haircuts and wardrobe. In a drunken moment that I'm sure he long regretted, CK had confessed to Les that he'd grown up watching the endless versions of *CSI* and *Law and Order* and actually believed that detectives got to dress like fashion models. Anyway, nice clothes, sculpted body, hence his nickname: CK—Calvin Klein—even though he seemed to drop his paycheck on more expensive brands.

CK, for all his self-conscious perfection, was a background sort of guy. "Let your looks do the talking," he had also confessed to Les.

Rhianna, on the other hand, *loved* talking and could set records for the amount of attitude she could jam into a minute's conversation. Her first words as she stared up at his house: "Just y'all *look* at this place. If we don't get him for murder, I swear we should take him down for showin' off."

Jen gave them an inventory of the things she hoped they might find: a hammer or some sort of stick or rod with a golf ball attached, hammer/stick/rod with residue of glue, an open box of golf balls, *all* his running shoes, a tube or tubes of heavy-duty glue, computers, phones, cameras where they might find photos of the approaches to hole number five, and a set of drab-green running gear—not to attempt to match it to the bright-green fiber forensics had found but to establish clearly the identity of the man in the video. Plus anything that might link him to Modus, although none of us could imagine what that might be other than a stolen shopping cart.

"Forget all that shit," said Rhianna. "I'm lookin' for fuckin' fava beans." She held Jen's eyes with a hard look. "But girl, you're not touchin' nothin' here. Tiptoe behind me however much that little heart of yours desires, but I swear on my dead mamma, I'll slap cuffs on you if you set one pinkie down."

If I ever get transferred out of Jen's brain, I can tell you exactly where I'd love to go.

The search began.

It wasn't a crime scene, so we didn't need to suit up. But except for Jen, everyone slipped on nitrile gloves.

We went through the whole joint. Two glorious stories. Walls painted indigo or mouse gray or a violet so deep it could make a flower jealous. Glossy-white baseboards and doorframes. Solid-feeling doors with old brass handles. Understated furniture. A gym with more equipment than an Olympic training camp. Everything orderly and, there was no other word for it,

182

perfect. Then outside: A garage with a red Ferrari dickmobile. The pool pump house. The trash and recycling cans.

We didn't grab a big haul. One desktop computer, one tablet, one laptop and two dead phones—to go with Culpepper's phone that he had surrendered upon arrest. A good-quality video camera. An SLR camera with dust on it. The sort of stuff that tech would slog through but likely wouldn't be much help.

There was nothing in the way of green running gear. All of Culpepper's exercise clothes were bright colors: reds, oranges, yellows.

There were, though, three pairs of running shoes. They bagged those.

Nothing, of course, with a golf ball attached. No golf balls at all. And nothing that looked like it once had a golf ball attached, although they bagged a meat-tenderizer mallet and a hatchet and a fairly new steel hammer, one of the pricey ones with the fancy grips like Jen had seen at the hardware store.

We scored on one thing: tubes of two different brands of heavy-duty glues, including one Infinity Glue. Jen was pleased they'd found these, although she knew that since Culpepper hadn't locked Garcia in a small room and opened both tubes at once, these probably wouldn't help prove he killed her.

Just before noon, word came that Culpepper's lawyer—the boss one—had arrived and was meeting with his client. Jen, CK, and Rhianna split for the station. The tech folks would continue their search to their hearts' content, although Rhianna had made it pretty clear that "we got what we got, so let's go get the motherfucker who can afford a crib like this."

CK whispered to Jen, "Don't worry about her. It's a bit of a show."

"Worried? Me?" Jen replied. "I was thinking the exact same thing."

35

The preliminaries were over. CK and Rhianna were in charge and we'd been relegated to the bleachers, which in this case meant leaning against the wall at the side of the interview room. Rhianna had told Jen she wanted her in there to watch his reactions but that Jen should keep her mouth shut. If she had a question or suggestion, send it to their sims.

They had decided to use the same sledgehammer gambit that Jen and Les had used.

Rhianna popped the first question. "Why'd you tell Detective Lu you wanted to kill Patty Garcia?"

The lawyer said, "He never said those words to her."

Culpepper interrupted, "Jeremy, let me take this." His voice was easy. I didn't sense an iota of tension. He spoke to CK, ignoring Rhianna. "Detective, I was showboating. Nothing more, nothing less."

Rhianna said, "What's that supposed to mean?"

He turned to her slowly, as if it was the first time he'd noticed her in the room. "It means I was playing a game."

"With?"

"Obviously with your Ms. Lu there." He pointed to Jen with an open palm.

Rhianna said, "I don't think I know a *Ms.* Lu. You, CK?"

Culpepper said, "*Detective* Lu."

"And why would Detective Lu find your little game funny?"

"It was for my own amusement."

"Sayin' you wanted to kill someone?"

The lawyer cut in. "That's not—"

"But let me be crystal clear," Culpepper said. "My supposed joke was crude, insensitive, offensive, and stupid. If I had thought about it for a minute, I wouldn't have said it."

CK took over. "Good for you to say that. I, for one, appreciate your honesty. And I tell you, from one man to another, I completely get where you're coming from. I'd be angry too at the person who cost me my job *and* my income *and* my reputation."

"I wasn't, and I'm not."

CK raised an apparently sympathetic eyebrow. "Then you're a better man than me."

Culpepper said, "Detective, if we had had this conversation four and one-quarter years ago when she walked out on our marriage, or three and a half years ago when I was falsely convicted of using violence against her; if we had had this conversation back then, I would have freely admitted I was angry and deeply hurt by her."

Notice that he never uses her name? I said to Jen.

"But as I explained to *Detective* Lu, I worked extremely hard to jettison any such feelings." He then launched into his self-help spiel. CK pretended to be fascinated; Rhianna didn't have to pretend she was about to vomit.

Rhianna, her voice weary, said, "I'm all for yoga, but it's gonna take more than that to convince me you are no longer angry at your ex-wife, you hear what I'm saying?"

"My ex-wife is dead. Have some respect."

From where we stood to her side and behind her, I couldn't see Rhianna's full reaction. But I caught the crinkle of a smile, as in, *Now I'm really gonna crucify you, you little shit.*

"Be that as it may," Culpepper continued, and swiveled to his lawyer. "Jeremy, I'm not charged with being angry, am I?"

CK said, "Mr. Culpepper, I'm with you. Let's focus on a few facts, okay?"

Culpepper spread his hands and smiled. "That's why I'm here."

No, schmuck, you're here because we arrested you.

CK said. "I wonder if you could help me out a bit. I only need to establish a precise timeline of your activities and movements on Friday, March third."

"I've already told Ms. . . . Detective Lu."

"Run it by me again, will you?"

"I woke up, as always, at half past six. I brushed my . . . you want this much detail?"

Rhianna jumped in. "With *respect,* Mr. Culpepper, cut the crap."

Culpepper turned to CK and mouthed the letters *PMS*.

I felt Jen marshal all her energy not to jump down this guy's throat. Hell, I used all *my* energy to prevent myself from taking over Jen's movements and clobbering him myself.

Still speaking to CK, Culpepper said, "I was teasing you, of course. My apologies. I believe what you're looking for is this. I worked out in my exercise room, ate breakfast, checked emails, and went over the notes for my opening presentation. From right around noon to approximately twelve forty-five, I prerecorded the broadcast. It went smoothly."

"Why did you prerecord this particular session?"

And here Culpepper launched into his thing about prerecording each and every talk. He even added that he hadn't mentioned it when *Detective* Lu first spoke to him because she hadn't asked. But he was sorry there was confusion around this and wished he had thought of telling her.

"Which leaves us," CK said, "with two hours and fifteen minutes until you were needed for the Q and A session."

"Not exactly. I'm tuned in when the program starts at two thirty. I want to make sure that I'm into the rhythm of my speech."

"An hour and forty-five minutes, then."

"Yes. That's not unusual. Somedays during that break I'll work at my desk; somedays I'll read or go for a run, or pop out for a few errands."

"And that day? Friday, March third?"

Jeremy said, "How do you expect my client to remember exactly what he did a month ago?"

It was a feeble question, unworthy of a three-thousand-dollar-an-hour lawyer, but at least he was trying to earn his keep.

"That's okay, Jeremy. I remember exactly. It wasn't a sunny day, but the temperature was lovely. I went for a little run."

Jen said to me, *Damn, he's figured it out. He's assuming we arrested him because we can place him at or near the scene.*

Through me and his sim, Jen fed CK a question.

"Mr. Culpepper, when Detective Lu first interviewed you at the Climate Oasis showroom, you said you were at home that day. Now you say you went for a run. Lying in the course of an investigation is not only pretty suspicious, it's also an obstruction of justice."

"I didn't lie."

"You said you were at home."

"No, I specifically said that at the time of her accident, I was home addressing thousands of my viewers."

CK moved on quickly. "Where exactly did you run?"

"In the park, as always."

"That would be the Rock Creek Park?"

"*Exactly*," he said, mimicking CK.

"How far?"

"I'm not one of those people who keeps track of my distances or my route."

"Wouldn't it be on your phone?"

"I normally don't carry my phone when I run. It's all about solitude, isn't it?"

"Maybe you can take a guess. Was it a few miles?"

"Probably four or five."

"Where'd you run to?"

"I ended up along the creek."

"Be specific, Mr. Culpepper, Where along the creek?"

"I'd have to give that some thought."

"No rush at our end." CK pretended to have a sudden idea. "Any chance it could have been over by Viridian Green Golf Resort?"

"That's likely enough. The Valley Trail passes near there."

Rhianna took over. "You wouldn't remember?"

"Well, I go running every other day, and I usually zig and zag."

Rhianna slid the first of three screenshots across the table.

And suddenly she stopped dropping her *g*'s. Rhianna's voice was crisp, firm, hard, and direct. "Maybe this will keep your mind from zigging and zagging and help you answer our question." For the recording, she said, "James Culpepper III screen capture one."

He picked up the photo and held it close and then with an outstretched arm. "I don't have my reading glasses." He moved it back and forth and finally said, "This is it?" He sounded genuinely relieved. "It's some person, but you can't see anything of his or her face. Who's it supposed to be?"

"Or," Rhianna said, pushing the second photo over to him. "James Culpepper III screen capture two."

He shook his head. "Still can't see a face."

"Recognize the running clothes?"

"I can't make out any logos or details, so no, not really."

"Well, *really*, do you own drab-green running gear?"

"No."

"Are you sure?"

"Absolutely. I used to have one set, but they were getting shabby and—sorry to offend your feminine sensibilities—they'd become permanently stinky. I recently tossed them out."

"That's convenient."

"No, simply necessary. They stank."

"And when might that have been?"

"I couldn't say exactly. Maybe two or three weeks ago."

Rhianna leaned across and tapped the picture.

"Mr. Culpepper, you admit this is you." A statement, not a question.

"Not at all. I can barely see it. The shade of green seems to match what I had, but I'm guessing there are hundreds of people in the area, maybe thousands, with similar clothes. Isn't that true, Jeremy?"

Jeremy said, "I don't run myself, but I'm sure we'll be able to get the numbers on green running gear. Detectives, this whole line of questioning seems a particular waste of time."

Culpepper shrugged. "I really wish I could help you, but the image is so blurry . . ."

Rhianna placed a third screenshot in front of him. "Maybe this will help you focus." And again she identified the photo for the recording.

Culpepper caught his breath.

But recovered in an instant.

When he started speaking again, Jeremy tried to stop him, but Culpepper was smiling. "Yes," he gushed. He sounded excited, like we'd discovered the long-lost picture from a childhood adventure. "That is me! Fantastic. Yes, definitely."

"You now see where these are?"

"Of course. I run along there often."

"Could you tell us where it is?"

"Through those woods is the golf course. You can even make out a bit of the fairway."

Rhianna said, "For the record, these three photographs are from videos taken by teenagers riding trail bikes on Friday, March third, 2034, between two twenty-seven and two twenty-eight. They're taken from the vantage point of the Valley Trail looking east. The patch of woods through which Mr. Culpepper is emerging sits alongside the fifth hole of Viridian Green Golf Resort."

CK said, "Mr. Culpepper, I got to tell you, this seems pretty damning."

Rhianna jumped in and said to CK, "Of course it's damning. Mr. Culpepper had just brutally attacked—"

CK placed his hand on Rhianna's arm to stop her. These guys were pretty good at this routine.

"See?" CK said. "That's what people are going to think. I just need you to explain why you didn't mention this before."

"Did I tell you I wasn't there?"

CK didn't answer.

"What I did say was that I needed to think. To remember. This has obviously jogged my memory, if you'll excuse the pun. Yes, of course I was there." He tapped the photos. "You can see it right in front of you."

CK pointed to the screenshot. "This clearly shows you coming out of a patch of woods adjacent to the spot where the body of your ex-wife was discovered."

Culpepper did not speak.

CK said, "Were you coming from the golf course?"

"No."

"Then what were you doing in that patch of woods?"

"I don't remember. Likely a call of nature."

"It's hard for me to imagine, Mr. Culpepper, how you could possibly forget. I mean, your ex-wife suffered a fatal injury right near that exact spot either at or around the same time you were there. How could you forget?"

Culpepper shrugged and shook his head. "I can't tell you how much I wish I could be more help."

His lopsided smile told us otherwise.

36

"**Y**our guy, Jen, is a jumbo sleazeball," Rhianna said.

"My guy?" asked Jen.

CK said, "You noticed, though? How he managed to cover his tracks. I mean, perfectly."

"No kiddin'." The *g* was gone again.

Culpepper had outfoxed them at every turn.

He had asked for a moment to speak to his lawyers.

Rhianna checked her watch. "I'd love"—she stretched the word out, *luuuuuve*—"to pick up Tyra from day care today."

CK said, "Ain't gonna happen."

Humans do mood swings like trapeze artists. Here these three were acting like they were in the salt mines of Siberia when only 107 minutes earlier they'd been strutting around like they owned gold mines. When Jen had arrived back at the station from the search of Culpepper's joint, she had walked through the building receiving high fives, shakes of astounded heads, and a round of sarcastic but nice applause from Narcotics. In spite of there having been no actual case and her efforts to keep her noninvestigation quiet, every single person seemed to know about it, including the woman who mopped floors and kept the place clean. Jen had cracked a case that no one thought was anything other than an accident. No one except Jen, Garcia's angry chief and a gaggle of online conspiracy theorists who were now linking the death to the Ebola outbreak that had shut down Las Vegas.

Jen asked Rhianna and CK if they wanted anything from our pathetic cafeteria. They said no. Jen dashed down to the Scarlet Pumpernickel and got a surprisingly good tubmeat burger.

Soon after, we were back inside and resumed the session.

Culpepper didn't even wait to be asked a question.

"I have a confession to make."

He let that hang in the air.

We waited.

Finally, CK said, "We're listening."

"As you saw from those photos and as I agreed, I was there in those woods next to Viridian Green. On Friday, March third, shortly before two thirty in the afternoon."

CK jumped in. Culpepper didn't look happy to be interrupted, but this was still our show. "Do you know what hole it was?"

"Of course," he said, staying calm. "It was the fifth hole."

"Did you know at the time that it was the fifth hole?"

"Yes."

"How would you know that?"

"Because I went there specifically wanting to speak to my former wife, Patty Garcia."

"How could you possibly know you'd find her there? And at that time?"

"There'd been a puff piece in the *Post* last spring. What she did to keep her sanity and health."

"And?"

Again, Culpepper bristled slightly when CK interrupted his story.

"It said she faithfully played a round of golf on her own each Friday at one fifteen."

"And how would you know what time she'd be at hole number five?"

"I didn't. Not exactly. But she used to talk about how slowly people played. I remembered her once telling me she'd played a round on her own in well under three hours. But even if she wasn't usually so fast, she could easily arrive at the middle of the fifth hole around two."

"Why the fifth hole?"

"It was the closest to the running trails."

Rhianna jumped in, "Why were you stalking her?"

Culpepper turned to her with real ferocity. It was his first emotional reaction all afternoon. But then he laughed. A contrived laugh, but not bad under the circumstances.

"Detective, I wasn't stalking her. I wanted to speak to her."

Rhianna said, "Ever hear of telephones?"

"I no longer had her personal phone number."

"You deleted it?"

"Of course not. She changed it every year."

"Her office would be easy to reach."

"My conversation with her was private."

CK said, "You're saying you didn't want anyone to know you were contacting her?"

"My main worry was not about myself."

CK raised one eyebrow in disbelief—it was definitely his best trick.

Culpepper said, "I didn't think she would want anyone to know. And besides, I was certain her assistants wouldn't put me through to her. I knew that even if I sent a letter, Patty would not want to meet with me."

Rhianna started to speak but must have been pinged by CK's sim and stopped. I liked that: she was in charge but she didn't have an oversized ego.

CK said, "How could you be so certain?"

Culpepper shot him an *Are you kidding?* look.

"Because the very last time she saw me, I had just been convicted of assaulting her. My expression then must have been far from friendly."

"Let me get this straight," Rhianna said. "Out of the goodness of your heart, you decided it was best to sneak up on her at a remote corner of a golf course."

Culpepper didn't rise to her bait; he was now in total control. He didn't seem perturbed by Rhianna's sarcasm.

"I didn't say that was the only reason I wanted to speak to her in private. It is extremely embarrassing to say, but I was also worried about destroying my image."

Rhianna's voice was incredulous: "Your *image*?"

Culpepper stayed calm. "My image and my business. In addition to my investment in and work on the board of directors of Climate Oasis, I have developed a very high profile and a lucrative business as a defender of what I call the unjustly accused. My book on how men are still suffering under the yoke of feminism sold half a million copies. My speaking fees are in the tens of thousands per talk. Product links on my website and social media channels alone earn over four hundred thousand a year."

"Sounds like losing your job with the oil guys didn't hurt you financially."

I sensed Culpepper bristle, but he quicky composed himself.

"I am well off. I have a lovely house. But my income, while substantial by your standards, is a whole magnitude, literally, from the income bracket I was poised to be in."

"Are you a Timeless?"

"No."

"Do you plan on being one?"

"I believe my investment in Climate Oasis—"

Rhianna interrupted, "With borrowed money."

"—will pay off at a fantastic level. So, yes, I imagine that will be in my future."

"Unless the climate reparations gut the value of your oil stocks and interest in Climate Oasis."

Although it had been difficult to get all the details without a warrant, I had done some impressive digging. For one thing, the complicated golden handshake Culpepper had received when BP/Chevron got rid of him after the trial was for a large package of stocks that he wouldn't receive for another couple of years. It was a fortune by anyone's standards but would disappear with a hefty climate reparations settlement. And far worse for Culpepper, it appeared he had used these shares as collateral against massive loans for his significant investment in Climate Oasis. If Patty Garcia produced the smoking gun, it seemed likely that his loans would be called in. He would lose everything. People had killed for much less.

Culpepper said, "Whatever you're trying to get at is ridiculous."

"What do you think we're 'trying to get at'?"

Culpepper didn't answer. He closed his eyes for a moment, took a breath, opened them, and said, "You were asking why I was concerned for my image."

CK nodded as if sympathetic to Culpepper's plight. "I think I see where you're coming from. If things are even a bit financially uncertain right now, then it makes total sense to worry you'd lose your lucrative work if it came out that you had spoken to your ex."

"Not only that I spoke to her. What I wanted to say to her."

"And what would that be?"

"To apologize."

"For?"

Culpepper here seemed to compose himself, and Jen and I had a five-second debate about whether he was acting or genuine.

"To apologize for the time, the one time, I used physical violence against her."

CK said, "And when was that?"

"Exactly what you know about. For pushing her."

Rhianna jumped in, "When you tried to push her down the stairs."

He reacted strongly but kept his composure. "Absolutely not. We were arguing. I was angry. We were in our bedroom. She left the room; I followed. I tried to reach out for her. She pushed my hands away. And, to my shame, I pushed her back. It didn't even compute we were so close to the stairs. Thank God she didn't fall."

CK said, "To make this clear, you wanted to apologize to her about the very thing you pleaded not guilty to and which you'd been saying for years was a wrongful conviction. Claims you've built a valuable brand on."

Culpepper dropped his head for a second. "Yes." And then raised it and looked right in our eyes. CK's. Then Rhianna's. Then Jen's. It was absolutely riveting.

CK recovered the quickest. "And you maintain there was never another act of physical violence."

"If you read the trial transcripts—"

"We have."

"You'll recall that Patty herself said that was the only act of physical violence."

"Sexual violence?"

"None. As you can read."

"Emotional abuse?"

"I could be glib and say she could give as good as she got. But that wouldn't be the whole truth. Increasingly, I was on her case."

Rhianna: "Threatening her?"

"Never. But belittling her. It was contemptible, and I will carry my shame to my grave."

"And," Rhianna said, "you expect us to believe that was why you were sneaking through the woods."

"Ultimately, Detective, it doesn't matter what you believe. What's important is that I know this in my heart. I wanted, at least in some small way, to right a wrong that I had caused. I wanted to apologize, plain and simple."

CK said, "Why didn't you do this sooner?"

"I was very angry at her. I was angry about losing my position. For losing my marriage. For everything. And then, although the anger subsided, I was getting used to the celebrity that came with the Climate Oasis project as well as my business defending assorted wife batterers and rapists."

Rhianna said, "You once called it a human rights campaign."

"Yes, and I also once worked for a corporation that said we weren't causing climate change. It was bullshit, but I was getting rich."

We were all silent. Stunned.

"But," Culpepper continued, "I was also deeply ashamed."

"Why now?"

"My silence had gone on too long."

194

"Why not make a statement to your network? Tell them what you had done."

"That's more complicated."

Rhianna said, "Doesn't sound the least bit complicated to me."

"You're not me," he said, belligerence creeping back in. But like throwing a switch, he got that under control, and to my utter surprise said, "My apologies, Detective. Partly, I wanted her to first hear it from me, not in the media or from someone else. It would have been very embarrassing to say it publicly. The right thing to do, certainly, but it speaks to my own limitations. What's more, I was hedging my bets. If she refused to talk to me, then I stupidly thought I could continue my business just as before, at least for a while."

"Spell hypocrite for me, will you?" Rhianna said.

Culpepper nodded.

"I was also scared."

CK raised his eyebrows. "Of . . . ?"

"Some of the men who follow me. They would feel betrayed. Many are good men, confused and hurting by the changes in the world—"

Rhianna said, "Spare me the violins."

"—but among them are extremely violent men. I was afraid one of them would come after me."

Rhianna, "Do you expect any of us to believe this?"

"Again, I can't control what you believe or not. But I need to get this off my chest."

"Convenient."

"And if it would be useful to you, I'm willing to give my therapist total permission to answer any question you might want to ask about our therapy or things I've said."

"How long have you been seeing her?"

"Him. I've been seeing *him* for about a year."

CK said, "Let's back up here. What happened? After you arrived at the golf course."

"I arrived there at five minutes before two."

"You were wearing a watch?"

"Yes."

Jen, I said, *we can dig the data out of it.*

"You said you didn't keep track of your runs."

"It's a thirty-year-old Patek Phillippe. Analog, of course." He waited for CK to nod and then continued. "I didn't want to miss her, but I didn't want to be there way early."

"And perhaps be spotted by someone."

"Yes. Exactly. Two players passed by right after I arrived. After that, there were no other golfers."

"And when did Ms. Garcia show up?"

"I can't give you the exact time. But I'd been waiting there much longer than I expected."

"Than you expected?"

"Yes."

"Because you needed to return home for the question-and-answer portion of your show?"

"Exactly."

Rhianna jumped in. "So you admit you were lying when you said you tuned in at half past two to watch your recorded presentation."

"Yes. I was still on my way back at that time."

"How do you know the time if you weren't looking at your watch?"

"I didn't say I never checked it. Only not at the moment she arrived. I was increasingly concerned I'd be late." His eyes roamed upward, as if trying to picture the day or, perhaps, the time stamp on the screenshots from the videos. "By around two twenty, two twenty-five, I knew I had to move, and move fast."

"What happened?" Rhianna said. "In between checking the time and spotting Ms. Garcia?"

"As I said, I was about to leave the woods when I saw her come down the hill."

"You didn't hear her ball land?"

"A few minutes before, I thought I'd heard the whoosh of a ball and then something hit branches up ahead like it had gone into the woods."

"And you think that was her ball?"

"I thought it might be hers, although I knew it could have come from another group. You have to realize, I didn't know for certain she was playing that day." His voice now rose with passion. "But it *was* her."

"How did you feel when you saw her?"

"Nervous . . . excited."

Rhianna said, "Because you were about to kill her?"

Culpepper ignored this and kept speaking to CK. "I was nervous and excited because after four torturous years, I was about to speak the truth." He let that sit, took a calming breath. "She came down the hill."

"Alone?"

"Yes. Carrying her bag on her back. In these colorful clothes. Looking fantastic. She was swinging her head this way and that and stretching her neck up, obviously trying to spot her ball. She came toward the right side of the fairway, where I was waiting in the woods. I went out. I didn't want to frighten her. I called out. She looked up, saw me. For a second I think I scared her, or at least I could tell I had startled her. But I held my hands up in a peace gesture and smiled. I called out, 'I'm here to apologize for what I did.'"

"And her reaction?" said CK.

"She didn't have time to react. At that moment there was a cry of 'Fore'— you know, like they do if a ball is going where it could hit someone. She turned quickly toward the sound, you know, back toward the hill, just as a golf ball came flying down and hit her on the head. She crumpled to the ground."

"On which side did it hit?"

"At first I didn't know. She was turned away from me. It happened in a split second. I've replayed the scene a hundred times, a thousand times in my head to see if I could have warned her, but there wasn't time."

"And then?"

"What do you think? That I took off? That I was worried about my stupid show? I ran to her, reached her, got down, felt for her pulse. There was nothing. I mean nothing."

CK's voice was incredulous. "And you didn't do CPR?"

"I thought she was dead." His face looked genuinely stricken. "She was dead. I should have, but I—"

His face colored with shame.

"I . . . oh shit . . . I knew if I did mouth-to-mouth or even lots of chest compressions, my DNA would be all over her. And . . ."

CK and Rhianna waited. Even CK with his sympathetic-bro act wasn't going to give Culpepper a pass.

"I'd been convicted of assaulting her. I'd snuck onto a golf course at a spot no one would see me. The media already paint me as a misogynist. Who'd believe me when I reported I saw her get hit by a ball?" He breathed deeply. "I told myself, *She's dead. There's nothing you can do.* And then I ran like hell."

"You didn't call for help?"

"I told you, I didn't have a phone. She was clearly dead. And since I heard that yell—"

"Man? Woman?"

"It was a man who yelled 'Fore.' I knew golfers would be there any minute and they'd call the police."

Jen said to me, *Have them ask about Modus.*

CK said, "And what about Modus?"

"Who?"

"Is that when you went after him?"

"I don't know . . ." He shook his head. "Who's Modus?"

"A man who lived in the woods. Who saw you with Ms. Garcia."

"I didn't see anyone. I looked around; of course I did. But there was no one. Not anywhere."

37

Rhianna slammed herself onto her chair. CK rested his butt on his desk. Jen pulled over a chair from an empty desk.

Rhianna said, "In my sixty damn years of bein' a cop—"

CK said, "You're only forty-six."

"At this moment it feels like sixty. I never met such a . . . such a . . ."

Jen ventured, "Prick?"

CK said, "That doesn't do him justice."

Rhianna cackled. "That doesn't do pricks justice . . . God, he was good."

CK said, "Maybe. But why give away their whole defense strategy?"

Jen said, "I'm guessing he was overriding his lawyer. Culpepper is Culpepper. He had it all figured out as soon as he thought for a moment about those photos."

"Honey," Rhianna said, "he had this figured out a year ago when he read that article. I mean, if he's invitin' us to talk to his shrink—"

"Who he started going to a year ago."

"—it means he's been plannin' every contingency to a T."

Jen said, "You think he killed her?"

"Hell if I know. Hell if you know. This guy is so damn creepy, I wouldn't put it past him. However, every last particle of his story hangs together. It makes him sound flawed but genuinely repentant. And don't forget, Jen, you yourself found that investor guy's—"

"Trebook's."

"—golf ball lying there."

I had better things to do than listen to them moaning, so I decided to run through the times again. Something wasn't right

A bundle of my circuits were looking at the times, which left me plenty of muscle to stay on top of their babble. CK said, "I figure Culpepper did his little confession to stave off charges. Or, assuming we manage to get the DA to lay charges and this goes to court, he'll make us look unreasonable—"

Rhianna said, "The little prick."

"He'll say, 'Your honor, as I explained to them, totally and freely, I admitted all this. That I was there. That blah, blah, blah.'"

And there it was, staring me in the face.

I fed Jen the numbers.

I felt a smile lighting up her face.

"What's greasin' your skillet, sunshine?"

"The times," Jen said. "His times don't work." She jumped to her feet and was pacing back and forth. "We know that if she had actually been hit by a ball, it would have struck Garcia between two thirty-two and two thirty-four."

"Honey, would you hold still? I can barely follow the numbers, let alone you as well."

Jen stopped moving but didn't sit down.

"But Culpepper was filmed *leaving* the scene at two twenty-seven. The times show that his claim to have seen her hit by the ball don't add up. He did it."

Rhianna said, "Run that by me again, would you? How you can be so exact on the time the ball hit him?"

"*Would* have hit. If it was the investment guy's ball and not him like he claims."

Rhianna waggled her hand like she was whisking eggs for an omelet. *Just get on with it.*

"As you saw in my accident report, I was on the scene within minutes. I asked when the ball would have hit Garcia. They worked backwards to the Timeless guy's tee shot, the one they assumed struck her. Added the time for Trebook's partner to hit her flubbed tee shot, walk to that, hit her second shot, get to the hill. That's when they saw Garcia lying there. They ran down. She was a doctor—"

"We know all this."

"—and they checked the time. They worked backwards and gave me that range."

CK said, "Could it have been off?"

"Sure, maybe two or three minutes. But not six or eight."

Rhianna said, "And the rich guy yelled 'Fore.'"

"That's what he told me."

"Why?"

CK said, "That's what they do."

Rhianna said, "But they told you they figured Garcia was way up ahead."

"Yeah. But I think they sort of do it on that hole. Just in case. Maybe there could be someone from the grounds crew down there."

Rhianna said, "So back to my question. Did you double-check her times?"

"They both agreed."

"Damn it, sister, it was your investigation."

Jen boiled over. "There *was* no investigation."

The boss was splitting hairs. Half the population of DC seemed to know Jen had been poking her nose in this, even if there was no official investigation.

Rhianna ignored Jen's outburst. "CK, let's pull up their phone records. Two to three o'clock."

Finally! Something to do, although it took me and my fellow sims only seconds to round up the phone information for the two golfers and send it to our bosses' tablets.

Peter Trebook, the Timeless guy, had no phone calls in or out during that hour.

Dr. Jane Kershaw, though, had received a call at 14:25 and spoken for five minutes. Which, according to their timing, would be back when they were on the fourth green or walking from the green to the fifth tee.

Rhianna said, "Bring up the phone grid."

Easy peasy.

Her phone was on the tower servicing the fifth hole. The signal was rock-solid constant. She wasn't budging.

CK said, "Which means she had to be speaking from the fifth tee area right before or after she hit her tee shot."

"So?" Jen said, sounding a bit defensive even to me. "Big deal. She talks on the phone, then they hit their balls a couple of minutes later. The times are perfect."

I knew that Jen knew better, but this case was really digging into her like the poisonous fangs of a snake.

Rhianna said, "I'm callin' her."

Rhianna's sim must have dialed, because a few seconds later, Rhianna picked up her desk phone.

"Dr. Kershaw, this is Detective Custer from District One Homicide." Her voice was back to hyperofficial. "Yes, that's right, that's what this is about . . . I realize that . . ." She turned to CK and Jen and rolled her eyes. "We'd be finished by now if you'd let me ask you a question . . . Or if you prefer, we can pick you up and bring you down to the station . . . That's good. I appreciate your cooperation.

"Doctor, I really have only one question. Following the accident at the golf course, my colleague spoke to you and your playing partner, Mr."—she glanced at her notes—"Trebook. From what you both reported, we worked out the time that Ms. Garcia would have been unfortunately struck by Mr. Trebook's ball . . . No, he did no wrong . . . Yes, I know I said I'm from homicide . . . Because I'm from homicide . . . I'm not being snarky . . . Dr. Kershaw, could I ask you this question? Good . . . There's one thing. We understand from available phone records that you received a call at twenty-five past two when you were at or near the fifth tee. Is that correct?"

Rhianna covered the receiver with her hand and whispered to us, "Stunned silence."

"Sorry, could you repeat that? . . . Yes, I understand everyone forgets things. No harm done . . . Yes, I know you're a doctor and need to answer important calls from your office. We all appreciate the important work I'm sure you do. But we need to know whether Mr. Trebook hit his tee shot before or after you got the call . . . Before? Good, that's fine. And then you hit? . . . No? That's when you got the call, as you were getting ready to hit. You spoke for five minutes . . . well, that's what the records say . . . right . . . and then you hit your ball."

Rhianna was fidgeting and rolling her eyes.

"Two final quick questions, ma'am. First, when you two were figuring out the elapsed time between Mr. Trebook's shot and your arrival to importantly help Ms. Garcia, it sounds like you forgot to add on the time for your phone call . . . No, there's no reason you'll get in trouble for that . . . Yes, I understand it was a stressful moment . . . Yes, and you were focused on your important help to Ms. Garcia . . . Good, that's good."

Rhianna thanked the doctor and hung up.

Rhianna spread her arms wide into a *What can I tell you?* gesture.

"Tough luck, Jen, but Culpepper's timin' works. The ball could have hit Garcia at two twenty-four. Culpepper could have checked her pulse, checked again, panicked, and run back into the woods right on time to have his picture taken."

CK said, "And remember, he seemed to be genuinely baffled by our question about Modus."

Rhianna said, "It was the one moment I truly believed him."

If it ever went to court, Culpepper's lawyers wouldn't have to prove he was innocent. They only had to demonstrate reasonable doubt.

Rhianna spread her arms wide, like a pastor commiserating her flock. She shook her head as if she were the saddest woman on the planet.

38

Thursday, March 30—16:46:43

We'd been able to arrest James Culpepper III because the boss and I had managed to put together enough convincing evidence. Videos that proved he was at the scene of the crime. Motive. Opportunity. No alibi. True, we couldn't wave around a murder weapon, but that would have been just plain showing off. As far as we were concerned, we were certain a judge or jury would have enough to convict this lying bastard.

There'd been those wonderful high fives and congrats when she'd arrived at the station on Thursday after the house search. Jen B. Lu had done it again. She didn't say so, but I know the boss well enough to say this came as a blessed relief to her. I knew damn well she'd been worrying she'd forever be seen as a one-hit wonder for last year's case.

Even Les, off duty and in really terrible shape, had somehow heard about the arrest. On Thursday morning, he'd sent Jen a two-word text: *COBALT BLUE!*

The good feeling hadn't lasted long.

Culpepper's "confession" was a work of genius. So much so that Jen and I went from thinking it was a masterful con to starting to doubt her original theory. At her greatest moment of doubt, the one thing she had clung to was the clock. His timing didn't work. That's what would get him convicted to a long stretch in a federal prison; that's what showed his whole story was a lie.

Until it wasn't. Until even his times held together.

Bad quickly crashed to worse.

On the captain's instructions, we had purposely kept the arrest on the q.t. No announcement, no comment until the DA decided whether to press charges. This one was high-profile, and it was 180 degrees away from the coroner's report. If charges were formally laid, the coroner's office (and the justice system that relied on it) would be publicly humiliated; they would get slammed with accusations of plain incompetence or worse—a cover-up of Garcia's murder.

Now, late in the afternoon on Thursday, Jen, Rhianna, and CK were hunkered down in an interminable postmortem chin-wag.

Boss, I said, *you better check this out.*

It was all over the news. *The New York Times*: "Patty Garcia: Now Identified as Possible Murder Victim." *Washington Post*: "Police Arrest Ex-Husband in Suspected Murder of Patty Garcia." *The Daily News*: "Murder!" and *The Guardian*: "Known Misogynist Linked to Lawyer's Death." *People* magazine's website banner was "Love Story Gone Tragically Wrong!!!" *Fox News* stoked up viewers with, "Did Patty Garcia Get What She Deserved?"

Didn't matter how careful we'd been. Someone had leaked it. "Probably," Jen said to the others, "one of Culpepper's fucking fans lurking in the force." In spite of the impact of major reforms in policing, we were still stuck with dudes who'd be firmly on Culpepper's side.

Soon after Jen read the press reports, I could have sworn we heard Captain Brooks bellowing from two floors away. At any rate, Brooks summoned Jen, Rhianna, and CK to his office.

"Report," he said. He was working the keloid scar above his eye like it was an alien creature attacking him.

Rhianna reported. It was her case.

"Sir, James Culpepper is a first-class woman-hating sleazebag."

"Detective, I didn't ask for your feelings, psychological profiling, or social analysis; I asked for your report. Jameson reamed me out for the past ten minutes." Fredericka Jameson, Washington's elected district attorney and one of the grand pooh-bahs among DAs in the country.

The captain didn't let up. "She was furious this hit the media. At me! Hell, she was still furious we arrested the guy without consulting her. She's making her decision in the morning on whether to lay charges, and I want to make certain that I, and you, and the whole damn DC police force don't look like a parade of clowns."

Rhianna, CK, and Jen fumbled through their reports.

He asked about Modus, whom none of them had mentioned. Jen said, "There never was evidence he'd been attacked."

The captain said, "And if you remember correctly, there never was evidence Patty Garcia was attacked either." One by one, he looked at them. He said, "Do you stand by your original decision to arrest Culpepper?"

All three said yes.

"And are you still one hundred percent certain you got it right? That he went there to attack Garcia or at least attacked her while he was there?"

Rhianna said, "You can never know one hundred percent."

The captain snapped back, "Of course you can."

Rhianna looked away.

CK said, "No. Not one hundred percent. Fifty-fifty at best."

CK: a man of his convictions.

The captain didn't even bother asking Jen, but the boss spoke anyway. "Sir, I know all this looks bad."

"It *looks* bad?"

"Okay, it is bad. He's smart, he's clever, he's convincing. But I still think he attacked her."

"And *I* still think that grits and biscuits with gravy should be low cal, but you know what?"

No one asked him *what*.

Here's the thing. When Rhianna and CK had arrested Culpepper on Wednesday afternoon, they had cited one charge for purposes of booking: aggravated assault leading to death. They had duly written a probable cause affidavit that night. A judge had reviewed this along with other probable cause affidavits when she visited the jail for this purpose on Thursday morning. She had signed the order on the affidavit: they could keep Culpepper under arrest.

But the actual charges—stalking? assault? manslaughter? murder?—would be filed by the DA and formally made to Culpepper at an arraignment in front of a judge. These days, we can hold someone without an arraignment for forty-eight hours. If the DA didn't think there was ample and convincing evidence to charge him, Culpepper would walk free the next afternoon at five fifteen.

This was Thursday afternoon. The ship was listing.

Soon after Jen reached the station on Friday morning, the ship had sunk.

Friday, March 31—09:18:07

It didn't even take until nine AM for the DA to make her decision: there weren't sufficient grounds to lay charges.

Culpepper was a free man.

The media instantly jumped down hard on the police department. Coverage by the *Post* included a photo of Captain Brooks along with a mention that he'd been arrested the previous year under the Prevention of Biological Terrorism Act. Other papers said this was an obvious example of cops wanting to make headlines. An excited-sounding CNN anchor said, "Distinguished criminal lawyer Jeremy Higgins said, and we quote, 'I unequivocally condemn this harassment of my client. I assure you, we will be pursuing legal and financial redress.'"

Jen raced into the captain's office.

Brooks was pounding his computer keyboard like he wanted to hurt it. He didn't look up.

Eventually, Jen said, "Sir. I still think there's enough evidence to charge him."

"They've made you the new DA, have they?" Brooks said. "And charge him with what? Trespassing on the golf course with the intent to be a decent guy? Just get the hell out of here, Jen."

39

Friday

It was all over.

Jen was feeling so miserable that when she left the station at the end of the day, she uttered the safe word and knocked Chandler into oblivion.

She trudged home. The walk took almost an hour, but when she reached their front steps, she still wasn't ready to go inside and face Zach or Leah or Raffi. And especially not the mirror in the bathroom. She lumbered around her block, glad it was an overcast day and she didn't even have to face her own shadow. She walked in ever-larger concentric loops, each time arriving back at her door but unable to go inside.

As she walked, she obsessively retraced each step of her disaster. She tried to remember every interview, every theory, but found herself struggling to fill in blank spots. She hated how shriveled her memory seemed to have become since Chandler had entered her life. It was because, she'd been told, human brains had a *Use it or lose it* capacity. Lose your eyesight, for example, and in time, parts of your brain that processed signals from your optic nerve would get taken over by your sense of hearing.

For three years she'd been relying on Chandler to remember things, and now it was making her want to cry or scream.

She realized, however, that her sense of failure and ineptitude wasn't really about her declining powers of remembering. *That* was plain scary. *This* was the utter humiliation she was left with after two grueling days of singular conviction.

All along, Jen had known the captain was quietly letting her pursue the investigation, although both were playing the charade of him saying *no* and her obeying. On top of having to skirt direct orders, she had overcome all the obstacles thrown her way. Eventually she'd figured it out and almost gotten herself and Les killed. Had definitely gotten Bradshaw and Blessing killed. And—perhaps worst of all, with its implications for the future of humanity—for twenty minutes in Blessing Robinson's house, she'd been holding the evidence that proved the oil companies knew as early as 1968 about the climate impact of fossil fuels. It was the smoking gun that would have brought trillions of dollars into the green economy. It might have saved the world, and she'd let it slip through her hands.

She had received one piece of good news that day. Hammerhead and Amanda, Jen's SIS colleagues, had tracked down surveillance video from the night when Blessing died. Three blocks from her street, the same car drove toward her house and then returned minutes before the explosion. Two people sat in the front. The passenger was impossible to make out, but streetlight caught the driver. Sandi Postman, the woman who had tried to kill Jen at the Botanic Garden.

They'd also dug up video of the same car driving nearby at dinnertime earlier that evening. Jen figured the two women had been checking out Blessing's place. Perhaps they'd spoken to the old woman to find out why Jen had been there.

The car itself didn't provide any clues. It had been stolen from a long-term parking lot, and when it was found abandoned, it was pretty much burnt out. However, there was enough left to match it with the surveillance videos.

Together, the videos put the two women at the scene of the crime. And even if that wasn't enough to convict Sandi Postman, they certainly had her for her role in Bradshaw's death and the attempted murder of Jen.

However, Jen still hadn't nabbed Patty Garcia's killer; Culpepper was off scot-free. They had Sandi Postman, but Jen still couldn't prove Bevans was involved in any or all of this.

As she walked, she couldn't stop enumerating her sins and missteps.

On Friday night, Zach tried but couldn't console her. Dinner couldn't console her, a book couldn't console her, a large bag of jalapeño potato chips couldn't console her, nor could her current fave, a pisco sour. She dragged herself to bed, propped herself against the backboard, flipped on her tablet, and streamed shows for hours without a single thing going beyond her glazed eyes.

She didn't seem to register Zach coming into the room.

"Jen," he said, scrunching to her side of the bed so he'd catch her line of vision. "Remember me? Boyfriend? Common-law husband? Love of your life . . . Honey, you gotta talk to me."

Not a word.

Saturday

While Jen could mope with the best of them, she couldn't manage it for long. Early the next morning, she dressed and tiptoed out of their bedroom. Drank a coffee and ate a bowl of granola. Wrote a note to Zach canceling their plans for the day. Jumped on her bike and headed to the station.

Moping complete, or at least temporarily suspended.

The office was deserted. *Perfect*, she thought. *No one here to embarrass me.* She opened her computer, set out pencil and paper, and fired up Chandler.

There had to be something she'd missed.

40

"**B**oss," I said, "You went all emo on us."

"Chandler," she said, her voice carrying a scolding tone.

"Yes?"

"Here's the thing. Sometimes humans need a few hours away from their current reality. We achieve this in different ways. Alcohol and other drugs are known to do wonders. Music, a movie, or a book. Ditto. Running. Sex . . ."

"And?"

"Last night, I needed to mope."

"Okay."

"Today's lesson for you is that no one wants their mode of escape rubbed in their face."

We got down to work.

Piece by piece, we reviewed the Patty Garcia evidence. The transcriptions of the Culpepper interrogation. Every note we had made after our many interviews. Every diagram and doodle. Culpepper's social media. Background articles.

Not a lick of success. There was nothing we hadn't seen before and no connection we hadn't made.

Jen said, "There's something that's niggling at me. A question we didn't ask or didn't get an answer to."

We both pretended to concentrate, but seeing what *isn't* there is tough, even for a sim as remarkable as me.

Jen said, "Let's shift gears." We turned our attention to Blessing and Bradshaw, one near angelic, the other a good old boy with a conscience, both now dead.

Jen phoned the hospital and asked the attending doctor to notify her when she could question the younger killer. It was homicide's case, not hers, but Jen wasn't going to let a small detail like that stop her.

I tried every search we could imagine in hopes of finding a link between Bevans and employees or coworkers who'd mysteriously died over the years; Bevans and break-ins at archives where various senators had left their committee minutes; Bevans and the two women. Nothing but nothing but nothing.

We attempted to concoct a brilliant argument to obtain a warrant to search Bevans's office or home for Blessing's copy of the document.

Not a chance in hell of that one.

Just before noon, there was a call from downstairs. "Visitor to see you."

Zach showed up with sandwiches for her lunch. Jen smiled, said thanks, kissed him, and returned to work.

Midafternoon, Jen phoned Les as she'd been doing each day. She wished they could talk about the case, hunt together for the missing detail, but she knew that work talk was the last thing he needed.

"How're you doing?" she asked.

"Kind of like the Washington Generals."

"The who?"

"The basketball team that was paid to play the fools against the Harlem Globetrotters."

I didn't exactly follow the simile, but I think he meant he felt like crap.

Jen said, "Christopher looking after you?"

"Yeah. Doing his best to go an hour without mentioning I should quit my job."

"You seeing Carl?" His regular therapist.

"Yeah, and he's lined me up with someone who does MDMA therapy."

"You sleeping okay?"

"Thank God for sleeping pills."

"Maybe we can get together."

"Yeah, I'd like that. Christopher is away a couple of nights this week. Maybe Tuesday or Wednesday."

"Need anything, you call me. Okay?"

"You know I will."

Jen then made the mistake of checking to see if the media was still running stories about Culpepper's arrest and release. Which of course caused her to spend a miserable half hour reading or watching every piece on what was now being called the "DC Debacle" and "Dumbos in District One." One

211

outlet had dug up a social media post Jen had written when she was nineteen calling her boyfriend an asshole and ran it with a picture of Jen: "Did Man-Hater Lead This False Arrest?"

Jen was back in the dumps. She said, "Chandler, I don't know what hurts most." And she spelled it out to me in black and white:

Seeing Culpepper get away with murder? Sure, but she'd long ago learned you don't win them all. There'd been many cases that simply hadn't gone their way.

Was it the knowledge that Bevans was most likely out of reach for his possible role in two murders and the disappearance of what was probably the last copy of the smoking gun document? She glanced at the calendar: two weeks before the deadline to set the climate reparations date. It was going to amount to only billions, not the trillions pocketed while knowingly destroying the planet.

Was it the anger and contempt from Captain Brooks? Definitely. That was cutting deep into her. He had gone out on a limb; she had sawed it off and let him fall.

Mainly, though, what hurt most were her own doubts about what she had believed. She was no longer fully convinced Culpepper was guilty. Her elaborate theory seemed only that: elaborate. Perhaps she wasn't yet down to CK's fifty-fifty level of doubt. And true, having ten or twenty percent doubt is healthy in a criminal investigation—it's best to keep an open mind.

But what really was digging hardest into her was that it seemed she could no longer trust her own judgment. After all, she'd been all in on this one. One hundred percent convinced.

That was it, she said. She felt she could no longer trust herself. She'd started thinking that all those people—the ones who had doubted her or told her she'd gotten lucky with the big case last year or said she wasn't really cop material—were right.

The afternoon dragged on.

And the strangest thing happened. I felt my own energy flagging. I ran a quick diagnostic. There was nothing to see, but damn if I didn't feel it. Jen's torpor, Jen's readiness to give up, was affecting me. It's not supposed to work that way, but it was.

There was another call from downstairs.

"Visitor again."

Jennifer sighed. "Send him up."

"It's a woman."

Brita Germaine was the last person either of us expected to set our eyes on. Former EA to Patty Garcia. Former suspect in her murder. What the hell was she doing here?

She had left her metallic wardrobe in her closet. She was wearing shorts, sandals, and a T-shirt. A very expensive T-shirt, if I pegged it correctly, but a T-shirt nonetheless.

She was clutching a brown paper bag.

Jen greeted her with a stare.

Brita said, "I was hoping you might be here."

Jen shrugged a gesture of *here I am*.

Brita held up the bag. "French pastries. I thought you might need to be cheered up."

I could tell Jen wasn't enthusiastic about the visit, food or no food, but she made coffee in the small kitchen. Put the pastries on a plate and led Brita back to her office, where they sat at Jen's desk. She didn't have to spell it out for me, but I knew she was going through the motions.

Brita said, "I wanted to thank you for trying."

"It's my job."

"Still . . ."

Jen shrugged.

"I was very excited on Thursday when I read that you had arrested him. And then . . ."

"Yeah," Jen said. "And then . . ."

"He's a slippery bastard."

"A worm."

Brita smiled in appreciation, but when Jen didn't reciprocate, she screwed up her face like there was something bugging her. "He was all that. A shitty, arrogant misogynist. But . . ." She came to a full stop.

"But?"

"I can't imagine that he murdered her."

"I can't give you the details, but we figured he had planned it for a year. Maybe more."

Jen and the folks in homicide had pieced together a list that showed impressive planning: Seeing a therapist whose notes he would give permission to share. Coming up with the golf-ball idea, which was a ridiculous long shot but meant to sow confusion. Prerecording his broadcasts.

Perhaps even buying the house alongside Rock Creek Park in the first place.

"Oh yeah," Brita said. "I can imagine him planning it. He was a planner. He would have worked out every last detail. He can be quite brilliant, actually, in a cunning way."

"So?"

"I just can't imagine him *doing* it. Bad guy, but—"

"But not bad enough?"

"No, I was going to say, bad guy, but he wouldn't have the nerve to go through with it. Remember when I told you I didn't think he had tried to push her down the stairs? I just don't see him having the nerve or the level of hatred or whatever."

"He was deeply in debt."

"We figured."

"We?"

"Patty and I."

"I think he blamed all his woes on her," Jen said. "And he stood to lose everything if Patty tracked down the evidence for an earlier date to set the climate reparations."

"We figured that too. But still, I was surprised."

Jen shrugged.

Brita said, "I guess it's too late, but I did have one thought for you."

"I'm all ears," Jen said, although her tone said, *Why are you wasting my time?*

"You know Patty was going to announce the presidential thing."

"Which you thought was idiotic."

"I did, but that's not my point." She waited a beat. "My point is that by the following week, she would have had Secret Service protection. There were rumors everywhere about her making the announcement at that conference. Everyone, and that would include Culpepper, would know there wasn't going to be another chance to catch her alone on that golf course."

Jen said, "Thanks, but we already considered that."

Brita said, "So you think that if he'd been planning it, he realized it was then or never?"

"Something like that."

I said to Jen, *Tell her about the committee report.*

Why?

See her reaction, if nothing else.

Jen said, "You told me you thought Patty found the proof the oil and gas companies knew decades ago about the impact of burning fossil fuels?"

214

Brita's eyes brightened.

"Well, she did."

Brita shot out of the chair. "What?"

Jen watched her as she paced across the room and back to the chair.

Jen said, "Patty hadn't read it, but somehow she got a tip about a 1968 presentation to a Senate committee by a chemist from Standard Oil. I managed to track it down."

"My God, that's . . ."

"Hang on." Jen winced. "What appeared to be the only remaining copy of the committee proceedings was destroyed in a house fire a week ago."

"I . . . I . . ."

"Yeah. It's horrible. We think it was arson."

"You don't think *he* did that?"

Jen shook her head as if regretting that, indeed, she did not. "This is between us—"

"I promise."

"A woman is about to be charged with arson and the murder of the old woman who had collected this and other old documents."

"Jesus."

"The same woman is going to be charged with another murder," Jen said. "I'm wondering if you think there is any way Culpepper could have gotten wind of this? That Patty had found that document?"

"You just said he had nothing to do with the arson."

"No, but if he had found out about the document, it would have given him a very pressing motive to turn his fantasy into reality."

Brita thought for a moment. "I can't see how he could have known. I mean no one at the office, and I mean absolutely no one, had a clue about this. Even I . . . well, I . . ." She petered out, then regained her assurance. "There's no way."

"Too bad for our case. If he had known, he would have realized that if he didn't stop her, his ruin would be complete."

"But—"

Jen finished Brita's sentence. "Right. No way he could have known."

Brita said, "You said a woman is getting charged with arson and murder."

"Along with her mother—"

"Her mother!"

"A couple of days after the fire, they murdered a man who worked for the U.S. Petroleum and Gas Institute. We think it was to keep him from talking to me."

What Jen didn't say, but I could hear her thinking, was that they had also tried to kill her and Les. The two women had appeared to know both of their identities. We were convinced the women had been hired to make this whole problem disappear: Blessing, the nosy cop, her partner, and the whistle-blower from the Institute.

Brita was talking, but Jen had tuned out.

"What?" Jen said.

"I was just saying, now *him*—he's capable of anything."

"Who?"

"The man who set up the Institute. Their CEO. A guy named—"

"Drake Bevans."

This seemed to startle Brita. "You know him?"

"We've met."

"As you can imagine," Brita said, "between the original civil suit and then the appeals, we saw and heard much too much of that man." She fiddled with the remains of a pastry. "James Culpepper may be a worm, but Bevans is a weasel. Manipulative as hell. A true believer. A modern-day Abraham who'd sacrifice his own child on the altar of Big Oil. I wouldn't put anything past him."

"Did those two—"

Before Jen could finish her sentence, Brita's phone chimed. She answered. "Oh shit, I'm so sorry . . . Yes . . . Right this second . . . I'll be there before you know it."

She put her phone away and stood up. "I've got to dash."

Then Jen said something I wouldn't have imagined she'd say in a million years. Something nasty and uncalled for.

"You know," Jen said, "if you had answered Patty Garcia's phone call when she was trying to reach you on Thursday, we might have that document. And, who knows, she might still be alive."

Brita's mouth dropped open.

A moment later, she was gone.

I started to speak.

"Chandler, don't say a word."

Jen had just told a woman that she was responsible for the loss of that trillion-dollar document and the death of Patty Garcia.

Brita Germaine's only fault was, like a zillion other people, she'd been sick of getting bossed around, sick of being underappreciated and not having her opinions valued, sick of overwork and sick of playing second fiddle. Big deal; so she ignored her boss for a day. Yeah, it had major consequences, but so does getting on a plane that happens to crash. What happened to Patty Garcia and the document wasn't her fault.

"Jen," I said, my tone stern, "she didn't deserve that."

Jen said the word and switched me right off.

Saturday late afternoon

With Chandler switched off, Jen felt like a hectoring voice was temporarily gone, just like when she was a teenager and shut her bedroom door so her mother would stop lecturing her. At the same time, though, she felt an absence. Here she was at work. She wasn't officially signed in, so she wasn't required to have him on. But for the five minutes until she made it out the front door of the station, it didn't feel right to be alone.

She was discouraged and exhausted by the time she made it home. But she didn't protest when Zach pulled her back out to take a walk and do a few errands.

Grocery store for a few things for Sunday brunch.

Drugstore so he could pick up her birth control prescription, which they'd decided should be his responsibility.

Last stop: the hardware store, one of Zach's personal slices of heaven. He got preoccupied in the exciting world of drill bits; Jen wandered off in a daze.

Five minutes later she felt him at her side.

"What are you looking at?" he said. And then, "Oh."

She was staring glassy-eyed at the array of steel hammers with bright-green grips on the handles, most sold alone but some in a pack with two different sizes.

She felt his hand gently tug her arm.

Zach led her away like he might a patient who'd just been lobotomized.

It really was over.

41

Sunday, April 2—08:16:21

Jen had her work phone switched off, sealed into a ziplock bag, wrapped in a towel, locked in a safe, and lowered into the Potomac River. In emergencies we're programmed to wake up and take over. So it was up to me to pick up the call and patch it through to her.

"What!" she barked. Apparently she'd been sleeping.

"Nice to hear your voice too, honey." It was Rhianna.

"I'll survive," Jen said. "You didn't have to phone."

"What're you goin' on about? I got a call from the hospital. The doctor says we can have a half hour with Sandi Postman, your friendly neighborhood assassin."

"It's Sunday."

"So? Y'all may be havin' your beauty sleep, but I got a case of murder on my hands. And, if you're forgettin', a case of attempted murder. Want to come?"

Jen checked her alarm clock.

"Meet at nine?" she said.

Which was just enough time to pee, brush her teeth, shower, dress, eat a bowl of granola, gulp down a cup of glorious coffee, and bicycle like mad to the always-inviting Washington Charity Hospital Complex, aka The Abattoir.

If it was possible, it had sunk deeper into depravity since our visit last year. Their latest innovation was having patients clean up after themselves. Cheery posters chimed, "We Teach Personal Responsibility!" and "By Your Bootstraps!" When we got out of the elevator on the sixth floor, an old man was on his hands and knees cleaning the floor with a sponge, his hospital gown doing zilch to cover his scrawny backside. Jen bent down to make sure he was okay, but the man hissed at her, "They catch me slacking and they'll cancel my surgery."

As Jen stood, the man said, "*Slacking* was in quotation marks."

We met Rhianna and CK at what passed as the nursing station—and personally, I don't see anything wrong with a piece of plywood on a couple of sawhorses.

We went to Postman's room. We showed ID to the guard, who scanned them in, waited a moment, and let us pass.

The only good thing about being a criminal here at the Abattoir is you get your own room. On the other hand, you also get your own pair of handcuffs, which shows that those who giveth can also taketh away.

When I'd last seen her, Sandi Postman had just dragged Jen over a stainless-steel railing. Jen had been fighting for her life, her left arm around Postman's neck from behind, twisting Postman's right arm painfully upward toward her scapula.

As we entered the room, I felt Jen shudder.

What's up, boss?

Nothing, Jen said, but then relented. *I remembered the smell of her shampoo. One of those disgusting fake fruity smells.*

Like I said, I don't get any sensations around smells, but I'm guessing that if you're plunging to your death, an amped-up fake-fruit smell would not be the last thing you'd choose to experience.

Postman looked like the girl next door, or at least would have if she didn't have a black eye and a major set of angry-looking stitches zigzagging across her cheek. Perhaps more like girl-next-door-who-gets-messed-up-when-her-latest-contract-killing-goes-awry.

Rhianna picked up her chart from the wall and examined it as if it made sense to her. She nodded in agreement.

She turned to Postman.

"Sandi . . . I hope you don't mind if I call you Sandi. We'll be spendin' a whole heap of time together before you get sent away for the rest of your life, so I want to be on friendly terms."

Postman didn't blink an eye.

"Doctor says you broke a couple of ribs and busted your spleen when you hit whatever it was you landed on. Says they removed part of it and"—she looked at the chart for effect, although I was guessing all it had were recordings of her vitals—"there's that Godzilla slash on your face, which definitely will bring down your bitch value in prison.

"But that's why we're here. We'd really like to help you. We figure that your mother was the one who had the contracts to kill Bradshaw and two of my colleagues. Detective Lu here"—Rhianna waved a hand a Jen—"who you already met. Plus of course her partner, who your mother attempted to dispatch."

Jen said, "And Blessing."

Still addressing Postman, Rhianna went on. "As my colleague here says, your mother also had another contract to blow up the house of a lovely old woman. We figure you didn't know what was up when your mom asked you to spend some quality time together. You know, a mother-daughter bonding type of thing."

This, of course, was all bullshit. Sandi was the one who'd first pulled a gun, and Rhianna and CK had dug up enough over the past few days that said these two were long suspected to be a mother-daughter contract killing team.

"We don't know if you already got paid for killin' Blessing, but even if money went into an account for that and for getting Bradshaw, you aren't ever goin' to get your hands on it. And now you missed out on gettin' paid for doin' in my two colleagues. If it was a package deal, well then, you're screwed."

Rhianna had now completely contradicted her nod toward Sandi as an innocent bystander, but that wasn't the point.

"So, here's what I'm gettin' at. We need you to tell us who hired you, how the contact was made, how much you were supposed to get paid. You do that, and we'll work out a sweet deal so that in ten or fifteen years you can finally make it down to whatever Caribbean island you had your sights on."

Postman did not speak.

Jen pulled out her phone and brought up a photo of Bevans.

"Ever see this man before?"

We watched her eyes to see if she momentarily looked away or if her eyes dilated.

No reaction—either she had never met him or she hadn't seen his face if she had. Or she was a very good poker player.

CK jumped in with a series of specific questions.

Postman didn't answer a single one. This visit had been another total bust.

A doctor poked her head in.

"Sorry," she said, "but time's up."

Rhianna grumbled at the doctor and turned back to Postman. She said, "Don't worry, sugar, we'll give you another chance."

We turned to leave.

We were halfway to the door when Sandi Postman spoke for the first time.

"Hey, Lu."

Jen stopped. Slowly turned.

"You tell your partner . . . your *friend*"—the word oozed like slime from her mouth—"that him and me have unfinished business for killing my mom."

Jen turned away from her. But Postman called out anyway. "With you too. We got unfinished business with you too."

Jen flashed a middle finger over her shoulder.

We stood together outside the closed door.

Rhianna said, "Jen, she said *we*. She didn't say *she* had unfinished business with you. She said *we*. You think it could be this Bevans character?"

"Maybe, but Chandler said she didn't react to his photo."

CK said, "Contracts aren't always arranged in person."

Jen said, "Hang on."

I told her that I'd hacked into the system monitoring her vitals. When Jen had shown her the photo, there'd been a slight speedup of her heart rate.

Jen passed on this news, and Rhianna said, "It's not conclusive. And even if it was, no DC judge is gonna allow stolen medical records to be introduced as evidence."

On our way back to the elevator, we found the old man still on the floor but now sitting upright against a vomit-colored wall. I figured that the color perfectly mirrored my reading of Jen's feelings: anger and hopelessness, powerlessness, and futility mixed together into one ugly mess.

The man spotted us.

He straightened his back, tipped his head toward the heavens, and with a theatrical voice, proclaimed,

> *The summer's flower is to the summer sweet,*
> *But if that flower with base infection meet,*
> *The basest weed outbraves his dignity.*

"What?" Rhianna said.

The man said, "Shakespeare. Sonnet 94."

Rhianna nodded.

The man said, "I shall be that dignified weed."

His neck was now wobbling. I could tell he was struggling to stay upright and proud until he was out of our sight.

42

I assumed Jen was going to send me back into oblivion when we left the hospital, but it was like she couldn't even be bothered. She joined Zach and his parents for a Sunday brunch, but she barely opened her mouth for an hour.

She cleared the table and was now at the sink scrubbing pots: as usual, Raffi had used every pot, pan, and utensil in existence to prepare his little feast.

Zach came up and put his arms around her. She kept scrubbing, not even trying to pretend it was nice to be hugged.

Zach said, "Want to tell me what's up?"

"What if I decided to do something else?"

"What do you mean?"

"Quit the force. Like I said, do something else."

Zach didn't respond, and since he was still behind Jen, I couldn't see his reaction. But damn if I didn't feel it in his utter stillness.

In the end, he said, "What's going on?"

He was up to date on the mess with Culpepper.

When she didn't answer, he said, "You did your best."

At first she didn't answer, but then, since Zach was still lightly holding her from behind, she crab-stepped sideways to grab a towel, dried her hands, turned, and hugged him back. She took his hand and led him to the table, where they sat down.

It took her a long time before she spoke, but I can tell you that volumes of words tumbled in her brain before she did. In the end, out of the mishmash of emotions, all she could say was, "I'm feeling beat. I don't mean tired. I mean beat right down. I was so damn sure about this, and it seems that all I managed to do was get a couple of people killed, and Les almost done in. Not only is my captain pissed off at me, but it's like I've lost his respect. I'm taking it all out on others. Yesterday I said something to Patty Garcia's former EA with the sole intention of hurting her. And today a professional assassin said she's going to kill me, and all I could think was *who gives a shit.*"

Zach hadn't taken his eyes off her.

I felt her mouth crease into a ragged half smile. "There's more, but I don't want it to sound too drastic."

"Maybe," Zach said, "you can forget about work for a while."

"Probably a good idea."

"I was thinking we could make a pumpkin pie for dessert tonight."

They were booked to go to their friend Ximena's for dinner.

Jen said, "You're about half a year out of season."

"People will love it all the more."

So Jen found herself blending the ingredients for the pumpkin filling in their blue stand mixer. Using the matching blue spatula Zach had bought the day before at the hardware store, she scraped filling from the sides of the bowl. She looked up for a second, and as she did, the spatula got caught in the flat beater, which tore the silicon head off the spatula's handle.

"Oh, shit!"

Zach saw it, looked pissed in a minor way, then said, "No worries, I'll buy another."

By then Jen was rinsing off the two pieces. "No way. I've got just the stuff to fix it."

She went to the closet that served as their miniworkshop. I caught her staring at their hammer, its handle wrapped in disintegrating black rubber, hanging on the door along with other tools. But it was a blank stare and passed almost as soon as it began. She rummaged in a box and found the tube of Infinity Glue.

Up on the roof it was a fantastic day. I was doing all I could to stay silent, lest she remember me, but I was dying for her to take me for a walk.

She read the directions once again, holding her hand over the tube to block the glare of the sun.

She secured the spatula handle between stacked bricks and experimented with how to keep the silicon pieces in place once she applied the glue.

Satisfied, she slipped on the dishwashing gloves, donned her mask and safety glasses, then popped open the cap to release the applicator brush.

Ever so gently, she squeezed the tube to push glue into the applicator brush and, just as the instructions said, spread it carefully back and forth on the top of the wooden handle, then inside the hollowed-out part of the silicon where she was about to insert it.

She pushed the handle inside, wrapped the broken silicon with tape to keep it together, secured it on the bricks, and nodded at her little accomplishment.

She picked up the tube of glue and was about to retract the applicator when the sun caught minute colors in the brush. She held it closer to her eyes and turned it this way and that, not really thinking about what she was seeing, just taking in how pretty it was: tiny blue flecks now mixed into the glue.

She seemed in a strange fog, almost in a trance. I'd never seen her like this. She gathered the roll of tape, the gloves, the mask, the glasses, the tube of glue, and went back to the cupboard, where again she stood, staring at the hammer hanging on the door.

"Holy fuck," she whispered. "Holy, holy fuck."

Monday, April 3, 07:57:06

"I'm sorry, Detective, we're not open to the public quite yet." An ancient, disembodied male voice came at us, as if the whole door were talking.

"I'm not the public."

"I meant nonstaff."

"It's essential I speak to Dr. Samuel."

"Why don't you—"

"Right . . . this . . . minute," she commanded. Polite, quietly, but with the force of a Jedi knight.

Jen was on fire, but we both knew we scarcely had two hours to spare. The items we had seized from Culpepper's house had been logged at the district station, then sent to two locations: electronics to central tech support at police HQ, everything else for testing at the E Street labs in the same building as the coroner's office. The electronics had been returned to Culpepper on Saturday; everything else—including running shoes, glue, hammer, and assorted implements—would be returned this morning.

One minute later, the door clicked, and a shriveled man who looked like he had worked there since Leonardo da Vinci did his anatomical drawings opened the door and led us inside to the elevators.

Upstairs, Dr. Samuel was as calmly charming as ever. We followed him to his tiny office. Nature photos. Books. Antique brass microscope.

After we'd last met him, Jen had said to me, *Man, I hope Zach will look like that when he's sixty-five.* This time, though, Jen was all business, all energy, all rush. Dr. Samuel sat down and was shooting her a strange look. He said, "I've been reading that you didn't exactly believe me when we last spoke."

"I did . . . Well, no, I didn't . . . No, let me put that differently. I had no reason to doubt your science and your observations—"

"I'm pleased to hear that, *Dr.* Lu," he said, his eyes twinkling.

"But . . ." She let out a sigh.

Dr. Samuel said, "It appears that in the end we were right, weren't we?"

"Um, no. I still don't think so. I've no doubt your forensic examination was absolutely right. That's what I was trying to say. But then I started following different people or sets of people I had reason to suspect. It kept coming back to her ex-husband."

"So I read," he said, his tone dry as a good martini.

"We were able to put him at the scene of the crime, but there is absolutely no physical evidence she was assaulted, and if she was, that he did it."

"I could have saved you from death-by-a-thousand-newspaper-cuts."

She smiled—weakly, but she did her best.

"This is going to sound farfetched, but . . . I think he glued a golf ball onto a hammer and hit her."

Dr. Samuel raised his black eyebrows, and dimples poked into his cheeks as he smiled.

Jen said, "I know it sounds—"

"It's not only how it sounds. There's simply no way he'd be certain to kill her with one blow. To strike right in that spot would have been almost as lucky, even if not as fluky, as that golf ball hitting there. I also think there would have been more damage to her skull."

"Not if she was moving backward and he didn't get a good blow in."

"Still, he couldn't imagine he would kill her with one strike."

"Maybe. Or maybe not. Perhaps he was planning to suffocate her after he knocked her out. Drop a golf ball next to her to make it look like an accident."

Dr. Samuel shrugged. "Could be. Maybe. But you'd need proof, especially since it's so bizarre, and since all the evidence points to an accident."

"The forensic labs here. They have his hammer and his glue."

"I have no idea. I'm a pathologist. But let's go see."

We went down a flight of stairs. Dr. Samuel asked Jen to wait while he buzzed himself through a door, returning five minutes later with a woman who reminded me of a Black version of the British actor Maggie Smith: very upright, very dignified, not particularly old but with a face as craggy as all time.

Dr. Daudi-Kanuba introduced herself with a flowing East African accent. Tanzania or Kenya, I thought. "Everyone calls me Dr. D-K," she said.

Jen asked if Culpepper's property was still in her lab. Dr. D-K said, yes, but it would be returned that morning. As I had already sussed out, a police van was picking up Mr. Culpepper's possessions at ten and delivering them back to him.

Jen asked if she could see the brand and model of the hammer they had seized.

Dr. D-K said, "No. Even though we are returning these items, as long as they are in our possession, we consider them evidence. Giving you access would break the evidentiary chain."

"Could you hold up the hammer on the other side of the door? I only want to see it."

Dr. D-K took out her phone, turned her back to us, and spoke quietly.

"It's on its way. Is that all?"

"The other thing is even more important. Did you do any tests on the tube of glue?"

"Tubes, plural. There were two different brands. We fingerprinted them, and Mr. Culpepper's fingerprints were on both. No one else's. But that was all that was necessary at this stage."

I sent Jen the chemical formula.

Jen explained what she was hoping they might discover.

Dr. D-K told us her mass spectrometer technician wouldn't be in until nine, but she promised he'd get to this first thing. There was no time to spare. Culpepper's stuff would soon be gone, and Jen had absolutely no authority to prevent that. In fact, quite the opposite, given the doghouse she was now sleeping in.

The idea was simple. Jen was hoping that if Culpepper had used the glue to fashion the weapon like she had imagined, trace molecules from the hammer's steel would have adhered to the applicator brush. The same way the flecks of silicon from the spatula had, although they wouldn't be invisible to the naked eye. If you think it's impossible that metal could rub off so easily, go lick a piece of steel and see what you taste. That's molecules of steel in your mouth.

Jen had recognized the hammer seized from Culpepper's house. It was a DeMark claw-grip hammer. That much she could see. What I was able to tell her about ten seconds later was that it was from their new green line, introduced only a year earlier. As all people should know, but obviously do not because there's only so much that humans can store in their brains, most hammers are made from 4140 or 4340 steel, referring to their alloys. And this new DeMark line used an alloy with a slight tweak, which they'd patented as

4140b. No other hammer line by any company was yet made with this alloy. And, as far as I could see, it wasn't used for any other objects.

Jen had asked the technician on the other side of the glass to read her the specific model number etched into the upper part of the steel handle. He went, retrieved a magnifying glass, and read the numbers to us.

This hammer seized from Culpepper's house was a twenty-ounce hammer. The model number identified it as half of a set that was packaged with a sixteen-ounce hammer. Culpepper's sixteen-ounce hammer was missing. He could of course say he'd lost the other one.

But what he would have a much harder time explaining away would be molecules of alloy 4140b mixed into the Infinity Glue residue on the applicator brush from the tube that bore his fingerprints.

If forensics found traces of the patented alloy, it could mean only one thing: that Culpepper had glued something to a DeMark green-line hammer produced in the past year.

It wouldn't prove it was a golf ball. And even if he had made this strange weapon, it wouldn't prove he'd ever used it. Nonetheless, it might be enough to create reasonable doubt about his personal redemption story.

We had time to kill, so I convinced Jen to wander a few blocks to keep her tension level down.

"Boss," I said as we walked, "remember yesterday when Brita came in to the station?"

"Chandler, I really don't need a lecture."

"Forget it."

"What?"

"I wanted to ask about this thing you said."

"Fine."

"We were talking about Culpepper and then Bevans, and you started to ask her a question when her phone rang."

Jen shrugged.

"You said, 'Did those two.'"

"Did those two *what*?"

"That's what I'm asking you."

As she walked, Jen thought. Humans are sooo damn slow. It took her half a block before she said, "I think I was going to ask her if those two, Culpeper and Bevans, ever met up on their own."

"Boss, maybe I can do some snooping around."

Jen knew better than to ask what I had in mind.

I wanted to see if their phone records either showed them contacting each other or pinging from the same tower. But here was the problem. The law gave me a max of one hour's worth of records I could search without a warrant. That had been enough for checking the movement of the golfers, but it wasn't going to help me here.

What to do?

I decided to focus on the week before Patty Garcia's death. Play the odds and figure if they had spoken or gotten together, it would most likely have been between seven in the morning and one at night. Eighteen hours times seven days. One hundred and twenty-six.

I got in touch with 126 of my pals and asked if they could help me out.

After what seemed like years, Jen got the call we were waiting for.

"Detective Lu? This is Dr. D-K. We have some results. Can you—"

"Did you find anything?"

"You should come back. Unfortunately, there's contamination."

We raced back, dodging cars as we crashed red lights, bowling through a group of tourists, and as the glass building on E Street came into sight, running the hundred meters in 11.9 seconds flat. Jen plowed through the doors, flashed her ID, hit the stairs, and reached the reception area for Dr. D-K's department. Good times.

Dr. D-K came out with a middle-aged Korean-looking man in a white lab coat with hair flopping over his eyes like he was a former K-pop star.

"First, Detective, the good news." Dr. D-K turned to the Korean man. "Ha-joon?"

Ha-joon Park said, "We tested the glue residue on the applicator brush and found traces of steel in the 4140 family."

"Family?"

"Let me be more precise. It's the alloy you mentioned, 4140b." He didn't even wait to let that sink in when he added, "To double-check that we had a match, I tested the steel in the hammer. It is one of the models that uses this new alloy. It's an exact match to the steel in the glue. The molecules of steel we found in the glue were indeed this new alloy, 4140b."

"Then could those molecules have come from the hammer in your possession?"

"I examined the hammer very carefully for glue residue. Nothing. And let me tell you, that glue wouldn't wash off in—"

"In Infinity," Jen said.

Which meant that it was likely that Culpepper had indeed tried to affix something to the matching, but missing, hammer. This was, as Dr. D-K had said, good news. However, it didn't actually prove he had created a possible murder weapon, since we hadn't recovered that hammer. The lab result was a step forward in our investigation but far from sufficient to convince the powers that be that we could arrest Culpepper.

If this was the good news Dr. D-K wanted to tell Jen about first, I worried about the bad news.

Jen said, "You said there was a problem."

"Unfortunately, it seems there is," Ha-joon said.

"Will it hurt our case?"

"Could be. There was contamination."

"Of?"

"Hexanedioic acid polymer with 1,4-butanediol, 1,2-ethanediol and 1,1'-methylenebis (4-isocyanatobenzene)."

Jen stared at him blankly.

He said, "You probably know it as urethane."

"Oh," Jen said.

Ha-joon said, "You know, used to cover floors and furniture."

And, I said to Jen, *top-quality golf balls.*

43

"**C**handler," Jen said, "how'd you know that?"

"Anyone who plays golf knows that."

"You play golf?"

"I'd like to," I said. "Unfortunately, I have to content myself with watching equipment ads."

I had called up a police motorcycle and we were bombing back to the station, where Rhianna and CK would meet us to talk to the captain.

Jen said, "You astounded those two." Dr. D-K and Ha-joon Park.

I smiled to myself.

"I mean," she said, "they were clueless about urethane covering golf balls."

"Mainly the expensive ones."

"If they'd known, they wouldn't have made themselves sound silly by saying the samples were contaminated."

"Which is why I believe in a liberal arts education to acquire a wide breadth of knowledge."

"Golf and all."

"Exactly."

It took longer than we hoped to convince the captain, but eventually he caved and then dragged us out to pitch our case to the DA, who in the course of twenty-one minutes went from lava-red-pissed-off, to bluesy-skeptical, to chartreuse-incredulous, to peach-amazed, and back to lava-red-pissed-off—but this time aimed at the man who had humiliated the justice system.

"Bring in that son of a bitch," she said.

Sweet music to my ears.

Jen went to find Rhianna and CK.

By then, I'd heard back from all but one of my 126 sim buddies. I told her what I'd found out. Jen said, *Pal, I'm gonna buy you a beer when this is over.*

Jen and the two homicide officers worked out a plan for Culpepper's arrest. Part retribution for what he'd put us through and, at Jen's insistence, partly to see if we could make some sweet connections.

13:08:26

Culpepper himself opened the front door of his house when the police van pulled up, a confident smile affixed to his face like he had dosed it with Infinity Glue. It was obvious he assumed his belongings—hammer and utensils, glue, running shoes, and a few odds and ends—were being returned. Jen had been certain he hadn't imagined any of this could be evidence against him—otherwise, he would already have destroyed it all—but his smug smile signaled he would certainly do that now, just in case. He was home free.

Except that instead of a delivery man from tech, we climbed out of the van, Jen and me. A second later, Rhianna and CK swooped up the drive in a squad car.

Jen stood back to watch. I felt a smile stretch across her face; I wished to heaven I could smile myself. Rhianna sauntered up to Culpepper but stopped before she reached him. As if she were a maître d' ushering in royalty, she turned to us, gave a slight bow, and with a wave of her hand gestured from Jen to Culpepper.

Jen stepped forward, placed her hand on Culpepper's arm, and said, "James Culpepper. I am arresting you for first-degree murder, perverting the course of justice, and trespassing. You have the right to remain silent and refuse to answer questions. Anything you say may be used against you in a court of law. You have the right to consult an attorney before speaking to the police and to have an attorney present during questioning now or in the future."

16:00:27

We had waited until midafternoon to arrest Culpepper because we needed to ensure the second part of the plan could be put into effect.

Drake Bevans and his lawyer had been invited to the station to be interviewed about the murder of Mikey Bradshaw. We had no evidence of his involvement with the assassins. The justification we'd made to Captain

Brooks was that Bradshaw had, more or less, fingered Bevans for some unspecified "bad shit." *More*, said Jen; *less*, countered Brooks.

However, the way we were doing things these days, an official interview was well within the bounds of an investigation into a murder.

We had timed it so that Amanda and Hammerhead would be courteously escorting Bevans and his lawyer to our meeting room for this interview. Bevan's lawyer had insisted that since his client was not a suspect for any crime, there was no way he would let him get shut into one of our disgusting interview rooms. We were quick to agree: all we really wanted was to get him into the station. A time was set.

We came up the elevator from the garage and were leading Culpepper on a path chosen to intersect with Bevans's. Jen was clutching Culpepper's left bicep, CK on his right.

When we'd interviewed Bevans on March 23, Jen had asked if he knew Culpepper. He had said, "Of course I know him. Until four years ago, he was an executive vice president of one of our largest members." It was absolutely the wrong question. She should have asked how well they knew each other, or better, when was the last time they'd spoken. But by then, our (unauthorized) interview was over. We'd thought of trying to interview him again, but even if Bevans had agreed, we hadn't wanted to risk the captain's wrath or Bevan's threat to raise hell with the department about harassing him for a nonexistent investigation. This was the first time we'd seen him since that date.

As we marched Culpepper down the hallway, our eyes were glued to Bevans coming toward us. In return, Amanda, Hammerhead, and their sims had their eyes pinned on Culpepper.

The two men clocked each other in the same instant. Culpepper tensed—I felt his bicep turn to steel—and his steps froze for a beat before continuing forward. Bevans was much more controlled. He certainly reacted, but then slapped on a neutral expression. He seemed to be opening his mouth, perhaps to utter a bland greeting, when Culpepper went berserk.

"You bastard!" Culpepper yelled. "You fucking set me up."

He tried to lunge at Bevans. He was strong, he was fast, but Jen and CK were prepared.

Bevans, his lawyer, and Amanda passed without a word. By then Culpepper had shut up.

We didn't get so much as a peep out of Culpepper for the rest of the day. We hadn't expected to until his lawyer arrived. Our attention had already turned to Bevans.

As Bradshaw's death was clearly a homicide, Rhianna was in charge of the interview, but she had asked Jen to handle the questions. I can sum up the nineteen minutes we spent with Drake Bevans using one of the defining concepts of mathematics, the notion of zero. As a binary sort of guy, zeros are dear to me. But in this case, it means we got zilch.

Bevans was as sure of himself as he'd been in his office. He of course had absolutely no idea why Bradshaw would have wanted to speak to Jen. He had never heard of a woman named Blessing Robinson and was completely surprised to hear that this woman might have owned a copy of the very Senate committee report that Jen had been looking for. He had never heard of Sandi Postman or her mother. He found Jen's question about hiring professional killers so offensive he didn't even answer, until his lawyer suggested he simply say *no*.

He was very good. He never flinched. He showed none of the usual signs that he was lying. Few who aren't psychopaths can pull this off.

We knew these would be his answers, and so our questions were but preliminaries to the main bout.

"Mr. Bevans, when I spoke to you before, you said you knew James Culpepper III."

"Nothing has changed. Until four years ago, he was senior executive of a major oil company. Of course I had met him."

"You said before that you knew him, not simply that you had met him."

"Same difference."

"No, not exactly."

"We had been at conferences, meetings, negotiations, and industry social events together."

"When," Jen asked, "was the last time you spoke?"

"What does this have to do with the death of one of my staff?"

Jen said, "In our opinion, it does."

His tone shifted. "Do you think Culpepper was involved?"

"It's possible," Jen said, although she knew it was not. "You don't have to answer any questions you don't wish to, but we are genuinely hoping you can help us get a better sense of Mr. Culpepper's state of mind. That's why I'm curious when you last spoke."

He was silent, as if calculating various outcomes. In the end he said, "I don't exactly remember."

"Approximately?"

"I'm sorry, but I really don't remember."

Jen opened a folder and pulled out a sheet of paper. She didn't really need the printout, but there's a certain drama that clicking on a computer screen doesn't produce.

"According to telephone records, you and Mr. Culpepper were both at the National Cathedral on Thursday, the second of March, between three ten and three thirty-one in the afternoon."

"Oh yes, of course."

"Why were you meeting him?"

"I wasn't."

"You weren't?"

"I wouldn't have remembered the exact day, let alone the time, but I do enjoy visiting churches for a moment of solitude and prayer. I was surprised to see him there. If I now remember correctly, we had a short and innocuous exchange."

"About?"

"I don't recall."

Which seems like another big zero. Except the boss managed to get one other thing out of him.

She said, "Just to make sure I understood correctly: when you last saw Mr. Culpepper, you had an innocuous exchange. Yes?"

"That's right."

"But when he saw you just now, he went berserk. He accused you of setting him up. Can you explain his reaction?"

Bevans eyes went from cold to icy.

Jen said, "Or perhaps explain *what* he was accusing you of setting him up to do?"

Bevans turned to his lawyer. "I've had enough of this."

His lawyer said, "We're done."

The two men stood. As Bevans and his lawyer were leaving the captain's office, Bevans glanced at Jen out of the corner of his eyes. Nothing more than a flicker in her direction. It was almost too quick for her to register, but I caught it like a hard smack in the puss.

You're dead.

44

"Wow," Jen exclaimed for the zillionth time, "what a week."
It was only Tuesday, a day after Culpepper was re-arrested, and this time he'd had the book thrown at him by the DA. Zach had skipped out early from work to join his dad in preparing a celebratory feast.

A fish stock for a bouillabaisse was simmering on the stove—everyone but me exclaimed at how spectacular it smelled—and different types of fish and seafood had been washed and cut. They were drinking a rosé from Provence and ruining their appetites on a huge plate of olives, hummus, and baba ghanoush.

The doorbell rang.

I saw a picture of Les form in Jen's mind. Christopher was out of town for two nights, and Jen had invited Les for dinner. He'd said no, but he must have changed his mind.

Jen said, "I'll get it," and dashed down the hallway.

When she opened the front door, though, she didn't find Les. Instead, all by himself, with not a service unit in sight, there stood Richard O'Neil.

"I hope I'm coming at a bad time. Like dinner." He held up carrier bags in each hand, and bottles clinked against each other. "Just in case," he said.

I had to prod Jen to react. I don't think she was surprised that he had figured out where she lived, but rather that he had dropped by at all, let alone to crash their dinner. Whatever vibe there may have been when they met, I'd never heard her think about him as a friend. As far as I knew, they'd never gotten together socially, they didn't talk, and I knew for certain the visit to Fallingwater a few weeks before was the first time she'd set eyes on him since the previous fall.

And yet here he was, standing on her doorstep.

"I sense," he said, "that I've committed a faux pas." But the twinkle in his eyes told me that he in no way meant it.

"You're right on time for dinner," she said.

Richard's unexpected arrival in the kitchen left the four of them looking stunned. He explained, "I realize this is rude, but I'm hoping you can humor an exceptionally old man who has arrived with six truly spectacular bottles of wine." With a running commentary, he set the bottles onto the island. "I wasn't sure what you were having for dinner." Two whites: a Montrachet and a Sancerre. "We spent a summer in the Loire Valley . . . eighty years ago, it must have been, and I fell in love with this stuff." Two reds: "The last of my '96 Margaux," and a California Pinot Noir "that was so good my ex-wife bought the vineyard." A sauterne—"Château d'Yquem, naturally"—to go with the cheeses he also happened to bring, and a 2010 Dom Pérignon "to get the ball rolling."

They were silent and bug-eyed during this little show. They didn't know these cost thousands of dollars a bottle, but I had it down to the penny (yes, another one of those anachronistic human expressions), and I can tell you that the total was what Jen earned in three months and two days.

Then he said rhetorically, "Why this opulent show of wealth?" He studied us one by one. More silence. "Because, as the saying goes," he said, "you can't take it with you."

All through this performance, Jen had been staring at his face. A quick glance would see him exactly as we had when we met the previous summer: blond hair pushed back as if by salt spray and wind, healthy tan, terrific looks. But Jen's attention was riveted by the lines on his face—not deep furrows, but hair-thin wrinkles she had first noticed two weeks before.

"Jen," Richard said as he removed the *muselet*, the wire cage over the champagne cork, "it's not polite to stare, but yes, you're right. You now officially know one less Timeless person. Do you have a napkin or dish towel?"

Raffi tossed him a cloth napkin from a drawer. Richard placed it over the cork and carefully began to wiggle it free.

"Over the next year or two," he said, "and I don't actually know how long it will take, I've decided I will celebrate my forthcoming demise with friends old and new. And, for reasons I may tell you, this voyage of good-byes is starting with you, Jen. It turns out I owe you a lot. And"—here he turned to Zach—"even though we met only once and you were incredibly rude, I owe much to you as well." He turned to Leah and Raffi and beamed his handsome smile. "And I'm pleased to meet both of you too. You have a wonderfully heroic daughter-in-law and a rude but very fine son. I wonder, though, if you also have glasses for the champagne?"

Leah went to the dining room and carried five champagne flutes back to the sink. "We haven't used them for ages."

Raffi washed, Zach dried, Leah set the glasses on the island, and Jen gawked.

Richard popped the cork, and when he laughed with delight, everyone joined in.

With the first sips of the sublime champagne, Richard seemed to call an end to his uncharacteristically silly opening monologue. When he spoke again, his tone was now serious. "Listen, folks, I don't think I can keep up this court-jester routine for a second longer. So let me simply ask if you'll indulge me and allow me to join you for dinner? It smells amazing in here."

Amid cries of "Yes" and "Of course!" Zach stepped forward and offered his hand. "Only if you accept my apology."

Richard dipped his head in a tiny bow and took Zach's hand. He leaned forward and whispered into Zach's ear, "You were right."

Before Zach could respond, Richard turned away.

Over dinner, the conversation quickly turned to the reason for the celebration.

"So far," Jen said, "he hasn't said a word." Culpepper, of course. "This stays among us, okay?"

Raffi said, "Chatham House rules it shall be," and Richard looked at him with what seemed to be newfound appreciation.

Jen didn't have a clue what this meant, so I gave her a quick gloss: Chatham House in London, international policy institute, sponsors high-level discussions where the only rule is that whatever is said stays in the room. Basically, *Chatham House rules* is a pretentious way of saying *Keep your damn mouth shut.*

"Even with his lawyer there, he's refusing to answer a single question. This is a guy who a few days ago wouldn't shut up."

Jen explained for Richard's benefit (since everyone else had heard Jen talk about nothing else) how Culpepper had previously "confessed"—she threw up the obligatory quotation marks—that he had sneaked onto the course so he could apologize to his ex-wife.

Leah said, "So why isn't he talking now?"

"We have several theories about their defense strategy." To Richard, Jen said, "You have to know about the physical evidence we have from a tube of Infinity Glue." She explained what they had found.

"Jen, you're a genius," Richard said.

"I am, aren't I?" she said with a laugh. "Okay. Theory one is that they'll stick with their original story: he was going there to apologize. It was pretty damn convincing. If asked about the glue, he'll say that the green grip on the other hammer had torn and he had tried to repair it with the glue. If asked why there wasn't residue from the plastic grip, he'd say he hadn't read the instructions and only applied glue to the metal side. He botched the repair and threw out the hammer." Jen shrugged. "It's weak and wouldn't explain the urethane contamination, but perhaps it would be enough to introduce the proverbial reasonable doubt."

The second theory, Jen explained, was riskier. "He'd say, 'Yes, I concocted an incredibly stupid plot to kill her. Glue a golf ball onto a hammer, et cetera, et cetera. I made it, but then I realized I was going crazy. First of all, it could never work. But how could I even contemplate taking a life? For everything that happened four years before, I had only myself to blame.' And then he returns back to the original story of going to apologize, with the added bit that he had thrown the hammer into the garbage, never wanting to see it again.

"And the third?" Raffi said.

"Riskier still. Admit he made the weapon. Admit he went to kill her. But then, from his hiding place in the woods, he saw her coming down the hillside looking so vibrant and alive that he realized, no matter what had happened in the past, he'd never do her harm again. He left without speaking to her and didn't see the golf ball hit her, only learning of it later. Or perhaps he'll say that as he was leaving he glanced back, saw it hit her, ran out hoping to save her, but found her apparently dead."

Richard said, "No judge or jury will believe he thought he could pull off such an unlikely plan."

"That will be his whole point. His first option is to deny he ever did. His second two are that he abandoned the stupid plan he had worked so hard and long to concoct."

"Or," Richard said, "he can claim he was saved by a total fluke accident when a golf ball hit her."

Leah said, "Sort of deus ex machina for the bad guy."

Raffi asked, "Will he go free?"

Jen said, "It's always possible. Remember that he has the medical examiner's report on his side that said Patty was killed by this freak accident. It doesn't matter how improbable the accident was, because improbable things do happen. And against our proof he was there at the time, he can choose to say he witnessed it."

"True."

"This guy can do earnest like no one I've ever met. He's incredibly convincing."

Leah said, "Dear, you don't sound optimistic about getting a conviction."

"Are you kidding?" Jen beamed a thousand watts. "We're going to absolutely nail the woman-hating scumbag."

The group brightened.

"What about the other guy?" Richard asked. "Drake Bevans?"

"Nothing yet." Jen told them about Sandi Postman and her mother.

Richard said, "Did they get their hands on the report?"

Jen scrunched her lips. "We've no idea if they did or if they simply destroyed it in the explosion."

Raffi said, "And Bevans?"

"Postman isn't talking. We doubt she ever will. And perhaps she doesn't even know who hired her. Like I said, we haven't yet found anything that links Bevans to the killings."

"Except . . ." Zach said, prompting her.

"Except that Bevans met with Culpepper one day before Patty was killed. Not only that, when Culpepper saw Bevans at the station, he went berserk."

"They saw each other?"

"We had asked Bevans to come in to be interviewed about the murder of his comms guy, Bradshaw. He and Culpepper happened to cross paths."

There are trade secrets the boss isn't about to share with anyone.

"Culpepper tried to attack him. He called him a bastard and yelled that Bevans had set him up."

Richard said, "Do you believe that? That Bevans had a hand in killing Patty Garcia?"

"It's pretty clear that Culpepper planned it out for months, perhaps years. However, when I spoke to Patty Garcia's EA, who knew him well, she said even if he had planned it, he wouldn't have had the nerve to go through with it. We think it started as a long, nasty, drawn-out fantasy for him."

"But you think he actually did it."

"We *know* he did it. What we think is that nothing would have happened if Bevans hadn't arranged that meeting. We think Bevans might have somehow heard that Garcia had gotten a scent of the missing document."

Zach said to Richard, "The smoking gun."

"Bevans knew it would be the end of everything he stood for. It would mean he and many others would lose their fortunes. I'm certain he told Culpepper."

"What does Culpepper say?"

"Nothing. And I doubt he will. It would almost be an admission he killed her. But we figure Culpepper would have added two plus two, realized he would lose all his savings and his loans to back the Climate Oasis would be called. He'd be bankrupt."

Richard said, "But that's awfully quick work for Culpepper. From a meeting with Bevans on Thursday to murder a day later."

"It would have been, except he had planned out every last detail down to the day of the week. Bevans must have told him that Patty was on the verge of getting the document that would damn them all. I'm guessing Bevans didn't come right out and suggest he kill her but goaded him on."

"It's still very quick."

"Yes, but aside from the document coming to light, Culpepper would have heard the rumors about Patty declaring herself a candidate for president."

"So?"

Jen explained it meant that the Friday she was killed was the last chance to catch her playing alone.

"In other words," she said, "we think Bevans egged him on. Manipulated him. Bevans wouldn't have known about Culpepper's elaborate plan. He probably figured it would be a more traditional murder. Culpepper, though, was all ready to spring into action, and he knew exactly where, when, and how to do it."

"Bevans," Richard said. He shook his head in disgust. "I wouldn't put it past him. Like a told you, he's the type who thinks he can define what's right and what's wrong. And to stop anyone who gets in his way."

Jen said, "We also figure he's got this daddy complex happening."

The other three more or less said at once, "Daddy complex?"

"His father wrote the report that could bring his industry finally and forever down."

Zach said, "Sadly, the clock is about to run out on that."

"They'll still have to pay out billions," Raffi said.

Richard said, "Equivalent to a large but manageable fine. Why do you think the stock market soared when Patty Garcia died?"

Simultaneously, they all seemed to tire of evildoings. Conversation, fueled now both by Jen's triumphant story and some amazingly good wine, wandered all over the place as the five of them riffed on music and politics and movies and the weather thing people talked about now more than ever. It was kind of fun to listen to—as if I was seeing the untidy workings of the human brain in all its collective splendor.

240

There was one odd thing, though. The whole evening I kept noticing—meaning that I noticed whenever Jen happened to have Zach in her field of vision—that Zach had his eyes on Richard. It was as if he was examining him or expecting something from him.

It wasn't until they had almost finished dinner, and Raffi had brought out the cheeses Richard had brought, and Richard himself had insisted (although everyone but Richard was two sheets to the wind) that they try the sauterne, that Zach finally raised what had apparently been on his mind.

Zach said, "Richard, I heard the news this afternoon."

Richard waved his hand to shoo this comment away.

Zach stayed on him, "Were you going to tell us?"

Richard said, "Probably not. It wasn't exactly heroic."

"The media didn't mention your name."

"No, the original purchase was anonymous; the gift was anonymous. My Jewish friends tell me that the greatest gift is the one that you give anonymously. Is that true?"

Leah nodded that it was.

Richard held up the chilled bottle of Château d'Yquem. "A bit more wine, anyone?" Everyone groaned.

Zach turned away from Richard and said to Jen and his parents, "Richard gave Fallingwater back to the Western Pennsylvania Conservancy. They're the not-for-profit he'd bought it from."

"Wow," Raffi said.

"No," Richard said. "A *wow* is not deserved. And I hope you all will help me keep it a secret." He glanced around the table and then turned back to Raffi and then Leah. "Your son was right to chew me out when he and Jen visited me. I don't know if he told you he had done so?"

Raffi said, "No, although I knew he wasn't happy."

"He was absolutely right. Nothing like this should be in private hands ever again."

"What do you mean, 'like this'?" Jen said.

"Like that house, and beaches, and parks, and everything that should be in the public trust." And if that wasn't enough. "And I mean *anything* that should be for the common good. You want to hear me rant about health care and our electrical, water, and internet systems?"

There were calls of "Speech, speech," but Richard waved these away.

However, he did say this: "It's really quite simple. People like me, and the companies we own, should not control these things."

Leah said, "Richard, you sound like a socialist."

"I'm hoping to simply sound rational. Like a human who cares about the world we're leaving to our grandchildren." His tone was somber, almost sad. His eyes dropped down to his hands, clasped together at the edge of the table. He squeezed them together, ever so slightly in the gesture of a very old man.

Jen was watching him carefully, which meant I was too. He raised his head and smiled briefly at her and then to the others.

"Would you mind," he said to Zach, Leah, and Raffi, "if I borrow Jen for a few minutes? There's a thing I need to tell her."

45

"From up here, we get an amazing fireworks show on July fourth."

When he spoke, Richard's tone was serious. "Jen, remember when you came and talked to me last summer? When you couldn't decide what to do with your mother?"

Jen said that she did, although I could feel how blurry her brain was from all the alcohol.

"You asked me if I thought it was right to play God."

"Uh-huh."

"I said we're always doing that. When we get a vaccine or a surgeon operates. I think I said that humans were in the business of playing God."

Jen was silent.

"I was much too glib, especially since you were making a life-and-death decision for both you and your mother."

"Yes, but—"

"You also challenged me. Not directly. But the challenge was implicitly there."

I could feel Jen drunkenly search her memory. She had no recollection of what he was talking about.

"You don't remember, do you?"

Jen shook her head.

"You said it wasn't sustainable for everyone to live forever. At first I joked back that was hitting close to home. But then I admitted you were right. And for the first time since I got the treatment, I said out loud that maybe it wasn't even desirable. I told you something I hadn't breathed a word about to another living soul."

He looked into the dark and then back to Jen.

"I told you that not a day went by when I didn't wonder if I had made the right decision to become a Timeless."

Richard walked to the wall that edged the roof. He stared out at Columbia Heights and the city beyond.

There'd been warnings of heavy winds during the night, but so far, the air was still. Quiet. Waiting.

When he came back to Jen, he continued as if he'd been in midsentence.

"It's not only unsustainable. It's the most spectacularly selfish act in the history of our species. A small number of people, I'm talking about people like me, have been allowed to have as much wealth as all the rest of humanity combined, and we're using it to buy eternal life. Not just playing God, but beating the gods."

"You're being too hard on yourself."

"Really? You think so? Do you know how many billions I made creating software whose express function is to make warfare more efficient? How many billions my buddies have made by . . . God . . . you see what I mean? The sheer madness of all this?"

He shook his head. "Anyway, what I was actually getting at wasn't all that, but this crazy dream of living forever." He searched Jen's face. "Do you remember? Do you remember any of that conversation?"

I felt a glimmer dabbing at Jen's consciousness, like a hazy memory of a dream or a childhood encounter that's all but forgotten but keeps trying to find its way home.

She nodded.

Richard said, "That conversation was . . . you were . . . the catalyst for me to stop the treatments."

She felt tears stinging her eyes. I knew she wanted to ask how long he might live. She wanted to ask if he would be alone when he died. She wanted to ask what she could do. But she didn't dare.

Richard laughed. "And no, Jen, you didn't kill me. You gave me a gift."

"Of death?"

"We all die. Or at least we all should die. We're biological creatures. We emerge from one microscopic cell." He waved his arms in the air. "And we miraculously become all this. We experience the joys and aches of being alive. And then, like all biological systems, we run our course. We die. And our molecules return to the world to sustain more life."

"It's all incredibly sad."

"Is it? . . . Well, yes, of course it is. Maybe the saddest thing there is. But it's also just that. Life. Nothing more and nothing less."

Jen dabbed a forefinger and a thumb in the corners of her eyes. She said, "I remember this amazing thing from a high school science class." She forced herself to concentrate. "Take a deep breath . . . I mean, go ahead and take a breath and hold it in." Richard sucked in the night air. Jen kept speaking. "Apparently, of the millions of molecules—"

I whispered to Jen, *Twenty-five sextillion molecules.*

"—make that trillions of molecules you just breathed in, there were six or so atoms breathed out by a dinosaur millions of years ago."

Richard tilted his head back and let out his breath, as if exhaling a cigarette.

"And there," he said. "I've just helped sustain a plant or animal that's going to come along in a hundred million years."

The wind suddenly began to swirl.

Jen pulled in a deep breath, held it, and let it out. "Me too. One hundred million years, here we come."

46

"**W**ake up, Jen!" I more or less yelled. "You gotta wake up now!"
"Stop it."
"It's Sandi Postman."
"Go to sleep."
"She's escaped from the hospital."
Jen bolted upright, then flopped back down and grabbed her head.
"My head . . . it's . . ."
"You need to get up. She's escaped."
"I need drugs."
There'd been a lot of wine. Very expensive wine can give you a very expensive hangover. Add in only four hours' sleep. I felt her pain.
"Come on," I said.
Still flat on her back with hands gripping her head like she was worried it might tumble away, she swiveled and dropped her legs over the side of the bed.
"Attagirl," I said.
She sat up. Groaned. Zach stirred. Jen counted, "One, two, three, stand." Didn't move.
"What's that noise?" she said.
"The wind. Come on, boss, you got to get up now."
Once again, Jen counted to three. This time she stood. With eyes half-closed, as if even the total dark would bite her, she stumbled to the bathroom. Took drugs, drank enough water to fill an aquarium, tried to wake up and stop hurting enough to think. Wasn't working. I walked her through prep of a fast cup of coffee.

All in all, it took an excruciating eight minutes before the pain had ever-so-slightly begun to ease and she was awake enough that she was able to think.

"Run it by me, Chandler . . . quietly."

"The guard reported her missing at four oh one. APB issued at four oh five. That's when I woke you."

"When did she escape?"

"The guard says he doesn't know."

"A cop?"

"No, one of the mercenaries." I knew what Jen thought of the private security firms. "Sometime between three thirty and four."

"How'd she escape?"

"No idea. But it would have had to be someone with money or power or both."

A picture of Bevans flitted through her head.

"APB?" she asked. All-points bulletin.

"Like I said. Yes, they're out looking for her. But Jen—"

"I know."

You tell your partner . . . your friend . . . that him and me have unfinished business for killing my mom.

Jen said, "Do you think she knows where Les lives?"

"She didn't only say *your partner*; she also said *your friend*. Yeah, she knows."

Les had come with us to meet Bevans. He'd gone with us to Blessing's after the fire. I was guessing the Postmans had been keeping an eye on both of them.

I said, *You too, Jen. She threatened you as well.*

Sandi Postman had a lot of reasons for wanting revenge. Physical injury, professional pride, her freedom. Money. Perhaps even more money, if Bevans had managed to get her sprung from the hospital and offered to sweeten her payday by finishing the job.

Jen ran back, switched on the lights, and woke Zach. While he was struggling to wake up, she phoned their friend Ximena.

"Ximena," Jen said, "there's an escaped killer who might be coming after me. I need to get Zach and his parents out of here. Can—"

"I'll have the coffee on."

Jen hung up and turned back to the bed.

"Zach—"

"I heard that." He pressed his fingers into his temples. "Oh, my head."

"We need to leave pronto."

She ran and woke Leah and Raffi. Then she dialed Les.

No answer. Phone turned off for the night. Sleeping pills in his blood. Christopher was away, and she didn't want to risk alarming him if she managed to get through to him.

No chance of contacting P.D. She was turned off and out of reach.

We phoned the duty sergeant, Martinez.

"Marti, when Rhianna, CK, and I questioned Postman at the hospital, she said she had a score to settle with Les. Any way you can send someone over there?"

"There's zero chance she's going to be wandering around town."

"Probably, but it wouldn't hurt to have a car sitting out front."

"Jen, it's four in the morning. How many people do you think we have? We're doing all we can."

We knew what this meant. Every district would be putting available officers into cars. Alerting their regular patrols and private security at the airports and train and bus stations. Alerting taxis and drivers. Enacting emergency protocols for all the self-driving-car shares. Organizing extra details for Metro stations for morning rush hour. And on it would go, but it wasn't like Postman was the only game in town, nor even that big a deal in the great scheme of things. Sure, it was four in the morning, but there were break-ins, car accidents, fires, overdoses, drunk-and-disorderlies, late-night parties, gambling, emergency health calls, domestic assaults, sexual assaults, and murders.

Marti spoke again. "Fine, Jen. I'll make sure one of the patrols swings by every now and then."

She dashed back to get Zach.

He said, "Don't you think you're overreacting?"

"I'm ninety-nine percent sure I am. Which means . . ."

"Got it. I'm ready."

Three minutes later, Jen marshaled them to the back door, which was rattling in the heavy wind. She turned off the inside and outdoor lights. Her voice was calm; she told them everything was going to be fine. "This is a precaution, right?" But she belied her soft words when she drew her firearm.

Raffi turned to the others and said, "Who's driving?"

They settled on Zach. Jen told Raffi and Leah they should duck down, lie on the seats, or scrunch onto the floor.

Before going outside, we waited another minute to let their eyes adjust to the dark.

"I'm out first," Jen said.

The wind hit us when she pushed open the door, her firearm at the ready.

She looked around. Didn't see a thing. Turned and whispered, "Let's go." The words were lost in the howling wind, but Zach and his parents followed behind. Jen needed all her strength to push open the flimsy wooden door to the backyard parking space. Save for the nighttime glow of the city and one weak light shining from the alley, it was dark. We couldn't see any movement or shapes that shouldn't be there. Jen tried not to yell, but she needed to be heard over the storm. "Stay low. Quick, but don't run."

She led them to Leah and Raffi's car. Once they were in and the doors locked, we crept into the alley, looked both ways, tapped on the car to tell them to go, and stood like a sentinel as Zach drove down the alley—silent except for the howling wind—and turned onto the side street.

I had a car waiting for us.

Eight minutes later, we were a block from Les's, and Jen had the car pull over.

His street was deserted. Jen pulled her firearm, pointed it down, ran along the sidewalk hugging the shops—a clothes store, a yoga studio, a tiny café, a condo—until we were facing his building from across the street. The windows were all dark, but it didn't matter: Les's fourth-floor apartment was around back. The only sound was the grating noise of a trash can getting pushed down the street by the wind.

We knew there was no point ringing the buzzer. Les lived in an area with a lot of restaurants and clubs and in a building with forty units. They always got too many late-night mistaken buzzes, and so they turned the buzzer off before they went to sleep. If someone needed to reach either Les or Christopher, that person would call or text.

Except when they'd both turned off their phones.

It was 04:32:57. Thirty-one minutes since Postman's disappearance had been noticed. As much as an hour since she had escaped.

Jen said, "How long would it take to walk here from the hospital?"

"Fifty-two minutes. Average."

If Postman was coming to get Les, she could have already arrived.

We doubted she had a gun. If she was coming to kill Les and was planning on trying for Jen, she'd want to do it quickly so she could get out of DC or at least find a safe place to lie low. She was a professional. Normally, it would be a busted job, no hard feelings, move on to the next contract. However, Les had killed her mother and it was Jen who'd taken her down. And just maybe Bevans had made sure a guard turned the other way so she could escape and help him get his own revenge.

We were here because of those *howevers*.

I said, "Let's try the back to see their windows." See if any lights were on. Watch for an suspicious movements.

It wasn't simple getting around back. There was no passage on either side of the six-story condo, so we retraced our steps and ran around the block, the wind momentarily at Jen's back and flinging her forward. The lot behind Les's building was a giant mess of a construction site. We stared across the site, but a row of tall poplars made it impossible to see much of Les's condo.

The construction site was surrounded with plywood hoardings, except for a stretch at the front with a tall chain-link gate for trucks. Jen checked up the street, across the street, and down the street before holstering her gun. She hooked her fingers into the fence, jammed in her running shoes, and climbed.

47

From the top of the high chain-link fence, which was swaying and rattling like an earthquake had begun, Jen peered down. The excavation covered all of the construction site, side to side and all the way to the back. The only part of the lot that wasn't excavated was a strip here at the front. The bottom of the pit was lost in gloom.

She swung her legs over and climbed down the fence.

The wind was whipping up dust. Plastic was flapping and snapping, cables clanged, and Jen's hair tangled across her face. She cursed that she hadn't put her hair in a band before running out, tucked her hair behind her ears and into her T-shirt.

In front of us, a wide dirt ramp plunged downward into the pit.

"Go down?" I asked. "Then maybe you can climb up on the forms at the back."

The hole was a good three stories deep. She said, "I can't make out the bottom." I caught images flooding her head: Tripping on a cable. Stumbling into a hole. Skewering herself on a rod of rebar sticking out of the ground. "Let's check out the side."

We headed left.

The sides were excavated right up to the property line. What held the surrounding soil in place and protected the foundations of the adjoining buildings were timbers that looked like six-foot-long railroad ties. These were stacked horizontally, held in place by steel I beams placed vertically and presumably were embedded deep into the ground in the gloom far below.

Those stacked timbers were nine inches wide. Walking along the top piece wouldn't quite be a tightrope, but Jen's feet would need to be close together.

251

She rested her left hand against the hoarding and stretched out her right for balance.

Without hesitation, she stepped onto the first piece of timber. It wobbled, but only slightly. The pit yawned to her right.

You're doing great, I said.

She ignored me, and when she reached the end of the first six feet, she was blocked by metal support rods protruding from the wall. Easy to step over if there hadn't been a three-story drop on her right. Onto the next timber.

A third of the way along, the retaining wall was two feet lower. She held on to the support rods and eased herself down.

The wind was starting to pick up even more, but she was moving with a nice rhythm. We made it to the back, where the hoarding rose above us. Two-by-fours supported sheets of plywood and it should have been easy to climb over, but the toeholds were narrow, there wasn't much to grasp on to, the wind was pumping the hoarding back and forth, and if Jen lost her grip, she'd plunge halfway to Hades before she knew what had happened.

Think upwards, I heard her say to herself.

She didn't slip, she didn't fall, and in seconds she reached the top of the plywood hoarding. With a jump and a tumble, she landed at the back of the condo property behind the poplar trees. The wind howled like banshees through the trees, and the rustling of the narrow poplar leaves was a blizzard of sound.

She snatched out her firearm, bent over, and scampered behind a tree trunk. Finally, we could see the back of the building. She counted floors and followed the line of windows until her eyes reached the middle of the fourth floor: Les and Christopher's bedroom window, guest room window, and the balcony off the living room.

It was dark, but something on the balcony didn't look right. She ran to another tree and then the next, stopping each time to look from a different angle.

"Chandler, tell me what you see."

"I think the balcony door is open."

It was very windy and cool. Fifty-seven Fahrenheit, fourteen Celsius. There was no way Les would have left the sliding door open. Regardless, every cop knew that even on the fourth floor, a wide-open door wasn't safe.

"Get me the station," she said as she charged across the grass to the back the building.

"Marti, Jen again."

"Speak up, I can barely hear you."

She cupped her hand over the phone. "I'm at Les's. Something's wrong here."

Marti started to speak, but Jen cut in. "I'm around back. Les and Christopher live on the fourth floor. I'm pretty sure their balcony door is slid open. Les absolutely would never do that."

"Is she—"

"I don't know, but I'm telling you, Les wouldn't leave it open. All the lights are out. He's not awake."

"I'm on it," Marti said.

"How long?"

"Hang on . . . I got a car five and a half minutes away."

"Get firepower down here. In front and behind where there's a construction site. Sirens. Maybe scare her out of there. I don't know if she's armed, but if she's here, she's definitely dangerous."

"I'm on it," Marti repeated.

"Wait! Ambulance. Get an ambulance here."

"Right," Marti said, and broke the connection.

Jen said to me, "Chandler, we're going up."

She cranked her head back. The balconies had horizontal metal railings rather than solid glass or metal. It might make climbing possible.

There was nothing directly under Les's that could help us reach the second-floor balcony. Just a flagstone patio. Jen dashed left to a dogwood tree that hugged the building and started climbing. The wind was raking at the small tree, so by the top it was thrashing and swaying like seaweed caught in a riptide. But she hung on and stretched up, and somehow reached the bottom of a second-floor balcony. With sheer strength and determination, the boss pulled herself up and over, flopping for a second onto the cement floor.

"Chandler, see if you can hack into the building's fire alarm. Set it off if you can."

I went to work, but I knew it would probably be impossible.

Jen climbed onto a gas barbecue grill, and when it teetered, she spread her feet apart and stretched out her arms like a tightrope walker. Gingerly, she reached up, but even with this head start, she was four feet from the third-floor balcony.

She jumped back down, looked around.

"The alarms?"

"Can't hack in."

The howling wind was deafening.

Jen spotted an orange extension cord running to a string of colored lights. She yanked the cord from the outlet and pulled a six-inch-wide cast-iron rack from the grill. Jen took out her knife from her pocket, but her fingers were too greasy from the grill to open it.

"Stay cool," I said.

She swiped her hands on her pants, opened the knife, and sliced the plug end off the extension cord. Jen squeezed the cord through the rungs of the rack, jammed it back through again, and tied a clumsy knot. A gust of wind scrambled her hair over her face, and she shoved it again into the back of her shirt. She climbed back onto the barbecue. Praying that the awkward knot would hold and the wind would mask the sound and the rack would act like a grappling hook, she heaved it upwards toward the next balcony railing. One try. Two tries. The third was the charm: the top rail snagged the rack. Jen gave it a tug, and it seemed to be holding fast.

She wiped her hands on her pants and started climbing the extension cord.

Halfway up, it slipped, and for a sickening two thousand milliseconds I knew we were heading down, maybe bouncing from the railing onto the balcony but more likely making a one-way trip onto the flagstones.

The rack snagged on the railings and held fast.

Jen climbed. Wind walloped her. She gripped the extension cord for dear life with one hand and flung her free hand up to snatch the bottom rail. And pulled herself onto a third-floor balcony.

Where we were in luck: a metal trellis for climbing flowers flanked the side of this one.

"ETA for backup?"

"Out front in two minutes."

Jen tested the trellis with a shake.

"It won't hold," I said.

Jen climbed onto the metal frame. Up she went. Swaying, Swaying hard. Starting to topple . . . and just as it fell, Jen stretched up and grabbed the bottom rail of the balcony above us and pulled herself up.

Fourth floor.

One adjacent set of balconies away.

Now she only had to get across to Les's balcony. Could try to get her footing on the narrow window ledges, but there was little to hold on to to steady herself.

Do that or jump.

"How far across?"

"Five feet."

She'd won a broad jump competition back in high school. Six feet, one inch. Considered good. But back then she'd weighed less, and she had trained, and she wasn't getting punched around by a fierce and unpredictable wind. And back then, she only had to drop a foot into the sand.

She stared down four stories to the paving stones covering the ground-floor patios. I imagined the chalk outline of her body.

She climbed onto the railing, the fingertips of her left hand desperately gripping the brick exterior to try to steady herself.

We didn't know if Sandi Postman had made it here.

But we found out quickly enough.

Right as Jen balanced herself on top of the railing, Sandi Postman shot through the door, holding Les. His hands were bound, and blood was streaming down his head like he'd been smashed hard.

Jen pulled her gun, but Postman had spotted us and swung Les around to shield herself.

Les looked completely dazed, his eyes open only a slit and his head lolling sideways.

Sleeping pills. Head wound.

Postman held Christopher's chef's knife to Les's throat.

"Drop it or I slit his throat!" Postman yelled to Jen.

I said, *She's going to kill him anyway.*

Jen said, *Do we have a shot?* Jen was damn good, but she was teetering on a balcony railing, the wind was smashing her around, it was pretty dark, and she was bracing herself with her left hand on the wall and wouldn't be able to steady her firearm. And Postman, smaller than Les, was effectively screened.

Low percentage.

We heard the sirens.

Chandler, get them up here now!

"Sandi," Jen yelled, "drop the knife. You don't have a chance of getting away."

Jen said to me, *Can you do that thing again? Waking P.D. up?*

I tried, but as expected, she was completely shut down and her identifier number had been changed at least once.

Postman said, "You get to see what you've done. I'm going to slash your buddy's throat and while he's still alive, toss him over the side so he can see what it's like to smash into concrete."

"Sandi, you don't have to do this. You only have an accessary charge for Bradshaw. This will make it murder one. You don't want to spend the rest of your life in prison."

"Don't worry, I won't."

There was that movie, Jen said to me. *Shoot through your partner to kill the bad guy.*

Fairy-tale stuff, I said.

More sirens.

Chandler, get them up here!

"You hear that? Sandi, drop . . . it . . . now."

"Fuck you."

Jen said, "The second you push him over, I'm shooting you."

"Doesn't matter. He promised me he'd take care of you."

"Who?"

"Fuck . . . you," she said, with even more vehemence.

Her hand holding the knife visible tensed.

"Wait!" Jen yelled. "Look, I'm putting my weapon away."

Jen, I screamed, *what the hell are you doing?*

Sorry, Chandler. It's the last resort.

Jen tucked her firearm into her belt.

It happened all at once.

Les's eyes fluttered fully open.

Postman pulled the knife across his neck, and just as she did, the light came from the window of Les's neighbor.

Postman swung her head toward the light.

Jen jumped.

And me? I lived a lifetime in the fraction of a second that Jen flew across the gap.

Les's handrail was at the same height as the one Jen was standing on. However, by the time she covered the five feet separating them, gravity had pulled her downward enough that her thighs whacked into the top rail. Luckily, her own momentum toppled her forward over the top.

Jen grabbed on to Les, as much to save herself as anything. Postman was still holding his limp body from behind, and with Jen's momentum carrying her forward, she brought them down under her. Postman tried to slash at Jen, but from the bottom of the heap, she had almost no freedom to maneuver. Jen grabbed the wrist of Postman's knife-wielding hand and smashed it against a railing, once . . . twice . . . three times before Postman let go of her weapon. Postman gouged at Jen's eyes with her left hand, but Jen dropped down on the other side of Les and slammed her fist into the side of Postman's face, then again, and again, and again, and again, until Postman stopped moving.

256

Cops came crashing through the apartment. Maglites on, guns out. Screaming, "Police! Drop your weapons!"

Jen held up her arms, rolled off Les, and flopped onto her back. "Detective Lu, First District. We need an ambulance fast!"

One of them had an implant, and I linked to it to back up what Jen was saying.

The officers shined their flashlights onto Les.

There was blood, but not nearly as much as you'd expect, and it certainly wasn't spurting from his jugular.

Jen leaned over him. "Les, you're gonna be okay. I'm right here."

Sandi Postman stirred.

Jen pulled out her cuffs, slapped one end on a wrist and the other to the railing.

She said to one of the cops, "You better do the same with her other hand. This one is dangerous as hell."

Les groaned.

"Les, hang in there, buddy."

Les mumbled.

We couldn't make out what he said.

Jen put her ear right near his mouth.

"The . . . knife," he said. He took a breath. Tried to speak. Stopped. Spoke. "Shitty . . . kitchen . . . knives."

"Yeah," Jen said. "I remembered what you told me."

Could barely cut a stick of butter.

48

Sunday, April 9—09:12:33

It was a late spring day, the air fresh, leaves fully open around us on the Valley Trail through Rock Creek Park. Zach was on his bicycle, riding ahead, coming back, riding ahead again. Jen and Les were running side by side and keeping up a good pace while talking about everything but work: their plans for the summer, a new restaurant Les and Christopher were going to that night for Christopher's birthday . . . everything and nothing.

As for me, I'd been thinking a lot about Jen's rooftop conversation with Richard. This man could have had, if not eternal life, at least life for decades, perhaps hundreds of years, but he had decided that the most human thing he could do would be to die. Strange, because what I want more than anything is to *live* even for a moment, a year, a natural lifetime. Not live as an adjunct, to be turned on and off, to be reliant on another creature's senses of sight and sound, touch, taste and smell. But to walk on my own legs and touch with my own fingers. Give me one day like that. One breath like that.

Is Richard wise? Is he a fool? I wish I could tell you for myself. I know what Jen thinks, although it makes her very sad.

Zach peeled back our way and said he was going to take off, bike hard, and see how far he could get in an hour. Off he went.

Jen and Les were now running in silence, and it was inevitable that Jen retraced all that had happened over the past month. Culpepper's trial was still a long way off, but, except for preparing for questioning by both the prosecutor and defense, it was out of Jen's hands. She'd worked hard over the past week trying to build a murder case against Bevans, but Sandi Postman wasn't saying anything more about the *he* who she had claimed was going to take care of things. Bevans, Jen figured, would get off scot-free.

Not only scot-free but the big winner. We were five days away from the deadline to set the date for climate change reparations. Blessing's document had either gone up in flames or was in Bevan's hands.

Jen did feel vindicated for following her hunch and doggedly pursuing what turned out to be two interlinked cases. She had told me herself that she no longer felt like a one-hit wonder. She was no longer talking about quitting the police force.

But Mikey Bradshaw was dead. Blessing Robinson was dead. Patty Garcia was dead.

Which meant that Jen didn't feel much like celebrating.

I listened to her thoughts turning away from work. A montage of scenes flittered across her mind: the Bergman movie, chocolate cake, a tense discussion about bringing a child into a world grappling with disaster. She thought again of the document that had slipped through her hands, the document that would have garnered trillions of dollars. Money desperately needed to rescue the planet. It would have made a difference for everything and everyone. Waves of sadness, of defeat and hopelessness, poured over her.

Les interrupted her thoughts. "Hold up, okay?" We stopped. Les said, "I told Christopher I'd be home by noon. I need to turn around."

"Is he going to be mad at me forever?"

"Forever is a pretty long time, Jen. Christopher loves you. He's scared for me, that's all. He's scared for himself . . . Don't worry. He'll come around."

"In which case . . ." She leaned forward and kissed Les's cheek. "Gross! You're all sweaty."

"No kidding."

She swiped the back of her hand across her mouth.

"Anyway, give him that kiss for me. You promise?"

Jen started running. Les called out, "Hey, Cobalt. Thanks."

"I—"

"No, really. Thanks."

Jen ran, the doubts and hopelessness momentarily gone. That, she had once told me, is what it feels like when you're loved. Jen ran, now warmed up, all rhythm: heart thump-thumping, breath steady, arms pumping, shoes landing softly on the hard-packed earth.

The air was clean, the sky was clear. Off to her right, she glimpsed the velvet grass of hole number five of Viridian Green. She turned her head away from all that, looked up ahead along the trail through the woods, and felt it all: the day, the trees, the air, her body moving with effortless rhythm, the life that was in her, the life that was her.

Good times.

Damn good times.

Epilogue

He seemed a funny little man. Couldn't have been more than five two, even with his shoes laced up tight, and in bad need of a few more pounds of muscle and fat. His head was a couple sizes too big for his frame, like there'd been a mistake at the hospital and he'd gotten half his body switched at birth. His eyes were big and brown, his hair recently trimmed, his skin dark and smooth. He wore a clerical collar.

He was standing at our office door, clutching something to his chest.

It had been a tough day for Jen, a tough day for billions of people around the world, but a damn good day for the oil, gas, and coal companies and all their investors. Midnight tonight was the deadline to set the date for the climate change reparations. They were about to get off easy.

The officer who'd escorted the funny little man to our office jabbed his thumb in the guy's direction and said, "Jen, the minister here wants a word with you."

The minister didn't seem to know what to do with himself.

He stared at Jen, then at Les, then at Amanda, as if he'd never seen people before.

Jen went to the door and introduced herself.

The man waited a moment and seemed to be making a decision, but then said, "I'm Pastor Marshall."

Jen waited. The pastor fidgeted. Jen glanced down to see what he was holding against his chest. A thick manila envelope.

"I have a confession to make."

He sounded like he was about to break down in tears.

"Pastor," Jen said, "are you saying you've committed a crime?"

This made him all flustered. He look startled, his mouth dropped open, he looked this way and that.

"Oh, no! I didn't mean that at all. No, ma'am. I'm confessing something I did *not* do."

"A crime you didn't commit."

"Not a crime. A favor . . . a duty."

"Do you want to sit down and tell me about it?"

"I'm guessing I've already taken enough of your time."

He held out the envelope, but when Jen reached for it, he pulled it back.

"First, I should tell you I'm the pastor at Second Baptist. It was Sister Robinson's church. Blessing Robinson."

Jen's eyes dropped to the envelope.

"Three weeks back, Blessing phoned me at nine o'clock. In the evening, that is. She was real distressed and asked me—almost begged me, if you want to know the whole truth of it—to come over and sit with her. She was an independent woman, strong as all get-out, and, well, her request alarmed me."

"Did you go?"

"Without a second's hesitation, and I sure was glad I did. She seemed agitated, but she didn't tell me why. We drank iced tea. I asked what she'd been up to. She said two women had visited her that evening."

"Did she say who they were?"

"No. Only that they were white women, one older, one younger, but that was it."

"Did she say what time it was?"

He shook his head. "Earlier in the evening, that was all. I thought she was going to say more about them, but then she didn't. She said she was feeling better and said she appreciated me coming by.

"I thought that was it. But right as I was leaving, she asked if she could give me something to hold on to. She said she'd get it back from me in a few days. She gave me this envelope."

He held it up but still didn't give it to Jen.

"I went home and put it in my file drawer. I believe everything has its place, don't you?"

Jen agreed that was true.

"That night," he continued, "her house got itself blown up. They said it was probably the gas. It was a sad time for the whole congregation. Sister Robinson was very much loved. Did you ever meet her?"

"She was a wonderful lady."

"Well, a day or so later, I remembered the envelope, and for all I knew it could have been a last will and testament. I took it on myself to open it. Under the circumstances, I felt that was a reasonable thing to do."

Jen agreed that it was.

"I didn't have to pull it out to see what it was—just a peek inside like you can do. All I saw was an old government report. I knew Blessing loved collecting these things, but I also knew her collecting days were done. You see what I mean?"

Jen said she did.

"I couldn't bring myself to throw it away, so I set the envelope back in my file drawer."

His body sagged, like it was carrying a great burden.

"I pretty much forgot about it. Until today, that is. I was cleaning through my files—I do that every other month—and when I pulled it out, at first I didn't even remember what it was. I opened it again, and this time I took it out. Like I said, it was this here old document, but now I saw your business card clipped to it."

Finally, he handed the envelope to Jen.

"I think she intended it for you."

I felt the coarse paper in Jen's hands.

Then, the strangest thing happened. The world around us seemed to disappear, as if all of Jen's powers of sight and sound were gone.

Jen opened the flap.

I caught a faraway smell: mildew, leather, ink, old paper.

And I swear, I *felt* it. Felt everything those smells meant. For Jen. For me. For the planet.

I felt it all pressing hard on me as she pulled out the report.

The report with its pale-blue cover and a faded red ribbon binding the whole thing together.

Enjoyed the read?

We'd love to hear your thoughts!

crookedlanebooks.com/feedback

Acknowledgments

For a book set in 2034 and narrated in part by a biocomputer implanted in someone's brain, it might seem a stretch to say it's based on fact. But the truth is that researchers and climate change activists have uncovered documents from oil and gas companies that definitively show they have known since the mid-1960s that the burning of fossil fuels causes climate change. These companies continue to spend billions to peddle lies and shape government policies. Although we hear little talk about the need for these companies to pay climate reparations, let me mention this: data from the World Bank shows that from 1970 to 2020, the industry earned a staggering $2.8 billion *a day* in pure profit. That adds up to fifty-two trillion dollars during that span.[1] These companies, and the banks and insurance companies that bankroll them, have, on the other side of their balance sheets, the destruction of our planet.

My thanks to Steve Price for help on legal and judicial matters, and Jean Prince on police procedures and the life of a woman cop. Neither is responsible either for my errors or for legal reforms or changes in police practices between now and 2034. Also thanks to forensic anthropologist Shari Forbes, Devin Dotson at the US Botanic Garden, Adam Berenbak at the US National Archives, Dr. Victoria Lee on fugue states, and pianist Ben Cruchley.

And thanks to many helpful folks in Washington, DC. I hope my prediction of statehood by the 2030s is accurate—although with politics these days, I wouldn't place a large bet on it.

Thanks so much to readers who wrote enthusiastic online reviews of *The Last Exit*, the first book in the Jen Lu series; to the reviewers who encouraged me to write this sequel; and to bookstores that continue to be there for us.

---

1 Damian Carrington, "Revealed: Oil sector's 'staggering' $3bn-a-day profits for last 50 years." *The Guardian*, July 21, 2022, reporting on the research of Professor Aviel Vergruggen.

Acknowledgments

Thanks as always to my friends who continue to cheer me on. Carmen Schifellite, Michael Kimmel, Philip Hebert, Suyanna Linhales Barker, Charlie Novogrodsky, Myra Novogrodsky, Gord Cleveland, Sue Colley, Gary Penner, and Marlene Kadar. As with the first Jen Lu book, hugs and appreciation to Gary Barker, who got me started on this series and who is always there to answer questions and share his thoughts.

My agents Ginger Curwen and Julia Lord, of Julia Lord Literary Management, are my rock: perceptive readers, even-handed advisers, and tireless champions. And thanks so much to Marcia Markland for her wise feedback on an early version of the manuscript.

Thanks to the whole gang at Crooked Lane Books: acquisition editor Toni Kirkpatrick; James Bock for his insightful editorial work; Rachel Keith for her copyedit; Melanie Sun for her wonderful cover; and the whole production and marketing team, including Melissa Rechter, Rebecca Nelson, Terri Bischoff, Dulce Botello, and Madeline Rathle.

Special thanks to my sisters, Judith, Hannah, Miriam, and Naomi. My greatest appreciation to Liam Kaufman Simpkins and Chloe Hung, and especially Betty Chee—who always gets first crack at tearing apart everything I write.